R.T. Mrs. ?. ?. McBryde

from

Agnes Sophie Luke

Christmas 1911

Chattanooga

Tenn

THE
BLACK BORDER

GULLAH STORIES OF
THE CAROLINA COAST
(With a Glossary)

BY

AMBROSE E. GONZALES

A FIREBIRD PRESS BOOK

PELICAN PUBLISHING COMPANY
Gretna 1998

Manufactured in the United States of America

Published by Pelican Publishing Company, Inc.
1000 Burmaster Street, Gretna, Louisiana 70053

TO
ROBERT ELLIOTT GONZALES

CONTENTS

CONTENTS

FOREWORD

Just under the left shoulder of Africa, which juts out boldly into the Atlantic, as though to meet half way the right shoulder of South America, lie, between Sierra Leone and the Bight of Benin, the Slave Coast, the Ivory Coast, and the Gold Coast. It was the lure of gold and ivory that brought to these shores the enterprising traders who first offered the African slave-holders a stable foreign market for the captives of bow and spear and knobkerrie.

Out of this fetid armpit of the Dark Continent came the first black bondsmen to curse the Western world. Thence, across the narrowing ocean, but a night's flight for Walt Whitman's "Man-of-War-Bird"—

"At dusk that look'st on Senegal, at morn America"— Portuguese and Spanish traders, but a few years after Columbus had set foot on San Salvador, transported their first human cargoes to the plantations of Brazil and the rich islands of the Caribbean. Here the labor of the blacks proved so profitable that the envious English soon engaged in the traffic, and during the reign of the virginal Elizabeth certain of her noble subjects sought concessions for the monopoly of the West Indian slave trade.

A generation or two later, the first slaves filtered through to the mainland colonies of North America from the Barbados, Antigua, and other West Indian Islands. After the institution had become firmly established, the New England eye, not lacking "speculation," saw the promise of the East, and New England, pocketing her prayer book while pouching her

7

musket balls, freighted her bluff-bowed ships with red
flannel and glass beads with which to accentuate, if not
to clothe, the heathen nakedness, and set sail for the
rising sun. Thenceforth the New England slavers
sailed in cycles, and their course was charted by rum,
slaves, and molasses. The "black-birders" bartered
their human cargoes for West Indian molasses, which,
by a spirituous, if not a spiritual, process, became New
England rum. "Old Medford" filled their holds, west-
erly winds filled their bellying sails, and the rum was
soon converted into more slaves, to be in turn converted again into molasses in completing the gainful
cycle.

For a hundred and fifty years Rhode Island and
Massachusetts competed successfully with England for
the North American trade, and these colonies (with
"God's grace") throve exceedingly. In the early years
of the last century, however, the importation of slaves
was interdicted and the last Yankee slaver converted
the last rum-bought slave into cash, then, converting
himself, he became an Abolitionist, and the well-
known "New England conscience" was developed.

But the Puritan slaver, whatever "woes unnum-
bered" he brought upon his own race, was, in trans-
ferring these bought or stolen blacks to the humane
Cavalier planters of the South, an unconscious bene-
factor to thousands of Negro captives and to mil-
lions of their descendants, whose masters gave them
Christianity and such a measure of civilization, that,
in the short space of two hundred years from the cannibal savagery of the stew-pot and the spit, they were
fitted, in the New England mind, at least, for man-
hood suffrage, which came to enlightened England only
after more than a thousand years of development!

FOREWORD

None of the encyclopedias mentions the Gullah Negroes, nor does the name appear in the dictionaries. Mr. John Bennett, the well-known writer of Charleston, who has, for twenty years, been gathering data concerning this interesting people, places the Gullahs among the Liberian group of tribes; "formerly powerful and numerous, they have been crowded and overrun; their remnant remains about thirty miles inward from Monrovia;" but in 1822, in a publication by the Charleston City Council at the time of the attempted Negro insurrection, reference is made to "Gullah Jack" and his company of "Gullah or Angola" Negroes, thereby making the suggestion that "Gullah" is a corruption of Angola. As Angola and Liberia are at least fifteen hundred miles apart, the former being nearly one thousand miles south of the Equator, these two opinions seem to be in hopeless conflict.

Mr. Bennett says further: "Among the many African tribes brought to this country, the presence of very many Gullah Negroes is apparent from the earliest times. On some plantations, before the days of experienced precaution, it is highly probable they formed a majority of the hands. As early as 1730 a plan had been hatched against Charleston by these Negroes....

"The dialect of the West Coast, from which came these Gullah Negroes, was early commented upon as peculiarly harsh, quacking, flat in intonation, quick, clipped and peculiar even in Africa. Bosman, the Dutch sailor, described its peculiar tonality, and calls its speakers the 'Qua-quas,' because they gabbled like ducks.

"The clinging together of these Gullah tribesmen, as indicated above, and their apparent resolute and per-

sistent character, evidently assisted in impressing their
dialectical peculiarities on weaker and more plastic
natures brought in contact with them, and fixed the
tonality of the Negro dialect of the Carolina low-country....

"For the above reason, of prevalence and domination
as a peculiar dialect with singular and marked tonality, the characteristic patois of the districts where these
Negroes most abounded, came to be universally referred
to as the Gullah dialect."

Whatever the origin of these Gullahs, Mr. Bennett
is probably correct in his estimate of their influence
upon low-country Negro speech.

Slovenly and careless of speech, these Gullahs seized
upon the peasant English used by some of the early
settlers and by the white servants of the wealthier
Colonists, wrapped their clumsy tongues about it as
well as they could, and, enriched with certain expressive African words, it issued through their flat noses
and thick lips as so workable a form of speech that it
was gradually adopted by the other slaves and became
in time the accepted Negro speech of the lower districts of South Carolina and Georgia. With characteristic laziness, these Gullah Negroes took short cuts
to the ears of their auditors, using as few words as
possible, sometimes making one gender serve for three,
one tense for several, and totally disregarding singular
and plural numbers. Yet, notwithstanding this econo-
my of words, the Gullah sometimes incorporates into
his speech grotesquely difficult and unnecessary English
words; again, he takes unusual pains to transpose numbers and genders.

FOREWORD

On some of the sea-islands and on portions of the
mainland, sparsely inhabited by whites, the Gullah
speech still persists in its original "purity." The
explanation for this is that the Negroes, before and
after the war, were in so tremendous a majority on the
great plantations of the low-country that only the
house servants came in frequent contact with their
masters' families, and these house servants, certainly
those who had been "in the house" for generations,
spoke with scarcely a taint of Negro speech. The field
hands, seldom coming in contact with whites, had
neither opportunity nor temptation to amend their
speech. There was none to "impeach" their language,
and so virile was this Gullah that, in some sections
higher up the state, as in Barnwell and Sumter counties, where, in the settlement of estates certain families or colonies of coast-bred Negroes were sold before
the war, the Gullah tongue, although with difficulty
understood by the other Negroes of the community,
still persists like lingual oases in the desert of up-
country Negro speech.

This Gullah dialect is interesting, not merely for
its richness, which falls upon the ear as opulently as
the Irish brogue, but also for the quaint and homely
similes in which it abounds and for the native wit and
philosophy of its users. Isolated from the whites as
were these coast Negroes, and having no contact with
the more advanced slaves of the up-country, who,
belonging as a rule to small slave-holders, were in
close touch with their masters' families, the coast
Negroes retained more of the habits and traditions of
their African ancestry and presented, therefore, a more
interesting study of the Negro as he was, and to a cer-

tain extent "ever shall be." Living close to nature, they were learned in woodcraft and the ways of animals and birds and fish, and used this knowledge to illustrate their dealings with their own kind.

The peasantry, the lower classes generally, are the conservators of speech. Writers who have exploited the white mountaineers of the Appalachian ranges of North Carolina and Tennessee have heard from their lips Biblical and Shakesperean English now almost forgotten among educated people. So these coast Negroes still use fragments of Shakesperean English long obsolete among their former masters.

To Mr. Bennett and other philological investigators must be committed the task of working out the sources of many words of this interesting tongue. The purpose here is simply to record the oddities of the dialect as the Coast Country Negroes use it. After all, grotesque and interesting as is this speech to those familiar with it, it is only a vehicle for carrying to the reader the thought and life of an isolated group among the varied peoples that make up the complex population of this Republic.

There have been many writers of Negro dialect. Some stories that have come out of the North, feminine effusions chiefly, have been fearfully and wonderfully made; the thoughts of white people, and very common-place thoughts at that, issuing from Negro mouths in such phonetic antics as to make the aural angels weep!

In fact, no Northern writer has ever succeeded even indifferently well in putting Negro thought into Negro dialect. Even Poe, in "the Goldbug," put into

FOREWORD

the mouth of a Charleston Negro such vocables as
might have been used by a black sailor on an English
ship a hundred years ago, or on the minstrel stage,
but were never current on the South Carolina coast.
To recent Southern writers, therefore, one must turn
for intelligent understanding of the Negro character
and the recording of his speech, which varies in the
different sections of the South.

Thomas Nelson Page, recognized as the outstanding
exponent of the Virginia Negro in literature, has yet
touched his field lightly, considering chiefly the old
family man servant and his relations with his master's
household. Very beautifully and tenderly, because very
truthfully, Mr. Page has portrayed the ante-bellum
Negro man servant; but as to the younger Negro,
Negro life before and since the war, and the relations
of Negroes to one another, it is to be regretted that he
has contributed little or nothing.

The genius of Joel Chandler Harris, who, with
Judge Longstreet and his "Georgia Scenes," fixed
Georgia firmly upon the literary map of the world,
embalmed the Negro myths and folk-tales of the South
so subtly in the amber of his understanding that
"Uncle Remus" is known and loved by the children
of half the civilized world. There was little creative
work in "Uncle Remus." Mr. Harris claimed to record
the stories only "like hit wer' gun ter me." These
myths were known and told by Negro nurses to the
white children over all the Southern states, and in the
West Indian Islands as well, but the artistry of
Harris lay in the sympathetic understanding of
children prompted by his kindly heart, and the human
appeal of the tender relations of "the little boy" and

13

the old Negro family servant was irresistible, not only to the children, but to those happy grown-ups who loved them.

It is interesting to know that in the low-country of South Carolina, instead of "Brer Rabbit and Brer Fox," it is invariably "Buh Rabbit en' Buh Wolf." Strange, too, because wolves must have been found in upper Georgia and Carolina for more than a hundred years after they were exterminated along the coast, within whose forests still abound the grey foxes whose natural prey is the rabbit.

Encouraged by the success of the "Uncle Remus" stories, which greatly surprised this singularly modest man, Mr. Harris wrote novels and other stories of Georgia life among whites and blacks. While these were published successfully, it is upon the animal tales of "Uncle Remus" that his fame has been permanently established.

In the introduction to one of his volumes Mr. Harris has made a rather exhaustive study and analysis of the origin of these Negro myths. That they are of African origin none can doubt, but as on the West Coast of Africa, whence the slaves came to the American continent and the West Indian Islands, there are neither wolves, foxes, nor rabbits, it would be interesting to know what African animals were their legendary prototypes. In Jamaica many of the "Uncle Remus" tales are current and have been told to English children by their black nurses for generations, but there the Anancy Spider, a black, hairy tarantula-like creature, is substituted for the rabbit in the mythical triumph of mind over matter—cunning over physical strength— while the tiger does duty for the outwitted fox. Whence

14

FOREWORD

comes the Jamaican tiger? One can only surmise that
tales of the strength and ferocity of the Jaguar ("el
tigre" to the Spaniards) the great spotted cat of
South and Central America, were brought from the
mainland to the West Indies by the Indians of the
Caribbean Coast or the earlier Negro slaves; but in
Jamaica even the saddle-horse story is told complete in
all its details, the spider, clapping spurs to the tiger's
flanks and riding him up to the house of the "nyung
ladies" (Mis' Meadows an de gals) hitching him to a
post and walking boldly in to love's conquest. For the
"Tar Baby" story, instead of the violated spring, the
drinking preserve of fox or wolf, a "tar pole" is set
up in a banana grove, and to this sticky lure the pil-
fering spider is found stuck fast by the lord of the
plantation when he makes his morning rounds.

Harry Stillwell Edwards, of Macon, is another
Georgian whose charming stories in the up-country
or cotton plantation dialect have given pleasure to
thousands. With an unusual knowledge of the Negro
character—the first consideration, if one would present
truthful pictures of Negro life—he combines a charming literary style, and his writings deservedly rank
high among Negro stories.

Harris touched the Gullah dialect very lightly and
not with authority. In "Nights with Uncle Remus,"
a later collection of Negro myths, he puts into the
mouth of "Daddy Jack" certain variants of the Uncle
Remus stories told in the dialect of the coast, and in
his introduction to this volume he acknowledges his
obligation to correspondents in Charleston and elsewhere on the Carolina and Georgia Coasts for
the Gullah stories. It is almost certain that he

15

lacked first-hand contact with the story-tellers, and thus missed some of the subtleties of their speech as well as the peculiar construction of their sentences, differing entirely, as they do, from those of the up-country Negroes. Mr. Harris also includes in his introduction a brief glossary of Gullah words, and expresses the opinion that this peculiar dialect is more easily read than the Georgia dialect of "Uncle Remus," an opinion in which, unfortunately for the popularity of "Gullah," few will concur.

In "Myths of the Georgia Coast," Col. Charles Colcock Jones, of Georgia (and South Carolina, also, by the way) has given, in generally correct Gullah dialect, the stories current along the coast, many of them variants of those told in "Uncle Remus." A careful lawyer, Col. Jones has set down, with most meticulous exactness, and without imagination or embellishment, the stories as they were told him on the plantation.

One familiar with Negro speech recognizes that these tales are recorded as they fell from Negro lips, and as such they must be regarded, as far as they go, as the most authentic record of Negro myths on the continent—probably the originals of many of the "Uncle Remus" stories, for the slaves first came from Africa to the coast, bringing with them their myths and legends which gradually infiltrated into the hinterland.

A comparison of Jones's story of the rabbit and the tar baby with Uncle Remus's version of the same tale will be interesting as showing, not only the richer and quainter dialect of the Gullah, but also his more direct and homely mode of thought.

16

FOREWORD

The "Coteney" sermons of the Reverend John G. Williams, of Barnwell County, which appeared in the Charleston News & Courier about twenty-five years ago and were subsequently published in pamphlet form, purporting to be pulpit deliverances and consequently showing chiefly the Negro's conception of his relation to religion, are full of homely wit, and, written in the language of the coast, constitute a noteworthy contribution to dialectal literature.

Mrs. A. M. H. Christensen, of Beaufort, although of Northern birth, enjoyed soon after the war unusual opportunities for acquiring folk-lore stories of the sea-islands and littoral, and she has set forth in a small volume certain of the tales that were told her, which are in the main variants of versions of those already related by Harris and Jones.

Another booklet, by the late J. Jenkins Hucks, of Georgetown, S. C., recording some of the cases that came before him as Magistrate, is, perhaps, the most humorous example extant of Gullah undefiled.

Following the Stories, will be found a fairly complete Glossary of the Gullah speech as used by the Negroes of the Carolina-Georgia Coast and sea-islands, perhaps the only extensive vocabulary of Gullah that has yet been compiled.

The words are, of course, not African, for the African brought over or retained only a few words of his jungle-tongue, and even these few are by no means authenticated as part of the original scant baggage of the Negro slaves.

What became of this jungle-speech? Why so few words should have survived is a mystery, for, even after freedom, a few native Africans of the later im-

17

portations were still living on the Carolina Coast, and the old family servants often spoke, during and after the war, of native Africans they had known; but, while they repeated many tales that came by word of mouth from the Dark Continent—the story-tellers were almost invariably of royal blood, and did not hesitate to own it—they seem to have picked from the mouths of their African brothers not a single jungle-word for the enrichment of their own speech.

As the small vocabulary of the jungle atrophied through disuse and was soon forgotten, the contribution to language made by the Gullah Negro is insignificant, except through the transformation wrought upon a large body of borrowed English words. Adopting, as needed and immediately when needed, whatever they could assimilate, they have reshaped perhaps 1,700 words of our language by virtue of an unwritten but a very definite and vigorous law of their own tongue.

In connection with the Glossary, certain characteristic features of this strange tongue are noted. Their consideration will facilitate the reader's exploration of "The Black Border."

Of the stories included in this volume, the last fourteen were written and published in The State in the Spring of 1892. The remaining twenty-eight were written and published during the year 1918.

Ambrose E. Gonzales.

Columbia, August, 1922.

THE BLACK BORDER

NOBLESSE OBLIGE

Joe Fields was the most onery looking darkey on Pon Pon. Squat, knock-kneed, lopsided, slew-footed, black as a crow, pop-eyed, with a few truculent looking yellow teeth set "slantindicularly" in a prognathous jaw, he was the embodiment of ramshackle inefficiency. Although he worked only now and then, thanks to the industry of a hardworking wife, he usually owned, encumbered by a chattel mortgage, a wretched half-starved horse upon which he rode to his occasional employments.

Joe, runt as he was, had two sources of pride—the aristocratic lineage of his "owners," for he had belonged to the Heywards, and the achievement, on his own behalf, of the paternity of twins. Poor, patient Philippa, being only the mother, and a person of no family to speak of, having been the slave of a Charleston baker—whose fortunes rose during the war, though his Confederate yeast didn't—Philippa, of the bourgeoisie, was not taken into account. "Dem two twin duh my'own," and "Me nyuse to blonx to Mass Clinch," were the Andante and Allegro of Joe's prideful song. When some lusty young wench, during the customary "chaffing" of the plantation dinner hour, would ridicule his small size, Joe would swell with importance, grin like a 'possum, and overwhelm her with the retort: "Little axe cut down big tree! You see dem two twin, enty? Dem duh *my'own*." But the "two twins," poor little dusky wights, were in evidence in the neighborhood and could be estimated at their true

19

THE BLACK BORDER

value and Joe's paternal prowess appraised accordingly, but "Mass Clinch" lived away off "een Walterburruh" and, later, as governor, in Columbia, and his name, mouthed unctuously by his former slave, carried with it a weird, mystical importance, a portentous something that held his auditors with staring eyes and dropping jaws till Joe reached his climax, when the tension relaxed and they returned to earth.

Once started, Joe's imagination fed upon his words as a dog upon his own fleas. One day when Philippa reprobated his want of industry, Joe, other negroes being present, began to brag: "Wunnuh haffuh wu'k 'cause wunnuh blan blonx to po' buckruh. Yo' maussuh *self* haffuh wu'k! Enty I shum een town one time duh stan' een 'e bake sto' duh mek bread, en' 'e kibbuh wid flour 'tell 'e baid stan' sukkuh deseyuh cedar hedge duh wintuhtime w'en w'ite fros' dey 'puntop'um?"

"Enty yo' maussuh wu'k, Joe?"

"*Who? My Maussuh? Mass Clinch?* 'Ooman, you mus' be fool! Enty wunnuh know him duh quality? You ebbuh yeddy 'bout *quality* wu'k? Wuffuh him haffuh wu'k? No, suh! Him hab him ob'shay, Mistuh Jokok, fuh wu'k. *My* maussuh tek 'e pledjuh. 'E ride hawss, 'e eat ricebu'd en' summuh duck en' t'ing'. Him hab t'irteen plantesshun 'puntop Cumbee Ribbuh. Him plant seb'n t'ous'n' acre' rice."

"*Seb'n t'ous'n' acre'!*"

"Yaas, enty uh tell wunnuh 'e plant nine t'ous'n' acre' rice? Wunnuh t'ink me duh lie, enty? Uh swaytogawd, w'en uh bin Cumbee one time uh count fo' t'ous'n' head uh nigguh' duh hoe rice een de baa'n-yaa'd fiel'. Nigguh' stan' een Mass Clinch' fiel' sukkuh crow' duh mustuh! En' him hab seb'n hund'ud mule'!"

20

NOBLESSE OBLIGE

"De mule' wu'k 'pun Cumbee?" asked an iconoclast.
"Co'se de mule' wu'k, en' de nigguh' wu'k, en' Mistuh
Jokok wu'k. Eb'rybody wu'k 'scusin' my maussuh.
Dem mule' hab long tail' duh summuhtime fuh switch
fly, but w'en wintuhtime come en' dem 'leb'n hund'ud
mule' tail' roach, de pyo' hair wuh shabe off'um mek
one pile stan' big mo'nuh rice rick!"
"Hukkuh yo' maussuh plant all dat rice en' t'ing' ef
'e yent wu'k?"
"Enty I tell wunnuh him lib een Walterburruh?
Duh summuhtime 'e does dribe duh plantesshun now
en' den fuh see how him crap stan'. Him dribe two
hawss', en' de buckle on 'e haa'ness shine lukkuh gol'.
One nigguh duh seddown behine 'e buggy wid alltwo
'e han' fol' befor'um lukkuh hog tie. Mass Clinch hab
on one kid glub 'pun 'e han' wuh come to 'e elbow.
W'en 'e git Cumbee, 'e light out 'e buggy. T'ree nigguh' run up fuh hol' 'e hawss' head. Mistuh Jokok
mek'um uh low bow. Mass Clinch iz uh berry mannussubble juntlemun, alldo' him *iz* quality, en' him 'spon'
to de bow. Den 'e biggin fuh walk. Him hab shishuh
rich walk! Den 'e cock 'e hat one side 'e head. You
nebbuh see nobody kin cock 'e hat stylish lukkuh
Mass Clinch. Den 'e onbutt'n 'e weskit. 'E pit 'e lef'
han' een 'e britchiz pocket, en' swing 'e walkin' stick
een 'e right han', en' biggin fuh quizzit him ob'shay.
By dis time 'e git 'puntop de baa'nyaa'd hill en' look
obuh 'e fiel'.
" 'Jokok'," 'e say, " 'dat de stretch flow you got on
my rice, enty?' "
" 'No, suh, dat de haa'bis' flow.' "
" 'De debble'!" 'e say. " ' 'E mus' be mos' time fuh
ricebu'd!' "
" 'Yaas, suh. We gwine hab some fuh dinnuh'."

21

" 'Wuh else you got fuh eat?' " Maussuh quizzit'um.

" 'We got one cootuh soup mek out'uh tarrypin' wuh bin een one pen duh fatten 'pun gritch en' t'ing,' en' one trout fish, en' summuh duck'."

" 'You hab enny mint?' "

" 'Yaas, suh, we hab 'nuf'."

" 'Berry well, mek we a few julip'," 'e say. " 'You got enny mo' 'pawtun' bidness dat 'quire my 'ten-shun?' "

" 'Yaas, suh; snake hole en' crawfish en' t'ing' spile one uh we bank, en' de trunk blow out, en' uh hab uh berry bad break, en' Cumbee ribbuh comin' een de fiel'. You wantuh shum, suh?' "

" 'No, I t'engk you'," 'e say. " 'Leh de ribbuh tek 'e co'se. Leh we eat'."

"W'en 'e gitt'ru 'e bittle, 'e hab 'e fo' hawss' hitch up, en' Mistuh Jokok pit two-t'ree bag uh cootuh en' rice-bu'd en' summuh duck een him cyaaridge, en' 'e gone *spang* Walterburruh, same lukkuh bu'd fly! Da' duh *my* maussuh!"

By the time Joe concluded his story the noon hour was over, and the awed negroes rose silently to resume their work. One old mauma, turning to Joe as she knocked the ashes out of her clay pipe and carefully stuck it in the knotty wool behind her ear, said, "Joe, dat duh Gawd you binnuh talk 'bout, enty?"

"No, enty I tell wunnuh duh Mass Clinch Heywu'd! Him duh my maussuh, me duh him nigguh. Me ain' haffuh wu'k, him ain' haffuh wu'k. W'en wunnuh look 'puntop'uh she, wunnuh look 'puntop'uh me. Me en' him alltwo stan' same fashi'n."

"I t'aw't," said the old woman, scornfully, "I t'aw't 'e mus' be de blessed Gawd you bin gib shishuh high praise, but I always yeddy suh Him duh de ainjul' maussuh, en' I yeddy suh de ainjul' w'ite en' shiny lukkuh staar een de sky, but *you*, nigguh! *YOU black ez* uh *buzzut!*"

"MY MAUSSUH"

How beneficent must have been the institution of slavery under kindly masters which could cause Joe Fields, black, yellow-eyed, knock-kneed, slew-footed, longtime husband of Philippa, sometime father of twins, to boast, 53 years after the war, of the prowess and attainments of his former master, Duncan Clinch Heyward, sometime governor of South Carolina, now collector of internal revenue and sitting at the receipt of customs in the tall Palmetto building at Columbia, with dominion over war tax, surtax and every other impost internally levied by a benevolent government upon its loyal people. Although, perhaps, an infant in arms when Joe first looked freedom in the face, this "master" was exalted in, the mind of his former slave to almost Godlike proportions. "Joe' maussuh duh him Jedus," conservatively remarked Philippa.

The negroes about Pon Pon had been considerably exercised over the lengthening of the daylight hours by pushing forward the hands of the clock. Always suspicious of a Caucasian in the woodpile, it was generally regarded as a device for increasing the hours of negro labor. At a recent gathering of the idle black at Adams Run station, the opinion was expressed that the President, although a "Dimmycrack," must be "a smaa't man" to have lengthened the days on the darkeys and taken over the railroads.

New York, in the minds of the coast negroes, is the *ultima Thule*— at once the farthest North, and the very core and center of Yankeedom, where, in awful majesty, the President of the United States is supposed to sit like Zeus upon Mt. Olympus, or "my maussuh" in Columbia.

"Yaas, man," said Joe, "de Prezzydent smaa't man, fuh true, but 'e yent smaa't lukkuh maussuh, 'cause my maussuh haffuh gone New Yawk fuh tell de Prezzydent wuh fuh do. Same lukkuh maussuh tell Mistuh Jokok, him ob'shay 'puntop Cumbee, hummuch rice en' t'ing' fuh plant, same fashi'n him tell de Prezzydent wuh fuh do, en' de Prezzydent smaa't 'nuf fuh do'um.

"Todduh day uh hab uh hebby disapp'int. Uh yeddy suh uh big buckruh wedd'n' bin fuh hab een Adam' Run billage, en' uh yeddy suh my maussuh fuh come spang f'um Cuhlumbia to de wedd'n'. Uh gone en' pit on me shoe' en' da' new britchiz wuh uh buy yeah 'fo' las', en' uh pit on uh old weskit wuh uh bin hab, so 'e kin mek me fuh look lukkuh maussuh, en' uh tek me two foot en' walk, 'cause da' las' oxin wuh uh buy done dead onduhneet' de mawgidge da' buckruh mek me fuh pit 'puntop'um, en' uh yent hab nutt'n' fuh ride, en' uh gone slam Adam' Run billage to de wedd'n', so uh kin see maussuh, en' uh stan' outside de 'Piskubble chu'ch en uh fast'n' alltwo me yeye 'pun de do' fuh see w'en de buckruh' gone een en' w'en dem come out, en' 'nuf buggy en' cyaaridge en' t'ing' dribe up to de do', en' some dem torruh t'ing wuh buckruh hab now—uh cyan' call 'e name, but 'e hab fo' w'eel en' 'e run lukkuh bu'd fly, en' 'e smell lukkuh kyarrysene— en' uh see de buckruh git out en' gone een de chu'ch en' de preechuh pit on 'e new shroud, 'cause 'e done buy anodduh one attuh Estelle t'ief de fus' one 'e hab. Bimeby, eb'rybody come out de do', en' uh look 'tell uh pop-eye,' but uh nebbuh see no maussuh; en' den uh fin' out suh maussuh ent hab uh chance fuh come to de

wedd'n' cause him haffuh gone New Yawk fuh tell de
Prezzydent wuh fuh do! Yaas, suh, da' duh my maussuh! Same way 'e mek Mistuh Jokok en' dem nigguh'
en' t'ing' fuh stan' 'roun' 'puntop'uh Cumbee ribbuh,
uh yeddy suh same fashi'n him fuh do een Cuhlumbia
en' New Yawk. Uh yeddy suh my maussuh fuh lib
een Cuhlumbia een one high house. 'E high mo'nuh
loblolly pine tree. De house hab seb'n hund'ud room',
but dem buckruh' wuh bin Cuhlumbia tell me de house
ent hab no step fuh climb. W'en maussuh ready fuh
go to de top uh 'e house, 'e gone een one leetle room,
en' 'e shet de do' en' 'e shet 'e yeye. Fus' t'ing you
know, 'e gone *spang* to de top uh 'e house. W'en 'e
op'n 'e yeye de do' op'n, en' 'e walk een 'e office en' 'e
hab 'nuf man en' nyung lady een 'e office. 'E seddown
befo' 'e table. 'E table big lukkuh winnuh-house flatfawm. 'E pit uh seegyaa' een 'e mout'. 'E cross 'e
foot. 'E call one dem nyung lady. 'You got any
match?' maussuh ax'um.

" 'Yaas, suh,' 'e say."

" 'Please gimme uh matches,' maussuh say, berry
puhlite, 'en' light'um fuh me.' De nyung lady g'em de
match, but him say suh maussuh hab mo' 'speriunce
fuh light match' den w'at him hab. Maussuh say,
'berry well,' en' him 'cratch' de match 'pun 'e britchiz.
'E ketch fire. 'E light 'e seegyaa'. 'E blow smoke! 'E
study! Bimeby 'e reach obuh 'e table. 'E tetch one
leetle sump'n'nurruh lukkuh rattlesnake' butt'n. De
t'ing hab lightnin' een'um, but 'e nebbuh t'unduh.
W'en maussuh tetch'um, de felluh go '*ping*,' same
lukkuh oonuh t'row stick 'puntop tallygraf wire.
Bimeby, fo' man' run een de room. 'Hummuch money
oonuh tek f'um de buckruh teday?' maussuh ax'um.
'You tek all dem got?' "

26

"MY MAUSSUH"

" 'Yaas, suh,' dem say. 'Eb'n so we tek dem fowl off de roos'!' "

" 'Berry well,' maussuh say. 'Ef you tek all dem got, uh haffuh study 'pun uh plan fuh git mo', en' 'e tell de fo' man' fuh gone. W'en dem gone, maussuh study. 'E pit 'e head one side sukkuh bluejay. 'E blow smoke, en' 'e study. Maussuh *too* schemy! Bimeby, 'e say to 'eself: 'Wuh me en' de Prezzydent gwine do? Us done ketch all de money wuh de buck-ruh got, en' us yent lef'um nutt'n' 'cep' de railroad. Nigguh' ent got nutt'n' but dem han' en' dem foot'. Nigguh' ent fuh hab no money. Nigguh' fuh w'uk. Leh we see,' 'e say. 'Fus' t'ing, me en' de Prezzydent haffuh wu'k! Alltwo uh we duh juntlemun, en' jun-tlemun ent fuh wu'k.' Maussuh pit on 'e hat. 'E gone deepo' een Cuhlumbia. 'E ride de westyblue strain, en' 'e nebbuh git off 'tell 'e git spang New Yawk! 'E gone to de Prezzydent' house. De Prezzydent mek'um uh bow. 'E ax'um, 'How you lef' yo' fambly en' yo' crap?' Maussuh treat'um berry mannussubble. 'E tell'um 'e fambly well, but 'e crap ent stan' so berry good, 'cause nigguh' seem lukkuh dem ent lub fuh wu'k 'fo' day clean een de mawnin', en' dem dat good-fuhnutt'n' dem wan' knock-off soon ez daa'k come. 'Dem eegnunt tuh dat,' de Prezzydent tell'um. 'Ent you hab moonlight night' 'puntop Cumbee ribbuh?' Maussuh tell'um yaas, him hab monlight, fuh true, but seem lukkuh moonlight night' duh summuhtime nigguh' fuhrebbuh duh shout en' beat stick. Maussuh tell'um ef him kin mek uh law fuh pit anodduh hour een eb'ry day, him kin git mo' wu'k out de nigguh'. 'Berry well,' de Prezzydent tell'um. En' 'e mek law fuh sattify maussuh, same lukkuh maussuh tell'um.

"Den maussuh cross 'e foot, en' 'e study some mo'. 'E git schemy 'gen! Maussuh tell'um t'engky fuh de law wuh 'e mek, but 'e tell'um one t'ing wuh bodduhr'um duh de railroad wuh run f'um W'ite Hall fuh gone town. 'E tell'um eb'ry Sattyday W'ite Hall deepo' black wid nigguh' fuh gone town fuh t'row'way dem money. Maussuh tell'um de ticket en' de 'scusshun too cheap, en' ef de Prezzydent gi' *him* de railroad, him will chaa'ge mo' money fuh de ticket, en' den de nigguh' cyan' trabble so fas'. De Prezzydent tell'um, yaas, 'e plan berry good, but him hab uh sonny-law wuh hab uh berry good ecknowledge fuh git money out'uh buckruh', en' ef him kin git'um out'uh buckruh', him kin git'um out'uh nigguh' alltwo, so 'e say 'e gwine tek de railroad f'um de buckruh' en' g'em to 'e sonny-law, en' maussuh tell'um berry well, him 'low'um fuh do dat, en' den maussuh come home en' write uh ansuh to Mistuh Jokok fuh tell'um nigguh' fuh wu'k one mo' hour eb'ry day Gawd sen', en' Mistuh Jokok pass de wu'd; en', please Gawd, de Prezzydent' sonny-law mek nigguh' fuh pay mo' fuh ride de railroad, en eb'rybody say suh de Prezzydent shishuh smaa't man fuh mek dem law, but, oonuh yeddy me! duh *my maussuh* mek de Prezzydent fuh mek law! Him schemy fuh t'ink all dem t'ing so him en' de Prezzydent ent haffuh wu'k! *My* maussuh ent fuh wu'k. No, *suh!*"

AN ANTEMORTEM DEMISE

Under whatever star Philippa had been born, she had known only ill luck since her acquisition of a husband in Joe Fields, the slew-footed former slave of former Governor Heyward. Joe's pride in his former master was too great to permit him to walk, and the mortgaged horse or mule which he usually owned seldom lived very long on the light rations and scant attention it received. Its demise would soon be followed by another animal purchase, another mortgage, and another death. Joe occasionally worked when it suited him, but Philippa toiled unceasingly, and, although she seldom lived at home, she was very proud of the little establishment which her labor maintained. Always distrustful of Joe, she yet gave him the custody of, and dominion over, the few material things she possessed, representing in her character the contradictions not infrequently met with among those of her sex in higher circles.

Once upon a time, Philippa aspired to animal husbandry. Tired of buying bacon for Joe at the Cross Roads store, she applied the savings of several months of hard labor to the purchase of a young sow, and, perhaps in compliment to Joe, she bought a Berkshire, the blackest pig she could find. During the months of anticipation, while she worked for the money with which to make the purchase, her mind was full of the little black pigs that some time would be running about her yard around the cabin in the woodland, furnishing meat in prospect, and immediate companionship for Joe and their taciturn black daughter, Chris-

29

topher Columbus, who kept the home fires burning with whatever lightwood knots she could pick up in the pineland, while the wife and mother worked for "de buckruh" several miles away.

"Joe en' Cuhlumbus sho' gwine hab uh good cump'ny w'en uh buy da' hog en' sen' um home," she thought. "Ef uh kin raise ten pig' dis'yeah, maybe nex' yeah uh kin raise two-t'ree hund'ud, en' dem kin git 'nuf fuh eat een de swamp en' de pinelan' bidout buy'um no bittle."

So her fancy pictured her humble premises teeming with little pigs, first squirming in their beds among the straw, then grunting and running about the place, while Joe and Columbus, squatting on the door step of the cabin, communed with them in spirit and watched them grow. Later, the husky shoats would forage the pinelands and swamps for mast and acorns, and root about in the muddy branches for slugs and crayfish, then, grown to fat porkers, they would be slaughtered, salted and smoked, and hams, shoulders, and flitches would hang in festoons from the cabin rafters. So they successively passed through the seven ages of swine. At last the sow that was to transmute Philippa's dreams into realities was bought and paid for, and a message dispatched to Joe to come and take her home. In due time he arrived with ox and cart and, admonished by Philippa to meet the responsibility placed upon him, he drove away, the guardian of her hopes.

But Joe was not a forward-looking man. His eyes, lacking speculation, were filled with the insistent materialism of the moment. A present pig was worth a hundred in prospect. His eyeballs popped and his lips leaked as he viewed Opportunity that grunted so tan-

talizingly at his door, and the gnawings of "Guamba"
(the meat hunger of the savage African tribes) played
Lady Macbeth to his halting thoughts of murder and
turned them into resolution.

"Yaas, ma'am, uh glad fuh git uh chance fuh wu'k
out 'gen, 'cause Joe' shishuh po' puhwiduh. 'E nebbuh
hab no bittle een de house fuh eat. 'E lub fuh eat, but
'e say suh 'cause him maussuh duh quality, suh him
ent fuh nyam no dry bittle. Cawn hom'ny ent wut'
fuh Joe 'scusin' 'e got hog meat 'long'um fuh greese 'e
mout', en' da' time we'n uh binnuh wu'k Pon Pon uh
lavuh' haa'd fuh two munt' fuh buy uh sow so uh kin
raise hog meat fuh keep f'um fuhrebbuh duh run duh
sto' fuh bodduh wid dem Jew' en' t'ing', en' w'en uh
done pay fuh de sow, uh sen' one metsidge fuh tell Joe
fuh come fuh fetch'um home. Yuh come Joe een 'e
oxin cyaa't! 'E *dat* swonguh, 'e mos' mek somebody
wuh ent know'um t'ink suh *himself* wu'k fuh buy de
hog. Joe tie all fo' de sow' foot, 'e pit'um een 'e cyaa't,
en' 'e gone! Attuh uh week done gone, uh sen' wu'd
fuh tell Joe fuh come fuh see me fuh tell me how de
hog git 'long. Bimeby Joe come, 'e tell me de hog hab
uh berry good he'lt'. Uh t'engkful fuh yeddy dat,
'cause uh study 'puntop da' hog tummuch. Anodduh
week done gone, uh sen' fuh Joe 'gen. 'E come. Uh
ax'um how de hog' he'lt'. 'E say 'e he'lt' ent so berry
good, 'e say seem lukkuh de hog kind'uh po'ly. Uh
baig'um fuh ent tek 'e yeye off de hog, en' 'e mek me
uh prommus suh 'e gwine watch'um same lukkuh de
sow duh 'e own chile. Anodduh week gone. Joe come
'gen. 'E fetch uh berry sad news f'um de hog, 'cause
'e say suh de hog duh leddown, en' him berry 'f'aid
suh 'e dey at de p'int uh de't'. W'en him tell me dat,

31

uh seddown en' uh cry, but w'en uh look 'puntop'um
uh see suh Joe hab uh berry sattify' face, en' 'e jaw
look hebby 'tell 'e stan' lukkuh mufflejaw fowl, but
stillyet uh nebbuh 'spishun nutt'n', en' uh ax Joe
wuffuh mek 'e jaw fat. 'E tell me 'e hab uh teet'ache,
en' dat w'ymekso 'e jaw swell. Joe gone. Nex' week
'e come 'gen. 'E jowl hebby ez uh buckruh' barruh
Chris'mus time, en' 'e face look berry sattify. Uh
ax'um how de hog? 'E say de hog dead 'tell buzzut done
eat'um. W'en uh yeddy dat wu'd, me h'aa't hebby 'tell
'e ready fuh drap out me t'roat 'pun de du't. Uh look
'pun Joe 'gen. Uh study 'pun how 'e jaw fat. Uh
biggin fuh 'spishun. Uh ax'um ef 'e still hab uh teet'-
ache een 'e jaw. 'E tell me yaas, 'e teet'ache hot'um 'tell
'e cyan' nyam 'e cawn hom'ny. Uh ax'um ef 'e teet'
hot'um to dat, hukkuh him mout' kin grin lukkuh possum mout' duh wintuhtime w'en 'e dey een possimmun
tree? 'E say suh 'e teet'ache hot'um 'tell 'e mek'um fuh
grin. W'en 'e tell me dat, uh know him duh lie, en' uh
know berry well weh de hog gone, 'cause him hab
shishuh selfish face uh know suh nutt'n' gwine mek'um
grin 'cep'n' 'e belly tight. Dat, en' brag 'bout 'e maussuh, duh de only two t'ing fuh sweet'n 'e face fuh mek
laugh come een 'e mout'! Uh tell'um, berry well, uh
fret 'bout de hog 'tell uh haffuh gone home en' look
'puntop de po' creetuh' bone. 'E tell me suh buzzut done
scattuh 'e bone. Uh tell'um, nemmine, uh gwine fin'um
ef uh haffuh hunt spang tuh Caw Caw Swamp! Joe
stick out 'e mout' 'tell 'e oagly ez uh catfish, but uh yent
mine'um, en' uh climb' een de oxin cyaa't en' mek'um
fuh dribe tuh de house. Uh know berry well suh uh kin
mek Cuhlumbus fuh tell me de straight 'bout de hog,
'cause uh train'um fuh watch 'e Pa same ez beebu'd
watch beehibe. W'en uh git home uh holluh fuh

AN ANTEMORTEM DEMISE

Cuhlumbus, but 'e yent mek no ansuh en' uh know 'e
mus'be gone deepo. Uh look fuh de key een de knot
hole een one de house' log weh 'e does lef'um w'en
'e gone out, but befo' uh gone een de house uh tell Joe
fuh show me weh de hog done dead, so uh kin look 'pun
'e bone. Joe look shameface' ez uh suck-aig dog w'en
oonuh ketch'um een uh hen nes,' but 'e nebbuh crack
'e teet', en' 'e gone tuh de aige uh de swamp en' 'e tell
me suh dey de hog dead, en' de buzzut mus'be flew 'way
'long 'e bone, 'cause none ain' lef'. Uh tell'um 'e buzzut
strong fuh true, but de nigguh lie so easy, uh haffuh
suck me teet' at'um. Uh gone duh house, uh onlock
de do' en' uh gone een. De fiah done out een de chimbly,
but een de cawnuh uh de chimbly uh see de big spiduh
duh set, kibbuh' up wid ashish en' dead coal'. Uh ax
Joe wuh 'e got fuh eat. 'E say 'e dunno wuh Cuhlumbus cook' befo' 'e gone out. 'E say 'e 'spec' Cuhlumbus
him roas' tettuh, eeduhso bile' hom'ny een de spiduh.
Uh tek off de kibbuh. Please me Jedus, uh see de hog'
head dey een de spiduh *done cook*, en' uh know 'e duh
my'own, 'cause 'e hab de w'ite people' maa'k wuh uh
buy'um f'um een alltwo 'e yez! W'en uh look 'puntop
de sow head, en' 'membuh all de t'ing uh bin agguhnize
'bout fuh git da' hog, uh hab uh berry hebby sperrit en'
water full' alltwo me yeye. Uh ax Joe weh da' hog meat
come f'um? 'E say him ent know nutt'n' 't'all 'bout'um,
'e say suh somebody mus'be gi' Cuhlumbus de meat. 'E
say suh him binnuh nyam de pyo' cawn hom'ny 'tell
him hab uh dry drought een 'e t'roat. Uh tell'um, 'Joe,
you sho' iz uh fait'ful liah fuh tell lie. Yo' jaw swell
wid de pyo' fat you git f'um eat my hog, en' da' berry
sow gwine ride you duh night time. 'E fuh haant you
long ez you lib.' Cuhlumbus come. Uh ax'um hukkuh

33

de sow git 'e de't'. 'E say suh ebbuh sence de hog come home, 'e Pa binnuh hankuh at'um fuh eat. 'E say suh eb'ry day 'e Pa seddown on de do' step duh watch de hog duh root 'bout de yaa'd, en' eb'ry time de hog grunt, 'e Pa dat hongry fuh eat'um, 'e gnash 'e teet' en' water run out 'e mout'. One time de hog git ketch een de fench en' squeal. W'en Joe yeddy 'e woice 'e run out, en' 'stead'uh 'e loose'um out de fench, 'e tek axe, knock'um een e' head, en' 'e tell Cuhlumbus 'e kill'um fuh pit'um out 'e mis'ry. Den 'e staa't fuh eat'um to 'e tail en' eat spang t'ru de hog 'tell 'e git to 'e head wuh uh fin' een de pot! De berry day da' nigguh tell me suh de sow eenjy uh berry po' he'lt', 'e done eat de hog' two hanch! Uh *done* wid feed Joe! Ef 'e maussuh lub'um tuh dat, *him* kin feed'um! Meself, *uh done!*"

Though the abandoned Joe made bones of Philippa's hopes, he made none about acknowledging the butchery, and boasting of it, away from home.

"Joe, you sho' iz fat."

"Yaas, man, uh fat fuh true. Uh binnuh eat hog meat. Philpuh him buy uh hog en' sen' um home, en' de hog meet uh acksident een de fench, en' uh 'f'aid 'e gwine dead lukkuh da' todduh hog 'e hab fuh dead on me han' one time, en' buzzut git'um 'fo' uh hab uh chance fuh eat'um. Buzzut git uhhead'uh me one time, but 'e nebbuh do'um two time! My maussuh' nigguh haffuh smaa't mo'nuh buzzut! Stepney* ain' fuh come een *my* house! Me fuh 'low my maussuh' nigguh fuh perish fuh hog meat? *Me* jaw fuh dry 'long cawn hom'ny, en' buzzut mout' fuh greesy 'long de 'ooman hog meat, enty? No suh! Uh gwine nyam'um fus'! *Uh kill'um 'fo' 'e dead!*

*A Gullah synonym for hunger.

34

THE LION OF LEWISBURG

Several years ago there lived on the "Lewisburg" rice plantation of former Governor Duncan Clinch Heyward, one Monday White, a yellow negro and a persistent and imaginative practical joker. The little "Devil's Fiddles" which boys construct of empty tin cans and rosined string emit unchristian squeaks and groans when played upon with smooth hardwood sticks, and Monday believed that a similar device on a larger scale could be so manipulated as to frighten into hysterics half the negro population along Combahee River. Begging from the store a large empty powder keg, he surreptitiously rigged it up with stout twine which, well rubbed with rosin and scraped with a dry hickory stick for a bow, produced a hoarse and horrible sound which might have passed among the uninitiated for the roar of a lion—or for anything else.

Monday knew that the superstitious negroes feared most the unknown. The negro who would have taken a chance with alligator or bull, or the even more dangerous hind legs of a mule, could be scared stiff by a weird, unfamiliar sound in the woods at night. So Monday decided that the ear-jarring sound emitted by his double-bass "Devil's Fiddle" should do service for the roar of a lion, as these creatures were unknown on Combahee, and the few negroes who had once seen lions when the circus visited Walterboro, brought back marvelous tales of their ferocity and their terrible voices.

Monday baited his victims skilfully. One Saturday night when the store was crowded with trading negroes, he led the conversation lionwards. He needed

35

tales of terror, and the two or three negroes who had
once seen lions were willing to oblige. One of them
had even seen them fed. "W'en uh bin Walterburruh,
uh look 'puntop one dem annimel fuh call lion, en' uh
shum w'en dem duh g'em 'e bittle fuh eat."

"Nigguh g'em 'e bittle?

"No man, buckruh feed'um. Nigguh ent fuh feed'um.
Da' t'ing dainjus tummuch! Nigguh duh him bittle.
Lion en' nigguh alltwo come f'um Aff'iky, en' w'en dem
Aff'ikin king en' t'ing hab lion een dem cage, 'e g'em uh
nigguh fuh eat eb'ry day Gawd sen', en' 'e crack nigguh' hambone een 'e jaw sukkuh dem Beefu't nigguh
crack crab claw' w'en 'e done bile. Him *done* fuh lub
nigguh! W'en dem sukkus man fuh feed'um een Walterburruh, dem fetch half uh bull yellin' fuh 'e bittle,
en' w'en da' t'ing look 'puntop de meat, 'e tail t'rash'
'pun de flo' sukkuh nigguh duh t'rash rice 'long flail,
en' 'e gyap 'e mout' same lukkuh Mistuh Jokok op'n 'e
trunk mout' fuh t'row uh flow 'puntop Mass Clinch'
rice! 'E woice roll lukkuh t'unduh roll, en' w'en 'e
holluh, eb'ry Chryce' nigguh t'row 'e han' obuh e' two'
yez en' run out de tent, en' gone!"

"Tengk Gawd dem annimel nebbuh come 'puntop
Cumbee!" a woman fervently exclaimed.

"Yaas, tittie," said another, "ef da' t'ing ebbuh come
yuh, me fuh run Sabannuh. Uh nebbuh stop run 'tell
uh done pass de Yamassee!"

Others joined in the trembling chorus and Monday,
when they had become sufficiently worked up, shrewdly
spilled the first spoonful of powder leading to his mine.
"Oonuh nigguh, one buckruh binnuh talk 'puntop de
flatfawm to W'ite Hall deepo dis mawnin', en' uh
yeddy'um tell dem torruh buckruh suh one sukkus hab

36

THE LION OF LEWISBURG

uh acksident to Orangebu'g, en' one lion git out 'e
cage en' run een de swamp en' gone, en' de buckruh try
fuh ketch'um but dem 'f'aid fuh gone een de swamp,
en' dem sen' dem dog attuhr'um, en' de lion kill t'irteen
beagle one time!"

"Oh Jedus!" cried an excited woman, "Uh berry
'f'aid da' t'ing gwine come Cumbee! Hummuch mile
Orangebu'g stan' f'um yuh?"

"Uh dunno hummuch mile," Monday replied, "but
uh know lion kin mek'um 'tween middlenight en' dayclean, en' ef uh ebbuh yeddy 'e woice roll een dish'yuh
swamp, meself gwine git een me trus'me'gawd coonoo
en' uh fuh gone down Cumbee ribbuh, en' uh nebbuh
stop paddle 'tell uh git Beefu't!"

A week passed. Like the waves from a stone thrown
into still waters, the lion stories spread among the outlying plantations in all directions. Saturday night
found Monday early at the store. Another convenient
buckra at White Hall station had told that morning of
the lion's escape from the Edisto and his crossing over
the intervening pinelands into the Salkehatchie
Swamp and, as most people know, the Salkehatchie
River, below the line of the Charleston and Savannah
railway, becomes the Combahee. The lion was loose,
therefore, in their own proper swamp, and might even
now be riding a floating log down the current of their
beloved river!

Monday stealthily slipped out. An hour later, when
the negroes in and about the store had worked themselves up to a delectable pitch of excitement, an
unearthly groaning roar came from the woods nearby.
The night was hot, but the negroes almost froze with
fear, and the clerk, in whom Monday had confided,

37

raised no objection when the negroes within the store called in their companions from the outside and asked permission to bar the door.

"Oonuh yeddy'um, enty! Wuh uh tell you 'bout da' t'ing' woice?" said the negro who had seen lions in Walterboro.

Monday's "Devil's Fiddle" groaned again, and as its dying notes trembled on the summer night, a rush was made to close and bolt the windows. The kerosene lamps smoked and flared in the fetid air. The men listened and shuddered as the recurrent roars, now muffled, reached their expectant ears. The women wailed. "O Gawd! uh lef' me t'ree chillun shet up een me house," cried one. "Uh 'spec' da' t'ing done nyam'um all by dis time!"

"Shet yo' mout', 'ooman," said a masculine comforter. "Hukkuh him kin eat en' holluh alltwo one time? Yo' chillun ent fuh eat."

"Me lef' my juntlemun een de house," said another woman, with resignation, "Uh 'spec' him done eat."

"Wuh you duh bodduh 'bout loss uh man?" said the mother. "Man easy fuh git tummuch. Me yent duh bodduh 'bout man. Uh kin git anodduh juntlemun ef da' t'ing nyam my'own, but weh uh fuh git mo' chillun?"

"Go'way, gal, ef you kin fuh git anodduh juntlemun, same fashi'n Gawd help you fuh git anodduh chillun."

After a while the roaring ceased and the clerk, being perilously near suffocation, calmed the fears of the negroes and opened the windows. The trembling darkeys cocked their ears and listened apprehensively, but the shrilling of the Cicada among the pines and the bellowing of the bullfrogs in the distant canals were the only sounds that broke the silence of the night so

recently full of terrors. After awhile the door also
was unbarred and opened, and a bold man borrowed an
axe from the storekeeper and adventured far enough
to cut some slabs of lightwood from a familiar stump.
The hero added to his popularity by splitting these up
and distributing them among the members of the
gentler sex, whose escorts lighted torches and convoyed
them in a body back to the quarters, where the children
and husbands whom they left at home were found
intact.

At church on Sunday, the Lewisburg negroes spread
among their brethren from the other plantations the
news of the coming of the lion, and the "locus pastuh"
fervently touched upon the king of beasts. "Puhtec'
we, Maussuh Jedus, f'um da' t'ing oonuh call lion.
Lead'um, Lawd, to weh de buckruh' cow en' t'ing' duh
bite grass so him kin full 'e belly bedout haffuh nyam
nigguh, en' ef 'e *yiz* haffuh tek nigguh fuh 'e bittle, do,
Lawd, mek'um fuh tek dem sinful nigguh wuh ent wut,
en' lef' de Lawd' renointed. Mek'um fuh do wid de
good sistuh en' bredduh 'puntop dis plantesshun same
lukkuh oonuh mek'um fuh do long Dannil—" "Yaas,
Lawd," shouted Monday, the hypocrite, "ef 'e *yiz* fuh
eat nigguh, mek'um fuh eat dem nigguh 'puntop'uh
Bonny Hall 'cross de ribbuh, en' tek 'e woice out'uh we
pinelan'." "Yaas, Lawd!" "Please suh fuh do'um,
Lawd!" shouted the fervent brethren and sisters. And
stealthily, about two hours after dark that night, while
the emotional negroes were alternately laughing, shouting and praying, Monday put his Devil's Fiddle into
a sack, slipped into his canoe, and, crossing to the
opposite shore of the river, roared frightfully along
the Bonny Hall water line, terrifying the negroes on

that plantation and filling the Lewisburg darkeys with thankfulness that their prayers had been answered.

Another week passed. Monday, playing with them as a cat plays with a mouse, kept quiet, until by Saturday night, no news having come of any damage at Bonny Hall, the Lewisburg negroes hoped that the lion had been captured by "de sukkus buckruh," or had left the neighborhood, and soon after nightfall, half the plantation gathered at the store.

About nine o'clock, when the store was jammed with briskly trading negroes, from afar in the woods came the ominous roar of the hand-made lion. It was distant, and the negroes, while badly frightened, stood their ground to await developments, but a few minutes later the awful sound came again from a nearer point, and by the time the roaring had come within a quarter of a mile of the place, the negroes were panic-stricken, and most of them hurried from the store and ran to the quarters, where they bolted themselves in, to pass a night in fear and trembling, for at intervals until past midnight, their ears carried terror to their souls. On Sunday, Monday, wearing the sanctimonious expression of a cat that has just swallowed the canary, moved among them, listening with sympathetic ears to the tales of perilous adventures that some of them had experienced. "Bredduh W'ite," said a church sister, "lemme tell you. Las' night uh gone to Sistuh Bulow' house attuh daa'k. Uh did'n' bin to de sto', 'cause las' week de buckruh credik me, en' uh 'f'aid 'e gwine ax'me fuh pay'um wuh uh owe'um, en' uh gi' Sistuh Bulow de money fuh buy me rashi'n' en' t'ing', en' uh seddown een 'e yaa'd fuh wait 'tell 'e come back. Him house ent dey een nigguhhouse yaa'd, 'e stan' to 'eself 'pun de aige uh de pinelan'. Bumby uh yeddy da' t'ing' woice. W'en uh yeddy'um fus', 'e bin fudduh, en' uh t'awt 'e bin Jackass duh holluh, but w'en 'e git close, uh ruckuhnize 'e woice, en' uh know 'e duh lion. Uh *dat* 'f'aid, uh cyan' talk. Uh trimble sukkuh mule' shoulduh duh shake off cowfly. W'en da' t'ing come t'ru de bush en' look 'puntop me, me two eye' pop' out me head! 'E stan' high mo'nuh Mass Clinch' mule. 'E yeye shine lukkuh dem fiah buckruh does mek 'puntop'uh Jackstan' duh pinelan' duh summuhtime fuh keep off muskittuh! W'en 'e op'n 'e jaw, 'e t'roat red lukkuh beef haslett! 'E mout' full'up wid teet' sukkuh harruh, en' blood duh drip out 'e jaw sukkuh water drap outuh nigguh mout' w'en 'e look 'puntop'uh watuhmilyun! W'en uh shum stan' so, uh drap' 'puntop me two knee' en' uh baig' me Jedus fuh sabe me! Uh dat 'f'aid, uh shet me yeye', en' w'en uh done pray en' op'n'um' 'gen, de t'ing gone!" And so on, each tale of dreadful experience told by one negro, being over-matched by the next, who, if one gave "free rein" to her imagination, would be sure to strip the bridle off her's and throw it away. "Meself shum," related a 20th Century Munchausen in petticoats. "Uh bin down de road uh piece 'bout two hour' attuh daa'k fuh try fuh ketch da' gal, 'cause uh kinduh 'spishun my juntlemun, en' uh binnuh folluh 'e track fuh ketch'um, but uh nebbuh ketch'um yet, but uh gwine fuh ketch'um, 'cause uh got me yeye 'puntop da' gal f'um W'ite Hall wuh tote dem bottle en' t'ing onduhneet' 'e frock fuh sell rum to all dese man eb'ry Satt'd'y night, en' mek'um fuh t'row 'way dem money 'stead'uh g'em to dem wife en' t'ing', en' uh bin swif' 'pun da' gal track, 'cause yistidd'y w'en my juntlemun git pay'off fuh 'e wu'k, 'e come en' pit half 'e money een me han' befo' uh kin ax'um fuhr'um, en' da' t'ing mek me fuh know him duh fool me. Uh look 'puntop'um en' uh shum duh grin. Sattifaction duh run roun' da' nigguh mout' same lukkuh puppy run roun' de yaa'd attuh 'e own tail! Uh know man tummuch, en' w'en 'e stan' so, 'e yent fuh trus'! Eb'ry time man gi' money to 'e lawfully lady, 'e h'aa't duh cry, en' w'en him look lukkuh 'e glad fuh g'em, 'e face duh lie, 'e try fuh kibbuh up 'e h'aa't, en' 'e done mek'up 'e min' fuh fool'um, but me! uh got uh ecknowledge fuh look t'ru 'e face, en' w'en uh look 'puntop 'e h'aa't, 'e stan' crookety ez uh cowpaat'! Da' gal kin fool some dem todduh 'ooman, but 'e yent fuh fool me! Him hab two petticoat', one mek out'uh homespun clawt', lukkuh we'own, en' todduh one hab skollup', lukkuh buckruh lady' own. W'en him hab on de clawt' petticoat, none de man nebbuh bodduhr'um, but w'en 'e walk t'ru Lewisbu'g nigguhhouse yaa'd wid da' skollup' petticoat staa'ch' *stiff*, en' 'e frock hice up high fuh show'um, en' dem man look 'puntop de skollup en' yeddy de staa'ch duh talk '*she, she, she*' w'en 'e walk, dem *know* suh 'e got rum fuh sell—dat duh 'e sign—dem t'roat' biggin fuh dry, en' dem eb'ry Gawd' one pick uh chance fuh folluhr'um, but dem todduh 'ooman, dem t'ink suh man lub da' skollup' t'ing 'cause 'e stylish, en' dem study 'bout git skollup' petticoat demself fuh mek man fuh folluhr'um, but duh nutt'n' but de pyo' rum dem man dey attuh. Dem fuh folluh da' gal ef 'e petticoat mek out'uh grano sack!

"W'en uh did'n' ketch de gal, uh staa't' fuh gone home, en' uh look 'way off t'ru de pinelan' en' uh see two t'ing duh shine sukkuh injine headlight! Uh look 'gen, 'e come close, en' uh see 'e duh annimel eye! Bumby 'e op'n' 'e mout' fuh holluh. Spaa'k' duh come out-uhr'um en' 'e woice roll 'tell de groun' shake. Uh neb-buh hab no time fuh pray. W'en uh see da' fiah come out 'e mout', uh tell'um, 'so long, bubbuh, *uh gone!*' en' uh hice me 'coat en' uh tek me two foot een me han' en' uh nebbuh study 'bout no road. Uh gone slam t'ru de bush! Briah 'cratch' me, uh dunkyuh. Jackwine' ketch' me foot en' obuht'row me, uh jump up, uh gone 'gen! One harricane tree bin 'cross de paat', uh bus' t'ru'um sukkuh fiah gone t'ru broom grass fiel'. Nutt'n' nebbuh stop me, 'cause, bubbuh, *uh run!* W'en uh git een de big road, uh hog binnuh leddown fuh tek 'e res'. W'en 'e yeddy me foot duh beat groun', 'e jump up fuh run, but uh obuhtek'um dat swif', me foot kick'um ez uh gwine, en' uh yeddy'um holluh behin' me sukkuh tar-rier duh graff'um by 'e yez! Briah tayre off me frock 'tell, time uh git nigguhhouse yaa'd, uh yent hab nutt'n' lef' but me shimmy, en' w'en dem nigguh look 'puntop me dem t'ink uh sperrit come out de 'ood. Uh run een me house, uh shet me do', en' uh nebbuh come out 'gen 'tell sunhigh!"

Monday inclined his ear and listened to the negroes, but he showed them no mercy, and before the end of the third week his lion became so bold that a roar came even in broad daylight from among the reeds along the river bank, frightening the laborers out of the fields and even prompting a neighboring planter to order his foreman to lock up the mules for safety when he saw the hands flying in terror from the ricefields! At last, to avoid industrial paralysis, the owner of the planta-tion, discovering Monday's plot, suppressed the powder keg lion. And the master saved his people, the Hal-cyon nested again on the waves of the Combahee, bringing peaceful days and peaceful ways to the Lewisburg plantation, with nothing more exciting than the quest of "da' skollup' petticoat," but—"that's another story."

THE LION KILLER

The lion of Lewisburg was dead. By order of former
Governor Duncan Clinch Heyward, the Devil's Fiddle
with which Monday White, yellow-skinned plantation
practical joker, had terrorized the negroes of the neighborhood for three weeks, had been hidden away, and
the groaning roar of the powder keg lion was no longer
heard in the land. Monday, the clerk at the store and
the master of the plantation, guarded the secret carefully and the negroes, who no longer heard the terrible voice echoing through the woods at night, or
along the reeds by the river, believed that the lion,
exorcised by the spirit of prayer, had departed from
among them and gone to some less regenerate community. Those who had told marvelous tales of the
fierce creature whose flaming eyes had burned into
their souls, whose bloody jaws had frozen them with
fright, told and retold with elaboration and close attention to detail,—and finally themselves believed, the first
told stories of their encounters with the monster. Some
of those who had had no personal experience with the
lion of Lewisburg believed only part of the oft told
tales. Others were frankly skeptical, for, while practically all of them believed in the lion, few were willing
to yield to the storytellers the prestige of having come
unscathed through such perilous adventures. These
stories are always liberally discounted among the
negroes, however. At a "baptizing" on the Combahee,
the big black pastor had doused in the canal one after
another of the "seeking" sisters. They emerged from
the turbid waters gurgling and choking, but all were

too full of water, or the spirit, for utterance. At last
one lusty wench with better breath control than the
others came up smiling, and with wind enough for
speech. "Oh Jedus!" she yelled, determined to create
a sensation, "uh see Gawd onduhneet' de water! Uh
fin' me Gawd. *'E look 'puntop me!*"

"You lie!" said the envious sister who had just preceded her, " *'tis cootuh!* Enty I shum?"

Gradually the negroes recovered their confidence,
and resumed their nocturnal rambles, visiting from one
plantation to another, but they usually went in small
companies and seldom adventured alone, save when
some bibulous man, glimpsing the "skollup' petticoat"
of the peripatetic bootlegger from White Hall as she
swished her starched symbol through the Lewisburg
quarters on Saturday nights, followed with parched
tongue and arid throat to some convenient spot where
coin could be exchanged for contraband.

In some way it was generally understood that, sup-
plementing the plantation prayers, "Mass Clinch,"
through personal magnetism or the exercise of some
former-gubernatorial authority, had had a great deal
to do with speeding the going leonine guest. This
rumor traveled by grapevine thirty-odd miles from
Combahee to Adams Run, the abiding place of Joe
Fields, the former governor's former slave, whose confidence in "Maussuh's" powers of accomplishment,
equalled the Mohammedan belief in the esteemed
Prophet's ability to stock the Hereafter with Houris.
It was true that "Maussuh" had commanded the roaring to cease—and it did, but Joe's imagination insisted
upon supplying all the "corroborative detail."

Joe foregathered with some of his friends at the rail-

THE LION KILLER

way station, for things were not going pleasantly at
home. His wife Philippa was one of those hard-work-
ing, aggravating creatures who, by her very industry
and self-abnegation, forced upon the lordly loafer by
whom she was husbanded a sense of his own inferior-
ity. Philippa worked out among the white people,
cooking and washing and scrubbing, while Joe rode
about on a mortgaged horse or ox and boasted as a Sir
Oracle at the Cross Roads or the station. Philippa
was always willing to feed Joe, but she was none the
less ready to season his food with the sauce of her
tongue, and whenever she came home, her sense of duty
urged her to remind Joe of his shortcomings. Once a
fighter, hard work and scanty food had worn her body
and somewhat broken her spirit, and she no longer
thrashed her grown daughter Christopher Columbus
as she once did, "jes' 'cause 'e look lukkuh 'e pa," but
Joe, having to take the sauce with the meat, seldom
wasted time in replying that he could utilize in eating,
and thus the more speedily put himself out of earshot.
Once away among his cronies, however, he expressed
himself boldly and truculently. "Da' 'ooman keep on
fuh onrabble 'e mout' 'tell uh w'ary fuh yeddy'um.
'E stan' sukkuh briah patch w'en blackberry ripe. 'E
gi' you bittle fuh eat, but 'e 'cratch you w'ile you duh
eat'um! Him iz uh fait'ful 'ooman fuh true, en' 'e lub
fuh wu'k, but w'en him dey home, uh yent fuh hab no
peace. Seem lukkuh nutt'n' wuh uh do nebbuh suit'um.
Ef uh seddown een me rockin' cheer duh fiah fuh tek
me res' w'ile uh duh nyam me bittle, 'e fau't me fuh
dat. Same fashi'n ef uh git 'puntop me oxin fuh ride
to de Cross Road, oonuh kin yeddy'um talk 'bout uh
lazy man ent wut!"

" 'E ebbuh fau't you w'en you got axe, eeduhso hoe een yo' han'?"

"Who, me? *Me* fuh hab hoe een me han'? No, suh! Maussuh' nigguh ent fuh hol' hoe! Wuffuh me haffuh hol' hoe w'en uh hab po'buckruh nigguh fuh wife? *Him* fuh hol' hoe! Philpuh' maussuh duh po' buckruh f'um town. Him binnuh bake bread ebbuh sence slabery time. Wuh him ebbuh do? *Him* ebbuh kill lion?"

"*Kill lion!* Wuh you duh talk 'bout nigguh? Who-ebbuh you ebbuh yeddy kin kill lion?"

"My maussuh fuh kill'um!"

"Go'way, Joe! You duh dream. Een de fus' place, no lion ent fuh dey een dis country, een de two place, you ent got no maussuh, en' een de t'ree place, ef you iz bin hab maussuh, him ent able fuh kill no lion."

"Me yent hab no maussuh! Enty you know suh uh nyuse to blonx to Mass Clinch Heywu'd to Lewisbu'g plantesshun 'puntop Cumbee? Oonuh eegnunt nigguh', oonuh yent know suh him hab t'ree t'ous'n' acre' rice en' mo'nuh t'ree t'ous'n' nigguh' en' mule en' t'ing'? Oonuh nebbuh yeddy 'bout da' lion wuh git'way f'um de sukkus to Orangebu'g todduh day en' gone down Sawlketchuh swamp 'tell 'e git Cumbee, en' 'e run all Maussuh' nigguh' out 'e fiel' en' 'e mek Maussuh' ob'shay, Mistuh Jokok, fuh climb tree?"

"Nobody nebbuh yeddy 'bout'um, Joe, en' *you* neb-buh yeddy 'bout'um. Hukkuh you fuh yeddy 'bout'um? You bin Cumbee?"

"Uh yent bin no Cumbee, but uh got uh tittie lib on Maussuh' place Cumbee, dat how uh yeddy 'bout'um."

"Wuh yo' tittie tell you, Joe?"

"W'en de lion git'way out de sukkus 'e gone spang

THE LION KILLER

f'um Orangebu'g to Sawlketchuh swamp en' 'e nebbuh stop 'tell 'e git Lewisbu'g!"

"Wuffuh him haffuh stop Lewisbu'g, Joe?"

"Enty you know suh Maussuh' nigguh' fat? Maussuh' nigguh' fat fuh sowl! Lion hab sense 'nuf fuh know fat nigguh w'en 'e shum, en' him kin smell *fat* nigguh mo' fudduh den him kin smell *po'* nigguh, en' Maussuh mek shishuh hebby crap uh rice en' 'tettuh en' t'ing dat him nigguh' fat mo'nuh all dem todduh nigguh' 'puntop Cumbee ribbuh!

"Soon ez de lion git Lewisbu'g, 'e stop. 'E know suh him bittle dey dey, en' 'e mout' biggin fuh run water. Bumbye duh nighttime, 'e woice roll een Maussuh' pinelan' en' all dem nigguh' tarrify' sukkuh chickin tarrify' w'en fu'lhawk' wing t'row shadduh obuhr'um! Dem nigguh' 'f'aid 'tell dem fool! Dem lock demself een dem house duh night, en', alldo' 'e duh summuh-time, dem mek fiah fuh bu'n so de lion cyan' come down de chimbly. W'en de lion cyan' git no nigguh' fuh eat 'cause dem all lock'up, 'e gone duh 'ood en' meet uh cow en' 'e kill *him* fuh 'e bittle. W'en 'e done nyam de t'ree cow—"

"*T'ree cow!* Joe, hukkuh him kin eat t'ree cow' w'en 'e only kill one?"

"Him nyam t'ree cow', enty? Him kin nyam'um uh dunkyuh ef 'e yent dead. You ebbuh see lion? Wuh Pon Pon nigguh know 'bout lion? Seem lukkuh w'en 'e done nyam dem t'ree cow', 'e jis' mek'um fuh hongry good, en' 'e gone back nigguhhouse yaa'd fuh see ef him kin git uh chance fuh nyam nigguh'. 'E walk up en' down, 'e t'rash' 'e tail, 'e gnash' 'e teet' en' 'e holluh sukkuh jackass en' alligettuh en' bull all t'ree one time! You kin yeddy dem nigguh' een dem house duh pray.

49

Dem eb'ry Gawd' one prommus dem Jedus fuh folluh Him wu'd, ef 'e only spayre dem life. One tell'um suh ef Him tek de lion' jaw off'um, him nebbuh t'ief Maussuh' rice no mo', en' eb'ry one tell de Lawd 'bout some uh dem light sin wuh dem willin' fuh t'row'way ef dem life sabe."

"Light sin! Mekso dem ent prommus fuh t'row'way dem hebby sin ?"

"No, man, dem ent fuh t'row'way dem hebby sin, uh dunkyuh ef lion crack dem bone'. Een slabery time nigguh baig 'e maussuh' paa'd'n fuh t'ief 'e fowl w'en 'e git ketch, but w'en 'e kill *cow*, 'e nebbuh crack 'e teet', en' eb'n so ef 'e maussuh ketch'um duh skin de cow, him fuh tell 'e maussuh 'e fin'um dead een de 'ood, en' 'e duh skin'um fuh tek de hide to 'e maussuh fuh sabe'um f'um buzzut! No, man; oonuh fuh hol' oonuh hebby sin sukkuh sheep buhr hol' mule' tail, 'tell Gabrull blow 'e hawn en' de Lawd tek'um off!"

"Bumbye w'en dayclean en' de lion nebbuh git no nigguh, 'e gone en' kill fo' mo' cow', en' w'en 'e done nyam'um 'e gone duh 'ood en' leddown fuh tek 'e res', en' nobody nebbuh yeddy'um 'gen 'tell Sat'd'y night come. All t'ru de week de nigguh' swonguh en' sattify een dem min' 'cause dem t'ink suh dem pray' mek de lion fuh gone'way en' le'm'lone, but 'e yent duh no pray' mek'um fuh gone, duh dem fo' cow' wuh 'e nyam, mek' 'e belly full 'tell 'e yent hab no room fuh nigguh!"

"W'en Sat'd'y night come, de lion holluh 'gen en' all de nigguh' run out de sto' en' gone een dem house fuh hide. Monday come, en' de nigguh' 'f'aid fuh gone een Maussuh' fiel' fuh wu'k. Mistuh Jokok dunno wuh fuh do. Him sen' uh ansuh to Cuhlumbia fuh tell Maussuh 'cep'n' him come Lewisbu'g, all him nigguh' fuh eat.

50

THE LION KILLER

Maussuh ride de train. 'E come. 'E git off W'ite Hall
deepo, 'e git 'pun 'e hawss, 'e tu'n to 'e ob'shay, 'Jokok,'
'e say, 'Weh da' annimel fuh hide? Lemme shum!'"

"Mistuh Jokok tell'um de las' time dem yeddy 'e
woice, 'e bin een de t'icket en' reed en' t'ing by de ribbuh bank. Maussuh nebbuh wait fuh yeddy no' mo'. 'E
snatch 'e rifle out'uh Mistuh Jokok' han', 'e jam 'e two
spuhr een e' hawss' belly, 'e hawss jump' nine foot off
de groun' een de ellyment, en' 'e gone! Maussuh run 'e
hawss 'tell 'e git 'cross de causeway 'pun de ribbuh
bank, den 'e biggin fuh ride slow en' t'row 'e yeye
befor'um fuh see weh da' t'ing fuh hide. W'en 'e git
close de briah en' t'ing, 'e hawss cock' 'e yez befor'um, 'e
snawt' en' 'e 'tan'up 'trait 'pun 'e hine foot. W'en 'e do
dat, Maussuh know suh de lion dey een dem bush! De
hawss come down 'pun 'e fo' foot. 'E duh shake sukkuh
rice t'rasher shake. Maussuh yeddy sump'nurruh duh
groan een de t'icket. Bumbye de lion come out. W'en
'e op'n' 'e mout' 'e teet' long sukkuh cawncob! Maussuh t'row 'e rifle to 'e yeye. 'E only hab one ball een'um
en' 'e know suh ef him ent kill da' t'ing *dead*, da' lion
fuh nyam him en' 'e hawss alltwo. Maussuh tek aim at
'e t'roat. 'E cut loose, *bam!* W'en de gun crack, 'e
look! De lion' head roll down de bank 'tell 'e fall een
de ditch! Maussuh cantuh up to Lewisbu'g. 'E tell
Mistuh Jokok fuh sen' uh waagin en' fo' mule' fuh
fetch'um to de yaa'd. Dem medjuhr'um en' 'e stan'
t'irteen foot long! W'en de nigguh' yeddy suh 'e dead,
dem stop wu'k en' dem fuh mek fiah en' shout roun' da'
lion de Gawd' night! Bumbye buckruh' come fuh look
'puntop'um en' w'en dem yeddy suh 'e seb'nteen foot
long, dem 'stonish!"

"Yaas, uh 'spec' nigguh' en' buckruh' alltwo fuh

'stonish ef dem kin yeddy you fuh tell'um, Joe. Da' lion duh git mo' longuh! W'ile ago you bin fuh mek'-um t'irteen foot long."

"Fus' time dem medjuhr'um 'e yent bin hab no head. Enty 'e fuh medjuh mo' attuh dem tie 'e head back 'pun 'e neck weh Maussuh' ball cut'um off? Oonuh mus'be fool!"

"Joe," said another doubting crony, "hukkuh da' leely ball kin fuh cut off da' lion' head? 'E tek soad, eeduhso axe, fuh do da' t'ing?"

"Who' Maussuh kill da lion! Duh yo' Maussuh, enty? Enty uh tell oonuh eegnunt nigguh' suh de hawss skayre 'tell 'e shake, en', same time Maussuh pull' 'e trigguh, de hawss trimble' 'tell 'e mek da' ball fuh wabble 'cross de lion' neck 'tell *'e cut 'e t'roat f'um yez to yez!*"

"OLD BARNEY"

Old Friday Giles was the English purist of Penny Creek. A former "driver" and slave of Mr. Edward Barnwell, his manners were pompous, though ingratiating. His speech was unusually good save for his ludicrous use of "she" and "her" for all things singular, animate or inanimate.

For many years "Old Barney," an Ayrshire bull acquired from the Barnwell family, was the terror of all the negroes roundabout. True to his Scottish breeding, Barney was both stubborn and acquisitive and lived up to

"The good old rule * * * the simple plan
That they should take who have the power
And they should keep who can."

Barney had the power. Therefore he took. He loved green peavines as the Scot loves his haggis, and whenever he fancied them he had but to lean against the miserable fences enclosing the negroes' patches, walk through, and help himself. The negroes would shoot him up with firearms and ammunition of all sorts and his hide was constantly full of lead of every size from mustard seed to swan shot, but fear kept the marksmen from getting near enough to hurt him seriously, so Barney philosophically took the lead without, and the peavines within, and after eating his fill would lie down in the field and chew his cud complacently, walking out later through the owner's front yard, pausing to paw the dirt contemptuously and pull a few mouthfuls from the Seewee bean vines that climbed about the garden palings.

One day Friday's field was invaded, and, hat in hand, he came to the doorstep to complain. "Missis," he said, "dat bull Baa'ney, she is ridickilus! Missis, I mek my fench ten rail high. I stake her and I rider her, but ole Baa'ney she put her breas' agains' my fench, she lean on her, she break her down. She enter my fiel', she eat my peas. I shoot her, but she is indifferent to my shot. When she conclude eatin' my peas, she lie down, and, Missis, she was so full that she could not rise!" But Friday was a gentlemanly old darkey and treated his sturdy, quick-talking wife, Minda, with great gallantry, *practical* gallantry, too, as she bore him (and raised) 17 sons and daughters, thereby earning the well-done of her kindly though thrifty old master. "Maussuh lub me 'cause uh hab chillun so fas'," she boasted. "I fetch'um uh fine nigguh eb'ry year Gawd sen'!"—meaning that the old gentleman had a pre-Rooseveltian objection to race suicide on the plantation.

Although old Bo'sun Smashum, the herdsman, who had raised Barney from a calf, would twist his tail in the barnyard and chevy him about with impunity, the bull was truculent toward outsiders and on more than one occasion disputed the highway with planters of the neighborhood, who were forced to turn back and drive a mile or so out of the way in the interest of safety; while negroes riding or driving oxen, on sighting Barney in the road half a mile away, would take to the woods or the fields and make a wide and respectful detour. The danger would be enhanced should the animal between the shafts of the primitive cart be one

54

of the "bull yellin's" so much affected by the freedmen
for combination purposes. The silly song, "Everybody
works but father," had not then been evolved from the
near-brain of the writer of music hall lyrics, and the
labors of a beast of burden were held not incompatible
with the paternity of a bovine family. So these little
creatures multiplied and continued to lead their double
lives. Barney held in utter contempt even the authenticated bulls of the community, but he so terrorized
the little harnessed scrubs that their owners could
hardly avert a stampede when the great bull bellowed
in the vicinity.

One hot Sunday afternoon three or four hundred
negroes were holding services at the old log church
near the Parker's Ferry cross-roads. Too numerous
for the building, they were using outdoor bush shelters
covered with green boughs and with hewn saplings for
seats. At the tail of a "distracted meetin'" that had
been running for several days, while grass grew in
their crops, they were in a state of exaltation, and the
high, sweet voices of the women blended in harmony
with the deep, rich basses of the men in the perfect
rhythm characteristic of African music. Old time
hymns and "sperrituals" alternated. At first, only two
or three voices followed the leader, then one by one
the singers joined in major and minor keys, until at
the last the entire congregation swelled the diapason
that floated away on the summer wind. The little oxen
and bulls, whose harness permitted the indulgence, lay
down at their hitching posts, the less fortunate stood
between the shafts and chewed their cuds, drowsing
with half-closed eyes in the soft, warm air of the pineland, fragrant with the blossoming partridge peas.

The singers walked up and down the aisles of the open-air church, working up enthusiasm in camp meeting fashion.

"Sistuh Chizzum, won't you meet me yonduh?" Sister Chisolm would, so she responded to the masculine invitation, "Oh yaas, Lawd!"

"Bredduh Hacklus, won't you meet me yonduh?" And Brother Hercules, a wizened little member of Sister Chisolm's "class," shouted in acquiescent gallantry, "Oh yaas, Lawd!"

The meeting drew to a close, the last inspiring "sperritual," of African suggestiveness, remained to be sung. Who should raise the tune? Simon Jenkins the "squerril" hunter, a devout old rascal, called to his brother-in-law, John Chisolm, "hice'um, Chizzum! You hice de chune."

John's resonant voice rolled out—

> "Jedus, hol' de lion jaw,
> Jedus, hol' de lion jaw,
> Jedus, hol' de lion jaw,
> 'Tell I git on de grazin' groun',
> Oh, 'tell I git on de grazin' groun',"

> "*Hol'um, Jedus!*"
> "*Don' tun'um loose, Lawd!*"
> "*Maussuh Jedus, hol' 'e jaw!*"

came the responses in bass and treble, then, as the refrain again swelled and died away, "Oh-h 'tell I git on de grazin' groun'," an ominous "mmmm, mmmm, mmmm, mmh! mmh! mmh!" rolled through the woods. "*Duh Baa'ney! Great Gawd, duh Baa'ney!*" shrieked the panic-stricken women who scattered in every direction, while the men ran to release their hitched animals as old Barney leisurely approached, routing sonorously. "Mek'ace, gal, mek'ace! Him duh walk sedate but 'e bex," shouted a man to a leggy, dry-boned black girl who, although guiltless of shoes and stockings, had worn to the meeting an antiquated hoopskirt which now impeded her progress. "Hice'um, gal! Hice yo' 'coat en' *run!*" She "hiced" her petticoat and ran, but the crinoline billowed about her knees as she passed Dick Smashum on her way to the Savage plantation. Dick was duck-legged and as slow of speech as of foot, but discretion had urged him to get an early start and he was well out of the danger zone. Later, when Atalanta's mother overtook him and asked, "You see my gal? Weh 'e gone?" he replied. "Uh yiz see one sump'nurruh duh run like de debble, gwine Sabbidge. 'E pass me duh paat', en' 'e binnuh trabble so swif' uh yent ruckuhnize um 'zackly, but 'e stan' sukkuh two blacksnake duh 'tretch out een one bu'dcage."

"BILLYBEDAM"

Billybedam was bibulous.

None knew how he achieved his devilmaycare nick-name—the only name he had, but everybody around Pocotaligo knew that he came by his thirst through patient industry, and that he loved his work. No round-paunched monk of the Middle Ages, no Falstaff of the English taverns, ever absorbed dusky Tuscan wine or Sherris Sack with more appreciative avidity than Billybedam soaked up the "Fus' X" corn sold on the sly by Yemassee blind tigers and bootleggers, for Billybedam had acquired his "liquorish mouth" during the days, the glorious, honorable days, of the State Dispensary, when, under the operation of that "Great Moral Institution," certain sons of "Grand old South Carolina" had shown the world that the Caucasian was not "played out," but could, upon occasion, graft like any freedman of the good old days of Reconstruction!

So the bibulousness of Billybedam became a byword all about "de Yamassee," where "de Po' Trial" Railway—significant name—crosses the Atlantic Coast Line, and, not infrequently, the tempers of passengers bound for Beaufort and Port Royal.

Perhaps it was the frequent pouring of libations—his gods were all in his gullet—that enabled Billybedam to crook his elbow so expertly, but this facility, and a marvelous twist of the wrist, contributed to his success as a fisherman, and the greater part of what he ate and drank and wore, came from the brown waters of the Salkehatchie, whose deep and narrow

58

current flowed between wooded banks a mile or so away. With rod and line he fished the stream by day, and many a string of bream and redbreast perch was sold at the station to buy the precious whiskey, while the narrow-mouthed "blue cats," caught on his set lines over night, were traded among the negroes in exchange for his scanty food and shelter, for Billybedam was a bachelor and a vagabond, unattached and unaffiliated, and called no roof his own.

Sometimes in the spring when the sturgeon were running, the fisherman would get the big-game fever, and, armed with a "grain" which he threw as the whaler throws a harpoon, stationed himself on some log that jutted out over the water, or in the fork of a low, overhanging tree, and took toll from the passing thousands. During the sturgeon run, when, too, mulberries and blackberries were plentiful, the negroes grew fat and "swonguh" and became more than usually irresponsible.

The heavy, sensuous Southern spring was in the air. The bayous or "backwaters," which irrigated the inland swamp ricefields, were dotted with the sweet white pond lilies, or aflame with the yellow lotus, while over the broad leaves of lily and lotus, purple gallinules tripped daintily. Every log that floated and every stump that rose above the water carried a string or a cluster of terrapins, their glistening backs reflecting the sunshine. The sloping trunks of the willows that fringed the banks were festooned with water snakes, basking in the grateful warmth. Here and there on tussock or muddy flat, rough-backed alligators lay dozing. Blue flags flaunted along the marges. Tall white cranes stalked slowly about the shallows, pausing now and then with spear-like bill poised, watching, waiting.

Billybedam was full of the magic of the springtime, but it was not altogether a satisfying fullness, and as he pushed the shallow flat-bottomed skiff off from shore, he laid down the paddle long enough to eat a hunk of coarse corn bread and swallow a nip from his "Fus' X" flask. And then, thoroughly satisfied with the world, he dipped his blade and, with alternate strokes to right and left, pushed the clumsy snub-nosed bateau across the backwater to a famous "drop," a deep pool just below a gap in the dam where the dark waters flowed slowly through from an upper reservoir. This was Billybedam's favorite preserve whenever high water in the Salkehatchie forced the river fishermen to seek their living elsewhere.

Today, however, he made an unpropitious start. After his earthworm bait had been repeatedly stripped from his hook by the troublesome silver fish, whose small mouths enabled them to nibble it away piecemeal without getting hooked, his cork bobbed furiously, and he jerked quickly, only to bring swinging over the boat one of the malodorous little black turtles commonly called "limus cootuh" by the low-country negroes. This unwelcome catch he disengaged from the hook and threw as far away from him as possible. "You good fuh nutt'n' *nigguh!* Yunnuh t'ink me come spang f'um Macfuss'nbil fuh ketch limus cootuh, enty? Who eenwite you fuh eat 'long fish? You ebbuh see nigguh eat 'long buckruh? De debble!" Running his cork a foot or two higher up the line, he fished at a deeper level and soon began to haul in fine perch, which he strung on the willow withes he had provided. At the end of two hours he had several strings of marketable fish, and, as the sun had set, he paddled to shore, threw away his now empty flask, tied his boat to a snag, and started for Yemassee to convert his catch into cash.

An hour later, with silver jingling in his pocket, he encountered in the dusk, Miss Maria Wineglass, a much sought-after ornament of colored society. Miss Wineglass was, in a manner of speaking, a peripatetic paradox. Altho' dour-looking and glum, she was noted for her spirits (80 proof); bootless and bare-legged, she was McPhersonville's most daring and accomplished bootlegger, and so circumspect and resourceful that she seldom met the law face to face.

When her course crossed that of Billybedam, she was traveling an unfrequented path on the outskirts of the settlement, and, with little need for caution, she walked rapidly, giving out as she moved a faint, hollow sound like the subdued tones of a xylophone. She hailed the bibulous one as a regular and valued customer.

"Weh you gwine, bubbuh?"

"Wuh you got? I gwine 'tell I fin'um."

"I got 'nuf."

"Gimme uh pint;" and he held out half a dollar.

"Gimme seb'nty fi' cent. Dishyuh t'ing hol' mo'n uh pint."

"Wuh kinduh t'ing dat? Lemme shum."

"Yuh him," and Miss Wineglass fumbled under her skirt and, from a marvelously durable and comprehensive pair of bloomers made of two cottonseed meal sacks sewed together at the top, produced a gourd holding about three half-pints, and passed it over. The gourd was bottle-shaped and cob-stoppered and ingeniously laced about with hickory bark, as flasks of Chianti are wrapped with flags. The knocking together of half a dozen of these gourds, tied around her waist and suspended within her bloomers, had produced the xylophone music. The money paid, they parted.

Billybedam went his ways. Whatever the nature of the nepenthe the "Fus X" extracted from the calabash, it so 'whelmed his wits that oblivion lurked in the bottom of the gourd and overcame him. He fell among thieves, who stripped him of a new shirt he wore and left him, in his trousers only, by the roadside, where a local constable found him next morning and haled him before the magistrate for being inadequately clothed on the public highway.

"What have you to say for yourself?"

"Cap'n, uh yent hab nutt'n' fuh say. Uh gone fish duh backwatuh, en' een de fus' gwinin' off, uh did'n' hab no luck, 'cause silbuhfish tek me bait en' uh nubbuh ketch'um, en' one limus cootuh grab de hook en' uh ketch *him* en' t'row'um'way, en' den uh ketch 'nuf fish, en' uh gone Yamassee en' sell'um, en' uh binnuh walk duh paat', en' uh meet one gal duh walk duh paat', name 'Riah Wineglass, en' uh yeddy'um befo' uh shum, 'cause 'e mek one soun' w'en 'e walk sukkuh cow foot crack w'en him duh run, en' w'en uh *yiz* shum close, 'e frock duh bunch out all roun'um sukkuh cootuh 'tring out 'puntop'uh log, en' uh ax'um, 'gal, wuh you got fuh fifty cent?' en' 'e say 'e yent got nutt'n' fuh fifty cent but 'e hab 'nuf fuh seb'nty fi' cent, en' I tell'um 'lemme shum,' en' 'e hice 'e frock, en' him hab one t'ing onduhneet' him frock, dem call'um bloomuh, uh nubbuh see shishuh debble'ub'uh t'ing befo' sence uh bawn! 'E hol' 'bout t'ree-fo' bushel, en' 'e mek outuh grano sack, en' britchiz duh 'e farruh en' frock duh 'e murruh, en' 'e stan' sukkuh alltwo. Den de gal graff een da' t'ing wunnuh call'um so, en' 'e full'uh de pyo' killybash 'long Fus' X, en' 'e ketch'out one en' gimme, en' uh gone off en' drink'um, en' fus' t'ing uh know uh yent know *nutt'n'*, 'tell de counstubble fin' me dis mawnin', en' las' night w'en uh bin een one strance, some dem Macfussn'nbil nigguh' t'ief' one new shu't off me back, en'," said Billybedam, "uh tengk Gawd uh did'n' bin hab on uh new *britchiz!*"

A SHORT CUT TO JUSTICE

Ever since the days of Solomon, the courts and tribunals of the law in all lands have sought short cuts to justice, but one of the straightest and strangest in the history of jurisprudence was achieved by one Daniel W. Robinson, colored, sometime Magistrate or Trial Justice of the sovereign State of South Carolina, for the Bailiwick of Jacksonboro, in lower Colleton County.

Under the trying days of Reconstruction in South Carolina, the white men and boys living in the so-called "black belt," comprising the coastal counties of the State, were constantly seeking to lure the black voters into the fold of Democracy, with but indifferent success, for the wary freedman, under the secret instructions given him by the leaders of his own race and the white-skinned spoilers, native and alien, who controlled his political activities for their own profit, was hard to wean away from the idols set up for him within "the awful circle" of the Republican fold.

These poor, deluded negroes, absolutely dependent upon their former masters, the landholders, for food, for clothing, for shelter, for remunerative work—often for free medicines and medical treatment in communities where there were no doctors and no drug stores— though making profuse lip service for benefits received, forgot them all on election day when, under the influence of the knaves who manipulated them, they turned away from their best friends and, hurdled at the polls like sheep, voted blindly the ballots put into their hands by the corruptionists.

A SHORT CUT TO JUSTICE

At one of these elections the Republican ballot was headed with the national flag in colors, swathed around the ample loins and spreading hips of the figure of Liberty, with the legend "Union Republican ticket." One of these flamboyant affairs was secured from the printer a day or two before the election and the Democratic tickets were also printed in red ink with a rooster at the top, in the hope that some of the negroes might accept and vote them for Republican ballots. One of these rooster ballots was offered an old darkey at the polls by a Democratic negro worker, but the wary old fellow had been rehearsed in his lesson too well, and he rejected it indignantly, saying: "No, man! uh yent want da' t'ing! Gimme da' ticket fuh wote wuh hab de gal wid de Balmuhral sku't wrop roun'um!" And he got it.

Then came '76 and the "Straight-Out" campaign. Every white man and boy who could raise two or three dollars to buy a few yards of flannel, sported a red shirt, usually put together by the loving hands of some member of his family, but, occasionally, fearfully and wonderfully made by a sweetheart or feminine acquaintance—some perhaps "a little more than kin," but all "less than kind." The boys, however, upon whom had been wished the needlework activities of their lady friends, wore them jauntily nevertheless, absolutely indifferent to the want of co-ordination of "seam and gusset and band."

As the campaign progressed and enthusiasm increased, an occasional courageous black, taking his life in his hands and braving the hatred and ostracism of his fellows, even of his church and his family, would boldly put on a red shirt and ride with the whites to political meetings or rallies. One of these, old Clitus Wilson, a life-long Democrat, who, as his master's body servant, fought with him in the battle of Gettysburg, flaunted his red shirt bravely and defiantly. Another was Paul Jenkins, a thrifty, property-owning negro, whose courageous work in the first Hampton campaign was remembered by the whites, who elected him county commissioner soon after the Democrats came into power. Paul, a wiry, coal-black negro, was once beset by several members of the Grant family, "Free-Issue" mulatto Republicans, and cruelly beaten. In the courts of radicalism there was no redress for a negro Democrat, but Paul bided his time and, meeting one of the Grants alone, retaliated so vigorously that the mulatto was laid up for a week. The victim went before Trial Justice Robinson, over the river at Jacksonboro, and swore out a warrant, charging Paul with aggravated assault and battery.

Paul, summoned to appear on the following Saturday, came in great trouble to a stripling planter of the neighborhood who willingly accompanied him to see that the Democrat got justice, and to go on his bond in case he should be sent up to a higher court.

On Saturday morning the deep and swift Edisto, lacking a ferry, was crossed in a shallow bateau, the saddle-horses, held by their bridles, swimming alongside, and the accused and his protector soon appeared before the august Court, sitting in a small shanty, facing an imposing layout of writing materials and a copy of the statutes. The young planter told the Court that he had come over with Paul to look after his interests and see that he got justice. The Court responded graciously that he was "glad to welcome the distinguished counsel from across the river" and took pleasure in extending to him the courtesies of his Court.

A jury was asked for and Justice Robinson, calling up some of the idle negroes who hung about his office, selected five elderly darkeys, all of them as black as crows. To these five jurors the magistrate added "the distinguished counsel from across the river," whom he graciously requested to consent to serve as foreman. In the interest of justice the request was complied with.

Grant, the aggrieved, appeared as prosecuting witness, "tore a passion to tatters" in describing the sudden and furious onslaught made upon him by the black Democrat, and rantingly demanded justice. Paul simply told the story of the attack made upon him by the Grant family and admitted his retaliation, which he held was justifiable, and the jury withdrew to a vacant room nearby which was indicated as the place of deliberation.

The foreman was given a primitive split white-oak chair with a rawhide seat, while his five dusky associates ranged themselves like roosting buzzards upon a teetering bench, whose supports, two short boards sawed into the semblance of legs at the bottom, were placed so close together that the utmost skill was required on the part of the sitters to maintain their equilibrium, for if the central section rose, both end men had to sit tight until they could rise simultaneously, else the laggard would be in jeopardy.

And now the jurors were ready for the case. Paul, having beaten his man fairly and in righteous retaliation, was entitled to an acquittal and to this end the foreman directed his efforts. As a preliminary, Paul was called to the shanty window, provided with sixty cents, and despatched to Arnold's store for a quart of corn whiskey. Upon his return with the pallid pop-skull, there was an excited shifting of five seats on the shaky bench and five pairs of eagerly expectant eyes rested their kindly regard upon the messenger of Bacchus as he withdrew, leaving his fate in their hands.

The lone and crafty Caucasian, playing Iago to five Othellos, picked out a gorilla-like old codger on the near end of the bench as the dominant personality among them, and extending the flask told him to take a drink and serve his fellows. Hacklus Manigo jumped up with such alacrity, and was followed so quickly by the negroes who sat next him, that the near end of the bench, relieved of their combined weight, flew up, and the two remaining jurors tumbled igno-miniously and indignantly to the floor. The grum-bling of the fallen and the derisive guffawing of the risen, ceased suddenly, however, as eight saucered and fascinated eyes fastened upon old Manigo's Adam's apple which moved up and down his neck in perfect unison with the "glug, glug," of the liquid flowing so easily down his throat. The drinker's ocular and auricular demonstration of hydraulics was too much for his associates, who cried out in indignant protest. "Tek'care, man! We'own dey een da' t'ing!" "Cap'n, please, suh, mek'um tek 'e mout' off da' bottle. 'E gwine drink eb'ry Gawd' drap!"

Manigo, having absorbed almost one-fourth of the contents of the flask, gave it into the nearest of the eager hands held out to receive it, drew his coat sleeve with a great swipe across his wet and glistening mouth, gave a grateful grunt, "umh, da' t'ing *good!* Tengky, Boss, tengky, suh!" accompanied by an elaborate scrape of the foot and a low obeisance, and took his seat in the center of the bench, where he was soon flanked by the four, whose watchful eyes, each upon the other, had not permitted their attainment of Manigo's state of exaltation.

"Now, Manigo, and you boys," said Iago. "This is a plain story. Three or four yellow men double-team a black man and beat him up. He doesn't take them to court but waits his chance, and when he catches one of these yellow men away from his gang, why the black man beats him to pay him back for what the yellow man helped to do to him. Now, that's what Paul did to this free-issue yellow fellow Grant. Paul is black like all of you. Do you want to send him to jail for laying hands on a mulatto, just because mulattoes think themselves better than you blacks?"

"Great Gawd, *no, suh!*" shouted Manigo, springing up. Turning half way round out of respect to the foreman, he alternately jumped in the air and squatted like a gigantic frog, while he whirled his arms and harangued his fellow blacks, cutting his eye around now and then for a nod of approval from Iago. "De debble! Punkin skin' nigguh fuh beat black nigguh en' black nigguh ent fuh beat'um back, enty? Oonuh ebbuh yeddy 'bout shishuh t'ing sence you bawn? Me fuh 'low yalluh nigguh fuh knock me en' me yent fuh knock'um back! No, man! Uh knock'um ef uh dead!"

"Yaas, man, *knock'um, knock'um!*" came the cries of approval as old Hacklus, having put up his yellow man of straw, leaped about as he proceeded to bowl him over.

"Uh yent fuh wait 'tell 'e knock me fus'. Uh gwine knock'um befo' 'e hice 'e han'! Uh knock'um een 'e yeye, uh kick'um on 'e shin, alltwo one time. Den uh butt'um een 'e belly. Uh double'um up 'cause 'e too swonguh, 'e too 'laagin'! Cap'n, who dis yalluh nigguh nyuse to blonx to een slabery time?" he asked the foreman.

"To nobody. He was free. He belonged to himself."

"Great Gawd! Cap'n, all dese'yuh mans blonx to quality! All uh we yuh nyuse to blonx to Baa'nwell, eeduhso Heywu'd en' Wandross. All duh juntlemun' nigguh. Nigguh stan' sukkuh 'e maussuh. Ef 'e blonx to juntlemun, him gwine mannusubble, ef 'e blonx to po'buckruh, him ent nutt'n', 'cause uh po'buckruh nigguh *ent wut*, but ef 'e blonx to 'eself, 'e blonx to nigguh, en' da' yalluh t'ing wuh blonx to nigguh tek 't'oruhty 'puntop 'eself fuh knock nigguh wuh blonx to juntlemun, en bex w'en de nigguh knock'um back! No, suh, 'e mus' be fool! Leh we tu'n Bredduh Paul loose!"

"Yaas, man, *tu'n'um loose, tu'n'um loose!*" came the chorus.

"Well, boys, before we go, you'd better finish the flask."

"*Tengk Gawd, suh!*" ejaculated old Hacklus whose mouth was now as cottony as a stump-tailed water moccasin's, as he lifted the flask to his lips, "me t'roat dry. Uh binnuh talk."

"*Hol' on, man!*"

"*Don' tek'um all!*"

"Manigo drink' too hebby!"

"'E gwine dreen'um dry!" came the protests, but

Manigo had swallowed the lion's share before he passed the flask to the next man. "Boss, we fuh pit da' yalluh Grant een jail, enty?" and he was much disappointed when told it couldn't be done.

The jury returned to the Court room with their verdict of acquittal, and received the thanks of the Court, who assured them all, "and especially the distinguished foreman," of his appreciation of the expedition with which they had dispatched the business of the Court. As Paul and his protector mounted their horses for the homeward ride, Daniel stood bareheaded at the Court room door, and expressed the hope that he might again welcome to his temple of justice "the distinguished counsel from across the river."

SAM DICKERSON

For many years after the war, Sam Dickerson, a former slave of the Horlbeck family, ranted around the courts of the lower counties of South Carolina in the practice of the legal profession, which he had acquired in a jack-leg sort of way soon after his emancipation. Tall, black, pompous, and as voluble as an overshot water-wheel, he cut his grotesque antics in higher and lower courts to the intense amusement of blacks as well as of whites. He habitually carried with him a bag of tawdry and greasy law books, which he hauled out and spread upon tables, wherever the space was available, to impress jurors and court-room spectators with his importance. With monkey-like imitativeness he copied the court-room gestures and mannerisms of prominent lawyers of the white race, and he had memorized certain passages from the statutes and the law blanks, which he spouted whenever opportunity offered. Upon one occasion Dickerson was defending in a magistrate's court a negro accused of larceny. The word written on the indictment pleased him and he mouthed and slobbered over it as one mouths the pit of a clingstone peach. "Dis man bin chaa'ge', yo' onnuh, wid laa'ceny! He bin chaa'ge' wid laa'ceny! W'at am laa'ceny, yo' onnuh?"

"Do you know what it is to steal?" retorted the court.

"Of co'se uh does, yo' onnuh. Laa'ceny is t'ief, en' t'ief is steal, en' uh man w'ich steal is uh man w'ich enter anodduh man' house een de dead ub night en' did mos' feloniously steal, tek, carry away en' appropriate to he own use de whole or uh paa't dereof uh de

72

juntlemun' proputty. But de chaa'ge, yo' onnuh, am laa'ceny!"

Dickerson was so well known about the magistrates' courts of the City of Charleston that many prominent white citizens were attracted to the trials when it was known that this simian-like advocate was going to participate in the proceedings, and it was quite the thing to take Northern visitors or the captains of vessels in port, to the court room to see the black perform, and sometimes the magistrate, or the opposing counsel, would be given a hint to stir him up for the entertainment of the visitors.

In a trial before a Charleston magistrate, the black lawyer once sought to have a bad case continued because of "the absence of a material witness," that threadbare plea so frequently urged in our courts. The magistrate, inclined to bait him, insisted that the material witness be produced in court forthwith.

"Yo' onnuh, I hope you will not insis' upun de material witness bein' produce' een dis co't."

The court demanded his reason.

"Yo' onnuh, de material witness am a female en' she cannot cunweenyuntly be produce' een dis co't."

"Why can't a female witness be produced in court? What is the matter with the witness?"

"Yo' onnuh, I hope you will not compel me to state w'at is de matter wid de material witness w'y she cannot be produce' een dis co't."

"Unless you can give me good reasons why the material witness should not be brought to court, I will insist upon going on with the case," said the court.

"Yo' onnuh, I appeal to you as a juntlemun ub delicacy not to fo'ce me to tell de co't w'y de material witness cannot be produce' een co't."

But the appeal to the magistrate's delicacy of mind was of no avail and he peremptorily ordered the case to proceed.

"Well, yo' onnuh, my delicacy will not permit me to state een de English langwidge w'at is de reason w'y de material witness cannot be produce' een co't."— just then a laugh from a gentleman of French extraction in the audience, caused him to turn his head, and he proceeded. "Yaas, suh, you kin laugh, but you cannot fo'ce me to use de English langwidge, en' I will haffuh fall back on my French." Then, wheeling around and facing the magistrate, "de reason, yo' onnuh, w'y de material witness cannot be produce' een co't, is 'cause de material witness is"—just then a negro woman entered the room, and, hurrying up to Dickerson pulled him by the sleeve and whispered in his ear. Turning dramatically, he shouted, "may it please yo' onnuh, I hab jus' hear from de material witness en' I kin now resume de English langwidge. De reason w'y de material witness cannot be produce' een dis co't, is 'cause *de material witness hab two twin!*"

On a certain summer day, twenty or thirty negroes from the Toogoodoo section, assembled at the office of the trial justice at Adams Run station to settle a legal matter. The dispute to be adjusted involved the ownership of a brindled ox, to which claims, apparently equally strong, were set up by two black ladies from "Down on de Salt." One, Bina Youngblood, the "lawfully lady" of Scipio Youngblood, the other the lone, though not lorn, Clara Jenkins, for the moment unaffiliated. Scipio, the "sea-lawyer" of the Swinton plantation, undertook to plead his wife's cause before the magistrate, while Clara, having money in her purse, because, perhaps, she had just then no man to support, had "done git de buckruh fuh write uh letter town, fuh tell Sam Dickuhsin fuh come fuh rupezunt me een de co't." At 9 o'clock Sam arrived from Charleston on "de shoofly strain," as the negroes call the local which stops at all way stations. The ox, having caused mutual wool-pulling on the part of both claimants, had been put in the custody of the magistrate's constable, and, tied to the picket fence surrounding a corn patch near the station, was chewing his cud complacently, viewing with drowsy eyes the human turmoil about him. Clara laid excited hands upon the Charleston advocate and pulled him into the presence of the ox, which she introduced. "Dish'yuh duh him, Mistuh Dickuhsin. Dish'yuh duh de oxin wuh me en' Mis' Nyungblood agguhnize 'bout. Uh buy dis oxin f'um Bredduh Izick Puhshay wuh lib tuh Slann' Ilun' en' Buh Izick him buy'um f'um de Jew wuh hab uh sto' to Wadmuhlaw, en' 'e buy'um f'um de Jew 'cause de oxin gone een de maa'sh fuh eat, en' 'e bog een de maa'sh, en' de Jew stan' 'puntop de bluff en' 'e look 'puntop de oxin, en' 'e 'f'aid 'e gwine drowndid, en' 'e shake alltwo 'e han' 'bout de oxin, en' Buh Izick binnuh stan'up close'um, en' de Jew try fuh sell-'um de oxin, 'cause 'e t'ink de oxin gwine dead een de maa'sh, en' Buh Izick tell'um him willin' fuh g'em fibe dolluh' fuh de oxin, en' him will tek'um out de maa'sh 'eself, eb'nso ef 'e dead, en' de Jew tell'um no, 'e yent fuh sell him oxin fuh no fibe dolluh' 'cause him kin sell 'e meat fuh mo'n fibe dolluh' eb'nso ef 'e done dead, but 'e say 'e willin' fuh tek ten dolluh' fuhr'um weh 'e stan'. Buh Izick tell'um him will nebbuh git'um out ef 'e dead, 'cause him well acquaintun wid uh quicksan'

75

dey een de maa'sh puhzackly weh de oxin duh bog'up
een de maa'sh, en' 'e say suh de quicksan' gwine swalluhr'um up, en' den de Jew ent fuh git nutt'n'. W'en de
Jew yeddy 'bout de quicksan', 'e dat 'f'aid him gwine
loss 'e oxin, 'e sell'um tuh Buh Izick fuh de fibe dolluh',
en' soon ez 'e buy'um en' 'e done pit de money een de
Jew' han', Buh Izick know berry well suh no quicksan'
dey een de maa'sh, en' e' gone weh de oxin duh stan'up
een de mud, en' ketch'um by 'e tail en' twis'um two't'ree
time, en' de oxin walk out de maa'sh jis' ez good ez
you en' me, en' Buh Izick git'um een de flat en'
fetch'um 'cross, en' 'e nebbuh stop 'tell 'e git'um spang
home weh 'e lib. Uh bin to Buh Izick house de berry
day w'en him fetch de oxin home, en' uh yent hab
nutt'n' fuh plow, en' uh buy de oxin f'um Buh Izick
fuh fifteen dolluh', en' pay'um ten dolluh', en' owe'um
de odduh res' uh de money.

"W'en de Jew fin'out how Buh Izick obuhreach'um,
'e dat bex 'e yent able fuh nyam 'e bittle, en' 'e study
all day 'bout how him kin git 'e oxin 'gen. 'E h'aa't
hebby 'bout de oxin, en' 'e jaw drap eb'ry time 'e t'ink
'pun Buh Izick, 'cause him t'ink suh nigguh ent fuh
smaa't 'nuf fuh cheat no Jew. Nex' day 'nuf nigguh
f'um Swintun en' Toale gone Wadmuhlaw fuh dig
Irish tettuh, en' dem gone tuh de Jew' sto' fuh buy
gunjuh en' nickynack en' t'ing. Mis' Nyungblood en'
'e juntlemun alltwo gone to de sto', en' de Jew yeddy-
'um duh talk 'bout one brinly oxin wuh buy een dem
nigguhhouse yaa'd, wuh come f'um Wadmuhlaw Ilun',
en' de Jew tell'um yaas, duh him oxin, en' 'e tell'um
de oxin sell fuh true, but all de money ent done pay,
en' 'e sen' ansuh fuh tell me wuh got de oxin fuh
sen'um ten dolluh' mo' fuh de oxin, 'scusin' him gwine

SAM DICKERSON

tek'um 'way en' sell'um 'gen. Buh Scipio en' 'e lady
alltwo fetch de Jew' metsidge jis' ez 'e come out 'e
mout', but uh nebbuh bodduh 'bout'um, 'cause uh know
uh hab witness fuh de money uh done pay Buh Izick,
en' uh look tuh Buh Izick fuh puhteck me, but de nex'
week Mis' Nyungblood gone Wadmuhlaw 'gen, en' de
Jew 'suade him fuh buy de oxin fuh fifteen dolluh',
en' him pay'um t'ree dolluh' on de oxin, en' de Jew
g'em uh paper fuh tek de oxin wehrebbuh 'e kin fin'um.
W'en 'e git home, de 'ooman walk een my yaa'd wid
de Jew' papuh een 'e han', en' e' walk swonguh, en',
please Gawd, 'e gone to de oxin weh 'e duh bite grass
een de fench cawnuh, en' 'e tek'um by 'e bridle en'
staa't fuh lead'um out de yaa'd. Bubbuh, uh yent got
no man 'bout de house fuh puhteck me, but uh got
dese ten finger 'puntop alltwo me han' fuh puhteck
meself, en' w'en uh see de 'ooman 'long de oxin, blood
full' alltwo me yeye! Uh peaceubble 'tell uh bex, but
w'en uh bex, uh ready fuh dead, en' uh light 'puntop'uh
da' 'ooman same lukkuh fu'lhawk light 'puntop'uh
chickin! Me en' him en' de oxin, alltwo tanglety'up
een de du't 'tell dem man een de nigguhhouse yaa'd
haffuh suffuhrate we. Nex' day me' en' de 'ooman hitch
'gen, w'en him come een de yaa'd fuh onhitch de oxin
de twotime, en' uh 'cratch' him face en' him 'cratch'
my'own, en' attuh dat, de trial jestuss yeddy 'bout'um
en' sen' 'e counstubble fuh tek'way de oxin, en' lef'
one metsidge fuh alltwo uh we fuh come Adam' Run
deepo fuh try de case, en' uh glad dem fuh try'um
teday, teday, 'cause me en' da' 'ooman en' da' oxin ent
fuh lib tuhgedduh 'puntop no Swintun plantesshun!"

"Come eento co't," yelled the constable, and Clara
and her counsel went within.

77

The two principals and their partisans, glowering at one another, ranged themselves on opposite sides of the little room, and the proceedings were opened. Bina came to the witness stand with a slowly healing gridiron of scratches covering her face, tokens of the efficiency of Clara's finger nails, which courtesies she had handsomely reciprocated.

"Uh gone Wadmuhlaw fuh dig Irish tettuh, en' w'en middleday come, me en' all dem todduh man en' 'ooman gone to de Jew fuh buy bittle fuh eat, en' him yeddy suh we come f'um Swintun place, en' him yeddy we duh talk 'bout one brinly oxin wuh come f'um Wadmuhlaw, wuh one uh we 'ooman buy f'um Izick Puhshay, en' de Jew say suh de oxin duh him'own, en' nex' time me en' my juntlemun gone Wadmuhlaw, de Jew say suh de oxin ent pay fuh, en' him fuh sell'um 'gen, en' w'en 'e say dat, uh buy'um en' pay t'ree dolluh' exwance on'um en' de Jew gimme uh papuh fuh tek de oxin wehrebbuh uh fin'um, en' w'en uh gone home uh tek de papuh en' gone een de 'ooman' yaa'd en' tek de oxin out de fench cawnuh en' staa't fuh gone, en' 'fo' uh kin git out de yaa'd, da' debble'ub'uh blacksnake ub uh 'ooman tek uh exwantidge w'en uh yent binnuh study 'bout'um, en' him git een de fus' lick, en' 'e yent sattify fuh 'cratch me eyeball' en' fight deestunt lukkuh lady fuh fight, but him haffuh bite me een de same time, en' 'e teet' shaa'p ez ottuh' teet', en' de 'ooman mek 'e fang' fuh meet een me yez, but me Jedus help me fuh obuht'row'um, en' befo' dem man suffuhrate we, uh done spile 'e face 'tell 'e maamy yent fuh know'um! Uh gone t'ru'um sukkuh bulltongue plow gone t'ru blackberry wine! You shum stan' dey? Duh me mek 'e mout' fuh twis'up oagly same lukkuh him binnuh chaw green possimmun!"

With a curtsy to the court and a scornful glance at her opponent, Bina retired, and after Clara had repeated word for word the story previously related to her attorney—for some negroes have the faculty of memorizing and repeating a romantic story over and over again, omitting none of the mendacious minutiæ—Scipio, a stout, self-conscious black, rose to match his plantation wit with that of the experienced advocate.

"Jedge, w'en my lady ubtain dis cow f'um de Jew tuh Wadmuhlaw—"

Old Sam rose impressively. "Do my distinguish' fr'en' frum Toogoodoo allude to de annimel dat is now een de custody ub dis honuhrubble co't ez *cow?*"

"Yaas, uh call'um cow! Cow duh 'e name! Mekso me yent fuh call'um cow! Uh call'um cow, uh dunkyuh ef e' duh *bull!* Enty roostuh en' hen alltwo is fowl? Uh call'um cow, yaas! Wuh de debble town nigguh' know 'bout annimel?"

"Kin de 'town nigguh' eenfawm de distinguish' counsel," observed Sam, sarcastically, "dat he is berry well acquaintun wid uh sutt'n annimel dat eenhabit de jungle ub Aff'iky, but, ontell teday, he hab always obserb dis annimel fuh hab tail. Puhhaps de specie' dat roam t'ru de fores' ub Toogoodoo is bawn bidout tail!"

"Great King! 'e fuh call me *monkey!*" protested Scipio, as the audience exploded with laughter, for however resentful they may be of such characterization by the whites, in their lighter moments, the coast negroes, at least, delight in the exchange among themselves of "monkey," "'ranguhtang," "crow," "buzzut," "blacksnake," "nigguh" and like terms of opprobrious endearment. "Da' 'ranguhtang f'um town fuh call me monkey! *Him gran'daddy 'self duh monkey!*"

The magistrate put a stop to these amenities between counsel, but Scipio's verbal machine gun was jammed and, too full for utterance, he took his seat, muttering wrathfully as Sam rose triumphant.

"Ef it please de co't," said Sam, "I repeah een dis tribunul fuh rupezunt dis defenseless female ub de Aff'ikin race f'um de paa'simony ub uh membuh ub de tribe dat tek Juhruzelum f'um de Christ'un t'ree t'ous'n' yeah' ago!"

"Now 'e duh talk'um!" commented a spectator.

"I am sattisfy', yo' onnuh, dat I kin repeal to yo' onnuh' sense ub jestuss fuh gib dis po' 'ooman de puhtekshun to w'ich de po' en' weak am eentitle' f'um de rich en' de strong, 'cause, yo' onnuh, een de lang-widge ub uh distinguish' membuh ub de Chaa'lstun baa', w'enebbuh we enter de sacrid premussis ub uh co't ub law, we all seddown onduhneet' de eagle ub jestuss as de chicken seddown onduhneet' de hen!

"Now, yo' onnuh, what am de fack? Dish'yuh ten-duh female, yo' onnuh, bidout de puhtekshun ub uh man fuh gyaa'd'um f'um de human race, is t'rowed on his back fuh puhteck 'eself, lukkuh de wil'cat t'row 'eself 'pun 'e back onduhneet' de harricane tree fuh refen' 'eself 'genst de pack ub houn' by whom she is attacktid."

"Yaas, him 'cratch lukkuh wil'cat fuh true!" commented Mrs. Youngblood.

"Yo' onnuh, dis tenduh female buy de ox een ques-chun f'um Izick Puhshay, uh respected citizen ub de Newnited State', en' she hab witness fuh proobe dat de

SAM DICKERSON

money wuz to him een han' pay, en' to 'stablish his
't'oruhty obuh de ox. De afo'sed Izick Puhshay buy
de ox f'um de Jew, de paa'ty ub de fus' paa't, residin'
een de premussis afo'sed 'pun de Ilun' ub Wadmuhlaw,
een de State ub Sous Cuhlina. De Jew' ox hab fall
eento de pit, yo' onnuh, en' 'less 'e is fuh perish, de ox
is sell to Izick Puhshay, dis respected citizen ub de
Newnited State' afo'sed, who by his ability twis' de tail
ub de ox en' mek'um fuh 'bandun he puhsishun een de
maa'sh, en' betake himself to de high groun'. W'en de
membuh ub de tribe ub Juhruzelum see dat de ability
ub de Aff'ikin race sabe de life ub de ox, he feel disapp'int' wid 'eself, en' he seek to agen ubtain de proputty dat he hab loss, en' 'e sell de 'denticul ox de two
time, to de paa'ty ub de secon' paa't.

"Deyfo', yo' onnuh, I mek uh plea fuh dis tenduh
female ub de human race, alldo' his skin is black, dat
jestuss be done, en' dat his ox shall not be tek away."

His plea was effective, for Clara returned joyfully
to Toogoodoo with the restored ox tied behind the cart
in which she had come, while Bina nursed her wrath
to keep it warm until she could return to Wadmalaw
to seek to recover her three dollars "exwance" from "de
membuh ub de tribe ub Juhruzelum."

SIMON, THE "SQUERRIL" HUNTER

As boys, a few years after the war, we knew him as a mighty squirrel hunter, and the negroes in the neighborhood knew him as a mighty slippery old scoundrel, whose smoothness had earned him the sobriquet of Okra—at once a tribute and a reproach—for the skill acquired in slaughtering "de buckruh' cow en' t'ing' " in the swamps, was sometimes used to lift a shoat from some nearby colored brother or sister when Simon did not care to hunt far afield, and, however commendable one's prowess in preying upon "de buckruh," who, for purposes of spoliation, stood in the same relation to the newly freed slaves that the esteemed Egyptians did to the children of Israel, it was regarded in dusky circles as somewhat unethical to steal from one's own color.

Although always suspected, old Okra was never caught. When he killed a cow or other large game, the hide, and the head with its telltale earmarks, were carefully buried in the woods, and part of the meat distributed among his cronies, insuring not only their protective silence, but a full crop of elaborate alibis for Simon, should suspicion ripen into accusation. "Nigguh haffuh stan' by we colluh," being the motto on all the plantations round about.

The squirrel hunter was as lean and hungry-looking as Cassius, with a shifty eye and a face deeply pock-marked. His footfall was stealthy and noiseless and he could walk the woods from dawn to dusk without tiring.

For several years following the war, many low-country negroes carried condemned army muskets which they bought for a dollar or two—long, heavy muzzle-loaders, straight of stock and hard of trigger. Although rifled, their proud owners rammed down and shot out of their grooved barrels anything and everything but ball. Shot of uniform size was not only held unnecessary, but really undesirable, an assortment of sizes running from No. 8 to No. 2, the latter called "high duckshot," being regarded as a mixed dose seriously jeoparding the safety of rabbit or "squerril" at a distance of "two tas'"—two tasks (½ an acre).

Most of the new-fledged negro sportsmen were content to hunt the little cat squirrels that were plentiful in the wooded swamps and the oak and hickory knolls, but Simon was ambitious and habitually hunted the beautiful fox squirrels, grays and blacks, wary creatures, rarely met with and found only among tall pines—sometimes in the long leaf *palustris* of the ridges, but oftener in the great "loblollies" skirting the bays, the height of the trees and the Spanish moss that clustered thick about their towering tops, making them safe retreats, once reached. One of these big squirrels would sometimes be surprised on or near the ground, offering a shot before he got far up the tall trunks which he always ascended rapidly with a great clatter of claws on the bark, cunningly keeping on the off side from the hunter, but never slackening speed till a fork or one of the higher branches was reached, upon which he would flatten out and keep absolutely still. Even a boy then knew it was wasting precious powder and shot to attempt to make him break sanctuary, but not so old Okra. He had implicit faith and infinite pride in the shooting powers of his old "muskick,"—"Ole Betsey, him cya' shot fuh sowl," and he would crack away as

long as his ammunition lasted, at a gray or black spot
at the tip-top of some forest giant; often indeed, at a
dead squirrel, for these "foxes" have an exceedingly in-
considerate habit of digging their claws so deeply into
the bark that they hang on after death and are hard to
dislodge. Often the boy hunter roaming the woods, day-
dreaming of the buck or big gobbler that was always
about to spring up just ahead of him, to fall gloriously
to his little single barrel, would hear at intervals the
heavy "*duhbaw!*" of Simon's ordnance and know that
the indefatigable old sinner was, like most of us, reaching up after the unattainable.

Curiosity to learn how he was faring would sometimes overcome caution, for Simon always begged for
powder, and his ingratiating "Mass—— so freehan',"
seldom failed to coax from the flask part of the boy's
scanty store, but woe to the scanty store if Simon was
permitted to "po'rum." "Berry well den, suh, you
po'rum," and into the deeply cupped palm of the
avaricious hand he held out, the precious powder would
trickle. Simon never stinted his gun, and as long as
the donor would pour, the recipient had no scruples
about drams running into ounces. Whatever you
poured into his hand went into the gun, and when she
responded in recalcitrance to a double charge, sending
her owner staggering back among the gallberry bushes,
he would grin proudly and remark, "Him duh tell we
tengky fuh wuh we g'em. Betsey him hab uh hebby
belly fuh powder."

One crisp winter's day, Simon and his half-grown
son, "Boyzie," were encountered on a high pineland
plateau dotted with a chain of shallow, sedgy ponds.
Suddenly, from the marge of a pond a hundred yards

away, the plume-like tail of a big gray fox squirrel was seen waving jerkily over the ground as he ran for the timber. The party gave chase and succeeded in putting him up in a clump of tall long-leaf saplings before he could reach the big trees. Simon's eyes shone like brown pebbles through the sunlit waters of a shallow brook. His slouch was gone and he was all alertness, apprehension.

"Weh him, Boyzie? Weh him?"

"Yuh him, Pa! Yuh him! Shum! Shum!"

"*Duhbaw!*" boomed Betsey, and Simon reeled from the recoil as the load cut the top from a sapling down which the squirrel raced to the ground and scampered off for a big pine not far away, rushing up the trunk in long spirals. "Watch'um, Boyzie! Don' tu'n yo' yeye loose off'um 'tell I git Betsey load'," and Simon hurriedly rammed down his charge with many furtive glances at the watching sentinel to see that he didn't "tu'n 'e yeye loose." Extracting from a greasy rag a huge copper cap of the grandfather's hat pattern, he fitted the nipple and cocked his musket, as strenuous an operation as pulling the trigger, for at half-cock Betsey's hammer leaned back like the head of a strutting gobbler, while at the full, the cup yawned toward the heavens like the crater of a miniature Mauna Loa. Circling the pine he tried to locate the squirrel now lying flat in a crotch near the crown of the long-leaf, his long tail hanging down while his body was securely hidden. Boyzie pointed out the drooping tail. "Dey him, pa, dey him, but 'e too fudduh. You cyan' reach-'um."

"*Who?* Dat squerril? *Watch'um!*" The piece was raised, two sinewy fingers clutched the trigger with a

THE BLACK BORDER

jerk that would have disconcerted any aim, and the hammer, describing a parabola, fell upon the cap which exploded with a report like a parlor rifle, but Betsey's muzzle remained glum and silent.

" 'S'mattuh, Betsey? You got 'ooman name en' you ent got 'ooman mout'? You cyan' talk? De debble!" Another cap was fitted; another hopeful aim taken and another futile "paow!" echoed among the pines. Simon, now having only two caps left, accepted the suggestion that priming might help. He also accepted the powder which he poured with a liberal hand down the capacious nipple and rammed home with a light-wood splinter.

"Now watch'um come down." Another careful sight at the tantalizing tail up aloft, another "popped" cap with a little blue smoke from the priming, and a sorely puzzled squirrel hunter.

"Witch mus' be pit bad mout' 'puntop Betsey. I 'spec' 'e done cunjuh."

"Pa, is you pit any powduh een dat gun?"

"Who? Me? Wuh gun? Betsey? C'ose I pit pow-duh een 'um."

"Bettuh try'um," said doubting youth, and he did. When the shot was drawn and the screw of the long iron ramrod clicked against the breech of the musket, old Okra's face was a study. "Yaas, ef I did'n' bin haffuh watch Boyzie duh watch de squerril, I wouldn't bin fuhgit fuh load'um." Consoling himself with this shifting of responsibility, he loaded deliberately and fired, bringing down, with a lot of pine needles, half the squirrel's tail, which he stuck in the cord which bound his old hat with the remark, "Well, ennyhow I git all wuh I shoot at. *Ef man kin git all wuh 'e try fuh git, him oughtuh tengkful!*"

86

THE "CUNJUH" THAT CAME BACK

Lucy Jones, of Pon Pon, square and stout and widowed, had in her youth been as frequently husbanded as the Wife of Bath. One by one, however, through death, incompatibility of temperament, or indifference, she had lost these affiliations, and now, a "settled woman," Lucy lacked the masterful ways and the loving club of a man about the house, for it is axiomatic among the Gullah ladies of the Carolina coast that love and physical chastisement are inseparable. "Ef man ent lick you, 'e yent lub you." So, yearning for the touch of a vanished hoe handle or axe helve, Lucy languished. There was no longer satisfaction in "cawnhom'ny" or "tu'n flour." There was no savor in "poke" greens or lamb's-quarter. Fat bacon, while greasing her mouth, no longer anointed her soul. Her cabin was snug and comfortable, her bed was wide, and covered with a patchwork quilt that would have made Joseph's coat look like a drab jacket of butternut jeans. This quilt, slowly fabricated of all the bits of bright cloth—silk, cotton and wool—that she had begged from "de buckruh" during a period of several years, she had stitched together with painstaking fingers and exalted soul, absolutely confident that with its completion would come a husband to share its chromatic glories. "All de time uh binnuh mek dat quilt uh bin agguhnize een me min' duh study 'pun wuh kinduh husbun' uh gwine git w'en 'e done finish. Sometime' uh t'ink uh gwine git uh nyung nigguh, en' den uh 'membuh suh dese'yuh nyung nigguh ent wut. Dem too lub fuh t'row bone. En' den, 'nod-

duh time uh study en' uh t'ink uh'll git uh settle' man,
but uh know berry well uh haffuh git some kind'uh
man 'cause uh lonesome tummuch, en' uh keep on sew
de quilt 'tell 'e done, en' uh pit'um on de bed, en' dat
night w'en uh gone'sleep onduhneet' de quilt, uh hab
one dream, en' one sperrit come to me een de dream en'
tell me suh me fuh marry Isaac Middletun."

So the notion got into her head. Isaac was tall, as
Lucy was short; Isaac was thin, as Lucy was stout, and
Isaac was wary, as Lucy was predaceous. Himself an
elderly widower, he was living alone when Lucy deli-
cately intimated to him her desire to change the Welsh
name of Jones for the aristocratic English patronymic
of Middleton. Middleton, acknowledging the compliment, politely declined the offer, preferring to keep his
lonely cabin to himself. "Uh tell'um wuh de sperrit
say," she said, "en' uh tell'um de sperrit say him fuh
come fuh marry me dat same night. Uh hab fait' een
de sperrit' wu'd, en' uh scour' out de house en' uh mek
de bed, en' uh pit de tea by de fiah, en' still yet Middletun ent come. Uh nebbuh know shishuh eegnunt nigguh. W'en uh fin' suh 'e yent come, uh gone deepo fuh
fin'um, en' uh tell'um 'gen wuh de sperrit say. Uh
tell'um 'bout de quilt en' de tea en' t'ing', en' uh tell'um
nemmine' 'bout him house, cause myself hab house fuh
alltwo uh we fuh lib een, but Middletun ent haa'kee to
wuh uh tell'um 'bout de sperrit. 'E say suh de sperrit
hab bidness fuh talk 'long nyung 'ooman ef de sperrit
fuh send wife fuh him. Uh tell'um uh nyung 'ooman
cyan' specify fuh wife fuh settle' man lukkuh Middletun, 'cause dem lub fuh dress tummuch, but seem lukkuh uh cyan' git Middletun' min' straight." So she
"took her foot in her hand" and went home, dejected

but not hopeless, for she determined to stick to the trail, as the hound to the slot, until she ran the wily quarry to earth, to wit, cabin, for she hankered after him with an intense hankering.

"Lucy Middletun," "Mis' Middletun," how it filled the mouth and the ear, and exalted the spirit with satisfaction! Ever since emancipation the negroes have laid great store by their "titles," prefaced by "Mistuh" or "Mis'." Very dear to their hearts was the evolution of "Cuffee," "Cudjo" and "Sancho" of slavery, into "Mistuh Scott," "Mistuh Hawlback" and "Mistuh Middletun," of freedom, and, in the twinkling of an eye, "Dinah" and "Bina" and "Bella," the grubs, were transformed into "Mis' Wineglass," "Mis' Chizzum" and "Mis' Manigo," the butterflies. So, as Lucy mused and spun the spider web of fancy in which she hoped to entrap the wary and unappreciative Isaac, her mind crossed the stormy seas of Endeavor, and, resting in the snug harbor of Achievement, she thought of the deed as done, and imagined herself as going to work on week days, to church on Sundays, and to class meetings in the evenings, carrying, as appurtenant to her person, the longed-for "title" of Isaac, and as she thought upon the occasions when on public road or by-path she should "pass the time of day" in the ceremonial salutations so dear to her kind, she was filled to the jowls with ecstasy and her eardrums vibrated with the melody of "Middleton."

"Mawnin', Mis' Jones, how you do, ma'am?"

"Mawnin', Mis' Wineglass, uh tengk Gawd fuh life, but you know uh yent name Mis' Jones now. Me duh Mis' Middletun."

"Dat so? I nebbuh yeddy 'bout Bredduh Jones dead."

"No, ma'am, 'e yent dead, ma'am, but him hab anod-duh lady, en' me hab Isaac Middletun. You know dat same Mistuh Middletun lib close Adam' Run deepo? Well, she duh my juntlemun now, en' me duh Mis' Mid-dletun."

"Yaas, ma'am, well, mawnin', ma'am," and so on.

And always as Lucy sat in the sunshine before the cabin door and smoked her short clay pipe, or in the loneliness of night lay pondering and ponderable under the quilt that looked like a county map of Texas, con-stantly she projected thought waves towards Adams Run station, near which abode the recalcitrant Middle-ton. Along this main-traveled roadway of the Atlantic Coast Line, many trains passed by day and by night. The shrill shriek of the local freight, as it took the sid-ing at the distant station, reminded her that Middle-ton's ears were filled with the same sound. The hoarse warning of the Florida Limited at the curve, as it rushed southward filled with Northern tourists, who,— viewing from observation cars the fruit-laden thickets of gallberry bushes covering the damp, flat pinelands— marveled at the prodigality of the Southern climate that ripened huckleberries in midwinter, every whis-tle that blew along the busy line reminded Lucy of the railroad, and the railroad reminded her of the station, and the station reminded her of Middleton. Theoreti-cally, a member of the gentler sex has only to wish herself upon a man and the man is as good as wived, and the dogma that "a woman has only to make up her mind to marry a man and she gets him," is probably as old as the Creation, for Adam, like the gentleman he was, accepted philosophically and uncomplainingly— even gallantly—the spouse which kind Heaven had wished upon him. But much thought had brought Lucy to the conclusion that in her chase of a husband she was after all a dachshund, while the elusive Middleton was a fox. His defenses having proved impenetrable by direct attack, she had tried sapping and mining without success, even the "sperrit" bomb projected Middletonwards had fizzled at the fuse, and her cabin and its encircling yard and garden were still, alas! "no man's land!"

In her desperation Lucy decided to conjure! Like old Lorenzo in "La Mascotte," she believed in "signs, omens, dreams, predictions," and also in the potency of the dried frog, the blacksnake skin and the kerosene-soaked red flannel rag, as charms to pull a bashful wooer up to the scratch, to put a "spell," resulting in sickness or death, upon an enemy, or for any other purpose suggested by the mind of the one preparing the charm, for, a sort of aftermath of voodooism, "cunjuhs" are still believed in by many of these superstitious people.

Lucy bethought her of old Simon, not an authenticated witch-doctor, for he demanded no fixed fees, but a wily old sinner, a sort of amateur in black magic, who gave advice free of charge, although his services were always rewarded with gifts of eggs, or sweet potatoes, or clean rice. As snake skins and dried frogs were component parts of almost all old Simon's "charms," the boys of the community frequently brought him those they killed or found dead by the roadside. These, at his convenience, old Simon skinned and salted, or rubbed with ashes and smoked and dried and put away, for use when occasion should require. The low-country negroes seldom pass a dead frog lying

on its back, believing that if so exposed for any length
of time, rain will inevitably follow, and those so found,
if not turned over to prevent the floods from Heaven,
were taken to old Simon and added to his store.

So in the dusk of the early night and the dark of the
moon, for Lucy did not wish the black sisterhood to
know her business, she locked her cabin door, put a
shawl over her head and slipped away to Simon.

The weather was cold and Simon's door was shut.
She rapped faintly and furtively, and a fierce bark
challenged from within. Simon hobbled to the door
and opened it, a black cur growling at his knee. Kicking the dog away, he bade Lucy enter.

"Come een, sistuh, how you do?"

"Tengk Gawd fuh life, Unk' Simun. Uh come yuh
fuh ax you fuh gimme uh cunjuh fuh t'row uh spell
'puntop Isaac Middletun wuh lib Adam' Run deepo,
fuh mek'um haa'kee to de sperrit' wu'd, wuh tell'um
fuh hab me fuh wife, 'cause uh done tell'um *two time*
wuh de sperrit hab fuh say, but him ent study 'bout no
sperrit, en' 'e suck 'e teet' at me, en' him say suh him
fuh marry nyung 'ooman 'cause him ent hab no appetite fuh marry settle' 'ooman, en' uh done tell'um suh
nyung 'ooman cyan' specify fuh settle' man, but Middletun dat eegnunt en' haa'dhead', uh cyan' git'um fuh
do nutt'n', en' please suh fuh mek one hebby cunjuh,
'cause Middletun stubbunt sukkuh oxin en' mule alltwo, en' w'en you gimme de cunjuh, tell me wuh fuh do
'long'um en' weh uh mus' pit'um fuh t'row de spell
'puntop'uh Middletun, en' uh fetch t'ree aig' en' some
yalluh yam tettuh fuh you fuh eat." And she took
these gifts out of her apron and presented them to the
weaver of spells.

THE "CUNJUH" THAT CAME BACK

Simon was a man of few words. Going to an old cupboard where he kept his store of raw materials, he fumbled about and at last drew forth the dried skin of a "copper-belly" moccasin, about three feet long. This he wound about a smoke-dried toad, to which had been added two rusty horseshoe nails. Around them all a dirty strip of red flannel, well soaked in kerosene, was tied, and the charm was ready. Wrapping it in a piece of brown paper he gave it to Lucy who, tremulous with happiness and excitement, tied it in a corner of her apron.

"Daughtuh, you f'aid fuh walk duh paat' duh middlenight?"

"No, suh, uh yent 'f'aid fuh go Middletun' house."

"Berry well den, you fuh go Middletun' house middlenight tenight. You fuh tek dis cunjuh en' pit'um 'puntop de do'step to Middletun' house, en' you fuh walk easy so him ent fuh yeddy you. Onduhstan'?"

"Yaas, suh, tengk Gawd." And she hurried homeward.

For awhile she dozed before her fire, and then, an hour before midnight, with that uncanny instinct which guides those who live close to nature, she roused herself, and with her precious charm, set out hot-foot for the station. As she hurried through the dark a raccoon padded noiselessly across the path. Farther on, a grey fox trotted fearlessly in front of her for a few yards then sprang into the bushes and disappeared. The terrifying shriek and wild laugh of a barred owl just overhead, as she passed along a dark aisle in the forest, made her heart stand still for an instant, but the thought of Middleton warmed its cockles again and she kept on her way. At last she reached Middleton's

93

cabin and, thanking her stars that he kept no dog, she cautiously lifted the latch of his yard gate and tiptoed up to the steps where, with a silent prayer for success, she deposited the precious "cunjuh" and quietly slipped away.

Just at the end of the "dog watch" of the mariners, just before the "day clean" of the negroes—the hour known to all night workers, when, with the imminence of the dawn, somewhat of the weight of the world seems lifted from their shoulders—Middleton rose from his cornshuck couch and opening his cabin door looked forth, as is the custom of the early-rising negroes, to scan the sky and appraise the promise of the coming day. A gibbous moon of dusky gold, new-risen, hung low in the East. Diana had been banting for ten days and altho' her waist was waning, she yet shed sufficient light to open the eyes and engage the throats of all the roosters round about, and from the yards of lonely woodland cabin, and plantation quarters, their voices, shrill and clear, deep and raucous, came to Middleton's ears as they saluted the fools' gold of the moonlight in the belief that they were heralding the dawn.

"Fowl' mus' be t'ink day' clean," commented Middleton, and as he opened the door wider to get a better outlook, his bare toe came into contact with the gelid snakeskin and he sprang back in fear. Striking a match, he lit a lightwood splinter and discovered the "cunjuh" mysteriously placed at his very threshold. He scratched his puzzled head. "Eh, eh! wuh dis t'ing? Me nebbuh do nutt'n' to nobody. Uh wonduh who duh try fuh t'row spell 'puntop me! Tengk Gawd, uh nebbuh 'tep obuhr'um," secure in the belief that as he had not stepped over it, no harm could come to him.

THE "CUNJUH" THAT CAME BACK

So, picking it up fearlessly, he put it away in a chink in the clay chimney until he should find use for the dread instrument which Providence had placed in his hands. All day he pondered, for, having no enemies, there was none to whom he wished harm. At last, as evening fell, dark thoughts came with the dusk, and a sinister purpose slid into his soul, which he lost no time in putting into execution. Venus was the evening star but she told him nothing, for there was no love in his heart and his mind held only the definite purpose to rid himself once and for all of the vexing importunities of the husband-hunter.

"Uh gwine tek dis t'ing to da' 'ooman' house en' t'row one spell 'puntop'um fuh mek'um pit 'e min' 'puntop some dem todduh man en' lemme 'lone," and walking briskly to Lucy's house, where she slept unsuspiciously beneath the unalluring quilt, he carefully placed the charm in the middle of the top step and went his ways under the starlit heavens.

THE RACCOON HUNTER

All through the autumn, when golden-rod and sumac flaunted the colors of Spain from every neglected fence corner, and the ripening sun burned from the blue through the haze that hung over the earth, when the crows, uttering their care-free harvest note, flew over the tawny fields of corn, and negroes with nimble fingers pulled the reluctant locks from the half-opened Sea Island cotton bolls, when squirrels chattered and barked contentedly among the hickories as they commenced to gather their winter's store, and wild pigs nosed about for acorns among the rustling leaves in the oak groves—all through these September and October days, the boy had pestered old Abram, the most successful 'coon hunter on Pon Pon, to organize a torchlight hunt and take him along. Abram White, or " 'Bram," as he was commonly called, was a slow-talking, slow-thinking, slow-moving old darkey; so deliberate that the mental effort involved in answering the simplest question would furrow his brow like an old-fashioned washboard. He had been allowed to clear up a piece of rich land on Cotton Hill, far removed from the "quarters" of the other negroes, and this field he held rent-free in return for the labor of bringing it under cultivation. The task occupied old 'Bram for several years. First building a substantial cabin for his smart wife, Delia, he proceeded to "ring" the forest trees and, leaving them to die, slowly grubbed up the smaller trees and undergrowth, planting in the little cleared plots patches of corn, peas and sweet potatoes, increasing his field bit by bit each year. He was employed regularly as night watchman for the plantation and, armed with his long "muskick"—a condemned army weapon—walked his beat about barn and stables from dark till dawn, returning from each round to drowse near the big fire which he invariably made in an open spot, summer as well as winter, for the coast negroes are true fire-worshipers and their love for the flames that leap and the embers that glow is as great as their skill in fire-making. Abram owned the best 'coon dog in the community, a black mongrel of medium size with a blaze in the face and a white ring around his neck. Devoted as he was to Delia, Abram's love for "Ring" was almost as great, and his pride in the dog's accomplishments and reliability was infinite. The abandoned rice field now overgrown, near old Abram's new-ground, was full of raccoons and 'possums and the old hunter often got permission to put on a substitute watchman for part of the night, while he foraged the woods with almost invariable success, and all through the winter the jambs of his wide-throated clay chimney were hung with the smoked flesh of his spoils, while their pelts—ring-tailed and rat-tailed—adorned the outer walls of his log cabin.

The veteran 'coon dog will rarely follow any other animal than raccoon or 'possum—the lawful prey of his negro master—ignoring the frequently crossed trails of deer or fox. Puppies and undisciplined dogs often break away and run rabbits, of course, but they are always caught and thrashed and the occasional lapse is held derogatory to the dog's master. Both objects of the chase are nocturnal feeders, sleeping most of the day in hollow trees or logs. Sometimes the hollow is high up in the fork of some forest giant, completely hidden by the lianas that run from the ground to the topmost branches. A dog will occasionally bark at a tree whence the 'coon has descended, or one from which the quarry has crossed on a limb or vine to another tree, and whenever the hunter finds that his dog has "treed" at a vacant tree, the poor animal is held to have "lied" and is given a severe whipping, so seasoned dogs make few mistakes and old Abram's Ring was always true.

At last, as October drew to a close and the first white frost nipped the potato vines, the boy's importunities bore fruit in a promise from Abram to take him on the first clear night in the dark of the moon, the condition being that the boy should furnish travel rations. The night appointed proved fine and frosty, with a sharp tang in the air, and an hour or two after dark the hunt assembled. Besides his single-barreled muzzleloader, the boy "packed" a knapsack filled with smoked herrings and hardtack from the plantation commissary. Abram had his musket, and Tom Ford and Joe Smashum, two young negroes, their axes. All three carried bundles of "fat" lightwood for torches strapped to their backs. Sike, a half-grown black boy, carried himself. All the negroes were bare-footed, the horny soles of their feet having become so toughened as to make them indifferent to briars and snags. Ring wagged his tail expectantly and, like his master, looked contemptuously upon the two young curs that followed Joe.

And now they started single file, the boy in front, then old 'Bram, the torch-bearers last, throwing a flood of light ahead of them, the dogs at heel close to their respective masters. So, down the broad avenue of liveoaks, the great trees heavily bearded with the gray Spanish moss, assuming fantastic shapes in the flare of the torches, on across the old King's Highway, past the Big Spring and over a low causeway that spanned an old rice field. Here the party hesitated between two "drives" that seemed equally promising, one to the right across the "half moon" dam to a thickly wooded island in the big savanna, the other with a slant to the left through a grove of big beeches toward the "Blue House" back water. While old Abram scratched his head for a decision which "the stubborn glebe" was slow to yield, Ring, who had been nosing about, dashed suddenly among the undergrowth of saw-palmettoes that covered the ground under the beeches and, giving tongue on a hot trail, ended his master's cogitations. The other dogs followed the veteran in full cry, and in a few minutes Ring's slow and measured barking apprised his master that he had "treed." The negroes shouted encouragingly, "*speak, Ring!*" "*Speak to'um, boy!*" as the party pushed through the thicket and found Ring sitting before a loblolly pine, one of a group of three which grew close together with their upper limbs almost touching.

There are three methods of getting a raccoon out of a tree. By "shining" his eyes, which is done by holding the torch behind one, and shooting him; by cutting down the tree and trusting to the dogs to capture him before he gets away; or by climbing the tree and shaking him down or making him jump off. As Tom Ford was a noted climber and the tree was not too large for him to "hug," it was decided to climb, after the "shining" method had been resorted to without success. Tom cut a stick about six feet long which he tied around his neck and dragged up after him. This

99

was to be used to poke the quarry off the limb in case
he came to close quarters. He threw off his jacket and
cap and commenced swarming up the trunk which
stretched full forty feet without a limb, lifting himself with his powerful ape-like arms and the cupped
hollows of his bare, horny feet, with which he gripped
the trunk. In a few minutes he reached the first limb
and the excitement below him increased, both hunters
and dogs looking earnestly upward as the climber stood
on the limb and looked above and around him, trying
to locate the quarry.

"Weh 'e dey, Tom?" called Abram. "You shum?"

"Uh yent shum," was the laconic response.

Tom again hugged the tree, whose narrowed trunk
now gave him a better hold, and went up ten or twelve
feet to the next limb. Just as he pulled himself over
it and got to his feet, there was a great rattling of
claws on the bark of a long outstretching limb a few
feet over his head, and, silhouetted against the patches
of starlight that broke the leafage above him, he could
make out the cunning 'coon running along the limb to
its very end where it touched a far-reaching bough
from the second tree of the group. Tom yelled, with
the hope that he might frighten the animal into miss-
ing its step and falling, but the sure-footed creature
passed safely and disappeared among the dark needles
that veiled his sanctuary.

"Look out, Unk' Ebbrum, look out! 'E done cross
to de todduh tree," Tom called, as he began to slide
toward the earth. The group on the ground flared
torches and looked anxiously at the new retreat, but
no shining eyes were visible, and the futility of further
pursuit of this particular 'coon was realized, as he

THE RACCOON HUNTER

had demonstrated that he could cross too readily from
one to another of the three sister pines. The short
chase had lasted only a few minutes and the hunt took
up its equipment and returned to the Caw Caw
Swamp Road, Abram, after much pondering, having
decided to exploit the "Tombs" drive, a noted hunting
ground. Half a mile farther and the party turned to
the right and in a few minutes passed near "the
Tombs," one of the Colonial burying grounds found
occasionally in the low-country forests.

The solitary negro will seldom pass one of these
graveyards at night, and even with companions and
torches the 'coon-hunters walked more rapidly until
"the Tombs" was passed. As they entered an old
field with several large persimmon trees full of ripening fruit, to Abram's experienced eye a presage of
'possums, sure enough, in a moment, one of Joe's curs,
with a shrill yelp, struck a hot trail and off they went
across the big field, followed rapidly by men and boys.
The dogs overtook the quarry at the edge of the clearing and treed at a young oak, near whose top the
torches revealed a big 'possum about thirty feet from
the ground. As the tree was easy, Sike, the fourteen-
year-old novice, was given the place of honor as
climber, and up he went, full of the pride that goeth
before a fall. Sike was short and fat, and spread-
eagled himself like a great black frog as he laboriously
worked his way upward. The going was heavy, and
having his hands or his arms full, he did not take the
precaution to look above him until he had almost put
his hand on the animal. A sudden snarl from the
hunted, and a frightened yell from the hunter, who
lost his hold and fell six or eight feet toward the

ground, clutching wildly at the branches on the way down, fortunately landing on one strong enough to bear his weight. He did not linger in the tree but slid to the ground as quickly as possible, where he was received with shouts of laughter. "Haw, Buck! ef oonuh 'f'aid *'possum*, how you gwine t'row down *rok-koon?*" But Sike said nothing, while Joe went up the tree and threw down the 'possum, which rolled into a ball as soon as he touched the ground, and, after having been mouthed over by the dogs, was tied up in a sack and given to Sike to carry.

And now into the big swamp that stretched from the Tombs to Long Life Spring, a noted water-hole that never failed in even the worst drought. Ring gave tongue querulously once or twice on a cold trail. "Rok-koon," Abram laconically remarked, and, as a shrill outcry from Joe's nondescripts rang through the woods in another direction, "rabbit," he added contemptuously. The younger negroes soon caught and thrashed the rabbit-chasers and, as Ring had now developed his trail and was giving tongue more freely, the other dogs were hied away to join him and soon added their voices to his. The cry skirted the swamp and in a few minutes their barking indicated that they had treed a quarter of a mile away. The 'coon had taken refuge in a big rosemary, whose smooth bark and thick trunk presented difficulties to a climber, and Abram decided to cut it down. Tom and Joe on opposite sides plied their axes vigorously. How many magnificent forest trees have been sacrificed since the war by the wasteful negro hunters who have no compunction about cutting down a ten dollar tree, belonging to some one else, to capture a "two-bit" raccoon! And

THE RACCOON HUNTER

the negro who would grunt grievously if had to fell
three or four big pines for a day's work, will throw
an equal number as a pastime, in an hour or two at
night! Soon the tree began to crack, and the dogs
were seized, to prevent them from rushing under the
falling trunk in their eagerness to be on hand when
the 'coon should jump out of the thick branches at the
top. They were released as the tree crashed to earth.
Although they quickly surrounded the top, the wary
'coon had already made a getaway, but the cry followed hot-foot and forced him up a white oak a
hundred yards distant. The tree, of moderate size,
was thickly branched and no glimpse of the 'coon could
be discerned through the heavy leafage. Tom tied a
long stick over his shoulder and was soon on the first
big limb which he proceeded to explore, "cooning" it
out, while the torch-bearers held their lights under the
end of the limb, and thus the second and third limbs
were explored, but no dark form appeared against the
light, and Tom climbed to a fork thirty feet from the
ground. He paused for a moment and looked about
him, then yelled "Great Gawd, Unk' Ebbrum, duh *two*
rokkoon!"

"Weh 'e dey, boy? *T'row'um down!*"

"Dem alltwo dey 'pun dish'yuh lef' han' limb."

"Shine dem eye, Joe, lemme shoot'um," said Abram.

"Tek'care oonuh ent shine my'own en' shoot me!"
cried Tom.

"Nigguh eye yent fuh shine," Abram replied, but he
was spared the embarrassment of having to distinguish
between Tom's eyes and the raccoons', for one of the
animals, a half grown individual, broke sanctuary,
and, dashing past Tom, slid down the tree to a lower
limb, from whose extremity he sprang to the ground,

unhappily for him, only a few feet distant from the watching Ring, who was on him before he could get started. There was a furious scuffle for a few minutes but the veteran dog soon choked the 'coon to death.

Tom now commenced crawling out on the limb after the big raccoon, who growled menacingly and backed as the negro neared him. At last the limb began to sag under Tom's weight and the 'coon at the very end, eight or ten feet beyond him, teetered uneasily, as the torches flared beneath him and the dogs yelped expectantly. The long stick was now brought into play and Tom straddled the bough while he tried to pry off the quarry, but in his zeal he overreached himself and slid too far. The bough buckled under him like a whip and he lost his balance, but while regaining his hold with monkey-like agility he clutched so frantically at the raccoon's end of the limb as to dislodge its occupant, who fell in the very teeth of the dogs. In the fierce fight that ensued, the raccoon slit the ears of the younger dogs and mauled them severely before Ring could get the throat-hold he wanted. Once secured, however, he soon choked the 'coon to death. As midnight approached, it was decided to eat supper and go home.

A lot of dry wood was gathered and a big fire made in a little glade. The younger negroes sat around the flames waiting for the coals upon which to broil the smoked herrings. Old 'Bram stretched out on the ground with the soles of his bare feet toward, and almost in, the fire, and, true to the traditions of a night watchman, he soon fell asleep. The flames crackled. Tom and Joe and the solemn Sike blinked at the light and nodded, the dogs licked their wounds and whim-

pered at the sharper twinges of pain. Suddenly old
Abram grunted and "sniffed the tainted gale."

"Eh, eh! Uh smell foot duh bu'n! Somebody' foot
mus' be duh bu'n! Uh wunduh who' foot duh bu'n?"
Then, as he sat up and saw the curling smoke rising
from the thick horny sole of one of his own feet, "Great
Gawd, duh *my'own! Duh my foot duh bu'n!* Tom,
oonuh binnuh seddown duh fiah duh look 'puntop my
foot duh bu'n, hukkuh you nubbuh tell me?"

"Me shum duh bu'n fuh true, Unk' Ebbrum, but
oonuh binnuh sleep en' uh t'awt 'e would bex you fuh
wake."

"Oonuh had no bidness fuh t'awt nutt'n'! You seddown duh fiah en' look 'puntop my foot duh bu'n en'
nubbuh tell me. Joe, oonuh binnuh seddown duh fiah
duh look 'puntop my foot duh bu'n, hukkuh you nubbuh tell me?"

"Unk' 'Bram, I shum duh smoke, but uh nebbuh
t'ink 'e bu'n bad 'nuf fuh hot you."

"Co'se 'e didn' bu'n bad 'nuf fuh hot me, but ef uh
yent bin had sense 'nuf fuh smell'um en' know suh
somebody' foot duh bu'n, 'e might uh bu'n off, en' you
seddown duh fiah en' look 'puntop my foot duh bu'n
en' nubbuh tell me. Sike, oonuh binnuh seddown duh
fiah duh look 'puntop my foot duh bu'n, hukkuh you
nubbuh tell me?"

"Me nebbuh shum, suh, uh binnuh sleep."

"Meself binnuh sleep. Enty uh smell somebody' foot
duh bu'n en' mek me fuh wake? Oonuh boy' grow up
sence freedum, oonuh *ent wut!*"

The herrings were broiled and eaten with the hardtack, the spoils were slung around the shoulders of the
hunters, the fire beaten out, the torches relit, and a

short cut taken for home. As old Abram relieved his substitute at the watchfire in the barnyard, his voice rumbled through his beard like the muttering of slow and distant thunder, "Uh done tell Mas' Rafe suh dese'yuh nigguh' grow' up sence freedum, dem ent wut! Dem good fuh nutt'n' *debble'ub'uh* no'count boy, dem seddown duh fiah duh look 'puntop my foot duh bu'n en' dem nubbuh tell me suh my foot duh bu'n. *Dem nubbuh tell me!*"

THE TURKEY HUNTER

Sabey, a queer, misshapen mulatto, almost an albino, with green eyes and yellow wool lighting and thatching a shrewd and twisted, though good-natured, monkey face, lived, a few years after the war, on Pon Pon. His wife, Bess, a good-looking black girl, was devoted to him as a good husband and a first-rate provider. When twitted by the other negro women with her husband's lack of personal pulchritude, she was always ready with a retort.

"Mekso you marri'd monkey fuh man, Bess?"

"Sabey oagly en' him look lukkuh monkey fuh true, but him iz uh good puhwiduh en' no odduh man haffuh come een him house fuh feed him wife, en' *Stepney* nebbuh come een needuh."

Sabey lived in a cabin at the edge of the woods, far away from the other plantation settlements, seldom mixing with the other negroes, who rather feared him, having a vague sort of belief in his ability to throw spells. When not hunting, he worked, but he was usually hunting in winter, and hunting successfully, for although his piece was one of the condemned army muskets carried by so many low-country negroes after Freedom, he was a good shot and possessed infinite patience and considerable woodcraft. Energetic, too, his twisted legs carried him for miles through the forests and along the backwaters and abandoned ricefields where, creeping on all-fours and worming his way through cane-brakes and briars, he frequently surprised summer ducks, and occasionally mallard and teal, feeding on the grass seeds along the margins, or

107

the rich acorns from the live-oaks whose far-flung boughs stretched over the canals, and Sabey was an economist and seldom wasted shot on a single bird. On frosty mornings when he peeped over the embankments and saw green-wing teal strung upon a floating log basking in the first rays of the wintry sun, he would maneuver and crawl around, regardless of bogs or briars, until he got into a position where he could line them up, when, after his old "muskick" had spoken, he would sometimes gather up a dozen or more, which he sold to "de buckruh" on the plantations, or at the railway station; but it was as a turkey hunter that Sabey achieved distinction in the community.

Wild turkeys were very plentiful in the low-country soon after the war, and in the winter season flocks sometimes came up in the live-oak avenues and tangled gardens of the war-ruined plantations, making a boy's heart thump against his ribs as he watched them picking up the acorns just out of gunshot of his little single-barrel. In roaming the woods, Sabey knew every dog-wood knoll between the Stackyard and Beaver Dam, and when, in midwinter or later, he saw where the turkeys had "scratched" among the leaf mould for the glossy red berries that form their favorite wild food, he scattered handfuls of peas or rough rice about and returned a day or two later to see if the turkeys had taken the bait. If the scattered grain was untouched, he would offer temptation elsewhere until the wary birds had overcome suspicion and established relations with the rich man-grown food placed before them. The bait once taken, Sabey returned at two or three-day intervals and spread the feast anew, which after a while came to be to the turkeys as their daily

bread. Then, behind some hurricane tree or old log
nearby, the hunter prepared the "blind"—usually a pit
three or four feet deep, camouflaged with boughs or
great pieces of pine bark, with a gun opening toward
an open space where, in a shallow trench, grain was
scattered. From the scratching ground under the dog-
woods, a trail would be laid to the trench, which was
visited and replenished day after day until the greedy
birds had become fearless and came regularly to their
breakfast table. Then "one fine day," just at dawn,
Sabey would shamble off to the forest and creep within
his blind, where he almost held his breath in "watchful waiting" for the coming of his quarry.

Nothing save Sir Walter's conception of the muta-
bility of the feminine mind, is quite so uncertain as
the hour of the coming of wild turkeys to a blind.
Sometimes at daylight, as they fly from their roosts
on the topmost limbs of the great pines, they go at
once to the bait. The next day, perhaps, they may
roam the woods for hours and not reach the blind until
noon, and on yet other days the fickle creatures resist
temptation altogether, so "it is well understood" that
whoso would shoot turkeys at a blind must have abun-
dant patience and a certain complacent attitude toward
his own society.

Who can tell what thoughts moved through Sabey's
brain cells as he sat "steadfast, unmovable" through
the waiting hours. Did the tips of Aurora's rosy
fingers mean anything to him as she lifted the somber
curtains of the night and ushered in the radiant God
of day? Did the harsh yet homey "chauw, chauw" of
the brown thrasher—the first winter bird to awaken in
copse or forest—take his thoughts to the lonely cabin

109

where Bess dreamed of the Sunday calico or the new shoes that would follow Sabey's successful shot? Did the last hoot of the barred owl as, his night hunting over, he slipped away on muffled wing to the thick woods to drowse his days away, tell him anything of the human prototypes of all birds of prey? They, too, the selfish and the predatory, clutter up the by-ways of the world, closing their eyes to the light of service and the pulsing of humanity about them till, with the falling shadows, their eyes open and they prowl in quest of the unwary!

But whatever Sabey's musings, he crept morning after morning into his blind and waited patiently as the hours slipped by, for the game that never came. Perhaps the wary birds had sensed danger at the blind—perhaps they had found a more convenient food supply elsewhere—but late every morning for a week Sabey had returned home weary and empty-handed, but, with a true sportsman's spirit, determined to try again. Sunday intervened. A strong superstition in the negro's mind, that to fire a gun on Sunday is to "hab sin," kept him out of the woods, and he shambled off to church, but four o'clock the next morning, an hour before dawn, found him at the tryst which, through thought-waves, he believed he had made with the flock of turkeys.

They kept the tryst. The dawn came up slowly and silently, bringing in one of those rare windless, low-country winter days, when all the air is pale blue and gold and the forests are green and purple and brown. The first rays of the sun touched with pallid flame the topmost boughs of the tall pines and glanced from the myriad glistening needles that hung motionless in the chilly air. As the sun climbed yet higher, its sensuous warmth drank up the white frost that lay like a crystal blanket upon the open spaces and the light vapors that hung over the dark places in the forest, and, as the warmer and softer air fell about Sabey, he drowsed at his post.

The outdoor negroes of the coast need neither watch nor clock to tell the time of day. From "middlenight" or "fus' fowl crow," on through the procession of the hours to "dayclean," "sun'up," "one," "two," "t'ree hour attuh sun'up," to "middleday," and then on, as the sun slants downward, through "t'ree hour," "two hour," "one hour to sundown," and "fus' daa'k," he makes a close approximation. So, as Phœbus shot with flat trajectory across the Southern sky, Sabey, snuggled down among the dry pine needles with which he had nearly filled his trench, dozed and listened and dozed, and waking, muttered "middleday," and dozed again.

A slight rustling of dead leaves like the whisper of gently falling rain, and ten beautiful gobblers entered the little glade and going straight to the trench, began picking up the grain greedily. The sunlight flashed from their gleaming breasts as from planished bronze. Their iridescent plumage showed all the tints of glorified autumn leaves, and, as they stooped to feed, their long beards touched the ground. A braver sight to a hunter's eye than bear or buck or any other game that roams the Southern forests!

Sabey slowly opened his eyes and stiffened like a setter at the point. His long musket, already aligned to rake the trench, rested securely in a forked stick driven into the ground. As a sibilant whistle came

from his twisted lips, ten heads uprose like the armed
men from the mythical dragon's teeth, and came in
line with the leveled gun. At a warning "putt" from
their suspicious leader, they stood on tiptoe for a
breakaway, but Sabey pulled his clumsy trigger, and
following the heavy roar, he clambered out of the blind
and ran forward to find seven great birds fluttering on
the ground, while the others ran at race-horse speed for
thirty or forty feet (your turkey, like your condor and
your aeroplane, must take wing from a running start)
and, rising on a long slant with a great beating of the
air, topped the pines a quarter of a mile away and
sailed off beyond "the Cypress." The big birds, shot
in the head, soon lay still and Sabey's simian face
wrinkled with satisfaction. "Tengk Gawd, uh git
oonuh at las'," he chuckled. "One, two, t'ree, fo', fibe,
six, seb'n," he slowly counted—"t'ree git'way." And
then he scratched his head. Sabey was undersized,
"him leetle but 'e ole," the negroes observed, and could
he pack far more than his weight in turkeys to the
"big house" a mile away? It seemed a task too great for
his strength, but his spirit was high, and, as he thought
of the wildcats and gray foxes that abounded in these
forests so seldom entered by hunter or woodman, he
shook his head, pulled out a formidable-looking clasp
knife and began to peel the bark from a young hickory.
"No," he said to himself, "uh yent fuh lef' none. Uh
tote'um all ef 'e tek me 'tell sundown fuh git Pon Pon.
All wuh Mas' Rafe ent buy, uh gwine tek deepo. No
fox, needuhso wil'cat, nebbuh git 'e teet' een dem tuckrey!" and he quickly removed the outer bark from the
long strips he had skinned from the sapling and
scraped and twisted the tough inner fibre into service-

able thongs. This strong hickory bark is the common cordage of the plantation negroes and serves for girths, bridles and harness for horse and ox, and is also plaited into the long whips used by herdsmen and bird-minders, the "pop" of whose lash or "cracker" is as far-sounding as the report of a rifle. Sabey tied six of the birds in pairs by their long necks, distributing them as comfortably as he could about his ungainly person—one pair over each shoulder, while the other, hanging forward, supported by the back of his neck, was balanced by the seventh bird hung at his back, suspended from the barrel of his musket. Thus laden like a pack donkey, he threaded the thick woods, avoiding as best he could the tangled vines and dangerous stump holes, and came at last to the open clearing of "Cotton Hill." Here he laid down his burden and rested, "fuh ketch me secun' win'." Half an hour later he took up his load and, mindful of the fact that he had been poaching, avoided the direct way through the fields to the settlement and, skirting the old ricefield, traversed with furtive eye the negro burying ground where, shaded by giant live-oaks, seven generations of slaves and freedmen slept under the thick mould. For many of the far-scattered family negroes still bring their dead to rest in these hallowed places on the old plantations. Apart from the sentiment, it gives them standing among the low-caste darkeys who had belonged to "po' buckruh" and whose forbears slept in no ancestral graveyards. Passing behind the "Echo Oak," Sabey reached the big road and, a quarter of a mile beyond, tramped boldly up the great avenue to sell "Mas' Rafe" his own game. He made a dramatic entrance into the yard, his deformed body completely covered by the splendid birds, their black beards hanging from their burnished breasts and their feet nearly touching the ground. The hounds, which had run out with bristling backs and open mouths at the unwonted sight, wagged their tails and whimpered as they caught the familiar scent of the game.

"Well, you copper-colored imp of Satan! Where did you shoot those turkeys?"

"Uh shoot'um Beabuh Dam."

"No, Sabey. Beaver Dam is more than two miles off, and I heard a gun in the Stackyard."

"Yaas, suh, but duh Beabuh Dam uh shoot'um. Uh mek uh bline' on da' po' buckruh' groun', 'cause him all-time duh mek bline' 'puntop'uh yo' groun', en' uh shoot him tuckrey fuh pay'um back, en' uh 'spec' da' gun you yeddy shoot duh da' po' buckruh wuh bin attuh da' gang uh tuckrey wuh use een dem dogwood t'icket. Meself been yeddy uh gun shoot Stackyaa'd w'en uh bin Beabuh Dam." "Mas' Rafe" passed his hand admiringly over the glossy breast of the largest bird while deftly feeling his crop. "What did you bait these turkeys with?"

"Uh bait'um wid cawn, 'cause uh nebbuh mek no peas las'yeah, needuhso no rice."

"Did you work here last week?"

"Yaas, suh, uh wu'k Chuesday and T'ursday eben-in'."

"What did you do?"

"Uh beat rice, suh."

"How much rice did you take home in that bag you carried?"

"Eh, eh, Mas' Rafe! You see me wid bag? You t'ink suh me t'ief yo' rice? Wuh nyuse me hab fuh rice? Me en' Bess alltwo lub fuh eat cawn hom'ny tummuch."

"You didn't bait these turkeys with rice, did you?"

"Who? Me! Mas' Rafe, you hu't me feelin's fuh talk 'bout bait dese tuckrey wid rice! Weh me fuh git rice? Dese tuckrey nebbuh see uh rice sence dem bawn!"

"How did the rice get in their crops?"

"Dem got rice een dem craw? Mas' Rafe, dem tuckrey mus'be bin spang Willtown dis mawnin' fuh use een Baa'nwell' ricefiel', en' full dem craw, en' attuh dat dem come six mile to de bline' weh uh kill'um."

"But it is only five miles from Willtown to Beaver Dam, Sabey, and six miles to the Stackyard, where you *didn't* kill the turkeys!"

Completely cornered, Sabey grinned. "Mas' Rafe, you sho' hab uh good onduhstan' fuh know nigguh! Nigguh ent fuh fool you! No, suh!"

And then the former slaveholder bought the game shot on his own land and baited with his own grain, from the freedman who had stolen both, which is not infrequently the way of former slaveholders in dealing with former slaves.

THE 'GATOR HUNTER

Crook-legged, pumpkin-colored, yellow-wooled, green-eyed Sabey—the mightiest turkey hunter on Pon Pon—sat in the midsummer sunshine at his cabin door and talked, partly to himself and partly to his black wife, Bess, who busied herself within. A protracted drought was over the land, and Sabey's summer harvest was at hand. Hunting turkeys and ducks in the winter, he was equally successful in his summer quest for the much-esteemed fresh water terrapins which abounded in the backwaters and the sluggish lily-covered canals that intersected the abandoned inland ricefields. They found a ready market on the plantations or at the railway station, whence they were shipped to Charleston, to appear on the tables of her discriminating gourmets in the form of highly spiced soups and stews. These big terrapins were frequently offered for sale by negroes who surprised the slow creatures while crossing the road or path on their way from one canal or pond to another, or trapped them in some shallow water hole. A few negroes even hunted them occasionally, the only equipment necessary being an empty crocus bag and a pair of legs—naked or trousered—with bare feet attached. Sneaking as close as possible to the floating log on which the terrapins sunned themselves, the hunter crept up until they became alarmed and slid off into the water, when he jumped in after them, and if the water was not more than three or four feet deep he could usually locate them by feeling about on the bottom near the log with his bare feet, when he would bob his head and his

116

hands under, and the prize would go into the sack hung about his neck. But Sabey followed successfully, not only the ordinary methods of capture, but during dry spells adopted the hazardous expedient of going down into the alligator holes after them. As Prairie dogs, owls and rattlesnakes live together in the same burrows on the Western plains, terrapins are always found in alligator holes with their hosts in dry spells when the water is low, and he who would secure them must either get the alligator out first, or go down into the hole with him—one a difficult, the other a dangerous, adventure.

In the cruel midsummer droughts that sometimes occurred in the low-country, even the wet savannas and backwaters were parched to desert dryness. The muddy bottoms, ordinarily covered with water, even the shallower canals and ditches, sun-baked and cracked open, were abandoned by the life that sometime swam or waded in the waters now receded. Only the deeper places held water, and these roiled with the teeming fish and eels and terrapins that cluttered up the muddy pools. Crane and heron—greater and lesser—flew squawking overhead, or stalked along the marges taking heavy toll of their helpless prey, while in the mud round about countless tracks of otter, mink and raccoon showed that, like lions at the African water holes, these lesser creatures, too, held nightly carnival at the water. Now came the human spoilers— negroes with "jampots" or "churnpots"—cylindrical contrivances about fifteen inches in diameter by thirty inches in height, made of canes tied together with hickory bark thongs, and looking like tall, bottomless waste-baskets. Wading in the shallow waters, the fisherman holds his jampot by the upper rim with both hands, churning the water in front of him. Apprised by splash or flutter that a fish has been trapped, he reaches one hand into the cage, withdraws his catch, which he bestows in a bag hung about his neck, and "churns" again. When conditions were favorable for this form of fishing, the negroes, in the years immediately following the war, caught not only the coarse mudfish and "cats" which they so affect, but destroyed also countless thousands of trout and bream and other fine food fish. In Sabey's time, almost every other negro in the well-watered districts owned a jam-pot, and the making of this was an important side line of the old plantation chair and basket-makers, but, synchronously perhaps with the destruction of the fish, the art, or the practice, of "churning" passed away, and it is seldom heard of now.

Now that a "hebby dry drought" was on, Sabey licked his chaps in pleasant anticipation. No rain was in prospect. The roaring of alligators is regarded by low-country weather sharps as a sign of coming rain, but, although the old bulls had bellowed lustily at dawn on several consecutive mornings, the sun still blazed from a cloudless sky and the heat waves danced and shimmered in the breathless air, giving point to the saw that in a drought all signs fail, which was once strikingly illustrated by an old-time plantation driver, whose master, needing rain, drew comfort from the persistent bellowing of the alligators. "Did you hear those 'gators this morning, Scipio? That should bring rain."

"Yaas, Maussuh, uh yeddy'um, but dis duh Dry Drought, enty?"

"Yes, a very severe drought."

THE 'GATOR HUNTER

"Berry well, suh. Enty you know, Maussuh, suh Dry Drought duh him own maussuh, en' him ent 'f'aid alligettuh? En', Maussuh, Dry Drought him haa'd-head' ez de berry Satan! Nobody ent fuh mek'um fuh do nutt'n'! All dem todduh kinduh wedduh dem berry 'f'aid alligettuh. W'en alligettuh belluh fuh rain, dem big Bloodynoun frog dem jine'um, *'come'yuh rain, come'yuh' rain, come'yuh rain!'* Den dem po' leely frog een de tree, dem hab shishuh mo'nful woice, dem biggin fuh cry. Bimeby, rain come. But Dry Drought, him ent stan' so. W'en Dry Drought come, bullfrog know suh alligettuh cyan' mek'um fuh wedduh, en' you yeddy'um holluh ' *'e yent fuh rain, 'e yent fuh rain, 'e yent fuh rain!'* Alligettuh bex. 'E holluh 'gen. Dry Drought suck 'e teet' at'um. 'Scuse me fuh cuss, Maussuh, but Dry Drought him ent care uh *dam* 'bout alligettuh, uh dunkyuh ef' 'e holluh 'tell 'e belly bus'!'"

So, as the unterrified "Dry Drought" burned about him, Sabey prepared to start his campaign. The waters, long drying up, were now low enough. Many alligators had been forced to move, and the smaller ones were frequently encountered in the road—sometimes even on the high pineland plateaus—as they traveled toward the river or adventured in search of deeper canals or water holes. They always showed fight, too, swelling up like pouter pigeons, standing high off the ground, and hissing like geese, while they watched for a chance to lash out with dangerous tail. But, with the conservatism of age and wealth, the big old fellows seldom moved from their favorite pools on which opened their subterranean holes or burrows, excavated with their forefeet, like those of other burrowing creatures. Here in the deep pools were fish at hand, and nearby were the pig paths

119

along which unwary shoats, going to the water, or nosing about in the soft earth for succulent roots, would often come in reach of the sweeping tail, and add to the variety of the big 'gator's fare. In these deep underground holes, the ugly creatures hibernated from autumn to spring, until, with the earliest warm sunshine, first the nose and eyes would appear cautiously above the water which covered the entrance to the hole, and, growing bolder day by day, as the weather became warmer, next the head, and, at last the entire body would be exposed, lying on the muddy bank, or on a tussock among the rushes. Here, perhaps, he would be descried by some adventurous boy, who, sighting carefully despite his palpitating heart, would shatter the 'gator's skull with a rifle bullet or reach his heart by a well-aimed charge of buckshot behind the shoulder; but, barring the boy, the days of the big 'gators were long in the land, for they became more wary with advancing years and seldom fell to the negroes' firearms.

While the drought was yet young, the heaviest alligator in the community had been located by Sabey at the "Half Moon" dam, and now the deep pool into which his hole opened contained all the water that was left in the great savanna. The yawning mouth of the big 'gator hole, ordinarily covered with water, now disclosed a parched throat wide enough to have taken in a barrel. From day to day during the pendency of the drought, Sabey had sneaked up to the pool hoping to surprise the 'gator out of his hole and by a lucky shot get him out of the way and clear the path to the terrapins, but he had not been fortunate enough to see him, although he knew he was there by the tracks and the impress of his great body in the baked mud that lay between the pool and the entrance to his hole. Even had Sabey found him, he could have slain him only with a close shot in the unprotected region just under the arm, for the negro seldom shoots anything larger than number two shot, which would have glanced harmlessly off the tough scales with which the 'gator was almost completely armored.

Forced to oust the householder, in order to get at his unbidden guests, the terrapin hunter was now turned 'gator hunter. Although almost invariably hunting alone, pulling the smaller 'gators out of their holes with an iron hook and killing them with his axe, the master of the Half Moon pool was too ugly a customer to be so easily disposed of, and, after pondering long, Sabey determined to organize a 'gator hunt for the following day and call to his aid some of the plantation negroes.

On Saturday morning a dozen negroes, men and boys, met Sabey at the Half Moon. They were making holiday and laughed and chaffed in high spirits. A few carried jampots, intending to churn the waters for their favorite mudfish. Others, directed by Sabey, had brought strong plow lines which they had borrowed without leave from "de buckruh'," and three or four were provided with axes. Besides his musket, Sabey carried on his shoulder a stout seven-foot hickory staff, at one end of which the village blacksmith had attached an iron ring, while at the other he had riveted a strong iron shaft shaped somewhat like a medieval pike—a spear-like point with which to prod and stir up his 'gatorship, and a sharp, though heavy, hook with which to drag him out of his retreat.

121

Although Sabey was the master craftsman of them all in this form of adventure, the two or three old darkeys in the bunch could not refrain from giving advice. "Git een de hole, Sabey, git een de hole," said old Cato Giles, the plantation foreman. "Tek de plow line en' tie'um to 'e foot, den we mans kin drag'um out."

"Duh me gwine een de hole, enty? Hukkuh uh gwine git at da' alligettuh' foot bedout git at 'e head fus'? Me fuh pit my head een 'e mout' w'ile uh duh tie 'e foot, enty? No, suh!"

Cutting a long, supple pole from a nearby thicket, Sabey ran it down the hole in order to determine its underground course and locate its occupant. He knelt at the opening and ran his sapling down carefully, listening for the scraping of the far end against the rough scales of the alligator. The hole, which slanted downward at an angle of 45 degrees, proved to be almost straight, and, when twelve feet of the pole had been shoved in, Sabey heard the grating sound he had been listening for, and knew what work was before him. Withdrawing the pole, he first made fast a double plow line to the ring end of his staff, while he tied another line around one of his ankles and prepared to go down into the hole. "Tek off yo' shu't, man," advised old Cato. "Ef da' 'gatuh bite you 'e gwine spile'um, en' no use fuh t'row'way uh shu't."

"Yaas, man," another said, "tek'um off. You kin slip een da' hole bettuh bedout'um."

So Sabey cast off shirt and hat, and, with a warning to his companions to pull him out quickly if he should call, went down on his hands and knees and crawled head-foremost into the hole, pushing his billhook before him. Wriggling like a snake, he dragged himself slowly and cautiously downward, and, about the time he had gone down far enough to leave only his toes sticking out of the mouth of the hole, the sharp point of his staff rattled against the 'gator's skull as he lay head on toward the entrance. The strong, musky smell of the great saurian would have suffocated one less tough than Sabey, but he paid no attention to it, and prodded with his staff until he had maneuvered the sharp point of his hook under the 'gator's throat when, with a quick upward jerk, he fastened it in the creature's lower jaw, and, as a hissing sigh met him in the face, he shouted and kicked his heels at the same time as a signal that he wished to come up. They pulled so lustily that his crooked leg was almost jerked out of its socket, and his head came out, grumbling and scolding, "Oonuh t'ink me duh alligettuh 'long fo' foot, enty? Wuh me fuh do fuh foot attuh oonuh pull off dem wuh uh got? Oonuh mus'be fool! Oonuh nebbuh pull nigguh outuh alligettuh hole befo'?"

But they were now too excited to quarrel, and, seizing the double plow lines, they began, under Sabey's direction, to pull slowly on the 'gator. Had Sabey hooked him in a less sensitive part, they could not have budged him. He was too well braced for hanging back, but his throat was comparatively tender, and inch by inch he began to come up, while the negroes shouted and chanted with delight, their excitement increasing as the line shortened and the quarry neared the mouth of the hole, till at last the ugly snout was pushed forward, and then the head, full two feet long, appeared as the fore feet followed, and the 'gator reared up. Frightened, the negroes retreated to the very end of the line. Meanwhile, Sabey had seized his mus-

ket and executed a flank movement, and realizing that,
as the 'gator's tail was still underground, there was little danger in a close approach, crept up and, firing
when the muzzle of his gun almost touched the 'gator's
side, tore a great hole just behind the shoulder. The
negroes shouted with joy, for they realized that the
wound was mortal. But 'gators take a long time to die,
and they kept pulling, and he kept crawling, until his
entire length of nine feet had been drawn out of the
hole. Sabey was wary, and insisted on their retaining
hold of the staff, which was still hooked in the 'gator's
throat, and he warned his companions of the danger
in approaching within reach of the treacherous tail,
but after awhile, as the great creature slowly bled to
death, several of the younger negroes walked too near,
and, while appraising with gastronomic appreciation
the great tail, which many of the negroes eat with
avidity, it lashed out suddenly. A feeble effort, but with
force enough to send the frightened negroes on both
sides of him sprawling and rubbing their bruised legs
which the 'gator's sweep, delivered with full force,
could have broken like pipe stems.

And now that the Dragon that guarded the treasure
had been haled from the dungeon and put *hors de
combat*, Sabey tied a couple of empty sacks, each to a
plow line, and essayed a second nose dive into the pit
of promise. There is always danger of getting jammed
or stuck in exploring a 'gator hole, but Sabey was
experienced and cautious, and the hole was large, so
down he went, taking the sacks with him, and soon
reached the bottom, which had widened into a considerable cavity eighteen feet from the mouth. His
exploring hands, feeling in front of him, found a small

pool of water literally alive with terrapins. Having ample room to turn around, Sabey lost no time in filling one of his sacks with terrapins, which, at a jerk of the line, was hauled up out of his way. The second sack held all that remained, and, when this had followed the first, he turned, and, facing upward, decided to go head-foremost, preferring to crawl out like a self-respecting caterpillar, under his own steam, rather than be hauled up by the heels like a slaughtered shoat. But, fearing suffocation in the close quarters underground, he had admonished the men above, who managed the rope attached to his foot, to pull him up quickly at the first jerk, and, as he turned upward, his free leg became entangled with the tied one. In kicking loose, he gave the line a jerk, to which his friends responded so suddenly that they hauled his legs up under him, trussing him into the semblance of a bronze statuette of a squatting Buddha. Sabey yelled with pain and anger, for the hole, while large enough for a man to pass extended, was too close for him doubled up, and Sabey was stuck in the barrel. His muffled cries reached his friends, but they thought them calls for more speed, and the harder they pulled, the tighter they jammed the unhappy wretch.

"Eh, eh! Da' felluh pull *hebby!*"

"Yaas, man, Buh Sabey pull hebby sukkuh alligettuh."

It was old Cato who noticed that they had not budged him an inch. " *'Top*, oonuh man, *'top!*" he shouted. " 'Ee yent duh moobe. Slack de rope."

As they stopped pulling, Sabey hauled in the slack, released his legs, and, hauling on the rope hand over

hand, was soon at the mouth of the hole, where he lay
for several minutes to fill up with fresh air. When,
recovered sufficiently to get mad, he rose on all-fours
like an alligator, he presented a fearful sight. His
yellow wool, his face, and his copper-colored arms and
torso were smeared and streaked with black mud, his
ragged trousers, water-soaked and muddy, clung to his
crooked legs, and he looked like a composite of iguana
and ape.

Though ordinarily a taciturn negro, Sabey, under
the spur of anger, galloped through his vocabulary of
invective at top speed. "Oonuh good fuh nutt'n' debble'ub'uh *no'count nigguh!* Oonuh ent *wut!* Uh tell
oonuh 'sponsubble fuh haul de rope w'en uh pull'um
'long me han', uh nebbuh tell oonuh fuh haul'um w'en
uh kick'um 'long me foot! Oonuh ent know de diff-
'unce 'twix' man' han' en' 'e foot? Ef man tell oonuh
fuh tek uh cucklebuhr outuh mule *yez*, oonuh gwine
saa'ch fuhr'um een 'e *tail*, enty? Oonuh mus'be tek
me fuh annimel!"

"Ef you ent wash off dem mud en' t'ing 'fo' you gone
home, Bess gwine tek you fuh cootuh, eeduhso fuh
'ranguhtang, en' him ent gwi' leh you fuh gone een
him house," they chaffed.

Sabey washed in the muddy pool, resumed his shirt,
tied the two sacks of terrapins together, hung them
over the gun barrel at his back, and prepared to shake
the mud of the Half Moon off his feet. "W'en uh done
sell dese yuh yalluhbelly cootuh en' gone een me house
wid alltwo me han' full'up wid money, Bess gwine lub
me tummuch, ef uh *yiz* look lukkuh 'ranguhtang.
Monkey hab fo' han', en' de mo'res' han' man hab, de
mo' 'ooman lub'um! Oonuh black Aff'ikin *Guinea nig-*

THE *'GATOR HUNTER*

guh! Oonuh kin nyam da' alligettuh, en' w'en oonuh
yiz nyam'um, *oonuh duh cannibel!*"

THE *'GATOR HUNTER*

guh! Oonuh kin nyam da' alligettuh, en' w'en oonuh
yiz nyam'um, *oonuh duh cannibel!*"

THE *'GATOR HUNTER*

guh! Oonuh kin nyam da' alligettuh, en' w'en oonuh
yiz nyam'um, *oonuh duh cannibel!*"

127

"THE WILES THAT IN THE WOMEN ARE"

For many years old John, as country coachman for
the late Governor Aiken, periodically drove a pair of
switch-tailed mules to the Governor's carriage, making round trips between Jehossee Island and Adams
Run station, whenever his employer came from
Charleston to visit the great rice plantation. John
was a trim and finicky old darkey, with quite a manner, and, in his old beaver hat and long-tailed coat,
made a notable figure among the darkeys usually loaf-
ing about the station.

Low-country negroes never miss a train. Journey-
ing by rail, they take no chances, but invariably reach
the station several hours ahead of train time, where,
chattering and gossiping, the waiting time passes
quickly and pleasantly.

Among these groups old John, with his long-handled
whip of plaited buckskin, correctly looped, and carried coachman fashion, moved and exchanged pleas-
antries. He, too, was always ahead of time, and his
docile mules, switching their long, untrimmed tails
about, and hitched to the only closed carriage in the
community, were always objects of interest to the
station idlers.

"Uncle John, mekso oonuh ent shabe dem mule
tail?" inquired one of a group that squatted upon the
platform.

"Sistuh, you ebbuh yeddy 'bout Johossee muskittuh'?"

"No, suh."

"Ahnhn, uh t'awt so. Gal, you ebbuh see blackbu'd'
'puntop'uh rice rick? You *is* shum, enty? Berry well;

128

dem muskittuh' een Johossee maa'sh stan' same fashi'n.
W'en dem light 'puntop'uh mule, dem kibbuhr'um 'tell
oonuh cyan' see dem haa'ness! One time, jis' attuh
daa'k, uh binnuh dribe comin' een late f'um Adam'
Run, en' w'en uh 'trike de causeway, all ub uh sudd'nt
uh nebbuh yeddy no mule' foot duh trot 'puntop'uh de
groun'! De cyaaridge duh moobe, but uh yent yeddy
no soun' f'um de mule' foot. Uh say tuh mese'f, eh, eh,
duh warruh dish'yuh? Uh look 'gen, en', uh 'cla' tuh
goodness, de muskittuh' *dat* t'ick 'puntop de mule'
belly, dem hice'um up off de groun', en' duh flew t'ru
de ellyment duh cya'um 'long! Dem wing' duh sing
sukkuh bee duh swawm, en' de mule' duh trot wid all
fo' dem foot, but 'e nebbuh tetch no groun'! Uh nebbuh do nutt'n' 'tell uh cross de bridge, 'cause de bridge
mek out'uh pole, en' dem berry slip'ry duh night time,
en' uh glad de mule' ent haffuh pit dem foot 'puntop'-
um, but attuh uh done cross de bridge, uh tek me lash
en' uh cut de mule' two't'ree time onduhneet' dem belly,
en', uh 'cla' tuh my Mastuh, t'ree peck uh muskittuh'
drap 'puntop de groun' en' uh yeddy de mule' foot duh
trot 'gen een de road! So, attuh dat, uh nebbuh shabe
de Gub'nuh' cyaaridge mule' tail no mo', en' now you
shum stan' dey, dem kin lick muskittuh', fly en' t'ing'
same lukkuh hawss."

So old John, coachman and raconteur, a faithful and
respected servant, lived his days, which were long, and
when at last he was gathered to his fathers, his
funeral was the talk of the colored countryside, and
his grave, ornately decorated with broken bits of old
blue china and the stone bottles in which Bass' ale
had once been imported, was much admired by those
whose sad occasions brought them to the plantation

God's-Acre under the spreading live-oaks.

"Eh, eh, Buh John sho' hab uh fine grabe."

"Yaas, tittie, 'e fine fuh true. You see da' blue chaney, enty? Dat chaney bin 'e Missis' pitchuh 'tell de pitchuh' mout' done bruk out. One time 'e missis sen' one leely nigguh gal duh big spring wid 'e blue pitchuh fuh fetch watuh. De gal full' de pitchuh en' pit'um 'puntop 'e head duh walk duh paat' comin' fuh de house. De gal duh walk ca'less like, duh swing 'e han', en' 'e yeye high, en' 'e nebbuh look 'puntop de paat', en' one limus cootuh binnuh cross 'e paat', en' him git to de paat' same time de gal git dey, en' de gal 'tump 'e toe 'puntop de cootuh, en' de cootuh t'row'um down, en' de pitchuh fall off de gal' head en' 'trike 'puntop'uh root, en' de pitchuh' mout' bruk out en' de gal gone back duh big spring en' full' de pitchuh 'gen, en' pit'um 'puntop 'e head en' gone big house duh paat', but 'e dat 'f'aid suh limus cootuh gwine hit'um 'gen, 'e 'tep' high, en' w'en 'e 'tep' high de watuh wuh 'e fetch f'um big spring 'plash' out de pitchuh' bruk mout' en' drap' 'puntop de gal two eye' en' run down 'e face en' gone een 'e mout', en' w'en de gal git duh big house, 'e missis look 'puntop all de watuh en' t'ing' dey 'puntop 'e face en' 'e missis t'ink de gal cry tuh dat, en' 'e missis sorry fuhr'um en' 'e nebbuh lick'um nuh nutt'n', en' 'e gi' de bruk mout' pitchuh to de gal, en' w'en de gal grow up, Buh John hab'um fuh wife, en' da' de way Buh John git de pitchuh, en' attuh Buh John done dead, 'e wife wuh 'e lef' tek hatchitch en' bruk de pitchuh 'gen, en' pit eb'ry Gawd piece 'puntop Buh John' grabe, en' da' w'ymekso 'e stan' so."

" 'E grabe look stylish fuh true, but uh know berry well w'en *my* juntlemun dead me yent fuh bruk no pitchuh en' t'ing fuh pit 'puntop *him* cawpse, 'cause da' nigguh *ent wut*, 'e too lub fuh drink rum, en' w'en 'e fetch'um home, him fuhrebbuh duh fall down en' bruk de bottle wuh 'e fetch'um een, en' uh hab all dem bruk bottle pile' een de fench cawnuh fuh pit 'puntop him grabe w'en 'e dead. Two't'ree time Joe seem luk-kuh 'e kinduh spishus 'bout de bruk bottle, en' 'e ax me wuffuh uh duh sabe'um, but uh tell'um uh sabe'um fuh beat'um up 'long pessle, fuh pizen buckruh' dog, en' dat sattify 'e mine' en' 'e lemme 'lone."

"You sho' hab uh good onduhstan', tittie, 'cause man ent fuh know tummuch. Ef 'ooman tell'um de trute 'e nebbuh sattify. 'Ooman haffuh fool'um fuh mek'um easy een 'e mine'!"

"You duh talk trute, tittie, him *lub* you fuh fool'um. Fool'um duh de only t'ing him gwine b'leebe."

"Yaas, man, meself hab uh good ecknowledge fuh fool'um. One time Paul, him duh my juntlemun, bin-nuh wu'k to de maa'l, duh dig rock, down to John Ilun'. Monday mawnin', him git up soon, 'e gone deepo, 'e ketch de shoofly strain, en' 'e gone! Uh neb-buh shum 'gen 'tell Sattyday night. Wuh me fuh do? Seddown een me house 'tell him come home en' watch 'tettuh duh bile? No, suh! Uh lub fuh talk tummuch! Soon ez uh yeddy de strain blow, en' uh sattify' my juntlemun gone, uh tek me two foot en' uh gone Paa'ker' Ferry Cross Road' weh da' buckruh hab 'e big sto'. All dem boy' wuh ent hab nutt'n' fuh do, dey dey duh talk, en' 'nuf 'ooman' dey dey duh hol' cumpuh-shashun 'long de man en' t'ing. W'en daa'k come, uh gone home. Uh cook, uh eat, uh leddown duh bed, uh sleep. Chuesday mawnin', uh gone same fashi'n, en' eb'ry Gawd' day 'tell bimeby Sattyday come 'gen. Uh

clean de house, uh wash, uh sweep de yaa'd, en' uh gone
Cross Road'. Uh pass de time uh day 'long dem todduh nigguh' 'tell uh yeddy de strain f'um town blow
deepo, den uh gone home fuh wait 'tell Paul come.
Befo' uh lef' de sto', Sancho Frajuh binnuh drink rum
en' 'e t'row'way 'e money berry freehan', en' 'e buy
'bout two quawt' uh candy, dese'yuh 'ticky kind'uh
t'ing, dem hab 'ooman name, de buckruh call'um Carrie
Mel, but eb'n so, 'e mek out'uh pinegum en' muhlassis,
en' ef oonuh chaw'um 'e gwine hol' yo' jaw 'tell t'unduh
roll. De buckruh hab'um een 'e sto' sence las' yeah en
de t'ing haa'd ez uh i'un. Sancho gi' eb'ry 'ooman two
han'ful'. Uh wrop one de han'ful' een uh papuh en'
drap'um een me ap'un pocket. Uh t'row de todduh
han'ful een me mout' en' biggin fuh chaw. Uh chaw,
en' uh chaw, uh chaw, en' uh chaw. De t'ing sweet'n'
me fuh true, but 'e ketch me jaw' en' 'e hol'um same
lukkuh pinegum plastuh! De mo' uh chaw'um de mo'
'e swell. Time uh git tuh me house, de t'ing wrop
roun' eb'ry teet' een me head lukkuh jackwine wrop
roun' tree. Alltwo me jaw' stan' same fashi'n ez mufflejaw fowl, en' me mout' swell'up same lukkuh Buh
Quash' mout' stick out w'en 'e bex! W'en uh git tuh
de do', Paul dey dey duh wait fuh me! 'Fo' him kin
ax me no squeschun, uh smaa't 'nuf fuh t'row me ap'un
tuh me mout' fuh hide'um, en' uh kibbuhr'um up en'
biggin fuh moan. Uh moan, en' uh moan. Paul ax me
wuffuh uh mek shishuh hebby cumplain. Uh 'ca'cely
kin able fuh talk, but uh tell'um uh binnuh walk roun'
de fench en' uh walk 'puntop yalluh jacket nes' en' de
t'ing 'ting me tuh dat. 'E ax me w'ich one de jaw' 'e
'ting me 'pun. Uh p'int tuh me lef' han' jaw. 'E ax me
'smattuh mek alltwo de jaw' swell. Uh tell'um gum-

bile mek todduh one fuh swell. Den uh biggin fuh
cry. Watuh stan' een me two eye'. Uh baig'um fuh
gone deepo en' baig some dem buckruh' fuh g'em some
linniment fuh de mis'ry een alltwo me jaw'. Paul say
suh him kin gone Cross Road' en' buy'um, but uh 'f'aid
ef him gone Cross Road', Sancho dem gwine tell'um
suh me bin dey, en' uh tell'um no, uh yent want'um fuh
t'row'way him money 'cause uh lub'um tummuch, en'
uh mo' redduh him fuh baig de buckruh', den fuh
buy'um out him own money. Dat mek'um sattify, en'
'e gone deepo. Soon ez 'e gone, uh try fuh git da' debble'ub'uh 'ceitful Carrie Mel out me mout'. De t'ing
'tick same lukkuh Buh Rabbit 'tick tuh Taar Baby.
'E won' tu'n me loose! Den me bline'gawd tell me fuh
greese'um. Uh gone duh house, uh mek fiah, uh pit
one fat bakin een de pan, en' w'en de meat done fry,
uh tek'um een me mout' en' biggin fuh chaw. Bimeby
de greese biggin fuh loose de Carrie Mel, en' uh tek
alltwo me han' en' uh pull'um out me mout', en' uh
t'row'um 'way, en' uh t'row'um *fudduh!*

"W'en Paul come back wid de buckruh linniment, uh
duh hol' me two jaw' en' uh duh moan. Him gimme
de t'ing, uh rub'um, en' attuhw'ile, w'en him done cook
de bittle wuh 'e fetch f'um John Ilun', uh call'um fuh
look 'puntop me two jaw' weh de swell' done gone, en'
'e dat sattify, 'e gimme de money wuh him bin fuh buy
linniment duh Cross Road, en' 'e nebbuh yeddy 'bout
no Sancho!"

"Yaas, tittie, 'ooman fool'um fuh true! Him *done*
fuh fool'um!"

A RICEFIELD IDYLL

A brilliant tropical day in late August. A strong breeze from the river moved the glistening leaves and swayed the long pennons of gray Spanish moss that swung from every bough and twig of the great live-oaks, whose spreading arms stretched their protecting shade over the plateau upon which stood the Big House, crowning the highest point of Prospect Hill. A mile away swept the flowing tide of the broad and beautiful Edisto, whose shimmering waters, opposed by the summer wind, danced and sparkled in the sunlight. Upon the lower levels between the uplands and the river lay the great fields of early rice, now ready for the sickle. Intersecting the fields or "squares" at regular intervals, and contrasting with their green and gold opulence, shining silver-blue canals ran from river to headland. Far across the river on "the Island," the eye rested upon an emerald expanse of June rice which would come to harvest six weeks later. From the ripening fields the "harvest flow" had been taken off, the squares dried, and on this Monday morning 100 hands had gathered by sunrise, for, by the mysterious grapevine telegraph through which negroes on one plantation hear almost instantaneously what is going forward on other plantations miles away, the news had gone about that rice-cutting was to commence at Prospect Hill, and the gregarious negroes, deserting the smaller settlements, flocked hither to the big plantation where, working in gangs, they could exchange quip and jest and gather the gossip of the countryside. Some of the best rice-cutters were the

134

sturdy young women, who, with skirts tied up above their knees and wearing men's wool hats to mitigate the heat of the sun, kept pace with the best of their masculine associates. Cutting and tying by piece work, an active hand could readily complete his task, the allotment for a day's work, an hour before noon, and some of those who had walked six or seven miles in the morning would knock off as soon as the task was finished and loaf around the quarters until sundown, while others, pushing their luck, held on until the evening, putting two days' work into one. Armed with the saw-edged, sickle-like "rice hooks," the cutters stretched across the squares, each seizing with her left hand as large a bundle of the heavy-headed stalks as she could conveniently grasp, which, with one stroke of her right arm, she quickly severed a few inches above the ground, laid the bundle on the stubble ready for those who tied into sheaves behind her, and, with a sweep of her left, gathered another handful for the embrace of the crescent-shaped blade. Down the steaming field moved a skirmish line of lusty black wenches, bare-armed, bare-footed and bare-legged, their skirts drawn above their knees by a cord about the waist, which took up the slack. Here and there among them worked men, and these, often physically inferior to the females of the species, were subjected to constant raillery and frequent challenges to equal the self-appointed tasks of the women.

Venus Chisolm and Diana Smashum, two strapping Amazons, were the most expert of the women rice-cutters, and excelled most of the men in efficiency. Scipio Jenkins, a smart young buck, was the special butt of the gang of which Diana and Venus were the leaders. Scipio was unusually black, with the common combination of yellow eyes and blue gums, and upon this color scheme his tormentors lit like bee martins on a crow.

> "Blue gum, yalluh eye,
> Black nigguh berry sly;
> Yalluh eye, blue gum,
> Black nigguh lub rum."
>
> Yalluh eye, w'en you shum,
> Black nigguh lub rum."

"Yaas, tittie, 'e stan' so fuh true. Sat'd'y night da' nigguh gone Cross Road'. 'E buy uh killybash full uh rum f'um de buckruh. 'E drink'um eb'ry Gawd' drap. 'E nebbuh gi' nobody none. 'E gone home. Sunday, *'e dead!* 'E nebbuh know nutt'n' 'tell Sunday night 'e maamy full' uh piggin full uh watuh out de well en' t'row'um 'puntop'uh Scipio, weh 'e duh leddown 'puntop de flo', fuh mek'um fuh wake. De nigguh binnuh leddown 'puntop 'e back fuh sleep. 'E sleep' haa'd. 'E groan' en' 'e groan! 'E groan' en' 'e groan'! 'E mout' op'n roun' same lukkuh snake hole. W'en de watuh full' 'e mout', 'e blow lukkuh de 'strucshun strain injine duh blow off steam w'en 'e duh load grabble! De t'ing 'trangle'um. 'E choke! 'E jump out 'e maamy' do' en' 'e gone t'ru de briah-patch dat fas' 'e lef' half 'e britchiz 'puntop de briah! Bumbye, w'en 'e maamy gone duh 'ood fuh fine'um, please Gawd, de nigguh binnuh leddown flat 'puntop 'e belly een de du't, duh swim! Da' piggin full uh watuh hab shishuh cuntrady tas'e een 'e mout', 'e mek'um t'ink suh him dey een de ribbuh! 'E 'tretch out all fo' 'e han' en' 'e foot. 'E ten finguh' duh grabble een de du't. Bumbye, w'en 'e han' loos'n de du't, 'e feel uh pinetree root. 'E graff'um een alltwo 'e han'! 'E holluh. '*Tengk Gawd*,' 'e say, '*uh done sabe! Uh yent fuh drowndid no mo!*' En' da' fool nigguh pull 'pun de pine-tree root fuh hice 'eself out de ribbuh! Da' rum do'um *bad!*"

Scipio swelled with wrath, but at first "too full for sound or foam," bent to his task and, cutting savagely at the thickest stalks, under the impetus of anger, soon forged ahead of the others and led the line. Before he drew away, however, he projected this Parthian shot with a torpedo in its tail: "Benus en' Diana, oonuh alltwo duh bodduh me, w'ymekso oonuh ent study 'bout Paul? Him duh alltwo oonuh sweeth'aa't en' t'ing. Diana t'ink suh Paul duh him'own 'cause 'e ge'm da' catfish 'e ketch las' Sat'd'y, en' Benus t'ink suh him duh she'own, 'cause 'e buy gunjuh fuhr'um duh Cross Road', but Paul nebbuh buy no frock fuh Diana, en' 'e nebbuh buy none fuh Benus, but him buy'um fuh Minda, en' 'e duh keep cump'ny 'long Minda, en' him duh yalluh gal, en' Paul nebbuh fuh study 'bout no black nigguh' no mo'! Him duh fool oonuh alltwo!"

The torpedo exploded.

Two dusky faces quickly changed from smirking comedy to girding tragedy. Two stalwart forms stiffened in their tracks and stood astraddle like two Colossi of Rhodes. Two pairs of powerful arms akimboed, and two sets of sinewy fingers clutched the handles of their rice hooks!

"Hukkuh Paul happ'n fuh gi' you catfish? You mus'be baig fuhr'um, enty?"

"*Baig fuhr'um!* Me fuh baig man fuh catfish! *I* iz uh lady, uh wan' you fuh know, en' ef *you* haffuh baig-

'um fuh *gunjuh,* me yent haffuh baig'um fuh *catfish!*"

"Wuh you got fuh do wid wuh Paul gi' me? Him duh *yo'* juntlemun, enty?"

"Ef 'e yent my'own, uh know berry well suh him ent fuh blonx to no black nigguh lukkuh you!"

"*Nigguh!* Who you call nigguh? *De Debble is uh nigguh!*"

"Him duh nigguh fuh true, but dis ricefiel' full uh 'e chillun, en' 'e gran'chillun alltwo, en' uh 'spec' you duh one uh 'e gran'!"

A shriek of laughter from Scipio filled Diana's cup of anger to overflowing, and, with a savage rice-cutting swing, she sideswiped Venus with her saw-edged sickle, and cut her acquaintance below, and behind, the belt. Bustles were not then worn, but the victim was saved from a most inconvenient wound by the folds of her looped-up skirt, which, like a furled sail, hung just abaft the beam, and she received only a scratch. Starting at the scratch, however, Diana was twenty feet away and going strong when Venus, yelling with pain, turned and gave chase. Screams of laughter mingled with shouts of excitement, as Diana tripped and fell on the stubble, and Venus, too close to check her speed, stumbled over her prostrate assailant and came a cropper, the rice hook flying out of her hand as she fell. Diana's weapon, having been taken from her by one of the men, the two ladies were on equal terms with nature's weapons, and, both being on all-fours, literally and figuratively, they soon fastened their "ten commandments" in each other's wool. They fought viciously and silently, and not until, collapsed from exhaustion, they had been separated by the men, did they again become vocal. Venus' gingham skirt had suffered a cruel rent. As she reached behind her and felt the yawning gap in her sartorial hinterland, and realized the ignominy that had been put upon her by this "most unkindest cut of all," she shrieked in anger. "Uh gwine tek you Trial Jestuss! You fuh gone Adam' Run fuh dis t'ing wuh you done do!" and she flung wrathfully out of the field. Out of the babel of voices that arose among the partisans of the two goddesses, the dominant note was abuse of Scipio, who had flung Paul, the apple, or rather the Guinea squash, of discord among them.

"Wuh you haffuh do 'long Paul' name? Ef him *iz* buy gunjuh en' frock en' t'ing fuh t'ree 'ooman', uh sho' 'e mo' bettuh den fuh nebbuh buy nutt'n' fuh none!" showing the world-wide feminine appreciation of a free spender. "Wuh you ebbuh buy fuh 'ooman? Eb'ry Sat'd'y night da' buckruh' sto' duh Cross Road' full up wid 'ooman, en' *you* ebbuh buy uh tencent wut' uh bakin fuh greese dem mout'? No, suh! You lub fuh talk sweetmout' talk 'long'um, but you dat stingy you nebbuh buy uh candy, eeduhso uh sugar, fuh sweet'n dem mout'. Ent you know suh 'ooman lub uh freehan' man?"

"Yaas, tittie! You talk trute! 'Ooman redduh hab 'e mout' full'uh muhlassis den 'e yez full'uh sweetmout' talk!"

"Him lub'um alltwo," observed a sapient one. "Him mout' en' him yez alltwo fuh full one time!"

———

On the second Saturday thereafter, having been summoned by Big Jim Green, the negro constable, Venus and Diana, with their respective satellites, appeared before the Trial Justice at Adams Run station, where Diana, duly indicted, was charged in the comprehensive phraseology of the Criminal Code with such a string of offenses against the peace and dignity of the State of South Carolina and the proper person of Venus Chisolm that her ears tingled and her eyes popped with amazement.

"Guilty or not guilty?"

"Uh yent know wuh you call so, Jedge, but uh nebbuh do none uh dem t'ing wuh da' papuh call dem name. Ef Jedus yeddy me, uh nebbuh do uh Gawd' t'ing but cut da' 'ooman, en' uh nebbuh hab uh chance fuh cut'um *good*, 'cause 'e hab 'e frock tie'up 'roun' 'e wais', en' w'en uh cut at 'e hanch en' de rice hook ketch 'e frock weh 'e roll'up behine'um, dat sabe de 'ooman' meat, en' uh only able fuh 'cratch 'e skin, but uh 'cratch'um 'nuf fuh mek'um holluh same lukkuh hog' holluh w'en oonuh cut dem yez fuh maa'k'um, en' alldo' uh yent puhzac'ly *cut* de 'ooman, uh *try* fuh cut'um, but uh cut 'e frock en' uh only able fuh 'cratch'um, en' ef uh *yiz* bin cut'um, duh Scipio mek' me fuh do'um, 'cause him come duh ricefiel' wid da' bluegum mout' uh him'own full'uh pizen talk fuh bex me nuh Benus, en' uh always yeddy suh ef uh bluegum nigguh bite you 'e gwine pizen you same lukkuh moccasin, en' same fashi'n de talk wuh come out da' nigguh' jaw pizen alltwo uh we en' mek we fuh fight, but, Jedge, uh nebbuh cut Benus lukkuh da' papuh say, 'cause ef uh had'uh cut'um *fuh true, true!* da' 'ooman would'uh haffuh stan'up 'puntop'uh 'e two foot fuh t'ree week!"

"Received as information," observed the magistrate, and he called Venus, who came up smiling. "You have heard Diana's story. What have you to say?"

"Uh yeddy'um, suh. But 'e cut me."

A RICEFIELD IDYLL

"Where did she cut you?"

"Suh?"

"Where did she cut you?"

" 'E cut me een Mas' Edwu'd' ricefiel', suh."

"Yes, I know you were all in the ricefield, but where did she cut you?"

" 'E cut me een ten acre, suh."

"Cut you in ten acre!"

" 'E cut me een da' ten acre square wuh stan' close to de baa'nyaa'd, suh."

"Well, you have given the location in the ricefield, now, where on your person did Diana cut you with a rice hook?"

"Suh?"

"Your person is your body. Did she cut you on your body?"

"Yaas, suh, 'e cut me."

"Well, on what part of your body did she cut you?"

"Da' same place wuh you call 'e name, suh."

"What place?"

" 'E cut me on me *pussun*, suh, en', Jedge, de t'ing sweet'n' me so bad, ef uh could'uh ketch da' 'ooman 'fo' uh ketch me foot en' fall obuhr'um, da' 'ooman would uh *dead!*"

As there was murderous intent in the sudden heat and passion of both Venus and Diana, the court imposed upon the defendant a fine only sufficient to rehabilitate the wardrobe of the prosecuting witness, who sailed out of court thoroughly satisfied with the new frock in prospect and the present enrichment of her vocabulary by the buckra word "pussun."

141

THE DOWER HOUSE

The "Dower House," which Abram Drayton had inherited from his father, old John, now resting under the great live-oaks of the plantation burying ground, was quite a pretentious affair, two stories high, with two chimneys and a leak. The stories were not very high, only six or seven feet in the clear, but it was sometimes convenient to be able to reach up and touch the ceiling, and, after all, it was a two-story house and, like all two-story houses among the negroes, added greatly to the prestige of the owner's family. In the usual one-story negro cabin, the boarded-over "loft," reached by ladder, is at once the sleeping room for the children, the granary for corn and peas, and the hay mow for whatever straw or fodder the householder possesses, but the Dower House had a real second story, attained by steps, narrow and teetering 'tis true, which the ascending biped usually "cooned" on all-fours, but they were steps, not rungs, and, however vigorously the negro expresses in hymns and spirituals his willingness, indeed anxiety, to "climb up Jacob's ladder," in the present life he prefers the creak of a board under his foot.

Under the law of primogeniture, arbitrarily established by old John for the disposition and control of his landed property, the "Two-Chimbly House" was bequeathed by word of mouth to his eldest son, and similarly settled upon his eldest grandson, and so on, as long as the line lasted, or until the shingles fell off, when dynastic difficulties would inevitably intervene. Perhaps he had heard of primogeniture and dower

houses while waiting at the table of his English-bred
master in the old times, but however the idea came into
his kinky head, once in, it stuck, and he determined
that a Dower House he would leave, and a Dower
House entailed. "Uh gwine tie de 'tail 'puntop da'
house fuh hol'um *fas'!* Uh tie'um fus' 'puntop my boy,
Ebbrum, en' den 'e fuh tie 'puntop *him* boy, my gran',
en' de 'tail ent fuh tek'off! De 'tail ent fuh tie 'puntop no 'ooman. 'Ooman ent fuh hab no house. Man
fuh hab'um en' him fuh hol'um, so him kin fetch de
'ooman to 'e han'!"

So, the " 'tail" still tied to Abram, in due time he
came into the Dower House, and here, in the woods on
the road from Adams Run Station to Caw Caw
Swamp, he lived and reared a family.

At the tail of the summer his wife partook "not
wisely but too well" of watermelon and buttermilk,
and through the unfortunate combination was forthwith translated from the bosom of Abram to that of
Abraham. The widowed man resigned himself to the
will of the Lord, and accepted his bereavement not the
less philosophically that his crop was already made
and partly gathered. "Ef de Lawd haffuh tek'um, uh
glad 'E yent tek'um 'tell de crap done mek," he
reflected gratefully and reverently. In a week he had
picked and sold the last of his cotton, and out of the
proceeds outfitted his old mare with a new saddle,
bridle and cloth, notwithstanding which, the ungrate-
ful creature, with true feminine perversity, "gone en'
leddown en' *dead*, jis' 'cause uh yent feed'um fuh two'-
t'ree day. Uh nebbuh know da' mare gwine hongry
to dat! 'E hongry 'tell 'e dead, en' now uh haffuh tek
me two foot en' walk!"

Abram, being now more than a "settled" man, jogged along in single harness uneventfully for several months. "Not so young, sir, to love a woman for singing, nor so old as to dote on her for anything," he now, in the autumn of his days, became somewhat critical in the matter of feminine needlework. His grown daughter esteemed herself a competent, almost a skilful, patcher of broken, frayed or frazzled raiment. She knew very well how to put crocus or burlap patches on the knees of the jeans or blue denim trousers affected by her sire, but though she could attach them in such fashion that they would hold, the edges always overlapped like the strakes of a clinker-built whale boat. But whatever these patches lacked in symmetrical attachment, they served well enough, for, as Abram advanced in years, he did not kneel so often as he sat. The seats of his trousers, however, yawned in pathetic neglect for, however acceptably his daughter repaired his broken knees, the half-soling of the seats was a much more serious matter, which she lacked the high spirit to undertake, and he carried about with him, whithersoever he went, gaping wounds in his sartorial equipment where, according to Hudibras, "a kick in that part more hurts honor than deep wounds before." Not that anyone would ever have kicked him, for he was of a quiet and inoffensive disposition.

Most observers of humanity have noted with interest the close resemblance of certain types of the "wild (and tame) animals one has known." The horse, the ass, the bulldog, the pug, sheep and goat, fox, raccoon and rat, the 'possum, grinning with pious hypocrisy, and the Berkshire pig with slanting eyes and champing jowls, are all marked likenesses frequently reproduced in human faces, representing the stupid, the sly, the selfish, the grasping, the predaceous, the stubborn, the sensual, the combative, the treacherous—all of them to be avoided, or warily appraised, for the good of one's soul—and of one's pocket. Unhappily, those who have been blessed with so rich an experience as to have suffered both fools and knaves, seldom learn to read the buoys with which nature has wisely marked the dangerous reefs in her physiognomonic charts, until the keels of their craft grind upon the rocks! But Abram's face was that of the mild-eyed, introspective ox. There was no militant personality in the neighborhood to "walk a mile out of his way to kick a sheep," and, even had there been, to have kicked Abram would have been anatomically impossible, for the unsportsmanlike may shoot a sitting bird, but he cannot kick (offensively) a sitting man, and Abram was usually sitting! So, having held inviolate against the insulting toe the seats of his trousers, which he had lost only through the slow attrition of honest sloth, he retained his self-respect, though he was a peripatetic scandal whenever he went abroad upon his "peaceful occasions." With praiseworthy propriety, he now came in late to church or prayer-meeting, and, a vigorous and devout "class leader," coached his class from the bench, dreading the publicity of the sidelines. Then he sat discreetly at the close of the services until "de 'ooman en' t'ing" had gained an offing and sailed away, when, as he showed a fairly presentable front, he would follow after them and engage in long distance conversation.

"Come on, Bredduh Drayton. Mekso you walk so slow?"

"Uh haffuh walk slow, tittie, 'cause dese debble'ub'-uh britchiz bus', en' dem ent wut. Da' gal uh my'own able fuh pit uh berry deestunt patch 'puntop de knee, but seem lukkuh him ent able fuh do nutt'n' 'long de seat. Da' w'ymekso dish'yuh britchiz do berry well fuh man fuh seddown een'um, but dem cyan' specify fuh walk."

"Wuh mekso you ent tek anodduh lady fuh wife? You got big house en' 'nuf groun' fuh mek crap, mekso you ent fuh hab 'ooman?"

"Uh hab house en' groun,' fuh true. Uh got uh two-chimbly house, but 'ooman shishuh onsaa't'n t'ing, uh kinduh 'f'aid fuh tek anodduh chance. Ebbuh sence my lady nyam dem watuhmilyun en' buttuhmilk en' him Jedus tek'um, uh yent hab nutt'n' fuh bodduh me. Uh kin seddown een de sun-hot eenjurin' de whole day en' nebbuh yeddy no 'ooman' woice duh call fuh tell me fuh git'up. Uh kin seddown tell uh fuh gone 'sleep."

"Yaas, my Bredduh, you binnuh seddown, fuh true!" a church sister laughingly retorted. "Da' de reas'n w'ymekso you shame' fuh stan'up fuh lead yo' class! Long seddown mek short stan'up, you know."

"Go 'way, gal! 'Nuf man wuh hab wife een dem house, dem britchiz ent able fuh specify. Dem wife lazy tummuch fuh patch'um." And so Abram, always backward in company, put on the best front he could for a while and, unlike Edward Bellamy, never looked behind him. At last the raillery told on him, however, and he made up his mind to take another plunge into the roiling waters of married life. Not the "uncertain sea of matrimony" beloved of poets, but just the black and sluggish current of the branch or run, in which,

among snags and cypress knees, swam the slimy catfish
and the venomous moccasin. The hazard was not
great, for, however forbidding they looked, the waters
were shallow, and the low-country negro, stepping into
matrimony, keeps at least one big toe on dry ground,
and, if one steps in the wrong place, one can always
step out again, and try elsewhere. So, with more than
a toe-hold of mental reservation, Abram at last, like
the storied frog, "would a wooing go"—and he went.
"Uh gwine Cross Road'. Uh gwine Sat'd'y night w'en
'nuf 'ooman dey dey, en' uh gwine saa'ch dem eb'ry
Gawd' one 'tell uh git one wuh kin specify. Uh yent
wan' no settle' 'ooman, 'cause dem done hab 'nuf man
fuh marri'd, en' dem know tummuch. Dem too
schemy! Seem lukkuh de mo' husbun' en' t'ing dem
fuh hab, de mo' schemy dem git! Ef uh tek uh nyung
gal fuh wife, wuh ent know nutt'n', uh kin bruk'um
fuh suit, same lukkuh oxin bruk fuh pull plow. Uh
kin fetch'um onduhneet' me han'!"

With these masterful masculine reflections, Abram
went his ways to the Cross Roads, and having, like
Poe's Raven, acquired the sitting habit, down he sat
near the store on a convenient log which offered at
once rest for his weary bones and camouflage for his
sartorial infirmities. For an hour or more he watched
with an appraising eye the women coming and going,
acknowledging the salutations of those who passed
near him. At last, his approving regard rested upon
what the antebellum advertisements would have called
a "likely girl" who curtseyed as she came opposite him.
"Come'yuh, gal," he called. "Wuh you name?"

"Sukey, suh."

"You duh An' Minda' gal, enty?"

"Yaas, suh, him duh my Grumma en' me duh him gran'."

"You onduhstan' 'bout cook en' wash, enty?"

"Yaas, suh, uh well acquaintun wid alltwo."

"Berry well. You know how fuh patch man' britchiz en' t'ing?"

"No, suh, uh know how fuh patch 'ooman' frock, but uh yent know nutt'n' 'bout no britchiz 'cause none ent fuh dey een we house."

"You hab Pa, enty?"

"No, suh, uh yent hab no Pa. Uh yeddy 'bout'um but uh nebbuh shum. Grumma tell me suh one time uh bin hab Pa, but Ma run'um off en' 'e 'f'aid fuh come back, en' attuhw'ile w'en uh biggin fuh grow big, Ma sen' me fuh lib 'long Grumma, 'cause 'e say suh uh tek attuh Pa 'tell eb'ry time 'e look 'puntop me 'e bex 'tell him haffuh lick me, en' him say suh 'e yent hab time fuh fuhrebbuh duh lick me."

"You tek attuh yo' Pa, enty?"

"Yaas, suh, uh nebbuh shum, but eb'rybody say suh uh look luk'um en' tek attuhr'um alltwo."

"You ent tek attuh yo' Ma, iz you?"

"No, suh, uh yent tek attuh *him*."

"Berry well, uh gwine hab you fuh wife. You know who uh yiz, enty? Me duh Ebbrum Drayton, en' uh lib todduh side Adam' Run deepo, en' uh hab uh two-chimbly house en' 'e got two story, en' uh bin hab uh mare, but him gone en' dead. En' w'en you gone home, tell yo' Grumma uh gwine fuh shum Sunday night fuh tell'um uh gwine hab you fuh wife."

"Yaas, suh. Well, good ebenin', suh," and, with another curtsy, she was gone.

But Abram's plans they gang'd agley, for old John,

in putting the word-of-mouth entail on the Dower House, had tied the " 'tail" so loosely that its terms and conditions were constantly subject to family discussion and interpretation, and Abram's son now objected to his father's marriage, believing that it would break the entail and deprive him of the right of succession to "de Two-Chimbly House." "W'en Grumpa him tie de 'tail 'puntop de house, 'e say 'sponsubble suh 'e yent fuh tek off, en' suh 'e yent fuh tie 'puntop no 'ooman. Pa ent know uh Gawd' t'ing 'bout da' gal him duh talk 'bout hab fuh wife. 'E nebbuh see 'e Ma, 'e nebbuh shum fight. Da' gal' Ma iz de debble! W'en da' 'ooman fight da' gal' Pa, 'e run'um 'long hoe en' hatchitch alltwo! Da' nigguh run 'tell 'e cross Jacksinburruh. 'E nebbuh stop' 'tell 'e gone spang Ti Ti! W'en 'e bog up to 'e crotch 'mong dem waa'ment' en' t'ing 'e git sattify een 'e mine'. No, suh! Pa ent study nutt'n' 'cep' hab wife fuh sweep 'e house en' patch 'e britchiz. Bumbye, w'en da' gal' maamy' sperrit git een'um en' 'e bex fuh true! Ki! Da' gal gwine tek de 'tail off Grumpa' house en' none uh we gwine shum 'gen! W'en Pa duh bog up to 'e crotch een Ti Ti, wuh saa'bis den fuh hab patch 'puntop 'e britchiz? No, suh!"

His daughter sought to comfort Abram, who, in the short space of 36 hours, had loved and wooed, and won and lost. "Nemmine', Pa, you got yo' Two-Chimbly House."

"Yaas, but uh cyan' seddown befo' alltwo de chimbly one time."

AT THE CROSS ROADS STORE

For many years after freedom came to the negroes of the low-country, they were cruelly and ignobly cheated by the tradespeople who set up little Cross Roads stores in every community. Many of these were German corner-shopkeepers from the cities. Others were wandering Jews, whose predatory instincts took them wherever there were pickings to be had. Yet others, to their shame, were certain low-class South Carolinians that did not scruple to take advantage of the ignorant freedmen who, a wasteful and improvident people, whose needs had all been supplied under slavery, squandered the money they were unaccustomed to handling and unable to compute.

Imitative as monkeys, however, it is to the credit of their intelligence, if not of their morality, that they soon learned to retaliate, and many a brick and rusty plowshare was weighed in their bags of seed cotton and paid for by the tricky shopkeeper who, knowing that in many cases the cotton was stolen from the planter for whom the negro worked, and brought stealthily by night to the sophisticated merchant, did not scan his purchase too closely, and many an ancient nest egg, too, was sold to the shopkeeper as a new-laid "yaa'd aig" and shipped away to city customers.

The marks upon the brass beams of the counter-scales with which the negroes' purchases were weighed, were so obscured and tarnished that they could not be deciphered, even by customers who could read, but the wily shopman knew exactly where to put his weight to give a twelve-ounce pound, which is what the negro

150

usually got. Always suspecting "de buckruh" of cheating him, and being unable to do even the smallest addition, the negro soon learned to protect himself, if not from short weights, at least from short change, and it was interesting to observe a shopper making her week's purchases on Saturday nights at one of these neighborhood stores. The women, commonly more alert, and always more suspicious, than the men, were usually charged with the buying. If a customer had a dollar to spend, she would first price the various commodities under consideration.

"Hummuch you ax fuh sugar?"

"Ten cents a pound."

"Ten cent' uh poun'?"

"Yes."

"Hummuch fuh fibe cent'?"

"Half a pound."

"Gimme fibe cent' wut."

The short-weight sugar wrapped up and handed out, the customer would draw it to her bosom and, leaning on the counter, put her protecting arms around it. The dollar, ceremonially unwrapped from a corner of her apron, would be handed over, and ninety-five cents in change returned, which she would count over carefully before proceeding with her next purchase.

"You got any bakin'?"

"Yes."

"Wuh kind'uh bakin?"

"Side meat and shoulder meat."

"Hummuch fuh him?"

"Ten cents for the shoulders and twelve and a half cents for the sides."

"Gimme ten cent' wut uh side meat."

When that was delivered, ten cents would be slowly taken from the little pile and paid over.

"Wuh kinduh clawt' you got?"

"Homespun, gingham, calico. What kind you want?"

"Lemme shum."

Bolts of each would be placed before her.

"Hummuch da' speckly kin'?" (pointing to the gingham).

"Ten cents a yard."

"Gimme ten cent' wut."

A thirty-three-inch yard would be torn off.

"You got any salt?"

"Yes."

"Hummuch fuh him?"

"Five cents a quart."

"Gimme t'ree cent' wut."

"You got any flour?"

"Yes."

"Hummuch you ax fuh him?"

"Five cents a pound."

"Gimme ten cent' wut."

The flour and the salt would come within the encircling arms, fifteen cents be counted out, and all transactions suspended until the two cents change was returned to her.

"Wuh kinduh tubackuh you got?"

Two or three samples of plug tobacco, the only sort in common use, would be offered for inspection, and perhaps the advice of a colored sister asked before deciding upon a selection.

By the time the dollar was expended, the clerk had walked a hundred yards or so, had used up lots of

brown paper and paper twine and had had his patience
sorely tried, but he charged liberally for his time and
trouble, and the poor darkey got far less than she paid
for.

In the funny columns of Northern periodicals, and
in the immemorial minstrel jokes and songs, the negro
not only steals chickens, but eats them. The low-country negroes, however, while all of them keep chickens,
seldom, if ever, eat them, the coarsest fat bacon being
far more to the negro's taste than the juiciest broiler.
Then, too, eggs and chickens are currency in most
negro communities and can always be converted into
cash at the country store or at the back door of the
nearest white family.

The country negroes on the coast still speak of
"fo'punce" chickens and "seb'npunce" chickens, meaning the sizes that were sold for four pence and seven
pence respectively before the Revolution, when British
coinage was the currency of the country.

"Gal, ketch da' seb'npunce chickin en' dem t'ree
fo'punce chickin' en tek dese'yuh six aig', en' tek'um to
de Cross Road', en' buy de six aig' wut'uh tubackuh en'
de seb'npunce chickin wut'uh flour, en' one de fo'punce
chickin' wut'uh sugar, en' norruh one uh de fo'punce
chickin' wut'uh side meat, en' de todduh fo'punce
chickin wut'uh muhlassis, en' tek dish'yuh bucket fuh
fetch'um een, en' don' 'low de buckruh fuh cheat you,
en' tie de aig' een yo' hengkitchuh, en' tie all fo' de fowl'
foot so dem cyan' git'way, en' hol'um een yo' ap'un,
en' don' stay duh sto' too long, en' w'en you tek de
chickin' out de ap'un, hol'um by 'e two foot fuh mek
'e head heng down, so 'e wing' kin 'pread out fuh
mek'um look big so de buckruh t'ink suh de fo'punce

chickin' duh seb'npunce chickin', en' w'en de buckruh
po' out de muhlassis, mek'um fuh po'rum 'tell de muhlassis stop run out de medjuh, 'cause ef you ent
watch'um 'e sho' fuh lef' some een de quawt cup, en'
w'en you come back duh night'time, walk middle'uh de
paat', 'cause 'e rain' teday en' toadfrog does jump
'bout w'en de ground en' t'ing wet, en' moccasin does
folluhr'um fuh ketch'um, en' uh yent wan' you fuh git
'structed by no snake duh paat'."

The little girl leaned on the counter, slowly unrolled
an old bandanna handkerchief, and spread the six eggs
before her, carefully keeping the unhappy chickens
concealed in her apron.

"Ebenin', suh. Ma tell me fuh git uh plug'uh
tubackuh wid dese aig'."

"You can get only half a plug for half a dozen eggs.
Eggs are ten cents a dozen!"

"Yaas'suh, but Ma tell me fuh git'uh whole plug,"
said the shrewd little trader. "Ma tell me fuh ax you
ef you ent g'em uh whole plug uh tubackuh fuh de six
aig', please, suh, fuh gimme uh gunjuh—tengky, suh,"
as the obliging clerk handed her a big scalloped
molasses cake and short-cut the plug of tobacco enough
to pay for it.

The tobacco trade consummated, the girl fumbled
furtively in her apron, and, feeling about deftly,
located and drew forth the "seb'npunce" chicken. That
adolescent fowl, a rooster whose voice was changing,
alternately peeped and squawked, as the seller with
out-stretched arm dangled him by the legs high over
the counter, his outspread wings making him look a
full size larger, but the shopkeeper was country-bred,
and felt the rooster's breastbone. "Fifteen cents," he

said.

"Ma tell me fuh git twenty-fibe cent' wut uh flour 'long dish'yuh one," she fibbed.

"I'll give you twenty cents' worth," he countered, and, as she nodded in acquiescence, jubilant at the thought of having outwitted him, he plunged his scoop into a barrel and weighed out twelve cents' worth of flour. When this had been wrapped and delivered, the clerk, knowing by her expectant look that further commercial transactions were imminent, stood at attention, while the girl abstracted the first of the three "fo'punce" chickens from her apron and held the noisy fledgling, naked and unashamed, at arm's length above the counter. "Ma tell me fuh git dis seb'npunce chickin wut uh side meat," she ventured, craftily watching the face of the Caucasian whom she sought to overreach.

"Why, that's a fo'punce chicken. He ain't half the size of the other one."

"Yaas'suh, alltwo come out de same nes' en' alltwo hatch out de same time. Da' todduh one duh dish'yuh one bubbuh, en' dish'yuh one duh da' todduh one tittie. Him look big mo'nuh dish'yuh one 'cause him duh roostuh en' him hab comb, en' dish'yuh one duh pullet en' him ent hab no comb, en' de roostuh greedy mo'nuh de pullet, en' him nyam de mor'is' bittle, en' dat mek 'e stan' so," she prevaricated unblushingly. These earnest asseverations had no effect on the purchaser, however, and, appraising the gallinaceous juveniles at ten cents each, he stood pat, and one by one they were withdrawn from the apron and exchanged for bacon, sugar and molasses. Upon the pouring of the latter commodity, however, Aryan and African again locked horns. The weather was warm, and as even the thick "blackstrap" molasses flowed freely, the careless shopman very nearly gave his customer the full quart for which she had paid—an inadvertence which, it should be said in justice to his commercial acumen, he very seldom committed. Realizing too late that nearly all the molasses had run into the tin bucket out of the quart measure (false-bottomed as it was) he gave it a quick upward flirt to save what he could, and started back to the barrel, but was checked by the girl's scream of protest. "Ma tell' me fuh tell you 'sponsubble fuh mek you fuh po'rum out 'tell eb'ry drop done dreen een de bucket," she cried excitedly, and, in shame-faced compliance, he let her hold the measure till the uttermost drop had been "dreened" out. With a sideswipe of a very questionable finger, she garnered the dulcet drops that clung to the curved lip of the cup and, sucking the sweetened digit greedi-ly, she grinned with satisfaction. And now, with the packages carefully tied up in the bandanna in one hand, and the covered tin bucket in the other, she dropped a curtsy, for she was a polite little darkey, and went her ways homeward, sweetened in soul and saliva.

The night was dark, and the path traversed a small bay, where the sweetgums spread their limbs above the track, and their heavy foliage hid the stars and deep-ened the shadows along the way. Along the edge of the bay, in the sodden soil, grew lush water-grasses, and they were very sweet to a vagabond ox, as he cropped them, undisturbed by flies, in the cool night air. But the peaceful ox, playing truant, poor wretch, from his negro master, was full of tragedy, for the ox was white, and no solitary negro in the low-country,

156

AT THE CROSS ROADS STORE

where the forests are full of little negro graveyards, can bear the sight of anything white in the woods at night. The fear of ghosts is always with them, and a white cow, grazing in or near a graveyard, will often stampede a road full of worshipers returning from a prayer-meeting.

As she reached the shadowy places along the way, the child heard a rustling sound in the bushes that suggested snakes. She instinctively jumped to the other side of the path, at the same time looking over her shoulder in the direction of the sound. One glance was enough! The pallid ox loomed gigantic in her affrighted eyes, and, with a scream of terror, she fled homeward and was soon, wide-eyed and trembling, before her mother. Faithful to her trust, she had held on to bundle and tin bucket, but the molasses was spattered liberally over her bare legs and had soaked her homespun skirt and apron.

"*Wuh 'smattuh, gal?* You done t'row'way half de muhlassis! Wuh de debble mek you duh trimble?"

"Ma, w'en uh binnuh walk t'ru de branch, een da' daa'k t'icket onduhneet' dem gum tree, uh yeddy sump'nurruh duh shake de bush, en' uh t'ink 'e duh snake, en' uh jump en' look 'roun', en' uh see uh sperrit, one big w'ite sump'n' high mo'nuh dis house, en' de t'ing groan' at me, en' uh dat 'f'aid'um, uh run'way, en' 'e nebbuh ketch me, en' uh mek de buckruh gimme twenty cent' wut uh flour fuh de seb'npunce chickin, en' 'e gimme uh gunjuh!"

"Tell yo' bubbuh fuh git da' hom'ny spoon en' 'crape da' muhlassis off yo' two knee, en' pit'um een da' pan, en' tek off yo' ap'un, en' you en' yo' bubbuh alltwo kin chaw'um, so de muhlassis ent fuh t'rowway."

157

MINGO, THE DRILL MASTER

At the close of the war, thousands of disbanded negro troops, how many, only the Lord knows and the pension roll shows, swarmed over the Coast Counties comprising the South Carolina Black Belt. Swagger in their new-minted freedom, and resplendent in the light blue trousers and dark blue coats of the Federal uniform, with ridiculous little forage caps perched aslant upon the sides of their kinky heads, like chickens roosting on leaning poles, girdled with great brass-buckled U. S. Belts, and shouldering army muskets, full of insolence and of ribaldry, they took the highways and the by-ways for their own. Their former masters, however kindly they had been to them before and since freedom, were frequently spoken of behind their backs as "de rebel," and the days of slavery were referred to as "rebel time" (times). Some of these soldiers had served for years, perhaps, others for months or weeks, few of them had smelt powder, all of them had smelt and fattened upon the bad— wickedly bad—bacon with which the loyal sutlers had supplied the invading army. (And, by the way, thousands of tierces of that same sutler's bacon of the years '64 and '65 were still at large for full five years thereafter, supplied by the Charleston and Savannah factors to the low-country planters for their plantation commissaries.)

In addition to the disbanded troops, thousands of other negroes, who had never seen service, wore cheaply bought Federal uniforms and long, light blue overcoats, and sported caps and belts and condemned muskets, so that the whole countryside was black and blue, and they were constantly drilling, while the women, peahens that they were, worked for them and admired the strutting of their lordly peacocks. Often at night, from the quarters of a distant plantation, instead of the peaceful "tap, tap-a-tap, tap-a-tap, tap-a-tap," of the sticks which the negroes beat on the floor to mark time for their dancing and "shouting," there would come the rattle of a snaredrum, and one knew that an awkward squad was being put through awkward evolutions in the compound or "nigguhhouse yaa'd" for the edification of the quarters.

It was a psychological study to watch one of these squads or companies drilling or parading on the public highway, when a white man of a former slave-holding family approached. Neither stern disciplinary eye, nor sharp command, could keep the lines straight until after "de buckruh" had passed. There were sure to be some members of the squad whose hereditary respect—stronger far than the fear of the drill master—would impel them to scrape a foot or pull wool, till the alignment was as wabbly as a swimming moccasin.

One August day in the early '70s, Prince Manigo, captain of the Adams Run Company, ordered his command out for drill, inspection and maneuvers. Sixty-five men reported; these were of all ages from 17 to 70. Some of them belonged around the village, but most of them came from about Toogoodoo, "down on de Salt," as the inland negroes designate the sea coast and the contiguous lands lying along the salt rivers and creeks.

The place of assembly indicated by Captain Manigo was about a mile south of the village on the way to Toogoodoo. Once a member of Col Thomas Wentworth Higginson's negro regiment, the "First South Carolina Volunteers," organized at Beaufort in 1862, he had known picket duty about Port Royal Ferry during the war, and wished to familiarize his dusky outfit with service in the field. The road ran along the edge of a deep swamp, or bay. The growth on the rich lowlands was heavy, and beautiful magnolias, close-limbed and tall, as is their habit of growth in thick places, rose to a height of sometimes a hundred feet, the sunlight flashing from the curved backs of their dark and glossy leaves. Under these great trees, sweet bay, red bay, beech and maple grew in a tangle, and below these, tall canes and great sword ferns, with riotous vines of bamboo and wild grape, thickened into an almost impenetrable chaparral. In these woods, dimmed to a twilight darkness, Captain Manigo established his picket posts. Fifteen or twenty men were selected for this dangerous duty, for, at this season, the swamp was full of rattlesnakes and some of those picked for outpost duty objected. "Man, I cyan' go een da' t'icket. Snake dey dey tummuch."

"Snake cyan' see fuh bite now," said another. "Ent you know suh rattlesnake' hab skin 'puntop 'e yeye een Augus' munt'? 'E bline'. 'E cyan' see fuh bite."

"Uh dunkyuh ef 'e yiz bline', ef uh 'tep 'puntop'um 'e gwine bite me."

"Go 'way, man, snake ent gwine bite you w'en you hab muskick een you han' wid dat shaa'p bay'net en t'ing 'puntop'um."

So all objections were overruled, and the posts established at intervals of a few hundred yards, the password "raccoon" was given to the corporals, and the captain and his inspectors, dismissing the remaining

MINGO, THE DRILL MASTER

members of the company for a rest period, prepared
to test the line of outposts. Making a wide detour they
sneaked through the woods almost noiselessly. The
dead leaves, fallen during the preceding winter, had
softened long ago and were rapidly settling into the
thick mold that covered the damp earth. Sneaking up
on the farthest sentinel from the rear, Prince was
almost upon him before the startled negro challenged
"Halt! Weh oonuh gwine? Gimme de passwu'd!"

"Raccoon," Prince responded.

"Oonuh cyan' go t'ru 'puntop dat wu'd."

Prince expostulated. "Raccoon" was the password
he had given the corporals to pass on to their men, and
having been selected as a word of singular appeal to
the negroes, should have been one of the easiest to
remember, so he repeated petulantly "*Raccoon, raccoon, raccoon.*"

"'*E yent wut,*" insisted the sentinel, as the long
bayonet projected threateningly through the gum
bushes. "Dat passwu'd cyan' specify. Da' longmout'
nigguh f'um Slann' Ilun', name Mingo, him duh de
cawprul en' him done tell me de wu'd two time, en'
'scusin' oonuh hab dat wu'd, oonuh yent fuh pass."

As the corporal was several hundred yards away,
Prince retired grumbling, and attempted the line at
another point. He approached a wary old picket, a
noted 'coon hunter, whose experienced ear detected
even the soft footfalls of the inspectors, and he hailed
them at a distance of 50 yards, in most unmilitary
language. "Haw, buck! Oonuh try fuh sneak 'puntop
me, enty? Uh binnuh hunt rokkoon en' dem todduh
waa'ment en' t'ing 'fo' you bawn! Come out, bubbuh!
Uh yeddy you' foot en' uh see bush duh shake alltwo.

161

Come out de t'icket. Exwance en' gimme de passwu'd!"

But they couldn't give it; not at least intelligibly to the ear of old Cæsar. Prince spoke with only a slight taint of Gullah, and when he had given "raccoon" to his Toogoodoo corporals, who understood him only after several repetitions, he didn't realize that they would pass it on as "rokkoon" and that as "rokkoon" the "open sesame" of the countersign must be given. Again, therefore, with his own password correctly pronounced, the Captain had reached an impasse, and as Cæsar truculently stuck out both his mouth and his bayonet, the Corporal of the guard was demanded.

"Cawprul uh de gyaa'd! Pos' number t'ree!" he bellowed. "Mek'ace en' come'yuh! T'ree mans dey yuh duh try fuh git t'ru bedout no passwu'd. Ef dem got'um dem cyan' call 'e name. Uh dunkyuh ef one is de cap'n, oonuh done tell me 'sponsubble suh 'e yent fuh pass bedout 'e got de wu'd."

The thick-lipped corporal came.

"'Smattuh, Unk' Cæsar? Yuh fuh call me?"

"Yaas, uh fuh call you fuh true. Mek dese'yuh man fuh gi' we de sign."

"Raccoon!" bellowed Prince.

"You shum, enty! Enty uh tell you 'e yent hab'um!"

"Yaas, man, da' duh him! 'Rokkoon' duh de passwu'd wuh Buh Prince gi' we, but him ent call 'e name lukkuh we call'um, 'cause him bin Beefu't rebel time 'long dem Nyankee en' t'ing, en' duh so dem call'um."

"Uh dunkyuh how dem eegnunt Nyankee call rokkoon' name, demself cyan' pass dis t'icket 'scusin' dem call'um lukkuh we call'um 'puntop Toogoodoo. En' 'cause dis nigguh bin Beefu't, him fuh 'spute 'long me en' tell me how fuh call rokkoon' name w'en uh binnuh ketch rokkoon befo' 'e daddy hab 'e maamy! Ef 'e cyan' call rokkoon' name, uh keep'um yuh 'tell t'unduh roll!"

"*Rokkoon!*" conceded the chapfallen captain, and he passed, somewhat chagrined at the outcome of his picketing experiment.

The outposts were recalled, the other negroes aroused from among the roadside bushes where they had been resting, and the full company assembled for drill. The outfit was heavily officered, and the captain allowed them to take turns at putting the men through their paces. At last they were turned over to Mingo Brown, a pompous corporal, so puffed up with "a little brief authority" that most of the negroes grinned in his face, and some openly guffawed, "eh, eh, Buh Mingo swonguh fuh sowl!" The men, a ragged line, were ranged on one side of the road, and, facing them on the other, Mingo drew a great cavalry sabre and began to cut such anthropoidal antics before high heaven, that three gentlemen, returning from a successful hunt, reined in their horses a few yards away and paused to see the fun.

" 'Tenshun! 'Tan'up 'traight, oonuh man! Oonuh stan' crookety sukkuh wurrum fench w'en dem staa't fuh t'row off 'e riduh fuh tayre'um down fuh moobe cowpen!

"Shoulduh, *aam!* Pit oonuh muskick 'puntop oonuh shoulduh en' hol'um 'traight. You mus'be t'ink dem duh hoe, enty? Fo' man fuh stan' side en' side fuh mek one t'ickness. Faw-wud, *maa'ch!* 'Top! Weh de debble oonuh gwine? Uh done tu'n oonuh head fuh face Toogoodoo Bridge, en', please Gawd, oonuh w'eel sukkuh mule hab cucklebuhr een 'e yez, 'en fuh gone

Adam' Run billage!" Sure enough, as the execution of the command would have taken them over hunters and pack, they had reversed the order and started in the opposite direction.

"Fuh true, bubbuh, enty you see Mas' Rafe en' Mas' Tom en' dem duh paat'? Nigguh fuh maa'ch obuh buckruh, enty?"

"Buckruh, de debble! Enty de Freedmun Bruro mek we fuh free? Uh free tell uh fool! Prizzunt, *aam!*"

Some were shouldered, others ordered, a few "presented" with the butt of the piece against the waist, and the bayonet sticking out at right angles to the body. " 'Tenshun! Da' man f'um Slann' Ilun' wuh duh 'tan'up close da' 'tump fuh hol' 'e gun een alltwo 'e han'. Him mus'be t'ink suh gun duh oshtuh rake! Groun', *aam!*" And the whole perspiring line squatted and laid their pieces on the ground, rising just as the hunters gathered up their reins and rode along the line, while the hounds, with lofty tails, trotted after them, sniffing scornfully at the warriors' legs as they passed.

"Huddy, Mas' Rafe. How ole Missis en' dem?"

"Mas' Tom, you look nyung mo'nuh Mas' Rafe."

"Yaas, suh. Phyllis him well, suh, tengk Gawd."

"Mas' Dick, you sho' hab uh hebby buck," as the great velveted horns of a fine buck tied behind the hunter's saddle brushed against him. And all down the line, their hands being free, men touched their little monkey caps or tugged at their kinky forelocks and scraped their feet, in token of the kindly respect in which, spite of freedom and franchise, muskets and uniforms, and the poisonous propaganda of the Freedman's Bureau, they yet held those known throughout

MINGO, THE DRILL MASTER

the countryside as having been kindly masters to their slaves, and just and liberal employers of the freedmen.

"Mas' Rafe, please suh, gimme some tubackuh," and the outstretched hand received a generous share of the contents of the donor's pouch.

"Da' duh my maussuh," said the recipient proudly, filling his pipe as the hunters rode away.

"Cump'ny fawm two t'ickness' een de rank," shouted Mingo savagely. *"Don' look at de buckruh, look at yo' officer!"* and, turning to the smoker, he added: "Me yent hab no maussuh. *Uh free ez uh buzzut!"*

"Yaas, bubbuh. Buzzut free en' buzzut black, but buzzut ent free 'nuf fuh light 'puntop nutt'n' 'cep'n' 'e dead, en' nigguh ent free 'nuf fuh mek buckruh fuh bex!"

"OLD HARRISON"

A few years after the war old John Harrison came into the coast country from somewhere beyond Caw Caw Swamp. He boasted a strain of Indian blood, and he showed it in his pigeon-toed walk and the red, coppery tint that stained his bronzed face. Six feet tall and powerfully built, he carried his fifty-odd years lightly, although his high, heavy shoulders were somewhat hunched from the heavy burdens to which they were accustomed for, a noted "pot hunter," he thought nothing of "packing" a hundred and fifty-pound buck five or ten miles through the forest. During the close season for game he was not averse to working, and had quite a local reputation as a shingle-maker and rail-splitter. His speech was the ordinary "cracker" dialect of the low-country with a suggestion of the Gullah, but he clipped his words, and when excited, his sentences ran into a quick crescendo, almost unintelligible and defying reproduction in print.

When he came to Pon Pon he was allowed to clear a small field in a distant part of the plantation, a mile away from the "big house," now only a beautiful ruin, with ivy, woodbine, and Lamarque roses clambering 50 feet in the air over the 200-year-old chimneys of English brick. On his "new ground," old Harrison built a large and trim-looking log cabin, and here he took up residence with his motherless children, two small girls and a straight and strapping son of 18, who helped his father with his work, but not in the chase, for Harrison hunted alone, sometimes, with a single well-trained hound, disappearing for two or three days at a time, to return laden with venison or wild turkeys which were sold at the railway station.

"OLD HARRISON"

His dog, like those of most of the "pot hunters" who follow the chase on foot, was trained to silence, and never gave tongue. A small bell was attached to his collar and he was seldom out of sight of his master, who could tell by the movement of his ears and tail when the animal had found a trail, and when the lifting of the ears and the more rapid wagging of the tail indicated the near approach to the myrtle thicket where the deer lay in his bed, both barrels of the muzzle-loader were cocked and Harrison usually got a shot as the deer "jumped."

Ben Summers, a large black negro in late middle-age, was a "locus" preacher in the neighborhood and, a jackleg carpenter, worked as well as preached. Throughout his life he had been partial to wives, having been more or less affiliated with six or seven, whom he put away and took back again, with no more ceremony than his change of mind. Unruly and insubordinate as a slave, he became "swonguh" with freedom, and was more or less insolent, save to his former master's family. He was regarded as a rascal by whites and blacks, and when a calf or a shoat was missed in the community, Ben was not infrequently suspected of having shared the meat, either as a participant in the slaughter, or as a welcomed guest at the banqueting board of the thief.

One of Ben's wives had achieved a son by a former husband, before Ben took her over, and this stepson had acquired a wife, a husky, cornfed wench, an Amazon in strength and fierceness. Soon after her marriage, old Ben, a rough-talking, brutal fellow, who tyrannized over the women of his entourage, undertook to discipline this step-daughter-in-law with phy-

167

sical chastisement. Cutting a hickory, he proceeded to manhandle her as he had been accustomed to use his wives. She accepted two or three blows, and then turned upon him so swiftly that he was swept off his feet and mauled almost into unconsciousness. After he had been patched up and rehabilitated, and the first bitterness of defeat had worn off, he really liked to tell the story, laying the unction to his soul that only his Christian spirit had stayed his hand and saved the life of the virago.

"Ben, you are a big strong man, why did you let that woman beat you?"

"Gin'ul, lemme tell you de trute, Gawd bin wid me dat day. You know, all me life uh bin uh strong man. Uh nebbuh hab no man fuh outdo me fuh wu'k, eeduhso fuh fight, en' uh bin nyuse fuh lick 'ooman en' t'ing all me life. W'en 'ooman ent sattify me wid 'e wu'k, eeduhso 'e mannus, uh lick'um fuh mek'um mannusubble. W'en my wife Sarah' son John' wife come een my house dat day, 'e sassy 'tell 'e mek me bex. Uh nebbuh tek sassy f'um no 'ooman, uh dunkyuh ef 'e big ez cow, en' da' gal big 'ooman fuh true. So uh cut one 'tick en' uh graff'um by 'e sleebe en' biggin fuh lick'um. Gin'ul, de 'ooman tu'n on me en' box me same lukkuh him duh man. Blood bin een me yeye! Uh 'membuh de time w'en uh could'uh box'um en' kick'um alltwo one time, en' ef uh ebbuh leh de *foot* folluh de *han'*, uh would uh kill'um *dead*. But Gawd hol' me han' en' me foot, alltwo, Gawd tell me fuh peaceubble, en' spayre de 'ooman life. Gin'ul, me don' want no 'ooman life 'pun me han'. Enty you know, suh, ef uh had uh kick dat 'ooman 'e would uh dead? Gawd tek'care uh ol' Ben dat day. Da' 'ooman t'ink suh him lick me, Gin'ul, but

"OLD HARRISON"

enty you know suh him oughtuh tengk Gawd fuh sabe'-
um? Ef uh didn' bin hab 'lij'un, da' 'ooman' cawpse
would'uh gone Jacksinburruh een one oxin cyaa't weh
'e come f'um. All de time 'e binnuh box me, uh bin
study 'bout how da' 'ooman' cawpse would'uh look ef
uh had uh hit'um like de time w'en uh nyuse to be uh
Ben! En' uh study 'pun him husbun', my wife Sarah'
boy John, en' uh study 'pun John' maamy, en' uh t'ink
'bout how dem will mo'n ef uh kill dis 'ooman, en' wid
Gawd' help uh hab strengk 'nuf fuh hol' me han'.
Gin'ul, w'enebbuh uh look 'puntop de' dead 'ooman een
me mine', uh tengk Gawd eb'ry day fuh hol' me han'!"

Once a fine shoat strayed too near to Ben's little field
and soon found its way into the old man's larder, where
it was found by a search party in charge of old Harrison. An examination showed that the animal had been
shot with duck shot, and shot of the same size having
been found in the undischarged barrel of the negro's
double-barrel, Ben was arrested and sent to Walterboro jail and Harrison was summoned as a witness.
Harrison was fond of a dram and looked forward to
the approach of court week which would bring him a
visit to the county seat with witness fees of 50 cents a
day and mileage. Walterboro was 35 miles away, and
five cents a mile both ways meant $3.50, which loomed
large in the mind of the old hunter. On the Saturday
night before the convening of court, he prepared a
week's rations of cornbread, bacon and baked sweet
potatoes, and early Sunday morning filled a great
knapsack, and, with his long gun on his shoulder,
walked all the way to the county seat. On the following day the pig thief was duly arraigned, the jury
organized, and old Harrison, loaded to the muzzle with

169

Walterboro whiskey, to which he had been treated by
the youngsters who liked to hear him talk, came to the
witness stand, a 20-pound knapsack of provisions
around his shoulders and his long gun in his hand.
His direct testimony was:

"Sunday mornin' bin over t' Cap'n Elliott's, coz
mostly Sunday mornin' ef uh goes by th' house Cap'n
gennully gives me uh pow'ful drink, en' uh allus likes
me dram. W'en uh got through me dram, uh was
walkin' 'long by ol' Ben's house, en' uh heerd uh gun
shoot. Uh meet some boys and went to th' house en'
fin' th' shoat en' fin' number two duck shot een 'im.
Uh fin' ol' Ben's gun in the corner, one barrel been
fired, en' uh drawed th' load of t'other barrel en' fin'
number two duck shot, same size ez een th' shoat. Then
uh told Cap'n, he give me 'nother dram, we 'rested ol'
Ben in th' pulpit where he was preachin' to a raft uh
niggers, en' we send him to Walterboro."

Then came the cross-examination. The young lawyer for the defense baited old Harrison to the great
amusement of the court room.

"What do you know about duck shot?" he was asked.
"I don't believe you know the size of a duck shot."

"Uh don't know de size uv uh duck shot! *Course*
uh knows de size uv uh duck shot. Bin hunt'n' all me
life, bin shoot'n' *duck shot* all me life."

"If you know the size of a duck shot, take this pencil
and let the jury see you draw one on the court house
wall."

Harrison rose with bleary eyes and a fatuous smile
on his bronzed face. Unable to read or write, he held
the pencil as a small boy holds a sizzling firecracker,
but he was game and stepped up to the wall primed

with the confidence born of ignorance. Judge, jury and spectators craned their necks to see the performance. The draftsman stuck close to the wall and moved the pencil slowly and laboriously over the whitewashed surface. When at last he stepped back and turned around proudly to reveal his work, the court house exploded with laughter, from Judge Wallace on the bench, to the tipstaff at the door, for the tipsy old hunter's outline of a duck shot was about eight inches long and five inches wide and bore a striking resemblance to the continent of Africa. He returned to the witness chair. Taking the shouts of merriment as tributes to the accuracy of his sketch, he looked scornfully at the young lawyer.

"Ain't I tell ye uh know'd d'size uv uh duck shot? Bin shoot'n' duck shot all me life. *Course* uh knows d'size uv uh duck shot!" And there was more laughter.

The negro was convicted, and sent to the penitentiary for two years, but was soon leased to a railroad contractor, and, becoming a "trusty" and a cook, had an easy time. When he returned to Pon Pon he resumed his place in the pulpit without the slightest loss of caste, and often referred to his sojourn in the Capital City, telling many stories to the members of his flock about "de time w'en uh bin penitenshus," or "w'en uh bin Cuhlumbia."

One Christmas morning old Harrison came to the house with the portentous information that he intended to marry the widow Pendarvis, was then on his way to her habitation seven or eight miles away, and would bring back his bride the same evening.

"Dat whut uh yaim t'do Cap'n. Uh knows hits pow'ful resky t'marry uh widder, coz dey allus knows

toomuch, but uh needs uh 'ooman to clean up en' do
about d'house, en' look after d'children, en' de widder
Pendarvis is uh right peart creeter, en' she ain't got
uh lazy bone een her, so uh reck'n uh'll resk it. Den,
she's got a son, John Henry, 'bout d'age uh my
William. John Henry he ain't much account, but uh
needs anuther han' en' uh reck'n uh kin make out wid
John Henry, so uh yaims to tek d'widder."

The old adventurer was fitted out with a white shirt
and a handkerchief, a pocketful of Christmas candies
and a couple of stiff snifters, and so, fortified, he
started toward the widow, stepping high, gun on
shoulder. "Uh allus totes m'gun. Y'never knows whut
y'gwine t'see."

So the widow Pendarvis was duly acquired and
proved a faithful and useful spouse, but old Harrison
soon reached the conclusion that he had been gold-
bricked in John Henry. "He ain't no manner uv
account. Ain't wuth d'powder'n shot it ud'take t'kill-
'im! W'en uh married d'widder, uh didn' aim t'git
much uv uh bargin in John Henry, he was jus' kinder
throw'd een fuh good measure like, but now uh wisht
he mout uh bin throw'd out."

A year or two later William Harrison was walking
the woods one day, and from a shallow grave at the
edge of a negro's field, his dogs dug up the hide and
head of a stolen cow which the thief had buried to
hide the ear-marks and the brand. The negro was
sent to jail to await trial and William was subpœnæd
as the chief witness. Old Harrison protested. " 'Taint
uh bit uh use t'sen' William t'Walterboro fuh fifty
cents uh day, w'en 'e's makin' seventy-five cents uh
day now. W'y don't yuh take my stepson John Henry

"OLD HARRISON"

Pendarvis fer uh witness? He ain't a workin' en' he'll
be glad t'git d'fifty cents uh day." It was explained
to the old hunter that as John Henry had not found
the telltale hide and head, and knew nothing about the
case, he could not be accepted as proxy. "Don't make
uh bit uh diff'unce. William kin tell John Henry
whut he found en' John Henry kin go t'Walterboro en'
swear to it. John Henry he's a noble liar, en' he kin lie
en' stick to't. Them Walterboro lawyers can't shake
him."

After awhile, bad health came upon the former
widow, and in taking palliatives to relieve her pain,
she became addicted to opium and spent all she could
scrape for the drug at the village store. At last the
neighborhood doctor warned her husband, "Harrison,
if you don't look out, some day your wife will take an
overdose of laudanum and go up the spout."

"Well, Doctor, 'tain't fuh me to go ag'in her! She's
bin'uh noble 'ooman in 'er time. She's never had uh
lazy bone een 'er body. She's bin uh pow'ful hand to
do about, en' she's bin as peart uh 'ooman as ever was
wropped up in that much hide, but she's gitt'n kinder
poorly now, she ain't whut she used to be, she ain't
much account now, she can't scrub no mo', she's got
de rheumatism in de jints, so, Doctor, if she aims to
go, uh reck'n d'best thing to do is to let her take a
pow'ful dost en' *let 'er go!*" So—poor, tired soul—she
went.

A MARRIAGE OF CONVENIENCE

Twenty-five years ago, old Jane was the very efficient cook at the Pawley's Island hotel. A widow woman of fifty-odd, her black countenance, with its aquiline nose and sharp chin, was shrewd and witchlike.

"Old maids" are seldom met with among the low-country negroes, most of the women achieving matrimony, or having matrimony thrust upon them, at an early age in communities where marrying and unmarrying are but the merest incidents in their social and economic lives—and they are largely socio-economic relations,—"Uh haffuh hab wife fuh cook fuh me en' wash me clo'es, enty?" "Uh haffuh hab man fuh wu'k fuh me en' min' me, enty?"—"and so they were married."

Often, however, in early life, less frequently in middle age, women are, for the moment, unmarried, or, as one might more correctly say, unaffiliated, and if one of these "unaffiliations" should last long enough to constitute more than a very brief intermission in the matrimonial program, one, if of the fiercer sex, incurs the odium supposedly attaching to "oldmaidenhood."

Jane had in her time looked upon husbands in yellow and brown and black, and had almost run the chromatic scale in temperament as in pigmentation. The sharps had irritated, the flats had wearied her—the "naturals," being neither too sharp nor too flat, were, like the small wee bear's belongings, "just right," and Jane, like Chaucer's Wife of Bath, thanked the Lord for them while they lasted. "But pleasures are like poppies spread," and, as in Georgetown colored circles hus-

bands don't always "stay put," one by one Jane's poppies—perhaps she thought them snap-dragons—folded
their petals and their tents, and, forsaking the dusky
companionship of the old love, flitted away to present
freedom and prospective enslavement to the new—for
there's always a new—"ef rokkoon only hab one tree
fuh climb, dog ketch'um," being an axiom among them.
As Jane couldn't trot in double harness, she single-
footed successfully for several years—so successfully,
indeed, that she developed a fine scorn for the opposite
sex. "Dem ent wut," she thought, and *"dem ent wut,"*
she said, whenever men were mentioned. In her soli-
tude she found solace in industry, and, working at odd
jobs during the winter, supplemented her summer
earnings at the hotel and soon acquired enough to buy
"uh piece uh groun'" (the coast negroes never speak of
land) and built thereon a comfortable cabin, near
which, within a wattled clapboard fence, she enclosed
a plot where she grew the easy-going squashes and
beans in summer, and Georgia collards—the holly-
hocks of the vegetable garden—in winter.

Jane's domain was on the mainland in the flat pine
woods thick sown with clumps of the dark green tropi-
cal-looking saw-palmettoes, and bordered the marsh-
fringed inlet or tidal lagoon, beyond which, half a
mile distant, lay the broad ocean beach, the rolling
sand dunes and the dwarf live-oak and cedar scrub of
"the Island." Here, nestling among the thickets, and
sheltered under the protecting shoulders of the hills,
were the summer cottages of the Islanders, and here,
too, just opposite Jane's cottage, stood the hotel, where
all through the summer days she fried whiting, boiled
sheepshead, deviled crabs, and did sundry other things

to the sea-food that the fishermen constantly brought to her kitchen. Jane's riparian rights permitted her a landing where, moored to a primitive little pier, she kept the flat-bottomed skiff in which morning and evening she crossed the unvexed waters that lay between her home and her work.

Esau, a trifling, ramshackle, youngish negro, made an easy living by fishing, crabbing and doing odd jobs about the Island community. He was venturesome, as most saltwater negroes are, and often in the early mornings ran his leaky skiff through the breakers at the mouth of the inlet, and rowing—or wafted, when the wind favored, by a rag of a sail—adventured out to sea five miles from the beach, dropped an anchor made of two condemned iron pots tied together, and fished upon the blackfish rocks in the broiling sun till noon, returning to shore to sell the good fish to the Islanders and, later, eat the culls and odds and ends himself. On other days, when the East wind warned him that the fish wouldn't bite, he bogged about the little creeks and runs of the marsh, or along the edge of the lagoon, and caught crabs by the basketful, which usually found a ready market.

Bringing his fish often to the hotel, Esau was on pleasant conversational terms with old Jane, and she often handed him out toothsome bits of "buckruh bittle" that fell from the overflowing table. In return for these gastronomic courtesies, Esau would chop wood, split kindling, or do other manly things that chivalrous colored bucks not infrequently perform for the females outside of their own family circles.

One hot August morning, Esau gathered lines and bait as soon as it was broad daylight, and, slipping over the shallow bar at the mouth of the lagoon, sculled lazily out to the "drop" on the rocks. It was a windless dawn, the sea was without a ripple, and the slow, heaving swells reflected the opalescent tints of the eastern sky. The tide was still on the ebb, and its impulse, augmenting his speed, soon brought him to the drop where he cast anchor, and the boat swung round, bow to land, while Esau, in the stern, sat with his back to the rising sun and threw out his lines. The fish bit well, and at the end of two or three hours the bottom of Esau's boat was well covered with the shining catch, chiefly speckled sea trout, whiting and blackfish. The sun increased in warmth, and Esau nodded and dozed and then slept, although, with the turn of the tide, the prow of his boat now pointed seaward and the sunshine burned in his face. At last, at noon, when its beams fell vertically upon his kinky head, he awoke with a start as a big horse-mackerel leaped from the water so near him that he was drenched with its spray. He looked out upon a sea of molten silver. A great shark, as long as his boat, rose slowly from the depths to within a foot of the surface, and, lying motionless, regarded him with cold, expressionless eyes. Esau shuddered. *"Great Gawd,"* he muttered, *"time fuh gone home!"* and, as the sinister creature sank out of sight, he quickly hauled up anchor, shipped oars, and pulled lustily to shore. It was high tide when he reached the inlet, and he rode the long rollers over the bar, and soon ran the nose of his skiff ashore on the oyster shells of the landing. He strung his fish and set out to find a market, but the time lost while he slept had made him too late to supply the dinners of his usual customers, and, as his fish were now stale, he had no recourse but to eat them himself, so he set about cleaning them, and an hour later, when Jane, having served the hotel dinner, was dining alone in the kitchen, Esau appeared and ingratiatingly asked the loan of a frying pan, "please, ma'am, en' some greese fuh greese'um." As neither fat nor fuel cost Jane anything, she graciously complied, in the handsome spirit that prompts so many of us to be generous at the expense of others. Esau rubbed the greasy bacon-rind over the broad, generous bottom of the hotel frying pan and, having lubricated it sufficiently, cast in his fish, and the horrible sound and the horrible smell of frying soon filled the ears and the nostrils of every one about the establishment. Esau fried and he fried until, having filled a large tray with fish, he hung up the frying pan, took down his appetite, and began to eat. Esau was an eater, and had no half-dealings with his art. Seizing a fish by the head and tail, he moved it laterally across his mouth as some traveling men maneuver green corn on the cob, or as the village darkey plays the mouth-organ, until, in the twinkling of an eye, only the bones remained in his greasy fingers; then he played another mouth-organ, until in a few minutes he was filled to the neck, and only ten or twelve fried trout remained, and these he *cached* with old Jane for future attention, and betook himself to the shade of a scrubby live-oak nearby to rest. He threw himself on the sand and slept for several hours like a gorged Anaconda. At last, toward sundown, the land breeze brought the mosquitoes from the main-land across the lagoon, and they swarmed over him. Thrashing about in his troubled sleep, some of the cockspurs that grow everywhere in the Island sands worked their way through his thin homespun trousers and stung him into wakefulness. He arose grouchy and grumbling, and returned to the kitchen where Jane was already preparing supper. "Eh, eh, weh you bin, Esau?" she greeted him.

"Uh binnuh sleep, ma'am, en' muskittuh' en' cockspuhr' en' t'ing wake me en' mek me fuh git up."

"Wuh you gwine do wid dese fish wuh you lef', Esau? De buckruh sen' wu'd suh dem fish duh bodduhr'um, en' 'e tell me fuh t'row'um een de ribbuh."

"Uh had bidness fuh eat all dem fish one time, den uh wouldn' haffuh t'row'um 'way." And Esau sidled over to the tray of fish, and, looking at them regretfully, pinched off nibbling bits with his fingers and carried them to his mouth.

"You bettuh t'row'way da' t'ing, Esau," admonished Jane as she bustled about her work.

"Yaas, ma'am, uh gwine t'row'um 'way bumbye. Uh yent duh eat'um, uh jis' duh pinch'um." And he went slowly out toward the lagoon with the tray under his arm, but, as he walked, he pinched the fish so assiduously that, by the time he came to the water, little save the bones remained.

Two hours later, Jane approached the mistress of the house with an anxious face. "Please, ma'am, fuh gimme some ginjuh en' t'ing fuh gi' Esau 'fo' 'e dead. Da' nigguh sho' hab uh hebby appetite fuh eat bittle. 'E ketch all dem fish, en' 'e couldn' sell'um to de buckruh 'cause dem binnuh leddown all day een de sunhot, en' him fry'um en' nyam t'ree string by 'eself, en' 'e lef' one string 'tell aw'ile ago, en' uh tell'um fuh t'row-'way dat one, en' 'e staa't' fuh t'row'um 'way, but de fish cry out fuh Esau en' Esau yeddy de cry, en' 'e

pinch de fish, en' 'e keep on pinch'um, pinch'um, 'tell
'e done nyam mos' all de fish, en now de fish pinch
him! Uh bin hab uh bottle uh hawss linniment fuh
rub hawss, en' uh t'row dat een'um, but de bottle didn'
bin mo'nuh half full, en' uh 'f'aid de linniment ent
'nuf fuh do'um good, alldo' 'e strangle Esau w'en him
swalluhr'um, en' mek'um fuh spit sukkuh crab spit.
Now, 'e duh roll obuh en' obuh 'pun de groun' same
lukkuh mule roll w'en 'e tu'n out duh Sunday, en'
oonuh kin yeddy'um groan sukkuh dem 'ooman groan
to the sett'n'up, w'en dem husbun' en' t'ing dead. Ef
you please, ma'am, kin gimme some linniment, uh
sump'n'nurruh fuh g'em, uh dunkyuh ef 'tis kyarrysene, 'cause da' nigguh gwine dead!"

"What do you want, Jane—ginger, peppermint or
whiskey?"

"Wuh da' las' one you call 'e name, Missis?"

"Whiskey."

"Missis, da' t'ing too sca'ceful fuh t'row'um 'way ef
da' nigguh gwine dead. Ef you ent got de linniment,
please, ma'am, gimme de ginjuh en' de peppuhmint alltwo, so uh kin t'row'um een Esau."

"Don't give him too many things, Jane, one is
enough."

"Missis, enty da' nigguh eat *fo' kinduh fish?* Uh
wan' g'em meddisin fuh reach all de kinduh fish wuh
'e done eat. Uh yent want'um fuh dead on my han',
'cause him ent hab no fambly, en' 'e yent blonx to no
suhciety fuh bury'um, en' uh know berry well me yent
fuh t'row'way money fuh buy shroud en' cawpse en'
t'ing fuh no Esau, so please, ma'am, mek'ace en' gimme
de t'ing fuh t'row een'um en' see ef uh kin sabe 'e life!"

A liberal dose of mixed ginger and peppermint was
poured into a tin cup, the rim of which Jane forced

between Esau's teeth, and drenched him so successfully
that in a few minutes he was flopping over the ground
like a fish just pulled out of the water. His spasms
were soon over, however, and he lay in a state of semi-
coma. Jane was delighted. "Missis, me en' you done
sabe Esau' life. Da' nigguh blonx to me en' you, Missis,
en' uh gwine mek'um wu'k."

Summer passed into early autumn. The days shortened. September suns burned fiercely upon the ripening corn, and through the lengthening nights heavy
dews fell on the purple petticoat-grass and the golden-
rod. Between sunset and dusk, summer ducks flew
over from their feeding grounds to their roosts in the
pineland ponds, and all through the night sounded the
faint "tweet, tweet" of the ricebirds passing on to
their winter quarters.

So Jane, in the late summer of her days, looked
kindly upon the man she had saved, even though she
did not value the salvage very highly, and Esau gradually got in the habit of hanging about her kitchen
and submitting to the air of proprietorship which she
assumed toward him, chopping wood and doing other
little chores for her, as a matter of course.

At last, one Thursday evening toward the end of
the month, Jane bashfully appeared before her mistress, holding a corner of her apron against a corner
of her mouth, which widened almost from ear to ear.

"Missis, uh come fuh tell you, ma'am, uh gwine
marri'd Esau. Da' nigguh duh heng roun' de kitchen
'tell 'e git een me way. Uh cyan' tu'n roun' bidout
step 'puntop'um, so uh gwine tek'um fuh husbun'."

The announcement caused quite a flutter among the
ladies at the hotel, and, as Jane had fixed the following

THE BLACK BORDER

Saturday evening for the wedding, they hastened to overhaul their wardrobes for suitable material with which to deck out the bride. An old dotted-swiss muslin, found hidden away, was contributed by its owner as something sweet and virginal with which to rig out the craft that had sailed the seven seas of matrimony. Another guest of the hotel contributed a pair of white stockings, and, as Jane desired a veil, a breadth of old mosquito-netting, stiffly starched and skilfully laundered, was added to the outfit. On Saturday night, an hour after supper time, Jane, under the convoy of Esau and accompanied by the "locus pastuh" (the local preacher of her church) appeared before the hotel company assembled on the piazza, and announced her readiness to wed. The mosquito-net veil had been artistically looped about her by some of the ladies, and the dotted-swiss enveloped her with its starched stiffness. The knot was soon tied, and Jane, carrying the bride cake in her arms and followed by her new husband, floated away like a smutty coal-carrying brig, under a new suit of sails.

On the following morning, Jane appeared in the kitchen earlier than usual. The lady of the house asked what she had done with her new husband. "Uh run'um off, missis. Uh yent want'um. Wuh me fuh do wid man! Enty uh hab proputty! Uh marri'd Esau fuh git husbun', uh yent marry'um fuh git man! Nigguh' wuh grow up sence freedum, dem ent wut! Uh marry'um, den uh t'row'um 'way!"

"Why did you marry him, then, if you didn't want him?"

"Ki! Missis! *Uh marry'um fuh shet dem todduh 'ooman' mout'! You t'ink me wan' dem gal' fuh call me ole maid?*"

182

THE PLAT-EYE

All low-country negroes believe more or less in "sperrits," "haants" and other mysterious appearances, but the "plat-eye," peculiar to the Georgetown coast, is the weirdest and most fearsome that vexes the roaming negroes at night. Plat-eyes appear to old and young of both sexes, sometimes in the form of a small dog or other animal, while at other times they may float like wraiths along the marshes or unfrequented paths, or stoop like low-hung clouds and envelop the victim. Most frequently, however, the plat-eye appears in the form of some familiar animal which, glaring at the beholder with eyes of fire, springs upon him, frightening him into rigidity, and, just as he expects his vitals to be torn out, the apparition vanishes, and the trembling negro hurries on his way. The belief has been expressed that, in some instances, the negroes to whom plat-eyes appear have fallen asleep as they walked, and, dreaming of these terrors, awakened to find them gone. In whatsoever form they come, however, the negroes dread the visitations as Werewolves were feared in Europe not so long ago.

Now, old Jane, the cook at the Pawley's Island summer hotel, the many-times widowed woman who, having saved the life of Esau, the fisherman, by drenching him with horse liniment after he had partaken too freely of the spoils of his lines, had wedded that same Esau to save herself the reproach of old-maidenhood, and had chased him away the morning after her *Marriage de Convenance*, was a fervent and fearful believer in plat-eyes. Whenever and wherever she went her ways at night, she was on the lookout for them, and the expectation of their momentary appearance kept her nerves in a pleasant state of jumpiness. A stray calf at the edge of the clearing, a raccoon ambling along a woodland path, a sudden rabbit bouncing up before her, the horned owl that lifted her wayward fowls from their runaway roost on the ridgepole of her cabin, even the ghostly sandcrabs that drifted along the beaches at night as lightly as wind-blown foam, were all potential plat-eyes!

Two weeks had passed since Jane, the self-made celibate, had ejected the transitory husband of her bosom from the "bed and board" to which, under colored custom, if not under State law, he was supposed to be entitled. Esau wandered about, following his usual vagrant occupations, but vaguely conscious of his rather indefinite status as a husband—responsibilities there were none. Jane, to whom the marriage had brought wifehood—in the abstract, and very real things in the dotted-swiss and the white stockings of her bridal outfit—being withal as free and untrammeled in her property and her person as she had been before the episode, felt herself the gainer, and, to do her justice, regarded Esau rather as a slaughtered innocent. In respect of one small matter, however, Esau, too, had gained something. During his tentative courtship, or rather while, without his knowledge, Jane had had him under consideration, he chopped wood and did other chores for her without specific contract for compensation, for Jane was then an unrelated and unconnected female of the species, and he willingly performed these gallantries for her; but once married, even though she had so speedily and uncere-

moniously divorced, or put him away, she was yet his
woman—in thought at least, his chattel—and, harking
back to his African ancestry, he bethought him that
women were but hewers of wood and drawers of water,
the domestic slaves of the lordly males, and, before
laying hand to axe or stooping to pick up chips or
driftwood, he never failed to bargain and chaffer with
the cook for what she should pay him—at the expense
of the lady of the house.

"Esau, uh wish you please kin pick up some chip'
fuh me fuh staa't me fiah."

"Wuh you gwi' gimme?"

"Wuffuh me haffuh pay you fuh chop wood, Esau?"

"Enty uh done marri'd you fuh wife? Wuffuh man
haffuh chop wood fuh 'e own wife?"

"Uh marri'd you, fuh true, Esau, but enty uh done
run you off, en' now you stan' same lukkuh all dem
todduh man wuh uh nebbuh bin hab fuh husbun'?"

Esau scratched his head, the point being rather fine
for his comprehension, but he grunted stubbornly,
nevertheless.

"Man hab wife fuh cook 'e bittle fuhr'um, enty?
Hukkuh ooman kin cook bittle bidout 'e chop wood,
eeduhso pick up chip' fuh mek fiah? No, ma'am!
Wuh you gwine gimme fuh eat ef uh chop wood fuh
you?" Therefore, whenever Esau chopped wood, the
hotel kitchen paid the fee.

September burned and passed away. October came.
Among the brown and purple trunks of the pines, the
red-bronze foliage of blackgum and sourwood glowed
like dull fires. Tripods rose above the breakers, and,
from the vantage of their elevated tops, the Islanders
fished with rod and reel for the beautiful channel bass

which came up with the rising tide. The long rollers crashed upon the strand and broke into lace-like spray that the sea-wind tossed into a thousand miniature rainbows. The plaintive cry of the sea-birds, the whisper of the wild-oats as their ripening seed panicles rustled in the wind, and the sharp tang in the air, brought to the spirit the poignant sadness of autumn—"Falling Leaf and Fading Tree," and Tosti's haunting melody.

On a certain night, Jane permitted Esau's escort to a cottage two miles up the beach, whither she had undertaken an errand for her employer. The night was dark and overcast, and the air was heavy with a promise of coming rain. A fitful breeze picked up the loose sand above highwater mark into little whorls, sent them dancing about the upper beach, and set the clumps of wild-oats on the dunes above to shivering weirdly. The tide was at the flood, and the long dun rollers boomed sullenly on the beach and sucked at the sands as though loath to leave them.

As she got farther away from the comforting lights of the hotel and adventured into the creepy darkness that lay before her, Jane shuddered, and lifted the shawl from her shoulders over her bandanna-topped head as though to shut out from her apprehensive ears all fearsome sounds. Esau shuffled along beside her, but he, too, was uncomfortable, for he was a timid negro, and even the boldest are none too brave at night.

A sudden gust of wind lifted the foam cap from a breaking wave, blew it in their faces and whistled eerily through the wild-oats. A ghost crab sprang up at their very feet and scurried away, affrighted. Jane clutched Esau's arm. *"Great Gawd!"* she groaned, *"duh plat-eye!* Uh shum! uh shum!"

"Weh-weh 'e dey?" stammered her frightened but less imaginative escort.

Before she could point to the flying crab, another pallid, spider-like creature drifted across her path and followed the first. Jane was poised for flight, but Esau stood firm and steadied her nerves, and in a few moments they moved on again, but with wide eyes and hesitant steps. At last they had covered half the distance, and a mile away, beyond the dark, a spot of yellow light marked their goal, which they might have reached but for the raccoons' love for shell fish. At a low spot in the broad beach the tide had eaten out a narrow channel through which the waters rushed almost up to the sand-hills, bringing small fish and shrimp and clams far beyond the break of the rollers, and, at the entrance to this cut, facing the ocean, a big raccoon was fishing at the moment the negroes reached the tidal rivulet and paused to look for a crossing. Esau, with trousers rolled up to his knees, adventured first, and as Jane, "standing with reluctant feet," on the marge, called to him to ask the depth, she unhappily cast her eyes seaward just as the four-footed fisherman, startled by the voices behind him, wheeled, and turned his round, green eyes full upon them. As their sinister light shone fearsomely against the dark background of the waves, Jane shrieked in agony. *"Oh Jedus! de plat-eye! de plat-eye!"* And, turning tail, she fled along the back track, screaming at every jump. Esau's gallantry, and one look at the shining eyes, prompted him to follow Jane, which he did at top speed, while the wretched raccoon, frightened out of his supper by the havoc he had unwittingly wrought, lost no time in attaining sanctuary among the scrub beyond the sand-hills.

On sped Jane. Her screaming-wind gave out after the first hundred yards, and, save for her labored breathing, she ran silently, Esau, a black shadow, close behind. In an incredibly short time, Jane and her runner-up reached the hotel, speechless with exhaustion and fright. When she had recovered her breath, Jane hurried to her mistress. "Missis, ma'am, uh nebbuh tek de ansuh wuh you sen' to da' juntlemun todduh side de Ilun', 'cause uh nebbuh git dey, Missis; en', ef Jedus yeddy me, uh nebbuh fuh gone to da' place no mo' duh night-time! Missis, dem plat-eye t'ick 'puntop da' beach sukkuh fiddluh crab' t'ick een de maa'sh w'en tide low! Uh binnuh walk 'long Esau, en' one sumpn'nurruh come off de wabe' top, en' 'e float by me sukkuh cloud wuh hab uh sperrit een'um. Uh shet me yeye, en' 'e gone. Den de win' mek uh jump, en' 'e biggin fuh shake dem grass en' t'ing 'puntop de san'hill 'tell 'e mek me hair fuh rise! Same time uh see two w'ite sperrit run 'cross de paat'. Esau binnuh trimble 'tell uh graff'um by 'e sleebe fuh keep-'um f'um run'way, but none de t'ing nebbuh hab uh chance fuh t'row dem eye 'puntop me 'tell uh git to de place weh de tide bruk t'ru de beach. W'en uh git dey, Missis, Esau roll up 'e britchiz fuh cross. Me duh wait 'tell him git 'cross befo' uh staa't' fuh hice me 'coat fuh walk t'ru'um, en', ef me Jedus didn' tell me fuh t'row me yeye fuh look roun', uh nebbuh would'uh bin yuh, but w'en uh look, uh see da' t'ing' two eye' duh shine sukkuh lightship' eye' shine 'puntop'uh Rattlesnake shoal'! Missis, w'en uh fus' look

THE PLAT-EYE

'puntop'um uh t'ink 'e duh lightship fuh true, but
bumbye 'e shake 'e head en' uh know suh 'e duh plat-
eye, en' 'e duh try fuh t'row uh spell 'puntop me fuh
mek me fuh dead! Uh yent hab time fuh kneel down,
but uh staa't fuh pray een me h'aa't, en' uh baig Gawd,
ef da' plat-eye haffuh ketch nigguh, fuh mek'um fuh
ketch Esau en' lef' me, 'cause, Missis, eb'rybody know'
suh Esau ent wut! But seem lukkuh Gawd nebbuh
yeddy de pray', 'cause me mout' bin shet w'en uh
mek'um, 'cause uh yent wan' Esau fuh yeddy wuh uh
say, en' de plat-eye nebbuh tek 'e yeye off'uh my'own.
'E look en' 'e look, en' 'e yeye git mo' bigguh en' mo'
shiny, en' w'en uh see suh him duh look 'puntop'uh
me en' ent duh study 'bout Esau, Missis, *uh comin' fuh
home!* Missis, you see dog run, you see hawss run,
you see bu'd fly, en' you see pawpus jump een de ribbuh, but you nebbuh see none dem t'ing trabble lukkuh
me trabble w'en uh staa't fuh run! W'en me ten toe'
dig een de du't, 'e t'row de san' mo'nuh half uh acre
behin' me! De win' wuh uh mek t'row dem wil'oats
en' grass en' t'ing flat 'pun de groun', en' all de time uh
duh run uh yeddy Esau' foot duh beat drum behin'
me, en' w'en uh yeddy'um, uh tengkful, 'cause uh
know da' t'ing fuh ketch him fus' 'fo' 'e kin git me;
en', Missis, ef you ain' hab no 'jeckshun, ma'am, uh
gwine tek Esau fuh husbun' 'gen, 'cause, attuh tenight,
uh know suh me kin run fas' mo'nuh him, en' him will
be uh nyuseful t'ing fuh tek 'long w'en uh duh walk
duh paa't duh night-time, 'cause, ef plat-eye mek alltwo uh we fuh run, him *'bleege* fuh ketch Esau *fus'*,
en', alldo' da' nigguh ent wut, 'e hab shishuh slow foot,
Missis, uh kin mek'um fuh sabe me life!"

"OLD PICKETT"

Before the war, the low-country planters, migrating each summer to their mountain homes at Flat Rock, N. C., frequently bought horses and mules from the drovers as they passed along the Buncombe Road on their way South from the stock ranges of Kentucky and Tennessee. Sometimes beautiful ponies were brought from the Pink Beds, away back in the North Carolina mountains, others came from the nearer valleys of the French Broad, but most of the Seacoast planters supplied their needs from the Tennessee drovers as they moved down the main-traveled road.

From an old drover named Pickett, a mule was acquired to which the negroes gave the drover's name. Although a young mule, and of the opposite sex, she was christened "Old Pickett," and bore the name with distinction for nearly a quarter of a century. Long and low, and powerfully built, Old Pickett was a light bay in color, with the brown stripe down the back and the zebra legs which mule wranglers regard as evidence of toughness—and Old Pickett was tough.

Old Pickett came into the hands of the family late in October. A thin skin of ice had formed along the shores of the lakes. Flocks of blue-winged teal whistled through the air and splashed as they alighted on the clear waters. Chestnuts had fallen, and their green and brown burrs covered the ground under the far-spreading limbs of the big trees. Their little cousins, the chinquapins, had long been gathered and strung in necklaces, or roasted at the hearths of the glowing wood fires. The pheasant-shooting was nearly over, and Westly-Richards and Greener were cleaned and oiled and slipped into their buckskin covers, in readiness for the campaign against deer and duck and turkey in the low-country. With the first days of November, as the branches of the great oaks cracked under the weight of the roosting wild pigeons, and the sloping sides of old Pinnacle and all the lesser peaks burned with the flame-like foliage of the hickory and the ruby fires of the oaks, the family started down the mountain for Greenville, the first stop in the ten-day journey to the sea. Carriages for the ladies and the elders, saddle horses for the younger men, and comfortable covered wagons for the house servants, the cavalcade moved out, Old Pickett and her companions tethered behind the wagons to take their turn at the pole later on.

Arrived at the big plantation, Old Pickett became familiar with the plow, the cart and the Gullah negro, and for twelve years led an uneventful life, buckling to the tough "joint grass" of the uplands in summer, and bogging pastern deep in winter as the slim plowshare slid through the sticky soil of the ricefields and turned the stubble into long greasy-looking furrows. While a willing worker, Old Pickett took her time and always "gang'd her ain gait." She was nimble, too, with her heels, and the stable boys about the mule lot could always amuse themselves by throwing sticks or light clods of earth on Old Pickett's hindquarters to make her "kick up," when she came in to be unharnessed after her day's work, and she was always ready to oblige. Wearing a blind bridle, she could not see behind her, but she was strong for the uplift, and

191

whatever touched her in the rear had to go up, whether stick, or clod or stable boy!

Then the war! In the dawn of an April morning, came the sound of the big guns in Charleston harbor thirty miles away, and, a few months later, from another direction, rolled the thunder of yet heavier and more distant guns, bombarding Port Royal, and still Old Pickett plowed and carted, and otherwise plodded in the ways of peace, but not for long. The questing eye of the Confederate Government looked approvingly on Old Pickett's short legs, arched loins and well-sprung ribs, and, discerning an artillery mule, intimated a desire for ownership, but Old Pickett, compelling as she did the little negroes who walked behind and around her to become alert and watchful, was a plantation institution and could not be parted with permanently, but she was loaned to the Confederacy, and for a year or two hauled caissons and cannon and army wagons about the coast section wherever an attack was threatened by the invaders.

At last, the booming of cannon came nearer, an expedition having reached Willtown only seven miles away, and, as negroes from nearby plantations were "running away to the Yankees," a farm was leased in the far away land of Abbeville, and thither, for safekeeping, went a number of slaves under Zedekiah Johnson, a kindly and reliable overseer. With this venture went Old Pickett, and here, until the end of the war, she faithfully followed the curved and crooked furrows that ran around the terraced hills, and stubbed her unshod hoofs against the flinty stones thick sown about the ruddy soil. In the up-country, women sometimes plowed, and Old Pickett, blinkered and forward-look-

ing as she was forced to be, submitted to the indignity
of being "gee'd" and "haw'd" and chevied along by a
bare-footed, sun-bonneted female of the species.

Freedom came. The low-country negroes whom it
overtook in Abbeville, went their ways. The wagons
and mules, all save old Pickett, were sold for the pitiful greenbacks that the profiteering few who had them,
were willing to pay, and old Pickett came home. A
low-country freedman, wishing to return to his habitat, kindly consented to ride her the two hundred
miles, cannily exchanging his fore-knowledge of the
road for the use of her four legs. And what a home-
coming! The "big house" at the head of the wide
live-oak avenue lay in ruins, sentineled by the tall,
charred trunks of "Sherman's laurels," the two great
magnolias that sometime stood in their glossy green
liveries overhanging the hospitable hearths that once
glowed within. Wildcats lurked in the briar thickets
now upsprung from the fertile soil where once stood
the great stables. The plantation quarters, whose
streets formerly resounded with jest and laughter, at
the touch of the vandal's torch had flared into flame
and vanished, and among their ashes Jimpson weed
and other rank growths struggled.

In a rough stable, hastily improvised of blackgum
logs, Old Pickett was introduced to strange, young
Western mules, new to negro ways, but, from the time
of her home-coming, she seemed to grow resentful
toward all the world. While still performing her
tasks faithfully, she would not be hurried, and no
freedman was ever able to urge her into a trot, so, by
example, if not by precept, the younger mules asso-
ciated with her gradually acquired somewhat of trick-

iness and of truculence. Old Pickett still respected the
former slave-holding planters, and under one of these
(she was a good saddle animal) she would still conde-
scend to canter, but the small white boy of ten or
eleven years, and the negroes of all ages, she held in
utter contempt. Saddles and bridles were scarce after
the war, and spurs were rare. "The Captain" had a
single ante-bellum spur with which he urged recalcitrant horse or mule to such bursts of speed as a grass
diet would warrant. When rallied by his hunting companions on his lack of the twin spur, he shrewdly
observed that if he could make one side of his steed
travel fast enough to suit him, the other could always
be induced to go along, too. As this precious tool was
never loaned, the small boy who aspired to equestrian
exercise was forced to kick his steed in the ribs with
his bare heel, to which was sometimes tied, with a
piece of hickory bark, a forked stick shaped like a
wishbone, usually an effective goad with which to
tickle the equine flank, but Old Pickett was unrespon-
sive. She was, in a manner of speaking, on all-fours
with St. Paul. "None of these things move me," she
thought—and they didn't. The ambitious boy who expressed a willingness to adventure a trip to the railway
station, two miles away, for the mail, only for the
chance to ride, was sometimes offered Old Pickett, just
to chill his ardor. If he accepted the mount, he was
given a plow bridle, a folded crocus bag upon which
to sit, and was allotted a few hours in which to make
the trip. A stout switch was permitted him, which he
carried in his right-hand for style, rather than for any
impression he hoped to make on Old Pickett's tough
hide. Fortunately, the kindly amenities of war had

left the great avenue without a gate, or he could not
have passed, as no amount of urging could have
brought Old Pickett within arm's length of the latch,
so the way was clear to the old King's Highway. The
boy had plenty of time to admire the scenery as Old
Pickett walked sedately along between the willow-
fringed canals that flanked the approach to the "Two
Bridges." In the summer, water snakes dropped
quietly into their element from the overhanging
branches upon which they had been sunning themselves, terrapins slid from their floating logs, and now
and then a small alligator sank slowly downward,
leaving only his eyes above the water. Just beyond,
where the boughs of a grove of Spanish oaks stretched
above the road, squirrels sometimes played, alighting
among the smaller branches with a soft "swish" as
they sprang from tree to tree. Then, on to Jupiter
Hill, or "Town Hill," as the negroes called it, because
it lay in the direction of Charleston. Here, with a
clay hole on one side and a Colonial milestone on the
other—"31 M. to C Town" cut in its brown sandstone
face—the roads forked, the right-hand leading to the
Village, the left to the station. Although Old Pickett's
way always led to the station, she never failed to sub-
mit the selection of the road to argument, and invariably leaned to the right. Whether the memory of the
brave, hopeful, early days of the Confederacy, when
she had drawn artillery or army wagons along this
road, urged her to tread again the once familiar paths,
or whether she sought only to match her will and her
wits against the boy's, one may not know, but, as far
as the boy was concerned, the discipline was whole-
some, for loss of temper availed nothing against Old

Pickett. Her response to an application of the switch was to sidle up to the nearest tree or sapling, against which she would rub her rider's bare legs, so she was seldom switched. Sometimes the boy would sit on her back ten or fifteen minutes without moving, while she drowsed and dreamed of the past, and then, when, perhaps, she had forgotten the dispute between them, he would get her started in the way she should go. At other times, however, when she could not be wheedled out of the Village road, her rider let her have her way, and, after going two or three hundred yards, would slowly turn her head into the pineland and, gradually sweeping around in a wide semi-circle to the left, would reenter the road to the station a quarter of a mile beyond. Arrived at his destination, the boy would be fortunate to find some idle negro around who would bring out the mail to him, for, once dismounted, he could not remount without assistance, Old Pickett invariably backing her ears, baring her teeth, and altogether turning toward him "an unforgiving eye and a damned disinheriting countenance." To grown-ups Old Pickett was dangerous only at the rear, but to a dismounted boy she was loaded at both ends and—a revolver at that—she was so pivoted that head and tail could swap places with surprising facility. Old Pickett's tracks on her way home, however, were the prints of peace. Like so many of the human race, she knew the way to the trough, and thither she was willing to be guided.

On Sundays, Old Pickett was turned into the big pasture with the other mules, for rest and recreation, but, while her companions galloped or trotted and played, she kept away from them, grazing alone until satisfied, when, withdrawing to a far corner of the field, and resting her head upon the rider of the rail fence, she would gaze into space with restrospective eyes. Sometimes the Sunday outings would be in cornfields after harvest, where the slovenly freedmen usually left bunches of rank-growing sheep burrs, having a strong affinity for the manes and tails of horses and mules. Of these, Old Pickett acquired her share. The negro who plowed her extracted without difficulty those which lodged in her mane, but the taking of them out of her tail was an event in stableyard circles. Strongly tethered in her stall with a short halter, a stout bar was run into grooves behind her, so hampering her hindquarters that she could not extend herself. Thus helpless, she was ignominiously despoiled of the burrs that clung to her tail, even the small black boys participating in the spoliation, of which they did not fail to brag later to their companions at the quarters.

"You see dis sheep buhr, enty? Uh tek'um out'uh Ole Pickett' tail," said one, proudly pulling a burr out of the wool about his ears.

"No, you nebbuh! You duh Gawd fuh projick 'long Old Pickett' tail? 'E yent come out'um!"

" 'E yiz, now!"

" 'E yent!"

" 'E yiz!"

" 'E yent!" and then they fought.

Besides the burrs acquired by her mane and tail, Old Pickett sometimes got them in her ears, and then a circus act was necessary to get the bridle over her head in the morning.

One summer afternoon, crook-legged, yellow Sabey

came up to the house to borrow a mule with which to
drag from a distant backwater a large alligator he had
just killed, offering to recompense the favor by bringing a portion of the creature's oily flesh to be cooked
for the always hungry hounds. As all the other farm
animals were busy, Sabey was told that he might have
Old Pickett, who grazed alone in a distant pasture.
Not knowing Old Pickett intimately, the poor darkey
scraped his foot gratefully, and taking a bridle from
the rack, an ear of corn from the crib and a bundle of
fodder from the stack, he set out as gaily and as full
of faith as the small boy who, receiving from an elder
his first handful of "fresh salt," goes forth in quest of
the elusive robin's tail. Arrived at the pasture, Sabey
shambled toward Old Pickett, holding the ear of corn
and the blades coaxingly before him. The bridle was
hidden from sight at his back, tied to a hickory bark
suspender. As Sabey approached, though he looked
like no Greek that ever walked, or fought, or ran, Old
Pickett, appraising the provender as camouflage and
fearing even the Gullah bearing gifts, raised her head
and looked at him suspiciously, but, as Sabey slowed
down his pace and called "coab, coab, coab" softly and
appealingly, she let him come up to her and conde-
scended to nibble at the outstretched handful of blades.
The negro's favorite method of catching a loose mule
is to seize her firmly by the ear, and to this Old
Pickett, without an earful of sheep burrs, might have
submitted, but, as Sabey grabbed, the sharp burrs were
pressed so painfully into the inner lining of her ear,
that she wheeled as quick as a flash and, lashing out
with heels that had lost none of their youthful vigor,
would have lifted Sabey into the air had he not with

quick presence of mind thrown himself flat on the
ground, so that she kicked over him. When the immediate danger had passed, Sabey rose to his feet and
followed her about the pasture for two hours, in the
vain effort to coax her again within reach, or to drive
her into a fence corner, where he might, by getting a
rail behind her, so pen her up that the bridle could be
slipped over her head without danger. But Old
Pickett could neither be led nor driven, and, just as the
sun was setting, Sabey returned alone to the house.

"Mas' Rafe, uh bin ketch cootuh een me time, uh bin
ketch alligettuh, but uh yent fuh ketch no t'unduh en'
no lightnin', en' da' t'ing oonuh call Ole Pickett, him
duh t'unduh en' lightnin' *alltwo one time!* Uh gone
een de pastuh en' alltwo me han' full'up wid bittle fuh
da' mule fuh eat. Uh hab uh kin' feelin' een me h'aa't
fuh da' mule 'tell uh fin'um out, but now, uh nebbuh
fuh trus'um 'gen no mo'! Mas' Rafe, da' mule 'ceitful
ez uh 'ooman! 'E nyam de bittle out me han', en' w'en
uh graff 'e yez fuh ketch'um, please Gawd, 'e head en'
'e yez gone, en' me han' duh graff 'e two hin' foot!
Uh nebbuh see shishuh swif' hin' foot lukkuh da' mule
got. Ef me Jedus didn' bin tell me fuh fall flat 'puntop me belly, sukkuh alligettuh, uh would'uh dead;
but w'en uh do dat, een Gawd' mussy, de mule kick
obuh me, en' de du't en' t'ing wuh 'e kick up out de
pastuh, gone 'way up een de ellyment, en' w'en 'e fall
'puntop me 'e kibbuh me up same lukkuh dem t'row
du't 'puntop'uh man een 'e grabe! Mas' Rafe, uh
tengkful fuh you fuh len' me da' mule fuh ride, but
'fo' uh try fuh ketch'um 'gen, uh redduh walk on me
han' en' me foot frum yuh *spang* Caw Caw Swamp!"

Old Pickett had now passed her twenty-fifth year,

and day by day became sadder and wiser. She accepted
her daily tasks with resignation, but not with enthusiasm. The sockets above her weary eyes grew deeper,
and white hairs thickened among the tawny pelage
about her brow. Her ears, once so erect and responsive
to all the sounds of the world about her, now flopped
dejectedly like an unstarched "cracker" sunbonnet.
Her lips, as pendulous as those of the bull moose that
once tried to bite the Faunal Naturalist, hung lower
and lower, and the hour drew near when she must
shuffle off the mortal harness she had worn so long.
Her eyes had looked upon smiling Peace, upon grim
War, and—under Reconstruction, the once proud planters on foot and their quondam slaves on horseback—
it was time to go. Turned out in the pasture to spend
her last days in idleness, she walked listlessly about,
cropping here and there a bunch of tender grass,
while she waited for the summons. When it came, and
she lay down to rise no more, a black spot, slowly circling in the sky, stooped, and, on a lower level, sailed
again in narrowing circles. The keen eyes of other
questing vultures, miles away, watched the drop, and
followed. From the four corners of the heavens they
came, and, alighting on rail fence and blasted pine, or
hovering low on shadowy wings, they watched and
waited, until at last Old Pickett's glazing eyes told
them that her heart and her heels were stilled forever.

A month or two later in the Autumn, when the family returned to the plantation from the pineland village, the boy indignantly reproached the negroes for
not having given Old Pickett decent sepulture, and
two of them were induced to gather up her whitened
bones and bury them in a shallow grave at the edge of

the ante-bellum "horse burying ground," where the old family horses rested under the live-oaks. The negroes could not understand the boy's emotion as the clods fell on the bones of the faithful old mule. "Eh, eh, buckruh boy too commikil. Him duh cry 'cause mule dead!" They did not know that the passing of Old Pickett severed a link with the golden past, and that into her grave went something of The Lost Cause!

THE LOST BUCK

An hour after sunrise, hunters and pack assembled at the appointed rendezvous, a centrally situated plantation. There was the usual exchange of pleasant badinage as to the relative speed, stamina and other qualities of the different hounds, who, now united in an imposing pack of twenty, combined almost every type known to the deer hunter, and each had its admirers. The older men preferred the native low-country stock, a blend, perhaps, of the blood of fox hound and beagle, bred for a hundred years or more from dogs brought from England long, long ago. These were fine, high-bred looking animals, mostly "blue speckled," flecked with patches of black and fawn, whose twisted ears, soft as velvet, were long enough to tie under their wearers' throats—very aristocrats of the dog world, from their long muzzles to the tips of their slender "rat" tails, not very fast, perhaps, but with noses so "cold" that they could follow a deer trail more than twenty-four hours old. Then, too, their cry! "Rolling tongues," all of them, sweet and sonorous, whose blending of deep and high-pitched tones sent the blood tingling through the veins. The hard-riding youngsters, however, preferred the recently imported "English" dogs—thick-set, powerful creatures, white, with great patches of black and tan, broad-eared and "feather-tailed." Their noses were not cold, nor was the music of their yelping "chopped" tongues inspiring, but they had great speed, and their feet were so hard that they could be run day after day without becoming footsore. Here and there, a somber spot in

the pack, was a black and tan and—a touch of flame—
a big "red-bone" of a western North Carolina strain, a
rangy fellow, bred to speed and endurance in a rough,
red-fox country. So each type and each individual
had special qualities and special advocates, and all
were gathered—Countess, Echo, Music, Harper, Lead,
Luck, Modoc, Rowser, Blueman, the panther-like
Huntress, and many younger dogs—into a pack whose
all-round efficiency could not have been matched
between Ashley River and the tawny waters of the
Savannah!

At last the horns were sounded, and horsemen and
hounds passed up the Cypress road. Soon after crossing the two bridges a mile or so away, a short consul-
tation was had, and the "Elliott Big Drive" was
decided upon. The elder huntsmen directed the
standers to their positions and, after allowing sufficient
time for those who had been assigned the more distant
passes to reach their stands, the two expert and daring
riders who had been designated as the "drivers" put
in the eager pack and they spread fanlike among the
myrtles.

The old buck, whose trophies were the special object
of this day's hunt, had long baffled the Nimrods of the
neighborhood. Unusually large and with a magnificent head of "basket" horns, his resourcefulness had
always enabled him to escape his pursuers. He varied
his tactics as occasion required. In the early fall and
winter, while lying with does and yearlings in the
myrtles, or on the sunny side of some broomgrass field,
he would cunningly keep his place upon the approach
of hounds and hunters, allowing his companions to
spring up and lead the cry off on a long run for the
river. Then, when the danger was over, he would

sneak away and take sanctuary in some distant thicket. Later on, in February and March, when the bucks, having dropped their horns, herded together like timid sheep, he pursued the same course, allowing the younger and less experienced to "jump" at the approach of the pack and lead it away while he remained in safety. In his bachelor days, however, he changed his methods, and, at the first cry of a distant dog opening upon the trail, the wary buck would "sneak," and, by the time the pack reached his erstwhile bed, they found only the outline of his burly body in the petticoat grass where he had made his luxurious couch, while the old fellow would be perhaps six or seven miles away in the Ti Ti across the Edisto, or in some remote and inaccessible fastness beyond the Toogoodoo. In summer, when his great antlers in the "velvet" were tender and sensitive to the slightest touch of twig or foliage, he avoided thickets and tangled places, skirting the ridges that rose like shoulders on either side of the narrow bays that intersected the great forests of long-leaf pine.

But on this crisp November day, the woods were clean and clear, with no tangle of summer foliage, and the big buck, now carrying iron-hard horns, was as free to run through swamp or thicket as on the higher knolls and ridges, and, cunning and deceitful, he changed his tactics from chase to chase, and kept his pursuers guessing as to whether he would "jump" or "sneak," whether his course would be east, south or west. Northward he never ran, for thither lay the railway and the flat woods, with no rivers beyond whose waters lay sanctuary.

One of the standers, well-mounted, took up a distant pass at Elliott's Wells, the site of a settlement abandoned many generations ago. Concealing his horse in a thicket at the rear of the stand, he returned to the knoll, stood in front of a great pine, a giant among its lofty fellows, and listened for the cry of the pack. But listening was difficult and no cry came to his ears. The wind was high, and, singing among the pine tops like æolian harps, rose and swelled and softened and died away, now whispering of the wold with its peaceful sheep, and quiet meadows where cattle grazed, now thundering of stormswept mountain tops and the break of ocean surges on rockbound coasts, and again softened to the lap of sluggish wavelets on the shining shores of placid bays, and sighing told of those that grieved, and shrieked with the anguish of those that suffered, and softened again with the laughter of little children, and told the myriad stories and waked the thousand memories that the weird and mysterious songs of the wind among the pines bring to those whose hearts are attuned to nature. More than once the stander stood at attention, thinking he heard the cry of a distant hound, but, with a lull in the wind, the aural will-o'-the-wisp was gone, so misleading are the wind-sounds to even the trained ear. An hour passed. Two hours—but only the wind was heard, no bay of dog, no blast of horn betraying the presence of hunter or hound anywhere in the great expanse of forest.

Not far away was an old graveyard, one of the Colonial villages of the dead occasionally found in the low-country forests. The lettering on the marble slabs that covered the eternal sleepers revealed them as members of important families, many of them children who died of fever during the summer months before the days of quinine, deep wells and wire screens.

THE BLACK BORDER

The stander, while listening for the cry of the pack, read the lichen-covered inscriptions on the tombs and mused like Gray and Omar. With a whimsical smile, he looked at the towering crown of a great water-oak deep-rooted in the mould of a stout-hearted 17th century squire—a "five-bottle man" perhaps, and marveled at the alchemy of nature that could, from Madeira, Port and old Jamaica Rum, resolve a dew to nourish a Water Oak! Then, with ineffable sadness, he read the brief life-stories of God's little children, "Mary," "Anne," "William," "beloved daughter," "beloved son" "of —— and —— his wife," "died August 171—," "died September 172—." A cherub deep-carved in the marble, the line "Suffer little children to come unto Me"—no more! Seven, eight generations of men and women had lived their lives and passed since these little children were taken home 200 years ago! Yet, how near the tragedy seemed! The father returning from field or forest to find the mother in agony over the stricken child, no doctor, no ice, no effective medicines. The brilliant eyes, the burning cheeks, delirium, the end. The little mound in the woodland, wet with a mother's tears, the graver's chisel in the marble—and that was all. So men and women lived, and little children died—two hundred years ago!

At the end of the fourth hour of waiting, the stander, hearing only the wind-harps among the pine-tops, and realizing that, either the pack had jumped and been led by the chase out of the drive—a cunning old buck sometimes running contrary to all precedent—or that, striking no trail, the drivers had "blown out" of the Big Drive and called the hunt together for exploitation elsewhere, mounted his

206

THE LOST BUCK

horse and rode due west through the woods for the
Willtown road, which, running north and south, and
nearly parallel with the Edisto and its tributary
Penny Creek, would be crossed by any deer making
for the river. Just as he reached the road, he accosted
a negro walking toward Parker's Ferry X-Roads, and
asked if he had heard horns or hounds.

"Maussuh, uh binnuh stan' een Willtown road close
to Mas' Edwu'd Baa'nwell' Clifton place, w'en uh
yeddy de dog duh comin' fuh me, en' uh stop fuh
liss'n. Bimeby, uh see de mukkle duh shake, en', fus'
t'ing uh know, de deer jump out de t'icket en' light
een de big road en' look 'puntop me! 'E foot fall saaf'-
ly 'pun de groun' same lukkuh cat duh sneak 'puntop'uh bu'd. 'E tu'n 'e head en' 'e look 'puntop me
lukkuh somebody, 'cep'n' suh 'e yeye big lukkuh hawn
owl' eye. 'E look at me so positubble, uh t'ink mus'be
'e duh haant, en' uh dat 'f'aid 'e gwine t'row one spell
'puntop me, uh tu'n 'way me head. W'en uh look roun'
'gen, 'e gone! Yuh come de dog'! Uh nebbuh see summuch dog'! Dem full' de road, en' dem woice' roll 'tell
you nebbuh yeddy shishuh music. Dem cross' de road,
en' dem gone! Attuh leetle w'ile, uh yeddy'um duh gib
dem toung een de gyaa'd'n uh ole Maussuh' Clifton
house wuh dem Nyankee bu'n down eenjurin' uh de
wah. De gyaa'd'n big ez uh cawnfiel', en' 'e full'uh
high rose bush duh climb up 'pun de tree, en' all
kind'uh briah en' t'icket dey dey. Uh yeddy de dog'
mek uh sukkle roun' de gyaa'd'n, den dem stop.
Bimeby, yuh come de ole buck duh run puhzackly 'pun
'e back track, en', w'en 'e git to de big road weh him
lef' me duh stan'up, uh t'awt at de fus' 'e bin gwine
jump 'puntop me, but 'e tu'n shaa'p roun' en' light
down de road gwine Paa'kuh' Ferry Cross-road'. 'E

207

run 'traight een de big road, en' uh' spec' 'e gone 'way
todduh side Allstun' Abenue befo' de dog' git back to
de big road on 'e trail. De dog' comin' so fas' uh git
out 'e way fuh l'em pass, en' dem so hasty, dem nebbuh 'top fuh smell weh de deer tu'n off down de road,
en' dem gone uh bilin' t'ru de mukkle t'icket on de back
track weh dem come f'um, en' dem run 'bout uh mile
befo' dem fin' out suh dem bin 'puntop de back track,
den dem tu'n roun' en' come back fuh weh uh binnuh
stan' up. One leetle blue speckle' toad bus' out de
pack en' tek de fresh trail weh de buck jump off de
back track, en' gone! Soon ez dem todduh dog' yeddy
him woice, dem lef' de ole trail en' bu'n de win' down
de big road on de fresh track. Da' duh de las' uh
shum, en' uh nebbuh yeddy'um no mo' attuh 'e done
gone."

Sure enough, the veteran Echo, the most intelligent
dog in the pack, was running wide when she reached
the road for the second time and detected the old
buck's maneuver. With a roar, the pack followed her
at top speed down the open road, but, by the time the
cry reached the Allston place on Penny Creek, the
buck, with two or three miles the start of them, had
run directly through the negro quarters, causing general consternation in the settlement, and had taken the
water at the landing. Instead of crossing, however, he
swam rapidly up stream and, aided by the flood tide,
was a mile away before the pursuing pack reached the
water's edge. True to their usual practice, they crossed
the creek and spread over the swamp on the other side
in search of the trail, but trail there was none. The
puzzled hounds ran up and down the bank for several
hundred yards, whimpering with disappointment, but,
for them that day, the buck was lost as completely as

though the brown waters had swallowed him up, and
one by one the disappointed dogs reluctantly recrossed
the stream, and, as there was no sound of horn to summon them, singly and in groups they made their way
to their respective homes.

Realizing that the buck had run far out of the drive,
and, by giving all the passes a wide berth had lost the
hunt, the sometime stander of Elliott's Wells followed
the spreading slot of the deer in the "big road" as far
as Allston's, and, riding up to the quarters, sought
information of hounds and quarry from an old negress
who was seated on the steps of her cabin, trying to
loosen, with a tough horn comb, the kinky wool of a
little black girl who sat on a lower step between her
knees.

"Mauma, have you seen anything of a deer or dogs?"

The old woman, true to her training, tried to rise to
drop a curtsy before replying, but the wide-eyed imp
of darkness between her knees sat stolidly on the hem
of her homespun skirt and prevented her rising.

"Git up, gal, ent you hab sense 'nuf fuh mek yo'
mannus w'en you see w'ite people? Uh bin agguhnize
'long all dem fowl' fedduh en' t'ing you hab een you
head, en' dem tanglety up 'tell uh cyan' git 'um out,
en' you hab no bidness fuh gone en' creep t'ru da' fowl-
h'us' winduh fuh git dem aig'. Git up en' gone!"

But long before she reached the end of her sentence,
the girl was up and gone, and, with a deep curtsy, the
old woman answered the hunter.

"Maussuh, 'bout two hour attuh middleday, dish'yuh
nigguhhouse yaa'd bin full'uh nigguh', 'cause duh Sattyday, en' all dese'yuh 'ooman duh wash dem clo'es.
All ub uh sudd'nt, uh yeddy'um holluh same lukkuh

roostuh holluh w'en 'e see hawk' shadduh 'puntop de
groun', en' eb'ry Gawd' nigguh, 'ooman en' chillun alltwo, drap eb'ryt'ing wuh dem got een dem han' en' run
fuh dem house. Uh look 'roun' fuh see wuh 'smattuh
mek'um fuh holluh, en', ef you b'leebe me, suh, one
deer duh comin' down de paat', big same lukkuh ole
Baa'ney, Mas' Rafe dem bull! 'E hawn big 'nuf fuh
hol' bushel tub, en', w'en 'e jump, 'e rise een de ellyment high mo'nuh dem house ebe'. W'en 'e look 'puntop me wid alltwo 'e yeye, uh 'f'aid suh de debble dey
een'um, en' uh drap 'pun me knee een de du't en' uh
pray! Bimeby uh look 'roun', en' uh yent see nutt'n'
but 'e tail. De pyo' tail dat big 'e kibbuhr'um, en' 'e
'pread out w'ite lukkuh buckruh' shu't buzzum duh
Sunday w'en 'e yent got on no weskit! 'E gone duh
crick, 'e jump een, en' nobody shum no mo'! All de
nigguh' come out dem house fuh look, en' attuh w'ile
dem yeddy de dog' duh comin', en' dem run back 'gen.
De beagle' tayre up de street 'long dem foot, en' dem
mek shishuh woice de fowl' fly up 'puntop de roof, en'
dem jis' leely w'ile come down. Tengky, Maussuh,
Gawd bless you, suh!—Come'yuh, gal! Yo' head
full'uh fedduh' 'tell 'e stan' same lukkuh frizzle' hen!
Come'yuh!"

Meanwhile, the big buck's sensitive ears told him
what had happened. He knew that the pack, at fault
and silent, a mile behind him, was out of the running
for that day, at least as far as he was concerned, and,
touching bottom on a little wampee-covered spit of
land that thrust itself into the creek, his dun and drip-
ping body rose from the waters as he leisurely walked
to shore, landing conveniently near a dense canebrake,
within whose safe seclusion he found a dry bed until

nightfall. With the rising of the moon soon thereafter, he slowly fed his way homeward through the forest, pausing, first near the edge of the Baring backwater, and then on every knoll where he could find a grove of the beautiful swamp white-oaks, for his favorite autumn food, the great over-cup acorns. At last, as the morning star blazed in the east and the far off roosters—long before Maude Adams won her spurs and her tail-feathers in Edmond Rostand's Chanticler—heralded the coming of the dawn, the old fellow returned to his bed among the myrtles in the Big Drive, and, full of acorns and the satisfaction of having again outwitted his pursuers, lay down to his well-earned rest, undisturbed by dreams of horn or hound.

JIM MOULTRIE'S DIVORCE

The tail of a cold, blustering February day. In the creeks and leads of the Jehossee marshes the ducks sought protection from the wind until flushed by the hunter. Since early morning he had successfully explored every promising hiding place in the great marsh, under the guidance of Jim Moultrie, a skilled negro hunter and paddler, who pushed the nose of his clumsy dugout canoe up every little run that looked like a likely shelter for the wary game. As the sun sank below the horizon, staining the sky a dull red, the hunter quitted the marshes, and the bow of the canoe was turned toward Willtown, five miles away. Crouching low in the stern, Jim paddled silently and strenuously against the current for an hour. Like birdshot "patterns" thrown against the red sky, flocks of belated blackbirds hurried to their roosts.

Gradually the shadowy mantle of the dusk shrouded marsh and headland and the shimmering waters that slid by the struggling canoe; then night fell and healed the blood-red wound in the West. The dugout crept along the shore where the current was less swift. Now and then a raccoon hunting in the marsh sprang away affrighted. The whistling wings of a swift-flying teal cut through the icy air. Far up the river, like low-hung stars, twinkled the watchfires of a great timber raft outward bound for the estuary of the North Edisto. From a distant plantation came the sweet lu-la-lu of a happy negro freed from work. The raft, borne upon the bosom of the strong ebb-tide, neared rapidly, and, around its fires built on earth-covered

212

platforms, the negro raftsmen talked and laughed as they cooked their supper, and the flames lighted the face and magnified the figure of the black steersman who stood by the great sweep oar with which, at the stern of the raft, he guided its course down stream.

For an hour Jim had silently bucked the tide, impelling the boat under the powerful strokes of his paddle, alternately left and right.

"What are you thinking of, Jim?"

"Study 'bout 'ooman, suh." (A short silence.)

" 'Ooman shishuh cuntrady t'ing, dem nebbuh know w'en dem well off. You kin feed dem, you kin pit clo'es 'puntop dem back, you kin pit shoe 'puntop dem foot, you kin pit hat 'puntop dem head, you kin pit money een dem han', en' still yet oonuh nebbuh know de 'ooman, nebbuh know w'en dem min' gwine sattify. Dem fuhrebbuh duh lookout fuh trubble. Ef dem ent meet trubble duh paat', dem gwine hunt fuhr'um duh 'ood. I dunkyuh howsoeb'uh fudduh de trubble dey, dem gwine *fin'um.* Ef dem cyan' see 'e track fuh trail'um, dem gwine pit dem nose een de du't en' try fuh smell'um, but dem gwine *fin'um!* I duh study 'pun dat wife I nyuse fuh hab, name Mary. Look how him done, w'en him hab no cajun! You yeddy 'bout me trubble, enty, suh? Lemme tell you. One Sat'd'y night I gone home frum de ribbuh. I tek two duck', bakin, flour en' sugar en' tea, den I pit fibe dolluh' een Mary' lap. Enty you know, suh, dat is big money fuh t'row een nigguh' lap? W'en I binnuh boy en' you t'row uh 'ooman uh fifty cent, 'e t'ink 'e rich, but I bin all dat week wid one cump'ny uh dese yuh rich Nyankee buckruh' dat Mr. FitzSimmun hab yuh fuh shoot, en' dem buckruh' t'row me fibe dolluh bill same lukkuh

213

dem bin dime'! W'en I t'row de money in de 'ooman'
lap, en' pit de todduh t'ing wuh I fetch 'pun de flo',
Mary nebbuh crack 'e teet'. I ax'um 'smattuh mek'um
stan' so? 'E mek ansuh, 'nutt'n'. Nex' day de 'ooman
keep on same fashi'n. 'E nebbuh crack 'e bre't'. I
quizzit'um 'gen. I ax'um 'smattuh 'long'um. Him say,
'nutt'n'. Den I say 'berry well den.' Monday mawnin'
I tek me gun, I call me dog en' den I talk to de
'ooman. I say, 'Mary, I gwine duh ribbuh, en' I gwine
come back Sat'd'y two week'. I dunno 'smattuh mek
you stan' so, but I know suh de debble dey een you.
No 'ooman 'puntop dis ribbuh hab mo' den you, no
'ooman got so much, but I yent able fuh lib dis way
'long no 'ooman wuh tie'up 'e mout', en', w'en I come
back las' Sat'd'y two week', I gwine 'tarrygate you one
mo' time, en' I gwine ax you 'smattuh mek you stan' so,
en' ef oonuh still een de same min' ez now, den me
nuh you paa't.'

"Well, suh, Sat'd'y two week', I gone back en' I say,
'well, Mary, I come, how 'bout'um, wuh you got fuh
say?' Him mek ansuh: 'Ent nutt'n' 'bout'um. Yent
got nutt'n' fuh say.' Den I tell'um 'berry well, den, I
gone my way, en' you tek you'n. Now, Mary, I yent no
Wanderbilt fuh gi' you fibe t'ousan' dolluh' allimunny fuh lib off, so you is free fuh lib 'cawd'n' to yo' own
min', en' I is free fuh do ez I please.' Den I tek me
gun, I call me dog, en' I *gone!*

"De nex' week, I bin comin' out de maa'sh on Mr.
Rab'nel' place, w'en I meet Mary. Him binnuh wait
fuh me. I say 'hello! dat duh you?' Him say: 'Jim,
I come fuh tell you dat all dem t'ing I bin yeddy 'bout
you, I fin' out dem is lie, en' I want you fuh come back
to me.' I say, 'enty I tell you dat de finull wu'd would
be talk w'en I come back fuh me ansuh Sat'd'y two

week', en' ent dat time done pass? You bidness fuh fin' out 'bout dat lie een dem twelbe day' time wuh I done gib you. 'E too late now.' En' I walk off en' lef'um!"

"Have you another wife, Jim?"

"I hab dat gal you see wid me dis mawnin' een Mr. FitzSimmun' yaa'd. *Him* ent wut'!"

"BUH ALLIGETTUH EN' BUH DEER"

One time, w'en nutt'n' cep' de bu'd en' de annimel
en' de Injun bin yuh, buh deer en' buh alligettuh ain'
bin fr'en', en' buh alligettuh blan does kill buh deer en'
nyam'um w'enebbuh 'e git uh chance, en' buh deer does
'f'aid fuh swim 'cross ribbuh, en' w'enebbuh 'e go down
to de ribbuh' aige fuh drink, 'e does cock 'e yez en'
squint 'e yeye fuh buh alligettuh befo' 'e pit 'e mout'
down fuh drink; but, bimeby, yuh come de buckruh, en'
bimeby 'gen, de buckruh fetch de nigguh, en' bimeby
'e fetch houn' dog, en' den de Injun gone, en' de buckruh' biggin fuh hunt buh deer wid dem English houn',
en' de dog' so swif' en' dem blan push buh deer so close,
de only chance 'e hab fuh git'way is fuh tek de watuh
'spite uh buh alligettuh, so, w'edduh de ribbuh dey
close uh fudduh, buh deer mek fuhr'um w'enebbuh de
dog jump'um.

Now, de fus' time de buckruh' run buh deer wid
houn', buh deer ain' 'quaintun' wid'um, en' 'e leddown
een 'e bed een one mukkle t'icket on de aige uh de
broom grass fiel' duh tek 'e res', 'tell de dog mos' git up
tuhr'um, den 'e fin' him ain' able fuh hide, en' 'e buss'
out de mukkle en' lean fuh de ribbuh fuh who las' de
longes'! Yuh come de ole buck, yuh come de English
houn'! Buh deer 'f'aid. 'E jump. 'E run. 'E git dey
fus'. Jis' ez 'e ketch de bluff fuh jump off een de ribbuh, buh alligettuh' two eye' rise out de watuh duh
wait fuhr'um! De alligettuh hongry. Bittle berry
sca'ceful. 'E belly pinch'um. Buh deer fat. 'E fat fuh
sowl. Buh deer dey een one hebby trouble. Alligettuh
dey befor'um, beagle' dey behin'um, en' dem toung duh

216

roll t'ru de swamp en' dem comin' *fas'*. Wuh buh deer gwi' do? 'E yeye dey 'pun de alligettuh, 'e yez dey 'pun de beagle'. 'E mek uh sudd'n twis' jis' befo' de dog' sight'um, en' bu'n de win' down de ribbuh bank 'bout seb'n acre f'um de bluff and tek de watuh 'cross weh buh alligettuh nebbuh shum.

Yuh come de beagle' uh bilin' fuh de bluff. Dem come so fas' 'pun buh deer track dem nebbuh stop, en' two't'ree gone obuh de bank en' drap een de watuh close buh alligettuh' snout. Buh alligettuh reason wid 'eself. "Wuh dis t'ing? I nebbuh see shishuh annimel befo', but, duh bittle!" en' 'e graff one de beagle' en' pull'um onduhneet' de water. Todduh dog' swim out en' tek dem foot een dem han' en' gone home.

Buh deer git'way dis time. 'E gone! W'en 'e ready fuh tu'n back 'cross de ribbuh, 'e walk easy to de bank duh skin 'e yeye fuh buh alligettuh, en' bimeby 'e shum 'tretch out 'pun one mud bank een de sunhot. 'E belly full'uh beagle. 'E sattify. 'E duh sleep. Buh deer sneak close to de ribbuh fuh tek a chance fuh git 'cross, but befo' him kin wet 'e foot, buh alligettuh shum, en' 'e slip off de bank fuh meet'um. Yuh de debble now! How buh deer kin git 'cross to 'e fambly? Him biggin fuh study, but befo' him kin crack 'e teet' fuh talk, buh alligettuh op'n de cumposhashun.

"Budduh," 'e tell buh deer, "dat t'ing wuh I done eat, wunnuh call'um beagle, berry good bittle. Me lub um berry well. 'E easy fuh ketch, en' 'e ent gots no hawn fuh 'cratch me t'roat. Me *done* fuh lub'um!"

"Ef you lub'um, mekso wunnuh don' ketch'um, en' lef' me en' my fambly 'lone?" buh deer ax'um. Buh alligettuh mek ansuh: "Me cyan' ketch de dog 'cep'n' wunnuh fetch'um t'ru de ribbuh, so leh we mek 'greement fuh las' long ez de ribbuh run. Wunnuh tek de ribbuh, me tek de beagle'. Me fuh you, en' you fuh me, en' alltwo fuh one'nurruh."

Dat w'ymekso ebbuh sence de' 'greement mek, w'en-ebbuh dog run'um, buh deer tek de ribbuh en' buh alli-gettuh lem'lone, en' w'en de beagle' come 'e ketch'um, but ef buh deer ebbuh come duh ribbuh bidout dog dey att'um, him haffuh tek 'e chance.

BUH HAWSS EN' BUH MULE

A FABLE

Buh Hawss' tail long sukkuh willuh switch,
Buh Mule' own stan' lukkuh t'istle.

One time Buh Hawss en' Buh Mule tu'n out duh
pastuh duh Sunday. Dem alltwo blonx to high buckruh. Buh Hawss binnuh dribe een buggy, en' Buh
Mule binnuh wu'k duh plow. Dem alltwo glad fuh git
out en' dem alltwo kick up dem foot en' play 'bout de
fiel'. Buh Hawss cantuh. 'E bow 'e neck sukkuh gob-
bluh duh strut, en' 'e tail heng sukkuh willuh switch.
Buh Mule trot. 'E 'tretch 'e neck out 'traight sukkuh
Muscoby duck duh fly. 'E step high en' 'e tail stan'
up sukkuh t'istle. Buh Mule tail oagly, fuh true, but
da' duh all de tail wuh 'e got en' 'e berry well sattify
'long um. Buh Hawss biggin fuh brag. "Look 'puntop oonuh tail," 'e say. "Mekso oonuh ent hab tail
lukkuh my'own?" 'e ax'um. "Oonuh yent kin switch
fly 'long'um 'cause 'e shabe. Shishuh no'count tail ent
wut'," 'e tell'um. "Me duh buckruh, you duh nigguh!"
Buh Mule biggin fuh shame. 'E yent sattify 'long 'e
tail no mo'. Buh Mule cyan' switch fly, fuh true, but
'e skin tough, en' fly don' bodduhr'um, but Buh Hawss
git'um so agguhnize' een 'e min' 'e fuhgit fuh tell'um
suh 'e yent hab cajun fuh switch fly 'long 'e tail, en' 'e
heng 'e head en' 'e tail alltwo, en' 'e lef' Buh Hawss
en' 'e gone off todduh side de fiel' en' 'e study. Bimeby,
'e look obuh de pastuh, en' todduh side de fench 'e see
one las'yeah cawnfiel' weh de nigguh lef' 'nuf sheep

219

buhr duh stan' 'long de cawnstalk. Buh Mule biggin
fuh laugh. 'E op'n 'e mout'. 'E blow 'e hawn. *"Aw-e-
Aw-e-Aw-e!"* Buh Hawss cantuh. 'E come close. 'E
ax'um 'smattuh mek 'e duh laugh. Buh Mule say 'e
laugh 'cause Buh Hawss ent smaa't 'nuf fuh jump de
fench en' run'um uh race t'ru de cawnfiel'. Buh hawss
tek'um up. 'E jump de fench. 'E behin' foot ketch
de top rail en' knock'um off. Buh Mule tumble t'ru.
Yuh dem come! Buh Hawss cantuh, Buh Mule trot,
up en' down de fiel' t'ru de sheep buhr. Buh Mule
tail shabe 'tell 'e slick. 'E switch'um roun' en' roun'
'mong de buhr but none nebbuh stick. Bimeby, Buh
Hawss' tail biggin fuh hebby. 'E ketch full'uh buhr.
Dem tanglety een 'e tail 'tell 'e stan' sukkuh timbuh
cyaa't rope. 'E duh drag. Eb'ry time 'e switch'um
roun' 'e hanch, de buhr sting'um. 'E say to 'eself, "wuh
dis t'ing? Me fuh lick me own self! Me fuh hab spuhr
een me own tail! De debble! Me dey een trubble, fuh
true!" 'E talk trute. 'E tail lick'um en' spuhr'um
alltwo one time.

Buh Mule pass'um. 'E look 'puntop Buh Hawss'
tail, en' 'e yent shame no mo'. "Tengk Gawd," 'e say,
"fuh shabe tail. Low tree stan' high win'!"

LISS "BIN EENSULT"

From Olar, that favored spot in a fruitful section of the State, where, under the guidance of a Carolina Burbank, the amorous Iron pea, loving the "Shinny" despite her freckles, wooed and won her to wilt-resistance, where quiet farmers are classical scholars and hermits are hospitable, comes a story of Liss, a character as noted in local colored circles for oddity as for ugliness. A white neighbor, who recently met her, noticing that she was swelling with wrath, and, seeking to get a rise out of her, asked:

"What's the fun today, Liss?"

"No fun een dis t'ing; I done bin eensult."

"Who has insulted you?"

"Mimy' yalluh gal Clara eensult me, suh. Dat gal en' 'e maamy mek crap fuh Cap'n Willie. I bin to Mimy' house, en' one bale uh cotton bin fuh haul town fuh sell. Clara tell 'e maamy, 'Ma, lemme go town wid dat bale, en' lemme git a spo'tin' suit out dat bale uh cotton?'

"Now, Mimy swell up bex, same lukkuh bullfrog. 'Spo't suit de debble!' 'e say. 'You binnuh do nutt'n' but spo't de Gawd' blessed yeah. You don't git a shimmy out dat bale uh cotton.'

"Den de gal mek ansuh en' say:

" 'Ma, ef you don't lemme git dat spo'tin' suit, I gwi' do eb'ry bad t'ing I know 'bout. I gwi' do bad right now.'

"Clara hab on one deseyuh newfanglety kinduh t'ing dem call *middle-blouse.* You know um, suh. 'E stan' same lukkuh man shu't, wid 'e shu't tail heng out,

221

excusin' 'e got one kind'uh shoe string tie onduhneet'
de gal' buzzum. *My Gawd, w'at a gal!* Alldo' t'ree
man dey een 'e ma' house, Clara staa't fuh tek off 'e
middle-blouse. I tell'um:

" 'Gal, ef you tek off dat middle-blouse een dis house
befo' dese mans, you will sho' hab sin.'

" 'Sin, *nutt'n'!* I gwi' strip nakit ez a jaybu'd befo'
'e fedduh' grow! I gwi' do bad!' W'en de gal say dis
wu'd, 'e ketch 'e middle-blouse by 'e shu't tail wid
alltwo 'e han' en' hice'um obuh 'e head! Befo' 'e kin
git'um off, all t'ree de man jump out de do', en' w'en I
look out een de yaa'd, I shum duh roll obuh en' obuh
een de du't same lukkuh hawss roll, en' duh buss' demself wid laugh. Now, w'en I see de gal' yalluh skin
biggin fuh shine lukkuh dese yuh yalluh-belly cootuh,
myself git eensult, en' I lef' 'e ma' house, 'cause I is a
lady, suh, en' dat is a *ondeestunt gal!*"

THE RETORT COURTEOUS

Her name was Patty. She was as black as a tar baby, as oleaginous as a cotton oil mill and—like Captain Merrimac in Olivette—as broad in the beam and as square in the rig as a Dutch brig, when she appeared before a tidewater trial justice as the prosecuting witness *in re* the State of South Carolina *vs.* Cudjo Manigo, charged with malicious mischief.

Taking the stand, she put her head on one side and complacently smiled until the corners of her mouth—evidently designed for the wholesale trade—approached dangerously near her ears. Twisting his amber imperial, his Honor began:

Q. "What's your full name?"

A. "Mis' Wineglass, suh."

Q. "Where's your residence?"

A. " 'E yent come teday, suh."

Q. "I mean where do you live?"

A. "Yaas, suh. I lib on Mass Kit FitzSimmun' plantesshun, w'ich'n 'e jis' done buy'um de Chuesday een week befo' las' mek six munt' done gone, en' I glad 'e buy'um, too, bekasew'y jis' ez soon ez 'e buy'um 'e run dat las' husbun' w'ich I marry een Augus' off de place, w'ich'n me en' dat nigguh nebbuh could 'gree, 'cause, een de fus' place, 'e too lub fuh lick 'e lady; en', een de two place, 'e too oncommun lazy en' no'count, en', een de t'ree place, 'e fus' wife en' me nebbuh could git 'long, en', een de fo' place, him is a class-leaduh een de Baptis' chu'ch, en' eb'rybody know berry well dat wehreas class-leaduh mek a berry po' kind'uh husbun' fuh 'e own wife, en'—"

His Honor—"That will do. What is your charge against the defendant?"

A. "Bredduh Cudjo, suh?"

Q. "Yes. What's your charge?"

A. "I nebbuh chaa'g'um nutt'n', suh."

Q. "Well, what did Cudjo do?"

A. "B'Cudjo is a berry nomannus nigguh, suh. Him is de class-leaduh een my chu'ch, en w'en eeduhso de preachuh on de sukkus, elsehow de locus preechuh, onable to filfill de pulpit, den B'Cudjo does hol' saa'bis een de chu'ch, en' w'en B'Cudjo done resplain de Lawd' wu'd, 'e berry lub fuh talk sweetmout' talk to all 'e freemale sistuh een de chu'ch, en' eb'ry time 'e meet me een de road 'e baig me fuh kiss'um, en' I yent wantuh kiss no shishuh oagly, twis'mout' nigguh lukkuh B'Cudjo, en' I tell'um so, en' den 'e does cuss at me berry nomannusubble, en' de las' time I meet'um een de paat', 'e quizzit me berry rappit, en' I tell'um 'go'way, B'Cudjo, bekasew'y I ent wantuh yeddy no shishuh cumposhashun', en' yet B'Cudjo keep on peruse 'long de paat', en' 'e keep on ax'me shish squeschun, en' fus' t'ing I know 'e cuss me a berry bad cuss."

Q. "What did he curse you?"

A. " 'E tell me dat my mout' does wide same lukkuh Ashley ribbuh!"

Q. "What else?"

A. "Dat all 'e had chance fuh tell me, 'cause I tell'um, 'Haa'k'ee at me good fashi'n, B'Cudjo, 'fo' de Lawd, ef my mout' *is* stan' lukkuh Ashley ribbuh, *you cyan' paddle yo' boat cross'um*', en' den 'e git bex en' knock me wid 'e hoe handle, en' dat w'yso I fetch'um yuh."

At this stage of the proceedings, the Toogoodoo trial justice adjourned court to measure the Ashley River.

THE CAT WAS CRAZY

On a recent Sunday afternoon, an itinerant evangelist with a throat of brass was stationed at the corner of Richardson and Plain Streets in Columbia, singing hymns in the laudable endeavor to save a soul or two.

From an upper window of the Grand Central Hotel a fair face looked out to the westward, while a child tapped upon the pane.

At a club window opposite, a young bachelor banker sipped his Sunday cocktail while he eyed critically the passers-by on their way from church. How many of their financial secrets did he hold in his keeping! How many of their obligations were locked in his vaults! The note of that jauntily dressed young man, who held his head so high as he spurned the dust from his patent leathers, had gone to protest but yesterday. The extravagance of yonder portly lady, who, with silken sails spread to the breeze, towed after her, as a tug tows a coal barge, one of the fashionable fourteen-inch trains, scattering in her wake banana peel, cigar butts and other miscellaneous wreckage of the street, had cost her husband another mortgage.

The banker was of a thrifty mind, and he wondered why, in the name of Saint Peter—why, in the name of the patron saints of cleanliness and all the gods of common-sense, fashion should exact of its devotees the performance of the unæsthetic work of the street-sweeper and the scavenger! Thinking, with a sigh, that shorter skirts might have permitted longer bank accounts, he turned his eyes to the wooded hills of Lexington above which hung the setting sun, a great

disk of gold. With his mental coupon shears, the
speculative financier quickly clipped the "orb of day"
into gold treasury certificates, put them out at interest—compounded, of course—and, with one more
Vermouth cocktail to aid his imaginative computation,
he was, in a twinkling, possessed of the wealth of
Monte Cristo. And now the world and all beyond was
his! On fancy's wings he sailed away, away to
Arcadie. Instead of herding bulls and bears, a shepherd now was he. Like Strephon, he played upon a
pipe, while at his feet the lambkins played, or hud-
dled together in the sunshine "so warm and sleepy and
white."

Garlanded with roses, the shepherdess led him
through leafy bowers into an open glade, where, among
the buttercups and daisies, he fell asleep, and dreamed.
Ay, Dios! How few of us realize, until all too late,
that the simplest pleasures are the best, that in home
and friends we may make for ourselves happiness far
above that which must be sought beyond our circle.
How few of us realize that there is more exhilaration
in a five-mile spin than in a quart of champagne, that
'tis more blessed to swish the briefest cotton skirt in
Arcadie—if in Arcadie we belong—than to drag a
satin train in a Paris salon!

But the banker dreamed, and the strains of the
Santiago waltz were in his ears, and the houris of
Mahomet glided along before him wreathed in—smiles.
One, fairer than the rest, beckoned, and he followed
on and on. Out into the darkness he followed the
golden gleam of her beautiful bi-carbonated hair, followed through tangled forest and treacherous fen—
alas! the will-o'-the-wisp!

With a start, he awoke from his reverie to find—like

the market girl who stumbled and smashed the basket of eggs from which she had hatched out all her hopes—that his gold was gone, for suddenly the sharp edge of the horizon was drawn like a scimiter across the throat of the sinking sun, and in an instant the western sky, away up to the zenith, was stained as with his life blood!

With a shudder, as though chilled from sitting in the overdraft of his imagination, the banker took his hat and went out into the street, where the evangelist, having closed his song service, was exhorting the little group clustered around him.

Suddenly, on the edge of the gathering, an old negro, bent with age and with a face furrowed by grief, appeared. He led by the hand a little black girl about ten years old. Her eyes were round with fright, and about her thin legs a ragged red calico skirt flapped like a weather-stained flag at half-mast.

The old man skirted the group, eagerly scanning each face as though looking for a sympathetic ear into which to pour his sorrows. Not finding what he wanted, he hurried on toward the State House, dragging the child after him, until, in front of a newspaper office, he saw a round-waisted gentleman with a priestly look talking to a tall, long-bearded one of the old school. Detecting benevolence in the faces of both, he approached the shorter of the two, and, in an anxious voice, inquired—"Maussuh, please, suh, tell me ef cat kin git crazy?"

"Do you mean is it possible for a cat to have rabies?"

"No, suh, 'taint rabbit, 'tis cat."

"I apprehend," said the English purist, "that you desire to ascertain whether it is possible for a cat to have the rabies. I may say, for your information, that there are, literally and mathematically speaking, 18 phases of insanity to which humanity is subject, ranging from the emotional insanity of commerce, to the popular *mania a potu*, vulgarly called *delirium ine-briosa*. I do not care to give an off-hand opinion as to whether or not a cat may have one or more of these kinds of insanity, unless you will accurately describe the symptoms and put your questions categorically. It is manifestly a work of supererogation—"

"Great Gawd, maussuh!" said the old man, turning appealingly to the tall gentleman. "Please, suh, tell dis juntlemun dat my cat nebbuh had no rabbit, 'e only had kitten'. Yaas, suh. My cat name Jane, en' 'e b'long to dis leetle gal chile w'ich is my gran', en' him (dat is de gal) name Jane, en' Jane (dat is de cat) b'long to Jane (w'ich is de gal) en' Jane does use to folluh Jane eb'ryweh 'e go, en' Jane does berry lub Jane, en' w'enebbuh Jane does ketch rat, 'e fetch-'um een de house, en' w'enebbuh Jane does git 'e bittle fuh eat, 'e always keep some uh de bittle fuh Jane, en' w'en Jane (dat is de cat) had nine kitten' een Mistuh Claa'k' smokehouse on de t'ree Chuesday een dis same berry munt', den Jane (dat is de gal) set up all night fuh nuss Jane (dat is de cat) en', please Gawd, maus-suh, jis' as soon as de nyung kitten' eye' biggin fuh op'n, one shaa'pmout' black dog, wid 'e tail stan' like dese bu'd fedduh buckruh 'ooman does lub fuh pit on 'e hat w'en Sunday come, dis dog jump obuh de fench en' bite'um, en' Jane (dat is de cat en' de gal alltwo) git berry agguhnize en' twis' up een alltwo dem min', en' Jane (dat is de cat) him jump obuh de fench en' run'way, en' de dog en' Jane (dat is de gal)

THE CAT WAS CRAZY

run attuh Jane (dat is de cat) 'tell w'en Jane (dat is de cat) staa't fuh run down de lane, Jane (dat is de gal) see ole Unk' Bill Rose—w'ich'n him is de Gub'nuh' Claa'k, walkin' good fashi'n down de lane. Now, de gal holluh att'um fuh ketch de cat, but eb'ry-body know dat Unk' Bill Rose is leetle kinduh bow-leggit, en', alldo' him hol' alltwo 'e foot togedduh, 'e foot couldn' specify, en' Jane (dat is de cat) jump clean t'ru Unk Bill Rose' britchiz, en' 'e git'way en' gone, please Gawd, en' lef' Jane (dat is de gal) en' lef' 'e nine kitten', w'ich all dem eye' ent done open, een Mistuh Claa'k' smokehouse, en' gone en' jump obuh de fench w'ich run roun' de 'Sylum yaa'd—en' dat de reaz'n w'ymekso I know berry well Jane (dat is de cat) mus' be gone crazy, 'cause he gone *spang* een de 'Sylum!"

A CONGAREE WATER-COLOR

During the last freshet in the Congaree river, three negroes living on the Childs plantation five miles below Columbia took advantage of the high water to go rabbit hunting in a boat. Paddling about between the tree trunks, they scanned the knolls and tussocks that, rising above the flood, afforded sanctuary to the cotton-tail refugees.

So intent were they upon the chase, that the carelessly managed skiff struck a cypress "knee" and was instantly swamped. Fortunately, the trees were thick, and the wrecked crew climbed into a tall gum, where, far above the swelling flood, they spent the entire day, sending out from time to time across the waste of waters a piteous cry for help, until, late in the evening, their voices were heard from the highlands, and a boat was sent to their rescue by Mr. Childs.

Mingo Singletary, one of the treed nimrods, was in the city yesterday, and gave the following account of the adventure:

"Yaas, suh, me en' Silus Smit' en Hacklus Rab'nel, w'ich Hacklus is my niece, 'cause *him* gran' en' *my* gran' alltwo is de same man, en' *him* farruh en' *my* farruh is two twin; so, berrywellden, me en' dese two mans gone out een de bateau fuh hunt rabbit, 'cause w'en de ribbuh high, rabbit is a berry easy t'ing fuh ketch, 'cause dey berry 'f'aid fuh git dem foot wet, en' dey does climb high 'puntop de tussock. So we paddle 'long en' quizzit all de tussock, en' de same time w'en me en' Silus binnuh peep onduhneet' one briah bush weh rabbit does hide, fus' t'ing we know,

230

A CONGAREE WATER-COLOR

we ain' know *nutt'n'*, 'cause my niece Hacklus, w'ich
dat nigguh nebbuh did hab a Gawd' piece uh sense,
him paddle de boat 'puntop de snag, en' de boat' bottom couldn' specify, en' de boat' bottom buss', en' lef'
we een de water. Now, Silus had a fight wid he lady
las' week, en' he lady strong mo'den Silus, en' Silus'
lady lick'um en' mos' bruk 'e back, so w'en Silus try
fuh swim 'e back couldn' specify, en' jis' ez 'e biggin
to drowndid, my niece Hacklus ketch'um by 'e britchiz,
but de britchiz buss', en' Silus gone down onduhneet'
de water fuh de two time, en' w'en 'e rise 'gen I graff-
'um by 'e lef' han' foot en' hice'um up close to one big
gum tree, en' all t'ree uh we climb de tree 'tell we git
'puntop de limb, en' den, please Gawd, we seddown, en'
seddown, en' seddown; en' we all t'ree berry well
sattify fuh seddown, 'tell hongry biggin fuh ketch we,
en w'en *him* come, den we staa't fuh holluh' en' holluh' en' holluh. But de mo' we holluh, de mo' we
hongry, en' bimeby we see Silus' lady walkin' by de
ribbuh' aige wid dat yalluh boy Sam, w'ich lib to
Mistuh Hamptun' place, en' Silus holluh at 'e lady
en' scole'um, but you know berry well, suh, 'ooman
is de debble, en' dat 'ooman nebbuh had Silus een
de back uh 'e head. So, we stillyet seddown, en'
seddown, 'tell we mos' ready fuh drap off de tree limb;
en' Silus is a class-leader, en' him biggin fuh praise
de Lawd, en' bimeby him tell we 'bout how de rab'n
feed 'Lijah, en' we look high een de ellyment en' we
see 'nuf buzzut flyin' high obuh de tree top, en' Hacklus call to de buzzut fuh fetch de bittle, but de buzzut
keep on flew high een de ellyment, en' nebbuh bodduh
'e head 'bout Hacklus. Den, bimeby 'gen, Silus resplain de Scriptuh 'bout how Noah' dub fetch tree
branch en' all kinduh t'ing een 'e mout' w'en de water

231

high; en', fus' t'ing we know, we see one dub fly t'ru
de swamp, en' de sun shine on 'e breas' en' mek'um
look like gol', en', likewise also, we call to *him*, but
'e didn' hab nutt'n' een 'e mout', en' *him* fly 'way en'
gone, please Gawd! Den, w'en de sun biggin fuh
lean 'cross de tree top 'en staa't fuh walk down de
sky fuh go to 'e res', we git mos' skaytode't', en' we
staa't fuh sing sperritual' en' praise de Lawd, en' Silus
ketch 'e tex f'um de fo'teen chaptuh een Nickuhdemus, en' him tell we 'bout how de Lawd tu'n Nickuhdemus eento cow w'en him hongry, so 'e could git
grass fuh eat, but I tell'um dat tex' couldn' specify,
'cause how de debble—een de fus' place, man cyan'
eat grass w'en him dey high een de tree top.

"En' den de sun gone down, en' one leetle cat squerril
come out 'e hole een de gum tree en' tu'n 'e tail obuh
'e back en' say '*paak, paak, paak*', en' one big owl fly
close to we en' seddown een we tree en' say '*whaak,
whaak, whaak, whaak, whoo, whoo, whoo, whoo!*' en'
den I know de Lawd tek pity on we en' sen' we
cump'ny, en' we git mo' fait' een de Lawd, en' we
biggin fuh holluh 'gen, en' dis time, suh, Mistuh Chile
yeddy we woice en' sen' 'e boat en' tek we off, en' w'en
we git back to de nigguhhouse yaa'd, eb'rybody on de
plantesshun sing praise en' glad we come back—eb'rybody 'scusin' Silus' wife, en', you b'leebe me, suh!
Silus' lady him bex 'cause 'e husbun' britchiz buss', en'
'e lick Silus 'cause 'e didn' drowndid."

WAITING TILL THE BRIDEGROOMS COME

On a hot June day a year or two ago, a tall, pumpkin-colored negro was leisurely plowing an unambitious mule in a cornfield in Lower Carolina. Minzacter Singleton was his euphonious name, and he was about 55 years of age.

As he passed up and down the furrows he whistled cheerily, for the brown earth that curled away in long waves from his plowshare was mellow and rich, and the bourgeoning corn that bristled around him, a grand industrial army, uniformed in blue green, epauletted with crimson silk and plumed with cream white tassels, was full of promise for the autumn. Here and there a convolvolus vine that had escaped the last hoeing twined lovingly around a sturdy stalk and, clambering boldly up, swung its purple, white-throated cups among the feathery blooms of the corn, where the swift-winged honey bee and the yellow-barred bumblebee plied their busy trade.

These sights, however, affected not Minzacter. He was a materialist, not a poet; and, mindful of his one-third interest in the crop that he was "laying by," he concerned himself far more with the occasional bumping of his singletree against the corn stalks, than with the soft music of the wind harps that crept from among the broad blades as the breeze passed through them.

High up in the blue, a crow flew slowly over the field, twisting his head from side to side, while he critically inspected the work in progress; and, find-

ing that it was good, croaked out an occasional
"ckwarrow, ckwarrow."

As the friar of the middle ages—the prototype of
this black-robed fellow—unctuously took from the
fields of his flock a tithe of the garnered store, so,
when the blades should be stripped away and September suns harden the grain, would this "sukkus
preechuh" claim the reward of his interest in, and
inspection of, the growing crop. As the ominous
shadow passed between him and the sun, Minzacter,
looking up, said: "N'mine, bredduh! Tek care buzzut
don' dance at yo' fun'rul dis same berry fall! You
smaa't 'nuf fuh know w'en man got gun een 'e han', but
yo' eddycashun cyan' specify w'en 'e come fuh tell w'en
shell' cawn got pizen een um. You fly high een de
ellyment teday, tek care you don' flew low befo' Chris-
'mus come!"

Upon reaching the end of his row, Minzacter found
awaiting him the burly black constable of a neighboring Trial Justice, accompanied by a middle-aged
brown woman, who, as the plowman came to a halt,
accosted him with: "Mistuh Singleton, I t'awt you
was a juntlemun, but I come to fin' out you cyan'
specify as a juntlemun, 'cause you run'way en' lef'
me obuh to Goose Crik, en' gone en' marry Paul
Jenkin' grumma jes' 'cause 'e got fo' cow en' I ent got
no cow. You run'way en' lef' yo' lawfully lady, en'
I come to tek you to de Trial Jestuss fuh t'row you
een Walterburruh jail."

With apparent nonchalance, Minzacter said: "Go
'way, gal! Who you call husbun'? I nebbuh see you
sence I bawn. I gots no time fuh hol' cumposhashun
wid eb'ry w'ich en' w'y 'ooman dat come 'long de
road. Dis cawn gots to lay by."

WAITING TILL THE BRIDEGROOMS COME

Julia Singleton, the *ecru* claimant, left him with the threat that she would go home and fetch the marriage "stuhstiffikit" to prove that Minzacter was her lawful husband.

Sure enough, on the day set for the preliminary examination, she appeared with not only the marriage certificate, but accompanied by her brother and the Rev. Sancho Middleton, the Goose Creek "locus pastuh," who was alleged to have performed the ceremony.

Upon being arraigned for bigamy, Minzacter denied indignantly any knowledge of the woman. The "stuhstiffikit" was put in evidence, but as it read simply, "I marry Mistuh Singleton to Missis Singleton," the Trial Justice ruled that it couldn't "specify." The claimant's brother and the preacher had been tampered with by an agent of Minzacter's and, at the last moment, they went back on the prosecuting witness. The brother was put up first, and Julia did the questioning.

"Bredduh," said she, "ent you 'membuh dat een June munt' een de same year w'en us cut down dat new groun' 'cross Caw Caw Swamp, en' de same time w'en Sistuh Frayjuh him had two twin, ent you 'membuh dat de pastuh renite me to dis juntlemun?"

"I yent know nutt'n' 'bout'um," said the traitor, "nebbuh shum sence I bawn, ent know 'e name, needuhso 'e farruh, needuhso 'e murruh. Mo' den one punkin-skin nigguh lib een dis wull'. Yalluh nigguh' t'ick on de groun' same as yalluh-hammuh' t'ick on de tree, en', as fuh *dis* nigguh—nebbuh shum sence I bawn."

"Mistuh Jestuss," said Julia, ruefully, "I come to

235

ketch my juntlemun, en' my *juntlemun* lie. I gone en'
fetch my bredduh Sam, en' my bredduh *Sam* lie. I
gone en' fetch de stuhstiffikit, en' de *stuhstiffikit* lie.
Now, I will 'tarrygate my locus pastuh, en' I know
berry well *him* ent gwine lie. Pa Sancho," said
she, turning to the sleek divine, "ent you 'membuh,
suh, w'en Sistuh Frayjuh him had two twin?"

"Oh yaas, my sistuh, I 'membuh dat, 'cause dat
same time Nickuhdemus Wineglass' niece Joe, w'ich
'e had by 'e fus' lady, git 'e foot ketch een de ottuh
trap on Mistuh Fishpun' place, en' de doctuh haffuh
cut off 'e right han' feet close to 'e knee."

"Well, suh, ent you 'membuh w'en you renite me to
dis same juntlemun?"

"My sistuh," said he, slowly and deliberately, "you
see, dis is a berry onrabblin' t'ing fuh yo' pastuh fuh
'xamin' 'e min' 'bout. You know, all dese common
eb'ryday kind'uh nigguh' kin talk all dese gwinin'
en' gwinin', but de preechuh is de Lawd' *renointed*,
en', w'en him open he mout', e' gots to quizzit 'e min'
berry close, 'speshly w'en 'e talk wid 'ooman, 'cause
'ooman so 'ceitful, ef you ent min', him will fool de
two eye' out yo' head; en', fuh dictate now 'bout dis
juntlemun, I mos' kinduh t'ink I 'membuh leetle kinduh sump'n', 'bout de time w'en I marry you to a
kinduh punkin-skin juntlemun, en' w'en I fus' see dis
juntlemun, I mos' t'ink 'e look leetle like yo' juntlemun, but w'en I come to saa'ch'um close en' peruse'um
puhtickluh, I mos' kinduh t'ink maybe dis ent yo'
juntlemun."

"Please Gawd," said Julia despairingly, "I gone en
try fuh ketch my juntlemun en' I fetch'um yuh, en'
him lie. Den I gone en' ketch my bredduh en' fetch-

'um yuh, en' *him* lie. Den I gone en' ketch de stuh-stuffikit en' fetch'um yuh, en' *him* lie; en', fin'lly at las', I ketch de locus pastuh en 'fetch'um yuh, en', 'fo' de Lawd, *him* lie. Now, I gwine home en' fetch de six bridegroom' w'at bin to dis wedd'n' w'en I marry dis juntlemun—w'ich my sistuh Amy bin one uh de bridegroom'—en' I know berry well *dem* will crucify dat dis is my juntlemun."

At last accounts, the Justice was still awaiting their coming.

A GULLAH'S TALE OF WOE

From the clay chimney of a negro cabin in the lower part of Hampton County the blue smoke curled and floated away in graceful rings. Within, the flames crackled cheerily in the generous fireplace, and a woman, surrounded by half a dozen children, was preparing the evening meal. The building was of logs, with moss and clay plastered into the crevices, and the roof which covered it was of clapboards. An humble dwelling it was, but big enough and warm enough to shelter old Scipio Wineglass and his family, and it represented—together with the few acres of land surrounding it—the net earnings of twenty-seven years of toil "sence freedum fus' come een."

The crop had been gathered and locked in the little corn crib that nestled up under the eaves of the cabin, and among the shucks that lay around the door a few pigs were rooting. As the twilight fell on this crisp December evening, the querulous bark of a squirrel came from the swamp, and away down the road the sound of a horse's hoofs in a sharp canter became louder and louder, until, at last, a horseman rode up and asked for a drink of water, just as old Scipio came in from the woods with a log on his head and threw it down with a grunt.

Bringing a gourd of water out to the gate, he eyed the stranger closely as he drank, and as he took back the dipper he asked, "Maussuh, enty puhlicituh kin oughtuh able fuh read?"

"Certainly, solicitors are able to read. Why do you ask?"

A GULLAH'S TALE OF WOE

"Well, suh, please Gawd, I gots nutt'n' but trouble
all dis yeah done gone. Een de fus' place, jis' ez soon
ez I git de crap plant een de t'ree week een las' Epprull, de waa'ment en' t'ing biggin fuh onrabble en'
distruss me een me min' 'tell, please de Lawd, I yent
know Rebus frum Rebelashun! Soon ez I t'row de
cawn seed een de groun', de waa'ment biggin fuh
agguhnize me. I didn't had no coal taar fuh pit 'pun
de cawn, en' soon ez I pit'um een de groun', de debble-
'ub'uh'crow come 'long en' pull up half de cawn, en w'at
de crow ent pull up, de cut wurrum ketch, en w'at de
cut wurrum lef', de dry drought 'stroy'd *him*, en',
soon ez de dry drought gone'way, den my ole mare
Silby, *him* haffuh gone en' dead! Yaas'suh, dat old
mare done gone en' leddown en' dead, en' lef' me wid
de fiel' full'uh j'int grass, en' nott grass, en' crab grass
en' t'ing, en' I yent got a hawss fuh ride now 'cep'n'
'tis dese two foot, but stillyet I praise de Lawd en'
glorify'um, 'cause, ef dat mare didn't dead, de debble
would'uh had Scipio Wineglass done roas' en bu'n'up
een de fiah 'fo' dis time! Yaas'suh, one night een las'
Augus' een de daa'k uh de moon, jis' ez I biggin to
drap 'sleep, I yerry one rap 'pun de do', en' w'en I
tell de somebody fuh come een, one sperrit buss' op'n
de do', en' stan' on 'e two foot een de middle uh de flo!
W'en I shum wid dese two eye', I bin dat skay'to'de't'
dat I didn't 'membuh fuh ax'um 'e name, but I mos'
t'ink 'e bin eeduh de 'Postle Paul, elseso Pollido'. En'
dis sperrit 'tarrygate me good fashi'n, en' 'e say, sezzee,
'Scipio'; sezzi, 'Suh.' Sezzee, 'Scipio, you got a great
load uh sin 'puntop yo' soul!' Sezzi, 'Yaas'suh, I
know dat, suh.' Den 'e say, 'Scipio, ef dat load uh
sin ent tek off yo' soul, you cyan' specify w'en de
great day come, en' you will sho' to ebbuhlastin' dead

en' bu'n'up.' En' den I say 'Yaas, suh, maussuh
ainjul.' En' den I drap on dese two knee' en' pray de
Lawd fuh tell de sperrit fuh tek de sin off my soul,
en' den de ainjul say 'e couldn' tek de sin off my soul
'cep'n' 'e pit'um 'puntop somebody else' own, en'
den I baig'um fuh pit de sin on ole Unk' Hacklus
Pinesett' soul, 'cause Unk' Hacklus lub fuh t'ief fowl
en' t'ing, en' him is a nomannus nigguh, en' de sperrit
say 'berrywell,' en' 'e wawm 'e han' by de fiah en' gone
out de do', en', soon ez 'e gone, I yerry ole Silby duh
kick en' grunt een de stable, but I bin too twis'up in
me min' fuh pay 'tenshun to *him*, en', een de mawnin'
soon, w'en I gone out to de stable fuh feed ole Silby,
please de Mastuh, 'e stretch-out, *dead!* En' stillyet,
alldo' 'e dead en' gone, yet I glorify de Lawd en'
praise 'e name, 'cause I know 'e tek de sin off me en'
pit'um 'puntop ole Silby, en' all de time I yerry'um
binnuh grunt een de stable, dat sin binnuh ride'um
roun' en' roun', 'tell 'e kill'um. I wonduh w'ymekso
dat sperrit ent tek dat ansuh to de Lawd de way I
sen'um, 'cause I buy dat mare to Mistuh Larrissy'
place fuh seb'nty-fibe dollar, en' Unk' Hacklus Pinesett ent wut' a t'ree cent, stillyet de Lawd tek ole Silby,
en' lef' *him!*

"Now, w'en Silby dead, I tek de hoe een me han'
en' lay by de crap, en', tengk Gawd, I mek fo'teen
bushel' uh cawn een dis same fiel'. Well, suh, w'en de
cawn done lay by, I git 'long berrywell 'tell Mingo
Puhlite' son Sambo t'ief' de fattes' hog I got. Een
Septembuh munt', soon ez I ketch'um, I tek'um to de
Trial Jestuss, en' him sen'um to Hamptun jail.

"Now, w'en de trial come in de fall, Sambo git Mistuh
Tillin'ass' to refen' she, en I gone to Mistuh Muffey, de
puhlicituh, en' tell'um all 'bout de t'iefin'. Den Mistuh

A GULLAH'S TALE OF WOE

Tillin'ass' squizzit me en' ax me all kinduh squeschun, en' Mistuh Muffey squizzit Sambo en' ax *him* all kinduh squeschun, en den ole Judge Hutsin him put on one black frock same lukkuh 'ooman, en' him ax me all kinduh squeschun, en' den Mass Billy Causey, de Claa'k ub de Co't, tek de eenditement (dat w'at 'e call de papuh) een 'e han', en' 'e tu'n'um upside down en' 'e read'um wrong, en' den Mistuh Tillin'ass' tek de papuh en' tu'n'um upside down en' him read'um wrong, en' den Judge Hutsin tek de papuh en' tu'n'um upside down en' *him* read'um wrong, en' den, please Gawd, Mistuh Muffey, de puhlicituh, *Him* tek de papuh en' tu'n'um upside down en' *Him* read'um wrong! Yaas'-suh, de jury bin all buckruh', en' all dem care 'bout is fuh sen' one nigguh to de penetenshus fuh eb'ry hog w'at git t'ief', en' de Claa'k ub de Co't git my name en' Sambo' name tanglety'up on de papuh, en', fus' t'ing I know—'cep'n' dat Sambo own to t'ief de hog fuh git meat fuh eat to de passobuh preachin' w'ich was hol' to Sistuh Frajuh' house—please Gawd, de buckruh' would'uh sen' me to de penetenshus fuh t'ief me *own hog!* En' dat de reason, suh, w'ymekso I ax wedduh puhlicituh kin read, 'cause I didn't bex so much 'bout Mistuh Tillin'ass', en' Mass Billy Causey, en' ole Judge Hutsin wid 'e black frock sukkuh 'ooman, but I *did* t'ink dat Mistuh Muffey, de puhlicituh, could'uh *read.*"

THE DOCTOR DIDN'T "EXCEED"

Down upon the banks of the turbid Toogoodoo—one of the many creeks that indent the seacoast of Colleton County—lives June Middleton, a negro of the old school. As a body servant, he followed his master through Virginia "eenjurin' uh de wah," and, at its close, he received for his faithful service a few acres of the plantation upon which he had been reared. His little holding was as dear to him as was ever an entailed estate to an English noble, for, like all Southern negroes who had formerly belonged to families of culture and refinement, he shared the pride of his quondam owners in their ancestral acres and in their distinguished names.

The comfortable frame house, in which June had spent the days of his slavehood, had long since gone up in smoke, for no habitation of man or beast was too lowly to escape the torch of Sherman's bummers, who, in 1865 illumined the "benighted South." Upon its site now stands a clay-chimneyed log cabin, and by its door ebb and flow the waters of the creek from which June had for years drawn his sustenance. While he did not exactly "go down to the sea in ships," he paddled his little "dugout" canoe out to the mouth of the stream at nearly every low tide during the winter season, and shared with the raccoons the little sharp-shelled bunch oysters that covered the exposed mud banks.

In the spring, when the yellow jessamine swung its golden cups above the forest undergrowth, and the silver stars of the dogwood gleamed from the chaparral, he mended his nets and lines in preparation for the summer campaign, and, later, when the woods were odorous with the blossoms of the elder and the wild grape, he commenced his nocturnal forays against the finny tribes. On dark nights, when the piping of the marsh hens apprised him that the tide was out, he took with him a boy to paddle his cranky little craft, and, standing in the bow, threw his cast-net with a "swish" far out into the schools of shrimp and "finger mullet." His catch, together with an occasional string of whiting and yellowtail taken with the hook and line, he converted at a distant village into the necessaries of life.

For many years there had scarcely been a ripple on this placid life of June's, save when a "puppy-shark" would occasionally make away with his bait, sending the whiting line whizzing through his fingers and almost upsetting the little craft with his impetuous rush, or when, two or three times a year, the itinerant preacher would visit his cabin to swap ecclesiastical platitudes for fresh fish.

On a bright day in early summer, old June sat at his door-step basking in the sun and watching the glistening waters as they hurried by. Occasionally, a kingfisher would leave his station on a dead limb and, zig-zagging in his flight, would swoop down on some small fish that showed on the surface, and, having swallowed his prey, would leisurely return to his perch with a harsh note of triumph. The "preechuh on de sukkus" had just arrived to pay his periodical visit, and, scattering a group of half-naked children who were playing around the door, June brought out another three-legged stool and extended the hospitalities of the establishment.

"Reb'ren'," said he, "I berry glad you come teday."

"Why, bredduh, 'smattuh mekso?"

"Well, suh," said June, whose philosophical patience and faith might put to the blush many who quarrel with their lot, "I yent min' 'bout me myself, suh, 'cause I tengk Gawd fuh life en' de bre't' w'at Him lef' een dis body. My lady, w'ich dead een las' Augus', had de consumpshus en' de remonia alltwo, en' him en' me alltwo nyuse to smoke de same pipe befo' him dead, en' I berry 'f'aid dat I gwine likeso fuh ketch de consumpshus en' de remonia frum dat same berry pipe, en', den, I got mis'ry een de back, en' I sen' dat leetle gal 'Riah—dat is my gran'—to de cross road sto' fuh git fibe cent' wut' ub tup'mtime, but de buckruh tek de fibe cent frum de gal en' t'row water een de tup'mtime, en' w'en I rub de back wid de tup'mtime de tup'mtime couldn' specify, en' de mis'ry keep on jes' de same, en' I git so po'ly now dat I kin sca'cely git een de crik fuh ketch swimp en' t'ing, en' bittle git berry sca'ceful dese days, suh; but tengk Gawd fuh life, suh, tengk Gawd fuh life, en' I berry glad you come, 'cause I want'uh ax yo' 'pinion 'bout my gran', Sooky. You know'um, suh, him is uh 'leben yeahs ole gal chile, en' 'e git sick een de two week een las' Jinnywerry done gone mek one yeah, en' Doctuh Baa'nwell t'row one dollar en' sebenty-fi' cent' wut' uh med'sin een de gal, but somehow I don't t'ink de Doctuh exceed so well wid de gal, 'cause, een de fus' week een dis same Jinnywerry—befo' de yeah well out—de gal tek wid mo' mis'ry een 'e lef' han' foot, en' w'en I sen'um back to de Doctuh 'e want'uh chaa'ge anodduh

244

dolluh en' sebenty-fi' cent' fuh t'row mo' physic' een de gal, en' dat mek me bex, 'cause eb'rybody know 'tis too soon fuh t'row'way anodduh dolluh en' sebenty-fi' cent', en' likeso eb'rybody know dat Doctuh Baa'nwell couldn' be exceed so well wid de gal, en' 'e med'sin couldn' specify, elseso 'e wouldn' haffuh cyo' one en' de same gal two time een one en' de same yeah!"

THE LADY COULDN'T "SPECIFY"

The Rev. Nepchun Kinlaw, the "locus pastuh" of a Colleton County flock, sat in the sunshine at the door of his cabin, drawing from the sights and sounds around him inspiration for his next Sunday's sermon. Although he could not read, an open Bible was on his knee, and his head was bowed reverently over the well-thumbed pages. His only knowledge of their contents was acquired from the circuit preacher whose quarterly sermons furnished the "class-leaders" and local preachers with scriptural data wherewith to conduct the campaign against Satan until his next round. These Bible truths "Pa Kinlaw"—as the female members of his charge delighted to call him—instilled into his flock by homely illustrations. Out in the yard before him, a little ridge of earth, which gradually increased in length, indicated the presence of a groundmole that was burrowing through the hard ground. "Dat gru'mole hab fait'," said he. " 'E yent gots no eye een 'e head, en' 'e cyan' see de wurrum een de eart', but 'e hab fait', en' de Lawd lead'um 'long to weh de wurrum does lib, en' de gru'mole ketch de wurrum en' eat'um. Same fashi'n, man en' 'ooman gots to hab fait' een de Lawd, elsehow dem ent able fuh *specify* w'en Gabrull blow 'e hawn en' de great day come. Ef you ent got *fait'*, please Gawd, oonuh nebbuh ketch de wurrum ub Salwashun!"

His reflections were rudely interrupted by the advent of Jim Green, the colored constable of a neighboring trial justice, who, mounted on a razor-backed rat of a Texas pony, rode up to the door and, in the name of

246

THE LADY COULDN'T "SPECIFY"

the State of South Carolina, demanded from the "Reb'ren'" a dollar and a quarter, the balance due on a two-dollar marriage ceremony performed in October last by the aforesaid trial justice, "who did then and there, at the time and place aforesaid, unite one Nepchun Kinlaw to one Minda Manigo."

Not a red flag flaunted before a bull—nor a rival's becoming Easter bonnet before a society woman—could have been provocative of more wrath than was the constable's demand upon "Pa Kinlaw." Rising from his seat, with the natural color of his face deepened by anger until it was as dark as the hinges of Hades, he said: "Green, you kin go back to de Trial Jestuss en' tell'um dat de lady, w'at him renite me to een de two Chuesday een las' Octobuh, cyan' specify. Tell'um dat de only reason w'ymekso I hab dis lady is bekasew'y my fus' wife dead een las' June. Dat 'ooman w'at dead wuz de fait'fules' 'ooman I ebbuh come 'cross een dis wull'. I g'em praise fuh *dat!* De only fau't I had wid'um, is 'cause 'e gone en' dead een *June!* Ef de 'ooman had'uh dead een de fall w'en de crop done lay by, I wouldn' uh min' summuch, but 'e gone en' leddown en' dead een June, please Gawd, een *June* munt', w'en de grass duh grow, en' w'en de time haa'd, en bittle berry sca'ceful, en' 'e lef' seb'n chillun een de house, en' lef' de cawn een de fiel' befo' 'e gitt'ru hoe'um two time, en' de jaybu'd flew een de fiel' en' nyam de cawn, en' de redbu'd flew een de fiel' en' nyam de cawn, en de crow en' de rokkoon en de 'possum en' all de odduh'res' waa'ment nyam de cawn, 'cause I yent gots nobody fuh min'um out'n de fiel', en' stillyet dat 'ooman gone en' dead een *June!* Now, w'en I see all dese chillun, wid 'e mout' open same

247

lukkuh chuckwilluh' mout', en' I yent gots no bittle fuh pit een 'um, I mek up my min' dat I gots to git anodduh lady, en' sistuh Minda en' him fus' husbun' paa't, en' I quizzit de fus' husbun' 'bout'um en' 'e gib de lady uh berry good cyarrictuh, so I tek'um to de trial jestuss en' marri'd'um, but w'en I marri'd'um I t'aw't 'e could *specify*, so I pay de jestuss sebenty-fi' cent', en' owe'um dolluh en' uh quawtuh on de 'ooman, en' I tek de 'ooman home en' t'row'um een de fiel' fuh done lay by de crap en' plant peas een de cawn, but, please Gawd, soon ez I lef' de 'ooman 'e leddown flat 'puntop 'e back en' gone 'sleep een de sunhot, en' 'e 'low de crow en' t'ing fuh spile eb'ry Gawd' crop een de fiel' eenjurin' de week day, en', w'en Sunday come, de lady put one high brustle 'puntop 'e back en' gone chu'ch same lukkuh him duh buckruh! En' w'en I fin' all dese gwinin' en' gwinin' bout de 'ooman, I kinduh git disgus' wid, de 'ooman, en' I yent feel like pay out no mo' money fuh de 'ooman w'en 'e cyan' speci*fy*. W'en I 'gree fuh pay de jestuss two dolluh' fuh marri'd dis lady, I t'aw't 'e could speci*fy*, en' I didn' min' 'bout payin' two dolluh' fuh uh smaa't 'ooman, but sence I tek de 'ooman home en' try'um, I fin' dat de 'ooman cyan' speci*fy*, en' 'e yent wut' mo' den de sebenty-fi' cent' w'at I done pay on'um; en', ef de jestuss ent sattify wid dat—befo' I pay de odduh-'res' ub de money—befo' I pay'um de dolluh en' a quawtuh w'at I still jue on de 'ooman—*him kin tek de lady back!*"

A QUESTION OF PRIVILEGE

The Republican State Convention was in session in the hall of the House of Representatives at Columbia. There was a contest between two rival delegations from Berkeley County, the one representing the "old line" Republicans, the other the younger element which had recently affiliated with the conservative Democrats. The fight came up on the seating of the delegations, and it was agreed that five minutes should be allotted to the chairman of each delegation for the presentation of his claims to the convention.

A young African, fancifully arrayed in a spotless white flannel suit, rose in behalf of the younger delegation and arraigned his opponents in an "impassioned" speech.

Before his five minutes had expired, Mr. Thompson, the ape-like chairman of the elder statesmen, interrupted him with an appeal to the chair.

"Mistuh Chair," said he, "I rise to uh squeschun ub priblidge."

The Chair—"Does de juntlemun rise to de priblidge, eeduhso de squeschun?"

"Great Gawd," said the thoroughly aroused delegate, "I rise to de priblidge en' de squeschun, alltwo one time, en' I also rise to uh squeschun ub *inflummashun*, 'cause I bin pussonully *attacktid*. Mistuh Chair, dis ondelicate nyung juntlemun w'ich pusceed me has prizzunt to dis augus' body de credenshul ub de contestuss delegashun frum Bucksley County to Mount Pleasant presinck fuh sen' one delegashun to Cuhlumbia, fuh sen' anodduh delegashun to Chicagyo fuh nominashun de Prezzydent uh dese Newnited State! Mistuh Chair, de 'Publikin paa'ty een Bucksley County is gots fuh speci*fy*, en' I will likes to quizzit dis immaculate nyung juntlemun frum Bucksley County en' ax'um a few cumposhashun! I will likes fuh 'tarrygate'um en' ax she weh *him* bin een de yeah sebenty-stree, w'en I bayre my breas' to de bullet uh de Dimmycrack frum de mountain to de sea*boa'd!* I will like, suh, fuh peruse de min' uh dis ondeestunt nyung juntlemun en' ax'um how de debble him kin specify en' ruppezunt de 'Publikin paa'ty een Bucksley County to Mount Pleasant presinck, w'en him binnuh lib een Mistuh Puhshay Smit' yaa'd, en' binnuh nyam buckruh' bittle ebbuh sence 'e farruh gone penetenshus fuh t'iefin' hog een de yeah sebenteen-eighty-stree! I will likes to ax dis ondelicate *chillun-nigguh* how him kin come yuh wid 'e jaw teet' full uh Puhshay Smit' hog meat en' onduhtek fuh seddown him contestuss delegashun 'pun dis historicus *flo'!*

"W'en, Mistuh Chair, dis meetin' wuz hol' to Bucksley County to Mount Pleasant presinck, fuh sen' dis delegashun to Cuhlumbia fuh sen' anodduh delegashun to Chicagyo fuh nominashun de Prezzydent uh dese Newnited *State*, dis immaculate juntlemun, Mistuh Dannil T. Middletun, repose heself 'gense de conwenshun plan fuh nominashun, en' adswocate de primus ward* *plan.* Now, w'en de juntlemun fin' dat de conwenshun plan is wictoria obuh de primus ward plan. de juntlemun git disgus', en' de juntlemun lef' de flo' uh de conwenshun en' gone down de step, follow' by he cohort, Mistuh Gibbes! Now, Mistuh Chair, I punnounce shish ondeestunt behavior, on de paa't uh Mistuh Middletun, uh disgustuss splotch 'pun de 'Pub-

*Ward primary.

250

A QUESTION OF PRIVILEGE

likin paa'ty' cawpsus politicksus, en' ef de juntlemun will contuhdix de wu'd w'ich I nyuse, I will punnounce she to be a *lie!* Mistuh Chair, de juntlemun' mout' is too black for she to be a Dimmycrack, en' 'e yeye is too red fuh he to be a 'Publikin, en' I punnounce'um, on de flo' uh dis conwenshun, uh monstrosity politicuss *muffledice!*"*

*Hermaphrodite.

251

CONDUCTOR SMITH'S DILEMMA

Is there one, among the thousands that have traveled on his train, who does not know and, knowing, does not esteem, Conductor Smith—"Billy" Smith of the Blue Ridge Railroad? Surely not, for like his prototype, Baines Carew, the sympathetic attorney of the Bab Ballads, who was so overcome by the recital of his clients' woes that he "had scarcely strength to take his fee," Billy, the embodiment of courtesy and kindliness, never collected a fare or punched a ticket without a deprecatory smile and look of sympathy, as tho' it grieved him very much. This accommodating disposition has made him an easy prey to an exacting public. Other trains have passed over his road, but the cream of the travel has always been reserved for Billy. His the happiness of looking after tow-headed boys sent to visit distant relatives; his the honor of escorting to and from boarding-school, grown girls who have been provided with half-fare tickets by their thrifty mothers; his the privilege of hauling to and fro, ladies who have been blessed with twins by a prodigal Providence, ladies with bird-cages, ladies with baby-carriages, ladies with cats in baskets, ladies with geraniums in pots, ladies with home-made jams and pickles in jars, ladies with bundles and bandboxes, ladies with an overweening desire to pour into his sympathetic ear divers family secrets—the exact number of teeth the last baby but one has cut, the number and variety of fashionable ailments considerately diagnosed by their family physicians, etc., etc. With these and like confidences the patient conductor's time is not infrequently whiled away between stations.

CONDUCTOR SMITH'S DILEMMA

Thus for years has Billy Smith trod—or rather joggled along—the path of duty between Walhalla and Belton. In the spring-time, when rill and river are swollen by heavy rains, and the tawny waters rush down the hillsides, gullying the plowed lands and scattering the rich soil "out among the neighbors," when the pale blue wild violet and the waxen Easter lily peep from dell and dingle, and the peach and plum trees, clustering around the farmsteads, open their pink and white petals to the sunshine and the dew; in the summer, when the golden bees swarm over the clover blooms and the ripe grain falls before the sweep of the scythe; in the autumn, when the chestnut burrs lie on the sod and the dead leaves swirl in the blast; in the winter, when the Blue Ridge is wrapped in a slumber-robe of snow and the frost crystals, forced out of the icy earth, sparkle on the sides of the deep cuts— in all seasons and in all weathers—Billy Smith plods on. Time and toil have streaked his beard with gray, and deepened the lines in his face, but his smile is as sweet and his hands and feet as willing as ever they were in his younger days, and, until he shall run his last train through the golden gates of the new Jerusalem and pass in his manifests to be checked up by the Almighty Auditor, he will doubtless be seen at the termini of the Blue Ridge Railroad, loaded to the gunwales, like a lighter at a coaling station, with babies, pug dogs, flowering plants and all the miscellaneous paraphernalia apparently inseparable from itinerant femininity, and will still take a commanding position in the centre of his coach and diurnally sing, alas! "that old sweet song:" "Belton, Belton! Junction Columbia and Greenville Railroad! About fifty minutes, fifty minutes, before the train comes for Columbia! Passengers going in the direction of Columbia will have to git off now, you'll have to git off, as this train leaves in about ten minutes, ten minutes, for Greenville, for Greenville—which is in the opposite direction from Columbia!"

There are moments in every life when flowers are no longer sweet, and women no longer fair; when there is no music in the song of birds, no merriment in the laughter of children, and all the world seems dark.

One of these moments came to Billy Smith the other day, when Conductor Fielding of the main line unloaded at Belton, Diana Hawlback, an elderly black woman from Beaufort County, who, with her grand-daughter "Lizzybet'," a spotted pig in a bag, two barn-yard roosters and a hen, tied by the legs, four quarts of roasted peanuts, a bushel of "Crazy Jane" sweet potatoes, a large bundle of bedding, and divers and sundry other belongings, was on her way to Pendle-ton to visit relatives. "The fight came up," as the Congressional reporters say, "on the recurrence of the previous question," which was, in this case, an empha-tic demand for the payment of full fare for Diana's "gran'," "Lizzybet'," a leggy girl of apparently four-teen years of age. "Cap'n," said Diana, "dat gal is a 'leben yeahs old gal, en' wehrebbuh I does tek'um on de train, de buckruh nebbuh does chaa'ge me mo' den chillun money fuh de gal. Enty you 'membuh, suh, de yeah w'en de dry drought come? Well, dat gal bawn een dat same berry yeah een de middle paa't ub de summuh, 'cause I 'membuh berrywell de dry drought dry up all de swamp en' backwatuh en' t'ing een Augus', en' all de man on de plantesshun gone out

een de swamp en' ketch de alligettuh out'n 'e hole, en'
dis gal Lizzybet' ma—him name Benus—eat too much
alligettuh w'en Lizzybet' wuz a t'ree weeks' ole gal, en'
de 'ooman dead en' lef' dis gal on my han'. De gal' pa
wuz my nyoungis' son, Pollydo', en' alldo' de scriptuh
say, 'Paul kin plant en' Pollydo' kin water, but Gawd
duh de man w'at gib de greese,' stillyet Pollydo' en'
him bredduh Paul plant de crap en' watuhr'um alltwo
'tell de dry drought come, but Gawd nebbuh sen' de
greese 'tell Pollydo' ketch de alligettuh en' bile'um, en'
stillyet, alldo' 'e folluh' de scriptuh' wu'd en' gib 'e
lady de alligettuh greese w'at de Lawd sen', yet de
lady dead, so I don't t'ink dat tex', w'at my locus
pastuh resplain, could be specify, elseso I don't t'ink
Pa Kinlaw could be onduhstan' de scriptuh berry well,
or de greese nebbuh would'uh 'stroy'd de 'ooman.
Stan' up gal, en' 'low de buckruh fuh look 'puntop yo'
foot. Cap'n, you ebbuh see, sence you bawn, shishuh
feet lukkuh dat on a fo'teen yeahs ole gal? Ent you
know," said she, as Conductor Smith's eyes opened
at the size of the pedal extremities exhibited, "ent you
know dat a 'leben yeahs ole gal gots bigguh foot den
a fo'teen yeahs ole gal? Dis gal nebbuh had a shoe
'pun 'e foot, en' 'e foot gots nutt'n' fuh stop'um frum
grow. Befo' you tek'way all my money fuh tek dis
gal to Pendletun, I wish you, please, suh, kin eeduh
go yo'self, elseso sen' uh ansuh to my sistuhlaw, Miss
Frajuh, w'at lib to Mistuh Brissle place to Cumbee,
en' ax'um wedduh dis gal Lizzybet', w'ich him is my
gran', is mo' den 'leben yeah ole."

ONE WAS TAKEN—THE OTHER LEFT

On the hot white sand of a cart road that wound along the edge of a ricefield in lower Carolina, lay the stiffened body of a yellow, crop-eared cur. By his side, a companion in death, was a cottonmouth moccasin, beaten almost to a pulp.

The road was flanked on either side by a canal half filled with stagnant water, dotted here and there with water lilies and shaded by the feathery foliage of the pond willows, while, among the clumps of rushes that fringed the edges, blue flags nodded. Over all, the July sun glared fiercely, and up on the willow branches, where, here and there, his rays penetrated the dense foliage, lay a water snake basking in the golden light. Now and then a blue heron—the "Po' Joe" of the plantation negro—rose lazily from his fishing station out in the ricefield, and, trailing his long legs after him, moved on to another "drop." The whole world seemed to be asleep in the warm sunshine—all the world save old Ca'lina Manigo, who sat on a cypress log by the side of the road and gazed sorrowfully at the dead dog, and the snake that had caused its death, while he muttered to himself:

"Po' ole Hol'fas' dead, yaas, suh, dead en' gone! Ketch 'e de't' en' git 'structed by uh debble'ub'uh snake! De preechuh say dat w'en de Lawd tek'way good man en' good 'ooman frum dis wull' 'tis bekasew'y Him lub 'um en' gots nyuse fuhr'um, but I wunduh w'y mekso Him tek'way Hol'fas'? Cyan' be dem does ketch rokkoon en' 'possum en' t'ing een Heben! I nebbuh yerry 'bout no shishuh t'ing, but, my Mastuh! ef dem *is*

256

got'um dey, Hol'fas' will tree'um befo' dayclean
tomorruh mawnin', 'speshly ef 'e got sense 'nuf fuh
fin' Bredduh Cudjo, my class-leader, w'at de Lawd
tek las' Fibbywerry, 'cause B'Cudjo nyuse to lub fuh
folluh de waa'ment' track een de swamp same lukkuh
'e nyuse to lub fuh folluh de 'Postle Paul' en' Nickuhdemus' track een de Scriptuh, en', I tell you, suh,
w'en B'Cudjo git on a hot trail, wedduh'so 'e duh trail
'possum or 'postle, 'e berry haa'd fuh t'row'um off!

"Dat mek me 'membuh 'bout de las' time me en' him
en' Hol'fas' ketch de hebby rokkoon een de Cypress
swamp close to Beabuh dam. Yaas'suh, dat dog
couldn' *tu'ndown* fuh rokkoon! 'E wuz jes' 'bout fus'
fowlcrow; de mawnin' staar climb up de sky 'tell 'e
stan' 'puntop de treehead, en', 'way obuh de swamp
een de big dribe, we yerry de owl 'whoo, whoo, whoo,
whoo,' en' bimeby pres'n'ly, we list'n good en' we yerry
Hol'fas' comin' 'pun one hot trail, en', bimeby 'gen,
we know by 'e baa'k dat 'e done tree; so, w'en we come
to de dog, 'e bin at de biggis' sweetgum tree een de
swamp en' duh gib 'e tongue berry rappit. Now, w'en
we pit de light'ood junk behin' we fuh shine 'e yeye, we
see de rokkoon 'puntop de berry top uh de gum tree,
en' we yent gots no gun fuh shoot de rokkoon, so
B'Cudjo staa't' fuh climb de tree fuh t'row down de
rokkoon, en' 'e git'long berry well 'tell 'e git mos' to de
rokkoon, en' B'Cudjo so hongry fuh ketch de rokkoon,
dat 'e nebbuh quizzit de limb w'at him binnuh seddown 'puntop, en' w'en 'e *graff* at de rokkoon, please
Gawd, de limb couldn' specify, en' de limb bruk, en'
w'en B'Cudjo graff de rokkoon by 'e tail, him en' de
rokkoon alltwo drap out de tree, en' hit de groun'
'bim!' De rokkoon dead, but B'Cudjo, een Gawd'

mussy, fall 'puntop 'e head, en' dat hukkuh 'e didn'
bruk 'e back!

"Well, praise de Mastuh, Him tek'way Hol'fas'. I
yent grudge'um de dog, ef Him want'um, but I wish
'E had uh bin tek my lady Bina en' lef' de dog, 'cause
de dog nebbuh lie, en' de 'ooman *fuhrebbuh* duh lie,
en' de dog wuz a fait'ful dog, en' de 'ooman is a 'ceitful 'ooman, en' w'en you feed de dog, de dog wag 'e
tail, but de *'ooman!* him nebbuh tengkful fuh *nutt'n'*.
You nebbuh kin sattify *him!*"

EGG-ZACTLY

"Come'yuh, gal, en' lemme look 'puntop yo' foot. W'en I call you, yo' foot hebby ez i'on, en' w'en I tu'n you loose, 'e light ez uh fedduh. Wuh 'smattuh? Yo' two foot' mus' be tie togedduh, enty? Befo' de Lawd, you stan' same lukkuh yo' maamy en' yo' gran'-maamy alltwo. You is tarrypin w'en time come fuh wu'k, en' bu'd w'en time come fuh play!"

Old Carolina Manigo sat on a three-legged stool at the door of his cabin, as he thus addressed his grand-daughter, Lucinda, a scrawny negress of twelve or thirteen years. With reluctant feet, the girl, a pitiful object, approached him. Her dress and appearance were in keeping with the wretched poverty of her grandfather and all his surroundings, and evidenced the utter incapacity of the average negro, thrown by "freedom" upon his own resources, to care decently for his family. The frowzy wool on her unkempt head had been plaited weeks before into little pigtails that bristled all over her crown like black caterpillars. Her face was gray with dirt, around her thick lips lingered the encrusted remnants of her sweet-potato dinner of the day before, while down her cheeks lay, like the rills of resinous gum that streak the bark of the pine tree "boxed" for turpentine, the tracks of recent tears. Through the rifts in the ragged cotton dress that constituted her sole attire, her scraggy limbs showed as she walked, or limped, rather, toward her grandfather. Around her left foot was wrapped a piece of burlap bagging, and, whenever she stepped upon it, her pinched face contracted with pain.

259

" 'Smattuh, gal, snake bite you, enty? Dis house
mus'be hab sin, 'cause dis mek de two time Gawd, een
'e mussy, sen' mis'ry en' water-moccasin een dis fambly. Las' week dem 'stroy'd Hol'fas' (w'ich him wuz
de bes' rokkoon dog ebbuh git 'pun a trail) en' now,
please de Mastuh, de snake gone en' structid dis chillun gal, en' 'e gwine to dead on my han', en' 'e know
berry well 'e ma gone town, en', ef 'e *yiz* dead befo' 'e
ma git back frum town, him will lef' me bidout a
Gawd' somebody fuh min' bu'd out de cawnfiel', en' I
nebbuh see, sence I bawn, shishuh hebby gang uh
woodpeckuh', crow' en' all kind'uh annimel lukkuh
dis same Augus' munt'. Gal! You ent gots no eye een
yo' head 'scusin' fuh look fuh blackberry, enty? You
walk duh paat' en' tu'n yo' gaze 'puntop de sky,
'stead'uh quizzit de groun' weh you duh walk! W'en
you dead, who gwine keep jaybu'd' out'n dis fiel'? I
good min' to lick you!"

"Gran'puh," whimpered 'Cindy, "I nebbuh step
'puntop no snake, suh, 'tis briah w'at 'cratch me foot."

"Briah!" laughed old Ca'lina, derisively. *"Briah!*
Who'ebbuh yerry 'bout shishuh t'ing! Briah! I sway
to Gawd, gal, you mos' mek me laugh! Weh de debble
you ebbuh know briah kin 'cratch nigguh' foot? You
mus' be t'ink you is buckruh, enty? You binnuh walk
een briah en' t'ing ebbuh sence you bawn, 'tell de bottom uh yo' foot haa'd same lukkuh alligettuh' back,
en' you gots de impedin' to come'yuh en' tell yo' gran'-
puh dat briah 'cratch yo' foot! Step fas', gal. Slow
walkin' mek quick lickin', en' fus t'ing you know
briah will 'cratch you 'puntop yo' back 'stead'uh 'pun
yo' lef' han' feet. Mek'ace, gal, en' come'yuh. Ent you
'membuh dat, een de 'Postle Paul' 'Pistle to de

EGG-ZACTLY

'Feeshun', him resplain de wu'd dat 'long talk ketch run'way nigguh?' Ent you know dat dey ent uh Chryce' hom'ny een de house fuh eat? De las' fr'en' I got een dis wull' wuz ole Hol'fas', en' snake gone en' structid dat dog en' kill'um, en' ebbuh sence 'e dead, de waa'ment en' t'ing come en' 'stroy'd eb'ry Gawd' fowl on de place, en' las' night wil'cat come en' ketch de frizzle hen wat binnuh set onduhneet' de cedar bush een de fench cawnuh, en' de hen 'low de cat fuh ketch'um, en' t'ree uh de aig' is duck aig' en' two uh de odduh'res' is tuckrey aig', en' you bettuh tek de aig' to Mistuh Ram' sto' to de Cross Road', en' chaa'ge'um seb'npunce fuh de aig', 'cause I don't t'ink de aig' kin specify berry well, 'cause de hen w'at bin seddown 'puntop de aig' git ketch by de wil'cat en' de aig' binnuh seddown een de jew en' t'ing, but ef de buckruh 'tarrygate you en' quizzit you too ondeestunt 'bout de aig', you kin tell'um dat de aig' kin specify, 'cause de frizzle hen w'at de wil'cat ketch ent binnuh seddown 'puntop dem aig' mo'n t'ree week, en' you kin tell'um dat wehreas de hen aig' oughtuh hatch'out een t'ree week' de duck aig' en' de tuckrey aig' ent jue fuh hatch'out 'tell de fo' week done out, en' tell'um dat wehreas de hen aig' en' de duck aig' en' de tuckrey aig' all binnuh keep one'nudduh cump'ny, de hen aig' is too mannusubble fuh hatch'out befo' de odduh'res' aig', so de hen aig' keep 'e cyarrictuh f'um spile, 'tell all 'e cump'ny done hatch'out."

AN INTERRUPTED OFFERTORY

Out at the edge of the woods that fringed a sea-island cotton field in the lower part of Colleton County, stood a little bush church—a primitive affair, constructed by setting four ten-foot stakes at the corners of a square, laying ridgepoles in their forked tops, and covering the whole with green boughs of the sweetgum. Humble as it was, this summer sanctuary of the Rev. Nepchun Kinlaw's congregation was as dear to them as was ever minareted mosque to Moslem, or cloister to Monk. Here, during the warm weather, when the more pretentious clapboard church became unbearably hot, they assembled two or three times a week to receive the pearls of theological thought that, clothed in the Gullah dialect of the Carolina coast, fell from the thick lips of their beloved "locus pastuh." Here, sheltered from sunshine and shower, they sat, like roosting chickens, on pine poles that, upholstered only with the bark that covered them, rested upon upright stakes sawed square at the top and driven into the ground. When these "pews" were filled to the ends, the overflow found lodgment on the stumps and logs that lay within sound of the preacher's voice in the environing forest.

On a night in the early summer, an unusually large congregation had gathered at this trysting place of the faithful, for the news had spread that "Pa Kinlaw" was going to say something sensational on the subject of pastoral ways and means. The night was dark, the sky overcast, and now and then the low rumble of distant thunder and a fitful gust of wind from the south-east, that soughed through the tops of the pines for a moment and then died away, betokened the coming storm. Around the place of worship, two or three pine-knot fires blazed brightly, furnishing, at once, light for the comfort of the congregation, and smoke for the discomfiture of the gnats and sandflies that swarmed about the church. Around and between the fires, the negroes, men and women, moved, avoiding the smoke and sparks that the wind, from time to time, sent among them, the firelight falling on their dark faces recalling the "hot-pot" scene in Rider Haggard's "She." While they awaited the advent of their preacher, they discussed their daily pleasures, trials, hopes and fears—the reduced cost of bacon or calico at the country store, the demand for labor, and the increased price therefor, at the rice plantations along the river, the destruction of the early corn by the cutworms and the crows, etc.

"I yerry," said one old woman to another, "I yerry dat Mistuh FitzSimmun done tek de sprout flow off 'e rice, en' 'e gwine hoe'um nex' week, T'ursday."

"Dat so?" said her companion. "Den, I gwine dey sho' ez Gawd lemme go. Ef my juntlemun kin git uh hawss, eeduhso uh oxin, fuh knock de middle out'n 'e crap, I will mek she go 'long too, alldo' 'e gots de mis'ry een 'e back 'tell 'e cyan' specify wid 'e hoe lukkuh 'e nyuse to do."

"I 'spec'," said old Ca'lina Manigo, "I 'spec', I mos' sho', rokkoon duh walk duh paat' dis berry night! Please Gawd, ef Him didn' mek dat snake 'stroy'd Hol'fas' las' yeah, I could'uh ketch one tenight, tenight, duh de night!"

"Ef you so hongry fuh rokkoon meat, w'en de praise

done gitt'ru, we kin tek my dog Ring en' tek a leetle dribe," said Monday Parker, a stalwart black fellow.

"*Ring!*" said Ca'lina, scornfully. "*Ring!* Boy, ef you talk Ring' name een de same bre't' wid Hol'fas' name, you will mek me hab sin right yuh tenight! I kin tek ole Hol'fas' jawbone out'n de du't weh de buzzut done lef'um, en' I kin pit dat jawbone 'puntop uh rokkoon track, en' him will mek de rokkoon git een de tree top, befo' Ring kin ketch a fleas out'n 'e own tail! Go'way, Paa'kuh, man, you know berry well yo' dog cyan' specify!"

"'Nuf t'ing, 'scusin' dog, dey een dis wull' w'at cyan' specify," said a deep voice from the darkness without, and, in a moment more, the long-looked-for pastor, mounted on a raw-boned brindled ox, rode into the broad disk of fire-light that filled the glade. A grain sack stuffed with corn shucks was his saddle, and a long grapevine wound around and around the unhappy ox, together with martingales and crupper of the same, held it in place. A bridle and stirrups of frayed cotton rope completed the extraordinary equestrian equipment.

"Cow iz shishuh 'ceitful t'ing fuh ride, dat I mos' didn' mek me 'p'int," said the preacher, as he dismounted and hitched his animal to a bush.

"Paul Jinkin' got some shinny peas plant close by de road aige, en' dis cow bin so hongry dat, w'en I git to weh de fench bruk down, 'e tek 'eself en' me en' all, en' gone een de fiel' en' staa't fuh nyam de peas, en' I try fuh git'um out de fiel', 'cause Paul ent b'long to we chu'ch, but de cow haa'd-head ez a 'ooman, en' I couldn' git'um fuh lef' de fiel', ontel we yerry Paul call to 'e lady fuh git up en' he'p'um ketch de somebody w'at dey een de fiel', en' w'en I yerry *dat*, I yent want'uh git de cow' cyarrictuh spile, so I mek'um come out'n' de fiel'—en' dat how I git yuh late."

Taking his stand in the tall box of rough pine boards that served for a pulpit, he looked askance at the contributions to his support that various members of his congregation brought to the altar and laid on the ground beside him. A quart of grist, a dozen eggs, a chicken, a pint of "clean" rice, a nickle—ostentatiously brought forth from a knot in the corner of an apron and placed by the proud donor "een de Reb-'ren' han'"—such were the offerings of this simple people, but, although representing more than a tithe of their possessions, they found little favor in the pastor's eyes.

"Sistuh Wineglass," said he, as a bustling middle-aged woman smilingly presented a chicken, "Sistuh Wineglass, chickin' seems to sca'ceful een dis congregashun ez debble sca'ceful een heab'n! Dis mek only de t'ree chickin' w'at bin contri*butes* to dis chu'ch sence de las' quawt'ly preachin', en' I done tell oonuh one time 'ready dat dis pulpit cyan' filfill' bidout *bittle*. Ent de Scriptuh say een de fo'teen chaptuh een Nickuhdemus, dat de lab'ruh wut' 'e hire? I gots to lef' my crap kibbuh wid grass, en' come yuh fuh 'rassle en' agguhnize wid oonuh sinful soul en' t'ing, en' you gots de nomannus to come een de Lawd' house wid t'ree aig' en' one leetle fo'punce chickin een yo' han', en' 'spec' fuh ketch salwashun, enty? Ef you saa'ch Nickuhdemus' wu'd you will fin' dat 'e say 'sponsubble dat a fo'punce chickin cyan' specify fuh seb'npunce' wut' uh salwashun! You tell me week befo' las' dat you couldn' git no chickin' 'scusin' you git aig', en' you cyan' gots no aig' 'cep'n' de hen lay'um, but de Lawd' wu'd say, ef yo' right han', eed-uhso yo' right han' feet, refen' you, you mus' cut'um off, en' ef de hen cyan' specify, you mus' cut off him head same fashi'n en' " —

The pastor's prelude was brought to a sudden close by a deafening peal of thunder that echoed and re-echoed through the forest. A gust of wind lifted the sweetgum thatch from the rafters of the little church and scattered the boughs to leeward, and, as the big raindrops began to fall upon the assembled worshipers, Pa Kinlaw gathered together his prog, mounted his ox, and trotted off in the darkness, calling to his flock as he went, "de Lawd en' me alltwo cyan' talk one time! De nex' preachin' will be to Sis-tuh Rab'nel' house 'bout fus' daa'k Chuesday night!"

A FLAW IN THE "EENDITEMENT"

She came into the office of a Walterboro lawyer and engaged his services to reverse, upset and "spile" the decision of a trial justice who had just fined her "nine dolluh' en' de cawss', suh," for obstructing a public highway.

Grace Rivers was her "eentitlement." The color of her skin was so deep that a piece of charcoal drawn across her face would have left a pallid mark. Although literally on the "shady side" of seventy, she was not regardless of the advantages of dress, and her costume was, like Katisha's left elbow, worth "coming miles to see." The gray wool that covered her head was snarled and tangled like a burry merino pelt, but a man's black straw hat, battered and weather-stained, was set upon it as jauntily as was ever worn the rakish cap of Fra Diavolo! When a fashion-plate had last been seen in her habitat near Ion's Cross Roads, bustles were "the thing." Although these protuberances on the human form divine had long since been called in and relegated to the rear (?) they were still "the thing" for Grace. The balloon bustle of the society actress, the oscillating bustle, the coiled-spring variety that rebelled at being sat upon, and, when "crushed to earth," like truth, would "rise again," having passed away, were not now obtainable at the country stores; so the ingenuity of this dusky devotee of fashion was called into play, and she had constructed as unique a "dress improver" as was ever worn under the sun—or under a home-spun skirt, either, for that matter. A rift in the rear of her gown disclosed

the mechanism of this work of art, which was merely
a piece of an iron barrel hoop, bent into a half-elipse,
and wound with two or three thicknesses of cotton
bagging. Primitive as it was, it sufficed to elevate the
hind part of her skirt several inches above the level of
the lower periphery of the front breadth, which was
hidden by an apron made of a rough-dried guano sack,
on which appeared in bold stenciled letters, "Ashepoo
Acid Phosphate, 200 pounds—privilege tax paid."

Taking a seat in the counsellor's office, she said:
"Majuh, I come fuh git jestuss yuh teday, teday!
W'en my juntlemun, Mistuh Ribbuhs, dead yeah befo'
las', een Augus' munt' (en' 'e dead 'cause snake
structid'um on 'e lef' han' feet w'en 'e binnuh gwine
to praise meetin' to Sistuh Gibbes' house on Hawss
Shoe causeway) w'en him dead, 'e lef' me t'irty acre'
lan' w'ich 'e buy frum Cap'n Gracy befo' 'e dead. Now,
w'en my juntlemun binnuh lib, Cudjo Singletun en'
'e fambly buy a piece uh groun' close to weh we lib,
en' likeso Sambo Hawlback buy groun' eenjinin' de
same lan'. 'Long ez my juntlemun binnuh *lib*, dem
berry well sattify fuh trabble 'longside de aige uh my
groun' w'en dem duh gwine chu'ch, eeduhso to de sto',
but soon ez my juntlemun *dead*, de eegnunt nigguh'
git so swell'up en' 'laagin', dem come en' cut paat' t'ru
my pinelan', en' call'um pulblic road. W'en I see de
'ceitfulness' en' de ondeestunt gwinin' en' gwinin' uh
dese nomannus nigguh', I git disgus' wid de nigguh',
en' I mek a fench 'cross de road, 'tell de road couldn'
specify. Now, w'en Sunday night come, Sambo tek 'e
lady een 'e oxin cyaa't, en' staa't lukkuh him duh
gwine chu'ch, but 'e nebbuh git to chu'ch, suh, 'cause
'e oxin ent gots good eye duh night time, en' de oxin

268

git tanglety'up een de fench, befo' Sambo ruckuhnize weh 'e duh gwine, en' de oxin t'row Sambo' lady out'n de cyaa't, en' de lady fuhgit de 'lij'un w'at 'e staa't fuh tek to chu'ch, en' 'e git bex, en' Sambo git bex, en, fin'lly at las', dem didn' gone chu'ch, but dem tu'n back home, en' nex' mawnin' Sambo gone to de Trial Jestuss en' swayre out warrant fuh 'res' me en' my groun' fuh twis'up en' obstruck de pulblic highway, en' de Jestuss sen' a mufflejaw' nigguh counstubble to my house, en' him tek me off befo' I gitt'uh chance eb'nso fuh pit on me shoesh, en' I tell'um dat 'e yent deestunt, no, suh, fuh 'res' a lady en' tek'um to co't, bidout 'e shoesh 'puntop 'e foot, but dat counstubble raise' by po' buckruh en' 'e yent gots uh Chryce' man- nus to 'e name!"

"Well," said the attorney, when he had stemmed this torrent of speech, "did you tell him that you were not ready for trial; that you wished time to secure counsel and to summon witnesses to testify in your behalf?"

"I *baig'um*, I tell'um, 'Mistuh Awkuhmun, I want to quizzit you on dis p'int, how de debble you kin 'res' a lady fuh obstruck uh highway, w'en you know berry- well de road w'ich de nigguh' mek t'ru my lan', run t'ru *low groun'!* How, een de name uh Gawd, kin I eentuhfayre wid de pulblic *highway* w'en de road so *low* dat 'e full uh watuh 'tell limus cootuh en' t'ing duh swim een'um! No, suh! 'scusin' you kin ansuh me dat parable, yo' eenditement cyan' specify'."

"What was his reply," asked the lawyer.

" 'E didn' reply *nutt'n'*, suh. 'E jis' tell me I gots fuh specify wid nine dolluh' en' de cawss', 'scusin' I want'uh leddown een Walterburruh jail ontell de t'ree

Sat'd'y een June. I didn' gots no money fuh g'em, so I g'em mawgidge on my cow en' t'ing 'tell I kin come yuh to you, suh, en' git you fuh see me t'ru, 'cause dis ondelicate buckruh 'res' me', en' try me en' all, een one en' de same day. 'E wouldn' eb'n gimme time fuh go home en' reconstruck meself, en', please suh, Majuh, w'en my juntlemun dead, 'e tell me fuh fin' out w'at you will chaa'ge me fuh tek care uh me en' my cow en' my groun' en' t'ing by de yeah—eb'n so ef I duh sleep—I want you fuh see how much you will chaa'ge fuh keep nigguh, en' counstubble, en' po'buckruh en' all kind'uh waa'ment en' t'ing off my groun', 'tell I *dead*, suh."

The lawyer told her he would consider the matter, and, Ashepoo's "Nada, the Lily," with a curtsy to the stranger within the attorney's gate, drifted out into the brilliant sunlight that lay like a golden mantle on field and woodland.

OLD WINE—NEW BOTTLES

He lived in Spartanburg, and was the proud valet (pronounced "valley" in the up-country) of a young physician. Whether the charcoal hue of his face, or his employer's profession, prompted a clever woman to bestow upon him the appellation of "the valley of the shadow of death," I do not know, but it certainly seemed, to every one acquainted with him, a peculiarly appropriate "eentitle*ment*."

Whence he came was a mystery. He tramped into the town one day, with his kinky wool full of the red dust of the up-country roads and his mouth full of the Gullah dialect of the coast, and asked for work. Although not more than thirteen years of age, his hardened muscles and pinched face indicated that he had known both toil and starvation. "Gran'puh lick me en' I run'way en' lef'um," was all he said, and, as he proved industrious and reasonably honest, there was no further inquiry into his antecedents.

One day, soon after he had established himself in his Spartanburg sanctuary, I chanced, while on a visit to the low-country, to learn something of his history. Passing through a plantation, formerly the home of a distinguished South Carolina family, but now abandoned to the occupancy of a few negro squatters, whose slovenly agricultural methods extracted but a scanty subsistence from the naturally fertile soil, I came to a miserable cabin, half a mile away from the main settlement. On its site had once stood a comfortable frame house of the type in general use on Southern plantations for ante-bellum negro quarters,

271

but the woodwork had long since been destroyed by fire, and the brick chimney alone remained. Among the negroes of the coast, where brick are scarce and the cabin chimneys are generally made of clay or mud, the possession of a brick "chimbly" is a sort of badge of aristocracy and a passport to high position in colored society, and old Scipio Smashum, having been a house servant before the war, and, retaining through all the hardships that had come to him with freedom, a profound contempt for the coarser-fibred "field hands," preferred to live apart from them, and had reared around the isolated brick chimney a habitation which, even when new, was never weatherproof, and was now in a pitiable state of dilapidation.

From the pine saplings, of which the walls were constructed, the rotting bark had fallen away, disclosing the perforations of the wood borers or "sawyers," whose industry had almost honey-combed the sappy logs. The clapboards which covered the house were falling to pieces with decay, and here and there on the weather-worn roof lay, like oases in a desert of gray, patches of green mould.

The surroundings of the cabin were as unkempt and unattractive as the building itself. Dogfennel and "Jimpson" weed grew almost up to the threshold. A few rows of corn and beans in a garden nearby were choked with grass and had been abandoned soon after the plants were up. The "wattled" fence of clapboards surrounding it was tumbling down, and through the fallen panels the neighbors' cows and pigs roamed at will. On the top of a little log chicken coop, a young Dominique rooster cackled loudly while he awaited the coming of his partner, who was, at the moment, busied with domestic duties within.

On a bench near the door sat old Scipio. The wool which covered his head was as white as the back of a Cotswold sheep, and the face, in which his bleared and jaundiced eyes were deeply set, was seamed with care.

As I approached, he was upbraiding the boastful rooster. "You so 'laagin'. Soon ez yo' lady git on 'e nes' you biggin fuh cackle same lukkuh *you* duh specify, 'stead'uh *him*. You stan' dey wid yo' back speckle' lukkuh one dese red-head' woodpeckuh', en' t'ink you gots mo' eentruss' een dat aig den de hen 'eself.—Mawnin', maussuh, t'engk *Gawd* I see you teday. De time so berry haa'd, maussuh; ef you didn' bin come soon, I 'spec' you wouldn' uh fine' yo' ole nigguh yuh teday. I mos' t'ink de big Maussuh gwine to call me putty soon, 'cause de mis'ry een de back git mo' wuss den 'e nyuse to be, en' bittle git so sca'ceful dese day', en' I cyan' hol' de hoe like I could'uh do one time, en' I cyan' git no cow, needuhso no mule, fuh plow de groun', 'tell I cyan' raise no crop, en' eb'nso w'en de crop done plant, I yent gots no chillun en' t'ing' fuh keep de waa'*ment* out'n'um, en' I mos' t'ink ef you didn' come teday, *Stepney* would'uh git dis po' ole body. Trouble come sence you bin yuh las', sho' ez Gawd! Dat boy Joe run'way en' gone to de up-country jis' 'cause I lick'um, en' soon as *him* gone, old Sancho Haywu'd' lady dead, en' Sancho come en' tek'way my gran'daa'tuh 'Riah, en' tek'um home fuh wife. I t'aw't dat ole nigguh had mo' sense, but w'en I peruse 'e cyarrictuh close, I see 'e cyan' specify ez uh sensubble man."

"When did his wife die?" I asked.

" 'E dead een Fibbywerry, suh. 'E binnuh cook supper, en' 'e gone to de shelf fuh git salt fuh pit een de hom'ny, en' ebbuh sence 'e gots catt'rack' een 'e yeye 'e cyan' see berry well, en' 'stead'uh tek de can wid de salt, 'e tek de can wid de consecrate' lye, en' 'e pit de consecrate' lye een de hom'ny, en' fus' t'ing 'e know, 'e yent know *nutt'n'* 'cause 'e dead! Oh yaas'suh, 'e git relij'un jis' befo' 'e dead, en' 'e dead beautiful, yaas' suh, en' 'e had de biggis' fun'rul you ebbuh see, en' ole Pa Sancho pit 'e lady een de groun' lukkuh teday, en', please Gawd, ez 'e gwine home frum de fun'rul dat same berry day, 'e come by my house en' tek my gran' 'Riah en' tek she home fuh wife! Ef I had'uh bin home, I wouldn'uh let'um tek de gal befo' de munt' done out, 'e would'uh look mo' *deestunt*, yaas'suh. But I don' min' 'bout Sancho, 'cause dat gal gwine to mek'um t'ink t'unduhsnake got'um befo' dis yeah gone, yaas'suh. I tell'um, 'Sancho, you better min'! Tek care bettuh mo'nuh baig paa'd'n*, en' Paul' wu'd to Buhrabbus een de Scriptuh specify puhtickluh dat you cyan' pit uh nyung grapewine een uh ole killybash, en' you cyan' pit a nyung 'ooman een uh ole 'ooman' frock, 'cause dem alltwo will buss'. Sancho, you know berry well you cyan' specify, en' you ent gots de strengk fuh lick dat nyung 'ooman, en' likeso Buhrabbus say dat ef you don' lick yo' lady you will spile 'e chile,' but I sway-to-Gawd, suh, dat gal tu'n Pa Sancho staa't fool, en' 'e nebbuh had my exwice een de back'uh 'e head! En' now, maussuh, sence de gal gone, I ent gots nobody fuh do nutt'n' fuh me. Dese nigguh' w'at grow up sence freedom come een ent gots no mannus, en' dey would'uh lemme dead een dis house, ef de w'ite people didn' see me t'ru. W'en ole Missis binnuh lib, bress Gawd, 'e always 'membuh de ole nigguh, but

---

*"Take care" is better than "beg pardon."

now, sence him dead en' de grass duh grow obuh 'e grabe out yonduh onduhneet' de libe-oak tree, en' all de w'ite people w'at I raise lef' de ole plantesshun en' scattuh all obuh de wull', en' all kind'uh low-down buckruh, w'at couldn' 'sociate wid we w'ite people' fambly een ole time', come fuh lib on de place, please Gawd, I yent gots nutt'n' much fuh lib fuh now, dese days. T'engk you, nyung maussuh, t'engk you, suh, Gawd bress you!"

A GULLAH GLOSSARY

The Glossary included in this volume, while making no pretense to absolute accuracy, is offered as a workable list of the words in common use by the Negroes of the South Carolina coast. It is doubtful, however, if the vocabulary of any single individual comprises more than half the list, for many words in everyday use about Georgetown or Charleston occur rarely at Beaufort, or on the Combahee. Then, too, many terms and expressions have only a local significance. On the seacoast and along the lower reaches of the tidal rivers, "trus'-me-Gawd" (I trust my God) is the common name for the cranky, unseaworthy dugout canoe, the hazard of whose use on the rough waters of the coast implies faith in the watchful care of a divine Providence. Higher up the same river, however, where smoother waters exact smaller faith, the coffin-like craft is merely a "coo-noo," a "cun-noo," or a "con-noo."

He who adventures into Gullah and would "make head or tail" of its queer phonetics, must keep in mind the sounds "uh," "e," "um," and "a." In no other tongue, perhaps, can so much be expressed with so little strain upon brain or lips or glottis as by the Gullah's laconic use of these grunting jungle-sounds.

To the Gullah, the naked "a" at the top of the first column of the dictionary is "uh," the dominant note upon which his speech is pitched. With "uh" he boastfully proclaims the personal pronoun "I." As "bubbuh," or "budduh," or "buh," he greets his brethren; as "sistuh," or "tittuh," his sisters. Sweet potatoes he roasts and eats as "tettuh." His father, mother, daughter, are "farruh, murruh, daa'tuh;" his ever is "ebbuh," his never is "nebbuh;" forever, "fuhrebbuh." His answer is "ansuh," his master is "mastuh," his pastor is "pastuh" (and so is his pasture); his either is "eeduh," his neither is "needuh," his fever is "febuh," his river is "ribbuh," his cooter is "cootuh," his silver is "silbuh." If in daylight he falls asleep in an open place, the vulture's wing that hovers over him will cast a "shadduh." His neighbor is "navuh," his favor is "fabuh," his labor is "lavuh,"

277

his Savior is "Sabeyuh." His bother is "bodduh," his other is "odduh," his t'other is "todduh;" another, "anodduh." Otter is "ottuh," and 'gator is " 'gatuh;" better, "mo'bettuh," and alligator, "alligettuh." Barrow is "barruh," burrow is "burruh," furrow is "furruh," harrow is "harruh," borrow is "borruh;" tomorrow, "tomorruh." His mourner is "mo'nuh," and so is his more than (more nor) and corner is "cawnuh," "mauma" is "maumuh," "maussa" is "maussuh," cover is "kibbuh;" uncover, "onkibbuh," the white man is "buckruh," the Negro is "Nigguh." And finger is "finguh," as ginger is "ginjuh." Pshaw is "shuh," and sir is "suh." His feather is "fedduh," his weather is "wedduh," his measure is "medjuh," his pleasure is "pledjuh." And if, in pleasantry or wrath, he cries out upon a compatriot, he scornfully apostrophizes him as "uh Gulluh nigguh!"

Following "uh" in frequency of occurrence comes " 'e," a contraction of he, she (but used also for it)—usually pronounced as "ee" in see, but sometimes approaching "e" in set and "i" in sit; but, without the use of diacritical marks, the exact shading cannot be expressed. This " 'e" is ever in the Gullah mouth. If a man has shuffled off this mortal coil, " 'e dead;" if a fruitful woman has blessed the earth, " 'e hab chile;" if the dusky infant cries out upon the world, " 'e cry;" if a mule be too free with her hindlegs, " 'e kick." If winter comes, " 'e freeze," and in summer weather " 'e hot." If a storm approaches, " 'e gwine to wedduh;" when it breaks, " 'e t'unduh, 'e lightnin', 'e blow win', 'e rain."

In "Myths of the Georgia Coast," Colonel Jones's Gullahs pronounce this contraction "eh," but with this a clearer phonetic apprehension of the Gullah does not permit agreement. "Eh" is a good English word which the Gullah pronounces correctly and frequently utters in the ejaculation "eh, eh!" to express surprise or bewilderment.

Almost the twin of " 'e" is "um," expressing him, her, it and them. Did that man steal your pig? " 'E t'ief'um." Did the woman whip the boy? " 'E lick'um." Did the fire burn your house? " 'E bu'n'um." Have you finished your task? "Uh done'um." Did you shoot those crows? "Uh shoot'um." And "um" added to see or saw becomes "shum."

A GULLAH GLOSSARY

See that woman? "Uh shum." Did you see her yesterday? "Uh shum." Will you see her tomorrow? "Uh gwine shum." "Shum" expresses see, seeing, or saw him, her, it, or them.

If the Gullah Negro, in "fuh him" and "fuh she," changes the pronoun to "um," he adds an "r" for euphony and utters a rolling "fuhr'um;" and, similarly, "tuh him," "tuh she" are changed to "tuhr'um."

The Gullah's favorite pronunciation of our first vowel is that of "a" in at, hat, bat—words that, like all others having the same "a" sound, he invariably pronounces correctly. Drawled to the double "a" as in "baa," it does yeoman service in "paat'," path; "paa't," part; "smaa't," smart; "cyaa't," cart; "h'aa't," heart; "shaa'p," sharp; "baa'n," barn; "yaa'd," yard; "maamy," mother; "maa'k," mark; "staa't," start; and so in many other words.

In the Gullah there are many contradictions, the Negro sometimes taking surprisingly short-cuts, expressing himself succinctly and saying a great deal with but a mouthful of words; while at others he rambles interminably and wanders so far afield in his verbal intoxication that he can hardly come soberly again to his starting point.

In this tongue one word or combination of words frequently does duty for singular and plural numbers, past and present tenses, and for masculine, feminine, and neuter genders. Thus "Uh shum" may mean I saw him, I see him, I saw her, I see her, I saw it, I see it, I saw them, I see them. So "Uh tell'um" means I told or I tell him, her, or them. Oxen and bulls, as well as cows, are generally classified and denominated as "cow," oxen as "ox," "two ox," "ten ox," etc., while a single ox, if not called a "cow," is invariably "one oxin." " 'Ooman" is both woman and women; "man" stands also for men, although "mens" is sometimes used for the plural, as "t'ree man," or "fo' mens."

Many words the Gullahs pronounce correctly. These are here spelled in the normal way, as to respell them would result only in a useless mutilation of the text.

Very often the Gullah usage consists in new and peculiar applications of words, twisted to meet its own needs, and making a single vocable serve the purpose of many.

279

THE BLACK BORDER

With a single "knock," the Gullah knocks, has knocked, is knocking.

With but a "rock," he rocks, has rocked, is rocking.

With "fight," he fights, has fought, is fighting.

With "run," he runs, has run, is running; and so on with many other words, used to express singular and plural numbers, or all the simple tenses of the verb.

While the Gullah usually holds fast to his favorite pronunciation, he sometimes permits himself a grotesque variation. For example, his usual pronunciation of car is "cyaa'," which he utters as flatly as a Charlestonian of the Battery; but should he permit himself a "cyaar," he will roll you an "r" as raucously as any Ohioan.

Of course, all Gullah Negroes pronounce certain English words correctly, while others approximate, in varying degrees, the speech of their former masters. This fact accounts for the slight variations that will be noticed in the speech of different individuals in these stories, and in the several pronunciations sometimes occurring in the Glossary. For example, the Gullah word for you, ye, your, yours, is variously pronounced "ona, oona, oonuh, unnuh," and, among dyed-in-the-wool dialecticians, "yunnuh" and "wunnuh." So, the Orang-utan is called by some " 'Rangatang" and by the extremists " 'Ranguhtang."

Warm is "wawm;" form or inform, "fawm," "eenfawm;" morning is "mawnin';" corn, "cawn;" horse or horses, "hawss;" horn, "hawn;" born, "bawn;" cow is correctly pronounced, and calf is near enough to the Charleston usage to pass. Tore, torn, tears, and tearing are never used, tear taking the place of all. As: the girl tore her petticoat—"De gal tayre 'e 'coat." That man's shirt is torn—"Da' man' shu't tayre." This cloth tears badly—"Dis clawt' tayre bad." They are tearing off the boards—"Dem duh (does) tayre off de boa'd'."

Them ("dem") is universally used for they and their. They took off their shoes—"Dem tek off dem shoesh." Dog and hog, while sometimes drawled, are very rarely lengthened to "dawg" and "hawg," tho' God is almost invariably "Gawd." The contraction of your is "yo';" and yet, for

A GULLAH GLOSSARY

yours, instead of "yo'n"—the mountaineers' "yourn"—they prefer "you'own," as theirs or their own is always "dem'own."

Unlike Mr. Weller, the Gullah does not affect the letter V, which he always changes to W or B—Violet modestly shrinking to Wi'let or Bi'let, while, as Benus, the amorous Aphrodite doubtless loves quite as ardently in her humble way. And the soft and teasing vex suggests, as "bex," anger swift and passionate!

"Lukkuh," or "same lukkuh," a corruption of like unto or same like unto—"same lukkuh" occasionally shortened into "sukkuh" by an excited or rapid talker—express likeness, resemblance.

"Hukkuh" is, of course, how come, or how came.

" 'E fat" means that the man, the woman, the pig, or the lightwood, is or was fat. " 'E fat fuh true" (in truth) adds emphasis, while " 'E fat fuh sowl" brooks no contradiction.

" 'Puntop," sometimes " 'puntap," or " 'pantap," on or near Edisto Island, means not only on top and on, but at. As: "De squinch owl light 'puntop de chimbly;" "Him plant' 'puntop Cumbee ribbuh;" "W'en uh look 'puntop de 'ooman en' see 'e yeye red, uh know him bex." "Biggin" is equivalent to begin, began, begun, or beginning.

"Haffuh" is both have to and had to. "W'en de strain leff'um to John' Ilun', him haffuh tek him foot en' gone *spang* town," meaning when she missed the train at John's Island station she had to walk all the way to Charleston.

"Same fashi'n," expressing likeness, has no sartorial significance.

"Alltwo" may mean both or each; as: "alligettuh en' cootuh alltwo stan' same fashi'n, alltwo hab fo' foot en' one tail, en' alltwo trabble 'puntop dem belly." So "stan' lukkuh" and "stan' sukkuh" mean look alike or bear a close resemblance, whether standing, sitting, crawling, lying, flying, or swimming.

"Wuffuh," or "woffuh," means why, or what for.

At times, "duh" and "suh" (not the "suh" for sir) have peculiar usage. "Wuffuh you duh do dat?" What for, or why are you doing that? "Him gone duh ribbuh," he has gone to the river. "Him walk duh paat'," he walks in the path (or the road). So, too, "'e duh sleep" for he does sleep, or he sleeps; and "duh wintuh time" for in the winter or during the winter. "Nuh" is another oddity, "me nuh him" being he and I.

Many years ago, the Reverend Kinlaw, upon hearing an educated darkey reading aloud one of the Kinlaw sermons from a newspaper, exclaimed: "Uh 'cla' to Gawd da' buckruh do me too bad! Dem t'ing suh him suh suh me susso, me nubbuh susso. Me t'ink'um, aw, but uh nubbuh susso, en' how de debble him know suh me t'ink'um, w'en uh nubbuh susso?" Which, interpreted, means: "I declare that buckra did me too bad. Those things that he said I said, I never said so. I thought them, it is true, but I never said them, and how did he know that I thought them, when I never said them?" Kinlaw was an extremely uncouth creature and his Gullah was of the rankest, spoken with the hot-potato-in-the-mouth effect of the low-comedy stage Irishman, hence his use of "suh" for that as well as for said, and of "nubbuh" for never, instead of the usual "nebbuh."

"Aw," for true, or to be sure, is seldom used.

"Ki," rarely "kwi," or "kwoy," is an exclamation.

"Nyam," or "nyam-nyam," means to eat.

"Bittle," is, of course, victuals—food.

"Blan," pronounced with the nasal resonance of the French "blanc," but without the broad "a" sound, or as the French would pronounce "blin," is probably a corruption of belong, and means used to or accustomed to.

"Study" means to think, ponder, plan.

The Gullah, like the Queen of Spain, has no legs, "foot" serving for the lower limbs as well as for their extremities. "Deer hab long foot, him run fas';" "Cootuh hab shawt foot, him trabble slow."

"Yez" is ear or ears, and "yeddy," sometimes "yerry," is hear, or hearing, heard; while "haa'kee" (hark ye) is also hear, and so on, whether addressed to one or to more persons, and is used not only in admonition, as "haa'kee at me good fashi'n," but is sometimes spoken lightly, as certain modern flappers and their bifurcated companions say "listen!" "Haa'kee" also does duty interchangeably for "yeddy," as

A GULLAH GLOSSARY

"haa'kee att'um," "yeddy'um"—hearken to him! hear him! And one who holds a warning as of small account, will often say in response to an admonitory "haa'kee!" "Yaas, bubbuh, uh haa'kee, but uh yent yeddy"—literally, I hearken but I don't hear, while actually meaning I hear but I don't heed, going in one ear and coming out of the other.

" 'Nuf" means not only enough, sufficiency, but more often abundance. Thus "you hab enny mint?" "Yaas, suh, we hab 'nuf," carries assurance of not merely enough for a few juleps, but a patch of fragrant greenery that could cover the graves of a score of old-school Virginians!

"Specify," one of the most characteristic Gullah words, from the English "specify," serves for most of the varied meanings of "specifications"—"making good." If a woman proves an unsuitable mate, she "cyan' specify." If trousers are frail, and "de britchiz buss'," " 'e yent specify." If a "cunnoo" proves unseaworthy—"him cyan' specify." And even of a Bible text, the fulfilment of whose promise seems inadequate, the Gullah says: "Buhrabbus' wu'd, him ent specify berry well."

"Enty," "ent," "yent," sometimes "ain'," serve for isn't, aren't, didn't, don't, doesn't. "Ent you shum?" "enty you shum?" may mean didn't you see? or don't you see? him, her, it, or them.

Preceded by a soft vowel sound, "iz" and "ent" are changed to "yiz" and "yent;" as: "him iz," "him ent," become, by the substitution of " 'e" for him, " 'e yiz," " 'e yent."

" 'Cep'n' " is except or excepting, and so is " 'scusin' " or "excusin'."

There is no nephew in the Gullah vocabulary, "niece" being used instead.

"Wunnuh," "yunnuh," "oonuh," "unnuh," occasionally "hoonuh," probably from one and another, is used for you and ye, usually in addressing more than one, though sometimes also in the singular.

Except along the Georgia and Carolina sea-coast and the outlying islands, the older Negroes are almost invariably addressed as "uncle" and "auntie" by the whites of all ages, and by the younger Negroes, but, wherever the Gullah dialect

283

predominates, "daddy" and "mauma" take their places. For that reason, perhaps, white children in the low-country never call their fathers "daddy," pa or papa frequently taking the place of the more formal "father."

Where the name of the person addressed or spoken of is used, "mauma" is changed to "maum," as "Maum Kate."

The simple name of the month is seldom sufficient, but must be fortified by the addition of "munt'," as: "Uh hab da' gal een June munt'."

Second, third, etc., are seldom used, the preferred forms being "two-time," "t'ree-time," etc. "Uh done tell oonuh fuh de two-time fuh lef' da' gal 'lone"—I've told you for the second time to leave that girl alone; and "two-time" is invariably used for twice. "Uh done call you two-time"—I've called you twice. The third Tuesday in August would be "De t'ree Chuesday een Augus'."

"Onrabble 'e mout'"—unravel her mouth, for it's always a feminine skein that's to be unwound—is as comprehensive as it is picturesque. At times the verbal tide flows on unchecked from a full ball of yarn; again, the ravelings are pulled angrily, jerkily, from the warp of a threadbare subject. "Onrabble 'e mout'!"

"Lef'"—left—is given not only its own proper meaning, but serves for leave, leaving, as "loss" does extra duty for lose, losing, lost.

"She-she talk"—a contemptuous characterization by Gullah bucks of feminine gossip—is suggestive of the whispering *frou-frou* of silken petticoats.

"En' t'ing'"—and things—is a verbal grab-bag comprehensive enough to hold every etcetera, animate or inanimate, that one may lay tongue to. A woman's "chillun en' t'ing'" may cover her chickens as well as her children; her "husbun' en' t'ing'" may include also her gentlemen friends, while reference to King Solomon's "wife en' t'ing'" would assuredly have lumped in with his wives every petticoat on the "Proverbial" premises!

The Gullah contraction of defend, is "'fen'," yet, if that defense be inadequate, he will invariably "refen'" himself. If he anoint, 'tis "'n'int," yet his pastor is the Lord's "renointed."

A GULLAH GLOSSARY

As the Gullah's tongue has no trouble with "eart' "—his correctly pronounced contraction of "earth"—he should have no difficulty with dirt or shirt, but these are invariably pronounced "du't" and "shu't;" and, although the "uh" sound is so easily uttered, he always "shets" a door, and tries to "shet," but never shuts, his lady's mouth.

Among the Negroes on Pon Pon, Stepney—a man's name —is commonly used as a synonym for hunger, want. He who hoped to keep the wolf away would "haffuh wu'k haa'd fuh keep Stepney frum de do'," while the fabled ant would admonish *La Cigale*, the grasshopper, "tek care, gal, you duh sing duh summuhtime, tek care Stepney don' come een yo' house 'fo' wintuhtime!"

There are, of course, many variations, some Negroes using only a few Gullah words, while practically all the house servants spoke without a taint. During the Confederate War, Phyllis, a highly trained young maid who had been taught deportment under Maum Bella, a fine old family servant in Charleston, once "impeached" the language of the five-year old boy under her charge. "Mass———, you shouldn't say path, you should say parth." How a broad "a" got loose in Charleston one can't imagine, unless it came in with the buxom Virginia girls who periodically descended upon "the City" to marry her most eligible young men.

The Gullah grabs his prophets, his kings, and his apostles out of the Old and New Testaments, haphazard, and uses them as they come, "to point a moral or adorn a tale"—and he believes in elaborate adornment.

Himself unlettered, he catches the names as they come to his ears from the lips of the whites, or of educated Negroes, and frequently gets his personnel inextricably mixed, the mouth-filling "Nickuhdemus" being quite as frequently turned out to graze, "bite grass," as the esteemed "Nebuhkuhnezzuh." The Apostle Paul is most often quoted by the class-leaders and local preachers, but they love to mouth over "Buhrabbus," while entirely ignorant of the character.

What Old Testament book can it be that the Gullah calls "Rebus?" Perhaps some Bible student will hazard a guess. It may be a far-fetched corruption of Genesis, for, in giving

285

THE BLACK BORDER

assurance of his having pursued a subject or an investigation from beginning to end, he will often say: "Uh bin t'ru da' t'ing frum Rebus *spang* to Rebelashun!"

Edisto Island was, before the war, through the fine Sea Island cotton produced there, one of the garden spots of the earth, and has been for many generations noted for the hospitality, culture, and refinement of its families; but in old times it was also noted for an unusual provincialism and for the habitual use of Gullah dialect by many of the planters' young sons. These were in constant association with their slaves on hunting and fishing parties, and unconsciously adopted the highly picturesque and expressive speech of their black servitors. They were accordingly subjected to many hard stories by their neighbors on the main land, who declared that, when the tardy news of Napoleon's exile to St. Helena, one hundred years ago, reached Edisto, the young islanders, believing their neighboring island of St. Helena to be the place of safe-keeping, were apprehensive of another "return from Elba," and, fearing the great Corsican as a potential liberator of their precious slaves, held an indignation meeting and resolved that: "Ef dem buckruh' 'pantap Sa'leenuh choose fuh hab 'Poleon come 'pantap *dem* ilun', berry well, but, uh swaytoGawd, him cyan' come 'pantap *dis* ilun', 'cause dat duh dainjus buckruh, en', fus' t'ing wunnuh know, him set we Nigguh' free."

The Edisto marshes abounded in wild donkeys, and a favorite Sunday amusement used to be the chevying of these unhappy animals out of the marshes by the white and black boys who, using sections of jackvine for whips, chased them over the plantations. A story is told of a young Edisto Islander who, a few days after matriculation at the University of Virginia, was requested by his fellow students to tell them something about the favorite sports and amusements of the South Carolina coast. He enlightened them as follows: "Great King wunnuh boy! Me nuh Cudjo blan hab fun duh Sunday. Cudjo him ketch long tail' hawss, me ketch shawt tail' hawss; we tek dem jack-wine, run dem jackass out'uh maa'sh, run'um all obuh plantesshun; den we blan go duh crik, ketch dem *big* pap-eye mullet!"

286

Vocabulary

The following list contains some seventeen hundred words. About this vocabulary two things are to be noted:

First, the Gullah is entirely a spoken, never a written, language;

Second, these 1,700 and odd words are so extended and applied according to Gullah usage as to serve the purpose and scope of at least 5,000 English words.

A

AA'GYFY—argue, argues, argued, arguing.

AA'GYMENT—argument, arguments.

AA'M—arm, arms.

AA'MY—army, armies.

ABBUHTIZE—advertise, advertises, advertised, advertising.

AB'NUE—avenue, avenues.

ACKSIDENT—accident, accidents.

ACQUAINTUN—acquainted. (See " 'quaintun").

ADSWOCATE—advocate, advocates, advocated, advocating.

AFF'IKIN—African, Africans.

AFF'IKY—Africa.

AFO'SED—aforesaid.

AGGUHNIZE—agonize, agonizes, agonized, agonizing.

AIG—(n. and v.) egg, eggs, egged, egging; as "him aig'um on."

AIGE—(n. and v.) edge, edges, edged, edging.

AIN'—(ain't) is not, isn't. (See "ent" and "yent").

AINJUL—angel, angels.

ALLDO'—although. (See " 'do' ").

ALLIGETTUH—alligator, alligators. (See " 'gatuh").

ALLIMUNNY—alimony.

ALLTIME—all the time, always.

ALLTWO—both, also each.

ALL UB UH SUDD'N ⎫
ALL UB UH SUDD'NT ⎬ —all of a sudden, suddenly.
ALL UB UH SUTT'N ⎭

AMBRELLUH—umbrella, umbrellas.

ANNIMEL—animal, animals.

ANODDUH
ANUDDUH } —another.

ANSUH—answer, answers, answered, answering. Also used for message, especially for one requiring an answer; as: "Uh sen' uh ansuh to de gal fuh tell'um uh wan' hab'um fuh wife"—I sent a message to the girl to tell her that I wanted to marry her.

AP'UN—apron, aprons.

AREY
ARUH } —each, either.

ASHISH—ashes.

ATTACKTID—attacked. (See " 'tack' " and " 'tacktid").

ATTUH—after.

ATTUHR'UM—after him, her, it, them.

ATTUHW'ILE—after a while.

AUGUS'—August.

AW—a queer word, sometimes used instead of "fuh true;" meaning, it is true, in truth.

AWKUHMUN—Ackerman—name of a white family.

AX—ask, asks, asked, asking.

AXIL—axle, axles.

AX'ME—ask, asks, asked, asking me.

AX'UM—ask or asked him, her, it, them.

B

BAA'BUH—barber, barbers.

BAA'K—(n. and v.) bark, barks, barked, barking.

BAA'NWELL—Barnwell. A low-country family name.

BAA'NYAA'D
BA'NYAA'D } —barnyard, barnyards.

BACTIZE—baptize, baptizes, baptized, baptizing.

BAD MOUT'—bad mouth—a spell, a form of curse.

BAID—beard, beards.

BAIG—beg, begs, begged, begging.

BAIG'UM—beg, begs, begged, begging him, her, it, them.

BAIT'UM—bait, baits, baited, baiting him, her, it, them.

BAKIN—bacon.

BALMUHRAL SKU'T—Balmoral skirt—a dark worsted under-skirt with red stripes above the hem, of the time of Queen Victoria and named for her castle at Balmoral.

A GULLAH GLOSSARY

'BANDUN—abandon, abandons, abandoned, abandoning.

BAPTIS'—Baptist, Baptists.

BARRIL—barrel, barrels.

BARRUH—barrow, a bacon hog.

BAWN—born.

BAYRE—bare, bares, bared, baring.

BEABUH—beaver, beavers.

BEAGLE—fox hound, fox hounds.

BEDOUT
BIDOUT } —without, unless, except.

BEEBU'D—bee-martin, king bird or Tyrannus Tyrannus.

BEEFU'T—Beaufort.

BEEHIBE—beehive, beehives.

BEFO'—before; as: "Befo' de wah." (See "'fo'").

BEFO' DAY—before day. (See "crack-uh-day," and "'fo' day").

BEHABE—behave, behaves, behaved, behaving.

BEHIME
BEHIN' } —behind.
BEHINE

BEKASE
BEKASEW'Y } —because, because why.

BEHOL'—behold, beholds, beheld, beholding.

BELLUH—bellow, bellows, bellowed, bellowing.

BELLUS—bellows (blacksmith's).

BEMEAN—to be mean to any one, to slander, abuse.

BEN'—bend, bends, bent, bending.

BENUS—(sometimes "Wenus")—Venus.

BERRY—(sometimes "werry")—very.

BERRYWELL—very well.

BERRYWELLDEN—very well then.

BES'—best.

BETTUH—better.

BEX—vex, vexes, vexing; angry, anger, angers, angered, angering.

BIDNESS—business.

BIGGIN—begin, begins, begun, began.

BIGGUH—bigger.

BIGHOUSE—the Master's house.

BILE—boil, boils, boiled, boiling.

BILIN'—boiling.

BILLIGE ⎫
BILLAGE ⎭ —village, villages.

BIMEBYE ⎫
BUMBYE ⎭ —bye and bye.

BIN—been, was.

BINNUH—been, was, was a; as: "W'en uh binnuh boy"—when I was a boy.

BITTLE—victuals, food.

BLACKBU'D—blackbird, blackbirds.

BLAN—belong, belongs, belonged, belonging; used redundantly; as: "Da' gal him blan blonx to my Maussuh"—That girl she belonged to belong, or used to belong, to my Master.

B'LEEBE—believe, believes, believed, believing.

'BLEEGE—oblige, obliges, obliged, obliging.

BLINE—(n. and v.) blind, blinds, blinded, blinding.

BLINE GAWD—blind God—personal idol or fetish of African suggestiveness whose aid is invoked to further the desires of its owner.

B'LONG ⎫
BLONX ⎭ —belong, belongs, belonged, belonging.

BLOODYNOUN—the great bull-frog of the swamps.

BOA'D—(n. and v.) board, boards, boarded, boarding.

BODDUH—bother, bothers, bothered, bothering; worry, worries, worried, worrying.

BODDUHR'UM—bother, bothers, bothered, or bothering him, her, it, them.

BOFE—both. (See "alltwo").

BOL'—bold.

BORRUH—borrow, borrows, borrowed, borrowing.

BOUN'—bound, resolved upon.

'BOUT—about.

BOWRE—bore, bores, bored, boring.

BRAWTUS—broadus, lagniappe.

BREAS'—breast, breasts.

BREDDUH—(also brudduh) brother, brethren (formal).

A GULLAH GLOSSARY

BREKWUS'
BRUKWUS' } —breakfast, breakfasts.

BRESH—brush, brushwood; brush, brushes, brushed, brushing.

BRESS—bless, blesses, blessed, blessing.

BRE'T'—breath.

BRIAH—briar, briars.

BRINLY—brindled.

BRITCHIN'—breeching (harness).

BRITCHIS
BRITCHIZ } —breeches, trousers.

BRUK—break, breaks, broke, breaking, broken; "bruk-foot man"—a broken-legged man.

BRUK-AA'M—broken-arm.

BRUK-FOOT—broken-foot, or leg.

BRUK'UP—break up, broke up, broken up: "De meetin' done bruk'up."

BRURO—bureau, as "Freedmun' bruro."

BRUSTLE—bustle, bustles.

BUBBUH
BUDDUH } —(familiar) brother.

BUCKRUH—a white person or persons; the white people.

BUCKRUH-BITTLE—white man's food.

BUCKRUH-NIGGUH—white man's Negro, used contemptuously.

BUCKSLEY—Berkeley (county).

BUD—bud, buds, budded, budding.

BU'D—bird, birds.

BU'DCAGE—birdcage, birdcages.

BUH—brother, as "Buh Rabbit."

BUHHIME
BUHHINE } —behind.

BUHR—burr, burrs.

BULL-YELLIN'—bull-yearling, or yearlings.

BU'N—burn, burns, burned, burning.

BURRUH—burrow, burrows, burrowed, burrowing.

BUSS'
BUS' } —burst, bursts, bursting.

BUTT'N—button, buttons, buttoned, buttoning.

BUZZUM—bosom, bosoms.
BUZZUT—buzzard, buzzards; vulture, vultures.

C

'CAJUN—occasion, occasions.
CALLICRO—calico.
CANNIBEL—cannibal, cannibals.
CANTUH—canter, canters, cantered, cantering.
CATT'RACK—cataract, cataracts (eye).
'CAUSE—because. (See "bekase").
CAW CAW SWAMP—a great low-country savanna.
'CAWCH—scorch, scorches, scorched, scorching.
CAWN—corn.
CAWNFIEL'—corn field, corn fields.
CAWNSTALK—corn stalk, corn stalks.
CAWNUH—(n. and v.) corner, corners, cornered, cornering.
CAWPRUL—corporal, corporals.
CAWPSE—corpse, corpses; coffin, coffins.
CAWPSUS—"corpus;" as: "cawpsus politicksus"—body politic.
CAWSETT—corset, corsets.
CAWSS'—(n. and v.) cost, costs, costing.

'CEEBE
'CEIBE } —deceive, deceives, deceived.

'CEEBIN'
'CEIBIN' } —deceiving.

'CEITFUL—deceitful.

'CEP'
'CEP'M } —except, excepts, excepted, excepting; accept,
'CEP'N' } accepts, accepted, accepting; unless.
CHAA'GE—charge, charges, charged, charging.
CHAA'STUN—Charleston, S. C. (See "Town").
CHANY—china, chinaware.
CHANYBERRY—Chinaberry, or Pride of India tree.
CHAW—chew, chews, chewed, chewing; also noun, as of
        tobacco.
CHEEP—cheep, cheeps, cheeped, cheeping.
CHEER—chair, chairs.
CHICAGYO—Chicago.
CHICKIN—chicken, chickens.

A GULLAH GLOSSARY

CHILE—child, children.

CHILLUN—child, children.

CHIMBLY—chimney, chimneys.

CHINKYPEN—chinquapin, chinquapins.

CHIZZUM—Chisolm—a low country family name.

CHOP'TONGUE—hounds with short yelp; the cry of the modern English fox-hound, as distinguished from the long bell-like notes of the Carolina deer-hounds.

CHRIS'MUS—Christmas.

CHRYCE—Christ.

CHU'CH—church, churches.

CHU'CHYAA'D—churchyard, churchyards.

CHUCKWILLUH—Chuck-Will's Widow, used to indicate the wide-open mouth of a hungry child.

CHUESDAY—Tuesday.

CHUNE—(n. and v.) tune, tunes; tune, tunes, tuned, tuning (up).

CHUNK—(n. and v.) chunk, chunks, chunked, chunking.

CHUPID }
CHUPIT } —stupid.

CLAWT'—cloth.

'CLA' TO GAWD—declare to God—a mild oath.

CLIMB—climb, climbs, climbed, climbing.

COA'SE—coarse.

'COAT—petticoat, petticoats (man's "coat" is always "jacket").

COAX—coax, coaxes, coaxed, coaxing.

COCKSPUHR—cockspur, cockspurs.

COHOOT—cahoot, agreement, association with, as: "Me en' Joe gone een uh cohoot fuh kill de buckruh' cow."

COHORT—colleague, colleagues.

COL'—cold.

COLLUH—collar, collars, collared, collaring.

COLLUH—color, colors ("we colluh," our color, or Negroes).

COME—come, comes, came, coming.

COME'YUH—come here.

COMMIKIL—comical, peculiar.

CONKYWINE—concubine, concubines; used for masculine as well as for feminine affiliations.

CONNOO ⎫
COONOO ⎬ —canoe, canoes.
CUNNOO ⎭

CONSAA'N ⎫ —(n. and v.) concern, concerns, concerned, con-
CUNSAA'N ⎭ cerning.

CONSECRATE LYE—concentrated lye.

CONSUMPSHUS ⎫
CUNSUMPSHUS ⎬ —consumption.

CONTESTUSS—contested, contesting.

CONTUHDIX—contradict, contradicts, contradicted, contradict-
ing.

COOK—cook, cooks, cooked, cooking.

COOTUH—cooter, cooters; terrapin, terrapins.

CO'SE—course, courses, as of a stream.

'CO'SE—course, of course.

CO'T—(n. and v.) court, courts; court, courts, courted, court-
ing.

COULDN'—could not.

COULD'UH—could have.

COUNSTUBBLE—constable, constables.

COW—cow, cows; bull, bulls; ox, oxen; cattle.

COW-PAAT'—cow-path.

CRACK 'E BRE'T'—crack his or her breath; same as "crack 'e
teet'."

CRACK 'E TEET'—crack, cracks, cracked, cracking his, her or
their teeth, meaning opened her or his mouth to
speak; as: " 'E yent crack 'e teet' "—She never
opened her mouth.

CRACK-UH-DAY—crack or break of day.

CRAP—(n. and v.) crop, crops; crops, cropped, cropping.

'CRAPE—(n. and v.) scrape, scrapes, scraped, scraping.

'CRATCH—(n. and v.) scratch, scratches, scratched, scratching.

CREDENSHUL—credential, credentials.

CREDIK—(n. and v.) credit, credits, credited, crediting.

CREETUH—creature, creatures. Commonly applied to a beast
of burden.

CRIK—creek, creeks.

A GULLAH GLOSSARY

CROOKETY—crooked; also tricky, unreliable.

CROSS-ROAD—the cross roads.

CRUCIFY—crucify, crucifies, crucified, crucifying; also improperly used for testify, testifies, testified, testifying.

CUCKLEBUHR—cockleburr, cockleburrs.

CUHLUMBIA—Columbia.

CUHLUMBUS—Columbus.

CULLOO—curlew, curlews.

CULLUD—colored, colored people, the dark race.

CUMBEE—the Combahee river, also the lands lying along the stream. This is, by the way, the correct pronunciation.

CUMPLAIN—(n. and v.) complain, complains, complained, complaining; complaint, complaints.

CUMP'NY—company, companies.

CUMPOSHASHUN
CUMPUHSHASHUN }—conversation, talk, parley, interroga-
COMPUHSHASHUN tories, argument.

CUNDEMN
CONDEMN } —condemn, condemns, condemned, condemning; but more frequently used to denote guilt or the appearance of guilt; as: "W'en uh ketch Joe wid de hog, 'e look so cundemn."

CUNFUSHUN—confusion.

CUMPLAIN—(n. and v.) complain, complains, complained,

CUNTRADY—contrary, provoking.

CUNWEENYUNT—convenient, conveniently, convenience.

CUNWEENYUNTLY—conveniently.

CUNWENSHUN—convention, conventions.

CUSS—(n. and v.) curse, curses, cursed, cursing.

CUT'DOWN, or TEK'DOWN—dejected, chagrined.

CUZ
CUZ'N } —cousin, cousins. (Shakespeare's "coz").

CYA'—carry, carries, carried, carrying.

CYAA'
CYAAR } —car, cars.

CYAAF—(n. and v.) calf, calves; to calve, etc.

CYAAM—calm, calms; "uh cyaam sea."

CYAA'PENTUH
CYAA'P'NTUH } —carpenter, carpenters.

CYAARIDGE—carriage, carriages.

CYAA'T—cart, carts.

CYACKLY
CACKLE } —cackle, cackles, cackled, cackling.

CYAN'—can't.

CYAS'—cast, casts, casting.

CYAS'NET—cast-net used for taking shrimp and mullet from tidal creeks.

CYA'UM—carry, carried, etc., him, her, it, them.

CYO'—cure, cures, cured, curing.

D

DA'
DAT } —that.

DAA'K—dark.

DAA'KY—darken, darkens, darkened, darkening.

DAA'TUH—daughter, daughters.

DA' DEY—that there.

DAINJUS—dangerous.

DAMIDGE—(n. and v.) damage, damages, damaged, damaging.

DAY-BRUK—day-break, day has broken.

DAYCLEAN—broad daylight.

DEAD—dead; die, dies, died, dying.

DEBBLE'UB'UH—devil of a.

DECEMBUH—December.

DEEF—deaf.

DEEPO'—depot, railway station.

DEESTRUSS—distress. (See "distruss").

DEESTUNT—decent, respectable.

DEM—them, they, those, their, theirs. Also used for "and them," as "Sancho dem," meaning Sancho and his companions.

DEM'OWN—theirs, their own.

DEMSELF—them, they, themselves.

A GULLAH GLOSSARY

Den—then, than.

Den—(v.) to den, stay in a den.

'Denticul—identical.

De Rock—the "Rock," or phosphate mines near Charleston.

Des'—just, as "des' so," just so. (See also "jis' ").

Dese—these.

Deseyuh—these here.

Desso
Disso ⎫ —just so. (See "jesso").

De't'—death.

Dey—they.

Dey—there.

Dey dey—there, there; right there; a repetition for greater emphasis.

Deyfo'—therefore.

Dibe—dive, dives, dived, dove, diving.

Dictate—dictate, dictates, dictated, dictating; giving orders, overseeing; sometimes for explaining.

Diffuh
Diffunce ⎫ —differ, difference.

Dimmycrack—Democrat, Democrats, Democratic.

Dinnuh—dinner, dinners.

Dis'—this; just. (See "jis' ").

Disapp'int—(n. and v.) disappoint, disappoints, disappointed, disappointing, disappointment, disappointments.

Disgus'—disgust, disgusts, disgusted, disgusting.

Disgustuss—disgusting.

Dishyuh—this, this here.

Distrus'—distrust, distrusts, distrusted, distrusting.

Distruss—distress. (See "deestruss").

Distunt—distant, distance.

Do—do, does, did, doing.

Do'—door, doors.

'Do'—though, although. (See "alldo' ").

Doctuh—doctor, doctors.

Dog—(n. and v.) dog, dogs, dogged, dogging.

Don'—don't, doesn't.

Done—done, did, already, has, finish, finished, as: "W'en you gwine done da' t'ing?"—when are you going to finish that thing? "Uh done'um," or "Uh done-done'um"—I have done or finished it.

DONE FUH—done for—meaning excessively, as: "Da' 'ooman done fuh fat"—that woman is excessively or very fat.

DONE DONE'UM
DONE DO'UM } —did it, finished the job.

DONE'UM—did it.

DO'STEP—doorstep, doorsteps.

DO'UM—do it, does it, did it, doing it.

DRAP—(n. and v.) drop, drops, dropped, dropping.

DREEN—(n. and v.) drain, drains, drained, draining.

DRIBE—drive, drives, drove, driven, driving.

DRIBE—(n.) a run, cover, or section of woods where certain game is found or hunted.

DROBE—(n.) drove, droves, as of animals.

DROUGHT—drought, droughts; "dry drought," protracted drought.

DROWNDID—drown, drowns, drowned, drowning.

DRY-BONE—dry-boned—thin, lean, often applied to dusky ladies who do not incline to *embonpoint*.

DRY SO—just so.

DUB—dove, doves.

DUH—do, does; in, to, toward. Thus "duh paat'," means going in the path, walking in the path; "duh ribbuh," going to the river, going on the river; "duh fiah," going to the fire; "duh 'ood," going to the woods, going in or through the woods; "duh Sunday," on Sunday; "duh weekyday," on a week day, week days; "duh summuh," summer, or in the summer; "duh wintuh," winter, or in the winter.

DUNKYUH—don't care, doesn't care, didn't care.

DUNNO—don't know, doesn't know, didn't know.

DU'T—dirt, earth.

DU'TTY—dirty, soiled.

E

'**E**—he, she, it.

EART'—earth, world, or soil, ground. (See "ye't" and "yu't").

A GULLAH GLOSSARY

EBBRUM—Abraham, Abram.

EBBUH—ever.

EBBUHLASTIN'—everlasting.

EBE—Eve, woman's name; also eaves.

EBENIN'—evening, evenings; "good evening," a salutation.

EB'N—even.

EB'NSO—even so.

EB'RY—every.

EB'RYT'ING—everything.

EB'RYWEH—everywhere.

ECKNOWLEDGE—knowledge, ability, understanding.

EDDYCASHUN—education.

EEDUH—either.

EEDUHSO—either so, either, else, or.

EEGNUNT—ignorant.

EEN—in.

EENBITE—(also eenwite) invite, invites, invited, inviting.

EENFAWM—inform, informs, informed, informing.

EENHABIT—inhabit, inhabits, inhabited, inhabiting.

EENJINE—engine, engines. (See "injine").

EENJININ'—adjoining.

EENJURIN'
ENJURIN' } —enduring, during.

EENJY—enjoy, enjoys, enjoyed, enjoying; experience; as:
     "Uh eenjy uh berry oncomfuhtubble night' res'"
     —I had or experienced a very uncomfortable night's
     rest.

EENSIDE—inside.

EENSULT—(n. and v.) insult, insults, insulted, insulting.

EENTITLE—entitle, entitles, entitled, entitling.

EENTITLEMENT—entitlement, "title;" as "Mr. Chizzum," "Mis'
     Wineglass."

EENTRUSS—interest.

EENTUHFAYRE—interfere, interferes, interfered, interfering.

EF—if.

EH, EH!—an exclamation.

ELSESO—else, unless; either.

ELLYFUNT—elephant, elephants.
ELLYMENT—element, air, sky.
EN'—end, ends, and.
ENNY—any.
ENT—(also yent) ain't, are not, is not, isn't.
EN' T'ING'—and things, and everything.
ENTY—ain't it, isn't it, are they not, etc.
ENT WUT'—isn't worth, meaning totally worthless, of no
        account.
EPPRULL—April.
'ESE'F—himself, herself, itself.
'E STAN' SO—it, he or she, stands so, it is so, it looks so, etc.
EXCEED—succeed, succeeds, succeeded, succeeding.
EXCUSIN'—excusing, except, excepting. (See " 'scusin' ").
EXWANCE—advance, advances, advanced, advancing.
EXWANTIDGE—advantage, advantages.
EXWICE—advice.
EXWISE—advise, advises, advised, advising.
EZ—as.

F

FABUH—(n. and v.) favor, favors, favored, favoring.
'F'AID—afraid, afraid of.
FAIT'—faith.
FAIT'FUL—faithful, earnest.
FAITFULES'—faithfulest.
FAMBLY—family, families; family's, families'.
FANNUH—a wide, shallow basket used for winnowing beaten
        rice or separating the corn husks from grist after
        grinding.
FARRUH—father, fathers,
FARRUHLAW—father-in-law, fathers-in-law.
FAS'—fast.
FASHI'N—fashion, like, resemblance.
FAST'N—fasten, fastens, fastened, fastening.
FAU'T—fault, faults.
FAWK—(n. and v.) fork, forks, forked, forking.
FAWM—(n. and v.) form, forms, formed, forming.
FAWTY—forty.

A GULLAH GLOSSARY

FAWWU'D—forward.

FEBUH—fever, fevers.

FEBBYWERRY
FIBBYWERRY } —February.

FEDDUH—feather, feathers.

FEED'UM—feed, feeds, fed, feeding him, her, it, them.

'FEESHUN'—Ephesians—Paul's Epistle to.

FEET—frequently used for foot; as: "Snake bite da' gal 'pun 'e lef' han' feet"—The snake bit that girl on her left foot.

FELLUH—fellow, fellows.

'FEN'—fend, defend. (See "refen' ").

FENCH—(n. and v.) fence, fences, fenced, fencing.

FIAH—(n. and v.) fire, fires, fired, firing.

FIBE
FI' } —five; "fibe dolluh en' seb'nty-fi' cent'."

FIDDLUH—fiddler, fiddlers; violinists and fiddler crabs.

FIEL'—field, fields.

FIEL'HAN'—field hand, field hands.

FIEL'NIGGUH—a laborer in the fields—the "peasant" of the plantation.

FIGHT—fight, fights, fought, fighting.

FILFIL—fulfill, fulfills, fulfilled, fulfilling; also fill, as to fill a pulpit.

FIN'—find, finds, found, finding; also to find, found, in the sense of furnishing or supplying rations.

FIN'LLY AT LAS'—meaning at last, finally.

FIN'UM—find, finds, found, finding him, her, it, them.

FISHPON'—fishpond, fishponds.

FISHPUN—Fishburne—name of a low country family.

FITZSIMMUN—FitzSimons—a low-country family name.

FLABUH—(n. and v.) flavor, flavors, flavored, flavoring; as: "Da' buckruh' hogmeat flabuh me mout' 'tell uh done fuhgit uh hab sin fuh kill'um"—That white man's pork flavored my mouth so that I forgot the sin I committed in killing the hog.

FLATFAWM—platform, platforms.

FLEW—fly, flies, flew, flying.

FLO'—floor, floors, floored, flooring.

301

FLY—flies, flew, flying.

Fo'—four.

'Fo'—before. (See "befo'").

Fo'CE—force, forces, forced, forcing.

FODDUH—fodder, used only for cured corn-blades.

FOLLUH—follow, follows, followed, following.

FOOT—foot, almost universally used for feet; also for leg.

Fo'PUNCE—four pence. Used universally to indicate size of chickens sold for four pence before the Revolution, when British money was the currency of the Colonies. See, also, "seb'npunce," which was used in a similar way.

FORRUD—forehead, foreheads.

Fo'TEEN—fourteen.

FOWL—fowl, fowls; chicken, chickens.

FRAIL—to whip or lash.

FRAJUH—Fraser, Frazier—a low-country family name.

FRAZZLE—(n. and v.) frazzle, fray, etc.

FREEDMUN—freedman, freedmen.

FREEDMUN' BRURO—Freedman's Bureau.

FREEDUM—freedom.

FREEHAN'—freehanded, generous, liberal.

FREEMALE—female, females.

FR'EN'—friend, friends.

FRIZZLE—frizzle, frizzles, frizzled, frizzling.

FROS'—frost.

FRUM ⎫
F'UM ⎬ —from.

FRY-BAKIN—fried bacon.

FRY-BAKIN FROG—the small pond frogs, whose constant cry is interpreted by the Negroes as "fry-bacon, tea-table; fry-bacon, tea-table."

FUDDUH—far, farther, farthest; further.

FUH—for, for to.

FUHGIT—forget, forgets, forgot, forgetting, forgotten.

FUH HAB—for have: "One dance bin fuh hab deepo' las' night"—a dance was to have been had at the depot last night.

FUHR'EBBUH—forever, always, all the time.

A GULLAH GLOSSARY

FUHR'UM—for him, her, it, them.

FUH SOWL—for truth, truly, used as emphasis; as: "'E fat fuh sowl"—He, she, it or they is, was, were or are very fat. "Sowl" is perhaps from the Irish pronunciation of soul; as in "upon me sowl!"

FUH SUTT'N—for certain, sure.

FUH TRUE—in truth, for truth, it is so.

FU'LHAWK—fowlhawk, fowlhawks.

FU'LHUS'—fowl-house, fowl-houses.

FULL—fill, fills, filled, filling.

FULL'UP—filled up, as a hive with honey, or a lady with wrath.

FUN'RUL—funeral, funerals.

FUS'—first.

FUS' DAA'K
FUS' DUS' } —first dark, dusk, twilight in the evening.

FUS' FOWL CROW—first fowl crow—midnight, or soon thereafter.

FUS' GWININ' OFF—first going off, at the beginning.

G

GABRULL—Angel Gabriel—he of the horn.

'GAGE—engage, engages, engaged, engaging; hire, hired, etc.

GAL—girl, girls; girl's, girls'. Also used familiarly in addressing women.

'GATUH—alligator, alligators. (See "alligettuh").

GAWD—God, Gods, God's.

GEDDUH—gather, gathers, gathered, gathering.

GELT
GIRT' } —girth, girths.

G'EM—give, gives, gave, giving him, her, it, them.

'GEN—again.

'GENSE—against.

GI'
GIB' } —give, gives, gave, giving.

GIMME—give me, gives me, gave me, giving me.

GINJUH—ginger.

GIN'NLLY—generally, in general.

GIN'UL—general.

G<small>IT</small>—get, gets, getting, got.

G<small>ITTA</small>—get a (See "gittuh").

G<small>ITT'RU</small>—get through, got through; finish, finished.

G<small>ITTUH</small>—get a (See "gitta").

G<small>IT'WAY</small>—get, gets, getting, got away.

G<small>I'WE</small>—give us, gives us, gave us, giving us.

'G<small>LEC</small>'—neglect, neglects, neglected, neglecting.

G<small>LUB</small>—glove, gloves.

G<small>O</small>—go, goes, going, gone, went.

G<small>OL</small>'—gold, golden.

G<small>ONE</small>—go, goes, going, gone; "time fuh gone"—time for me to go.

G<small>ONE'WAY</small>—go away, goes away, gone away, went away.

G<small>ONNIL</small>—gunwale, gunwales.

G<small>OOD-FASHI'N</small>—good fashion—well, thoroughly; as: "Uh lick da' gal good-fashi'n"—I gave that girl a thorough whipping.

G<small>OT</small>
G<small>OTS</small> }—get, gets, have, had; also, has got to.

G<small>O'WAY</small>—go away! get out!

G<small>RABBLE</small>—(n. and v.) gravel, gravels, graveled, graveling.

G<small>RABE</small>—grave, graves.

G<small>RAFF</small>—grab, grabs, grabbed, grabbing; grasp, seize, seized.

G<small>RAMMA</small>—grandmother. (See "grumma").

G<small>RAN</small>'—grand—grandchild, grandson, or anyone in such relationships of "grand".

G<small>RAN'MAAMY</small>—grandmother.

G<small>RANNY</small>—grandmother, but used for any old Negro woman, whether related or not.

G<small>RANO</small>—guano, phosphate, commercial fertilizers.

G<small>RAN'PUH</small>—grandfather. (See "grumpa," "grumpuh").

'G<small>REE</small>—agree, agrees, agreed, agreeing.

'G<small>REEMENT</small>—agreement, agreements.

G<small>REESE</small>—(n. and v.) grease: "greese 'e mout'," to feed with fatness, as with bacon.

G<small>REESY</small>—greasy.

G<small>RIN'SALT</small>—"grinding salt," said of a hawk or vulture circling aloft.

A GULLAH GLOSSARY

GRITCH—grist, grits.

GROUN'—ground, land, piece of land.

GRUMMA—grandma.

GRUMMOLE
GRU'MOLE } —ground-mole, ground-moles.

GRUM'PA
GRUM'PUH } —grandpa, grandfather.

GRUNNOT
GRUNNUT } —groundnut, groundnuts, peanuts. (See "pinduh").

GUBNUH—governor, governors.

GUNJUH—the scalloped molasses cakes sold in Southern country stores and commissaries.

GWI'
GWINE } —going, going to.

GWININ' EN' GWININ'—goings and goings on. Usually characterizing the light conduct of idle or irresponsible persons.

GYAA'D—(n. and v.) guard, guards, guarded, guarding.

GYAA'D'N—garden, gardens.

GYAP—gap, gaps, as in a fence or hedge.

GYAP—gape, gapes, gaped, gaping; also for speech, as: "'E nebbuh gyap"—she never opened her mouth.

H

HAA'BIS'—harvest.

HAA'BIS'-FLOW—harvest-flow, or last irrigation of the rice-fields preceding the harvest.

HAA'D—hard.

HAA'D-HEAD—hard-head, hard-headed.

HAA'KEE—hark you or ye, hear.

HAA'NESS—(n. and v.) harness, harnesses, harnessed, harnessing.

HAANT—haunt, haunts; apparition; ghost, ghosts.

H'AA'T—heart, hearts.

H'AA'T—hearth, hearths.

HAB—have, has, had, having.

HACK'LUS—Hercules.

HAFFUH—have to, had to.

HAIR RIZ'—hair rose (with fright). An expression adopted from the whites, as upon the kinky heads of the coast Negroes there is nothing that even fright could cause to rise.

HALF-ACRE—half acre—210 feet square—a measure of distance or area.

HAN'—(n. and v.) hand, hands, handed, handing.

HANCH—haunch, haunches, hind quarters.

HANKUH—hanker, long, longs, longed, longing for; desire, desired, desiring.

HAPP'N—happen, happens, happened, happening.

HARRICANE—hurricane, hurricanes; "harricane tree," one thrown down by storm.

HARRUH—(n. and v.) harrow, harrows, harrowed, harrowing.

HATCHITCH—hatchet, hatchets.

HAWN—horn, horns.

HAWN'OWL—the great horned owl.

HAWSS—horse, horses.

HEAD—(n. and v.) head, heads; head, heads, headed, heading off.

HEAD'UM—get, gets, got, getting ahead of him, her, it, them.

HEBBY—heavy, great; as: "uh hebby cumplain' "—a great outcry.

HE'LT'—health.

HE'LT'Y—healthy.

HENDUH—hinder, hinders, hindered, hindering.

HENG—hang, hangs, hanged, hung, hanging.

HENGKITCHUH—handkerchief, handkerchiefs.

HICE—hoist, hoists, hoisted, hoisting.

HICE DE CHUNE—hoist or raise the tune.

HIGGUHRI-HEE—the great horned owl. (See "hawn-owl").

HIM—he, she, it, his, her's, its.

HIM'OWN—his, her's, his own, her own, its own.

HIN'
HINE }—hind, behind; as, "hine foot"—hind feet.

HISTORICUSS—historic, historical.

HITCH—hitch, hitches, hitched, hitching; also for marry, marrying.

A GULLAH GLOSSARY

HOL'—(n. and v.) hold, holds, held, holding.

HOL'FAS'—Hold Fast—a favorite dog name.

HOLLUH—(n. and v.) hollow, hollows, hollowed, hollowing.

HOLLUH—halloo, halloos, hallooed, hallooing.

HOM'NY—hominy.

HONGRY—hungry, hunger.

HOONUH—you, ye. (See "oonuh" and "wunnuh").

HOT—heat, heats, heated, heating.

HUCCOME
HUKKUH } —how come, how came; how does or did it come; how came it?

HUDDY—howdy, how do you do?—"tell'um heap'uh huddy."

HUMMUCH—how much, or how many.

HUND'UD—hundred, hundreds.

HU'T
HO'T } —(n. and v.) hurt, hurts, hurting.

I

IMPEDIN'—impudence, impudent.

INFLUMMASHUN—information.

INGINE—engine, engines. (See "eenjine").

INJUN—Indian, Indians.

INTUHCEDE—intercede, intercedes, interceded, interceding.

I'ON
I'UN } —(n. and v.) iron, irons, ironed, ironing.

IZ
YIZ } —is.

IZICK—Isaac.

J

JACK—(n. and v.) jack, jacks, jacked, jacking.

JACKSINBURRUH—Jacksonboro.

JACKSTAN'—jack-stand—stands on which fires are kept at night in summer settlements for protection against mosquitoes and other insects.

JACKY-LANTU'N—Jack-o'-lantern—will-o'-the-wisp.

JALLUS—jealous, jealousy.

JAYBU'D—jaybird, jaybirds.

'JECK'—reject, rejects; object, objects, objected, objecting; objection.

THE BLACK BORDER

'Jeckshun—objection, objections.

'Jeck'um—reject or rejected him, as an undesirable juror.

Jedge—(n. and v.) judge, judges, judged, judging.

Jedus—Jesus.

Jestuss—justice.

Jew—Jew, Jews.

Jew—dew.

Jimpsin-weed ⎱
Jimsin-weed ⎰ —Jimpson or Jamestown-weed.

Jine—join, joins, joined, joining.

Jinin'—joining; adjoining. (See "eenjinin'").

Jinnywerry—January.

Jis'—just. (See "dis'").

Jisso ⎱
Jesso ⎰ —just so. (See "disso").

Johossee—Jehossee—a rice-growing island of the South Carolina Coast.

Jokok—Jaycocks—the name of former Governor Heyward's overseer on the Combahee.

Jook—jab, jabs, jabbed, jabbing.

Jookass—jackass, jackasses.

Judus Caesar—Julius Caesar.

Jue—due, dues.

Juhruzelum—Jerusalem.

Ju'k—jerk, jerks, jerked, jerking.

Julip—the vanished mint julep.

Jully—July.

Junk—chunk, chunks, as of lightwood.

Juntlemun—gentleman, gentlemen; also a woman's "man" or husband; as, "him juntlemun," meaning her husband.

Juntlemun' nigguh—gentleman's Negro, meaning one who as a slave had belonged to people of position—the "quality."

K

'Kace—scarce. (See "sca'ce").

'Kacely—scarcely, hardly. (See "sca'cely").

308

A GULLAH GLOSSARY

KETCH—catch, catches, caught, catching; took, take; as: " 'E
    ketch 'e tex f'um de fus' chaptuh een Nickuhdemus"—
    He took his text from the first chapter of Nicodemus.
    Also for reach, reached; as: "Time uh ketch de ribbuh
    bank, de dog done gone."

KETCH'UM—catch, catches, caught, catching him, her, it,
    them.

KI—an exclamation. (Sometimes "kwi" or "kwoy").

KIBBUH—(n. and v.) cover, covers, covered, covering.

KIBBUHR'UM—cover, covers, covered, covering him, her, it,
    them.

KILLYBASH—calabash, calabashes; gourd, gourds.

KIN—can.

KIN—kin, kindred.

KIN'—kind, kinds; sort, sorts.

KIND'UH—kind of, sort of.

KNOCK—knock, knocks, knocked, knocking.

'KNOWLEDGE—acknowledge, acknowledges. acknowledged, ac-
    knowledging; admit, etc.

KNOW'UM—know, knows, knew him, her, it, them.

KYAG—keg, kegs.

KYARRYSENE—kerosene.

L

LAA'CENY—larceny.

LAA'D—lard.

LAA'GIN'—enlarging, swaggering, boastful.

LAA'N—learn, learns, learned, learning.

LAB'RUH—laborer, laborers.

LAM'QUAWTUH—lamb's-quarter—an edible wild herb of which,
    like the tender leaves of the pokeberry, the Negroes
    are very fond, using it for boiling.

LANGWIDGE—language, talk.

LAS'—last, lasts, lasted, lasting; last (adverb); shoemaker's
    last.

LAS'YEAH—last year, last year's.

LAUGH—(n. and v.) laugh, laughs, laughed, laughing.

LAVUH—(n. and v.) labor, labors, labored, laboring.

LAWFULLY LADY—a Negro's legally married wife.

LEABE—leaf, leaves.

LEABE—(n. and v.) leave, leaves, left, leaving (see "lef' ") ; permit, permission.

LEAN FUH—lean for—set out for with haste and speed.

'LEBEN ⎫
'LEB'N ⎬ —eleven.

LEDDOWN—lay, lays, laid or lie, lies, lay, lying down.

LEEK—lick, licks, licked, licking—with the tongue.

LEELY ⎫
LILLY ⎬ —little, in size or quantity.

LEETLE—little, in size or quantity.

LEF'—leave, leaves, left, leaving. (See "leabe").

LEF' HAN'—left hand or left handed, "lef' han' foot," or "lef' han' feet"—left foot or left leg.

LEF'UM—leave, leaves, left or leaving him, her, it, them.

LEGGO—let go, lets go, letting go.

LEH—let, lets, letting.

LEH WE—let us.

LE'M—let them.

LEM'LONE—let, lets him, her, it, them alone.

LEMME—let me.

LEN'—(v.) lend, lends, loaned, lending.

LENGK—length, lengths.

'LESS—(or onless) unless.

LIAH ⎫
LIE ⎬ —liar, liars.

LIB—live, lives, lived, living.

LIBBIN'—living.

'LIBE—alive.

LIBBUH—liver, livers.

'LIBBUH—deliver, delivers, delivered, delivering.

LICK—(n. and v.) a blow; to whip, whips, whipped.

LICK BACK—turn, turns, turned, turning back, while moving rapidly.

LICKIN'—(n. and v.) a licking, lickings, whipping, etc.

LIGHT ON—light on—mount, mounts, mounted, mounting.

LIGHT'OOD—lightwood—resinous pine-wood.

LIGHT OUT—to start, start off, or away.

A GULLAH GLOSSARY

'LIJAH
'LIJUH } —Elijah, the prophet.

'LIJUN—religion.

LIKESO
LIKEWISE ALSO } —likewise, also.

LIMUS-COOTUH—a small, malodorous black terrapin, held in contempt by both races.

LINNIMENT—liniment.

LISS'N—listen, listens, listened, listening.

LOBLOLLY-PINE—the great short-leaf pine growing in low ground.

LOCUS PASTUH—local pastor, or preacher.

'LONG—along, along with.

LONGIS'—longest.

LONGMOUT'—long mouth—descriptive of the surly or contemptuous pushing out of the lips of an angry or discontented Negro.

'LONGSIDE—alongside.

LONG TALK KETCH RUN'WAY NIGGUH—meaning long talk or conversation by the roadside often causes or caused runaway slaves to be caught by the "patrol."

LONGUH—longer.

'LONG'UM—along with, or with him, her, it, them.

LOSS—lose, loses, lost, losing.

'LOW'UM—allow, allows, allowed, allowing him, her, it, them.

LUB—(n. and v.) love, loves, loved, loving; like, likes, liked, liking.

LUK—like, alike.

LUKKUH—like, like unto, resembling.

LUK'UM—like or resembling him, her, it, them.

M

MAA'CH—March; march, marches, marched, marching.

MAA'K—(n. and v.) mark, marks, marked, marking.

MAA'L—the marl or phosphate mines. (See "de Rock").

MA'AM—madam.

MAAMY—mother, mothers.

MAA'SH—marsh, marshes.

MACFUSS'NBIL—McPhersonville—a summer village.

MAN—man, man's; men, men's.

MANGE—mane.

MANNUS—manners, politeness, courtesy.

MANNUSSUBBLE—well-mannered, polite.

MARRI'D—married, marry, marries, marrying.

MASS ⎱
MAS' ⎰ —master when used with a name; as, "Mass Clinch," "Mas' Rafe."

MASTUH—Master—used only for God.

MATCH—(n. and v.) match, matches, matched, matching. Yet "matches" is sometimes used for the singular; as, "Gimme uh matches"—give me a match.

MAUM—same as "maumuh," when used with the name of the person spoken to or of, as "Maum Kate."

MAUMUH—mauma, the equivalent of the up-country "mammy."

MAUSSUH—master, masters. NOTE: See above "Mastuh." While the Gullah can pronounce "mastuh," he reserves this for God, even saying "Maussuh Jedus" —Master Jesus.

MAWGIDGE—(n. and v.) mortgage, mortgages, mortgaged, mortgaging.

MAWNIN'—morning, mornings; also "good morning!"

ME—I, my.

MEAN—mean, meanness.

MEDDISIN ⎱
MED'SIN ⎰ —medicine, medicines, physic.

MEDJUH—(n. and v.) measure, measures, measured, measuring.

MEDJUHR'UM—measure, measures, measured, measuring him, her, it, them.

MEK—make, makes, made, making.

MEK'ACE—make haste.

MEK ANSUH—make, makes, making, made reply.

MEK FUH—make for; to go to, goes to, went to, going to.

MEK OUT—make, makes, made, making out, a makeshift.

MEK OUT—make, makes, made, making out; a makeshift.

MEK YO MANNUS—make your manners, your obeisance.

MEMBUH—member, members as of a church or society.

A GULLAH GLOSSARY

'MEMBUH—remember, remembers, remembered, remembering;
   remind, etc.

'MEMB'UNCE—remembrance, remembrances.

MEN' 'E PACE—mend his, her, its, their pace; hurry, hurry up,
   etc.

MENS—men.

MESELF
MUHSELF } —myself.

MET'DIS'—Methodist, Methodists.

METSIDGE—message, messages.

MIDDLEBLOUSE—middy-blouse, middy-blouses.

MIDDLEDAY—midday, noon.

MIDDLENIGHT—midnight.

MIN'—mind, minds, minded, minding; heed, etc.; take care of,
   protect, cherish, guard.

'MIRATION—admiration, wonder, astonishment.

MIS'
MISS } —Miss, Mrs., Mistress, when accompanied by a
   name, as Miss Anne, "Mis' Chizzum."

MISSIS—mistress, mistresses.

MISTUH—Mr.

MO'—more.

MOAN—moan, moans, moaned, moaning.

MO' BETTUH—more better, better.

MOCCASIN—water-moccasin, a venomous snake.

MO' LONGUH—more longer, longer.

MO'N—mourn, mourns, mourned, mourning.

MO'NFUL—mournful.

'MONG
'MOUNG } —among, amid.

MONGK'Y
MONK'Y } —monkey, monkeys.

MONSTROSITY—monstrous.

MO'NUH—mourner, mourners.

MO'NUH—more than.

MO'NUH DA'—more than that.

MOOBE—move, moves, moved, moving.

MO'OBUH—moreover.

Mo'ris' ⎫
Mo'res' ⎬ —most.

Mout'—mouth, mouths.

Muffey—Murphy.

Muffledice—hermaphrodite.

Mufflejaw—muffle-jawed—a strain of barnyard fowl, heavily
        feathered about the cheeks.

Muhlassis—molasses.

Mukkle—myrtle, myrtles; myrtle thickets.

Munt'—month, months.

Murruh—mother, mothers.

Murruhlaw—mother-in-law.

Mus'be—must be, must have, must have been.

Muscoby—Muscovy—a breed of domestic ducks much af-
        fected by low-country Negroes.

Muskick—musket, muskets.

Muskittuh—mosquito, mosquitoes.

Mussiful—merciful.

Mussy—mercy, mercies.

Mustu'd—mustard.

Mustuh—muster, musters, mustered, mustering.

My'own—mine, my.

N

Nakid ⎫
Nakit ⎬ —naked.

Nakity—naked, nakedness.

'Narruh—another. (See " 'nodduh" and " 'norruh").

Navuh—neighbor, neighbors.

Nebbuh—never. (See "nubbuh").

Needuh—neither.

Needuhso—neither so, neither, nor.

N'min' ⎫
N'mine ⎪
Nemmin' ⎬ —never mind.
Nemmine ⎪
Nummine ⎭

Nepchune—Neptune.

Nes'—(n. and v.) nest, nests, nested, nesting.

Newfanglety—newfangled.

Newnited States—United States.

A GULLAH GLOSSARY

NICKYNACK—"nic-nac" crackers, biscuit.

NIGGUHHOUSE—Negro house or houses, cabin or cabins.

NIGGUHHOUSE YAA'D—Negro house yard, the main street running through the plantation Negro quarters.

NIGH—near, also draw near to; as: "W'en de bull biggin fuh nigh'um de gal tek 'e foot een 'e han' en' run 'way."

NIGHT—night, night-time, at night.

NIGH'UM—near, or nearing him, her, it, them.

'N'INT—anoint, anoints, anointed, anointing. (See "renoint").

NO—any.

NO'COUNT—no account, worthless.

'NODDUH—another. (See " 'narruh" and " 'norruh").

NOMANNUS }
NOMANNUSSUBBLE } —impolite, without manners, rude.

NOMINASHUN—nominate, nominates, nominated, nominating; also nomination, nominations.

'NORRUH—another. (See " 'narruh" and " 'nodduh").

NOTT—nut, nuts; as "nott-grass," nut grass.

NOTUS—(n. and v.) notice, notices, noticed, noticing.

NOWEMBUH—November.

NUBBUH—never. (See "nebbuh").

'NUF—enough, abundance.

NUH—nor; also for and.

'NURRUH—another.

NUSS—(n. and v.) nurse, nurses, nursed, nursing.

NUSSUH }
NUSSO } —not so.

NUTT'N'—nothing.

NYAM—eat, eats, eating, ate; sometimes "nyam-nyam," a repetition for emphasis.

NYANKEE—Yankee, Yankees.

NYOUNG }
NYUNG } —young.

NYOUNGIS'—youngest.

NYUSE }
USE } —(n. and v.) use, uses, used, using. (See uz'n").

NYUZE ⎫
NYUZ'N ⎬ —(v.) used, using.

O

OAGLY—ugly.

OBJECK'—object. (See "'jeck'").

OBSERB'—observe, observes, observed, observing.

OB'SHAY—overseer, overseers.

OBUH—over, above.

OBUHTEK—overtake, overtakes, overtook, overtaking.

OBUHT'ROW—overthrow, overthrows, overthrew, overthrowing; overthrown.

OCTOBUH—October.

ODDUH—other, others.

ODDUHRES'—the other rest, the rest, remainder.

OFF'UH—off, off of.

OFFUH—offer, offers, offered, offering.

OFF'UM—off, or off of him, her, it, them.

OLE—old.

ONBUTT'N—unbutton, unbuttons, unbuttoned, unbuttoning.

ONCOMMUN—uncommon.

ONDEESTUNT—indecent, indecency.

ONDELICATE—indelicate, presumptuous.

ONDUH—under.

ONDUHNEET'—underneath.

ONDUHSTAN'—understand, understands, understood, understanding. Also, as an understanding.

ONDUHTEK—undertake, undertakes, undertook, undertaking.

ONE—only; "me one," I only.

ONE'NARRUH ⎫
ONE'NODDUH ⎪
ONE'NUDDUH ⎬ —one another.
ONE'NURRUH ⎭

ONETIME—once, once upon a time.

ONHITCH—unhitch, unhitches, unhitched, unhitching; also marital separation.

ONKIBBUH—uncover, uncovers, uncovered, uncovering.

ONLOCK—unlock, unlocks, unlocked, unlocking.

ONMANNUSSUBBLE—unmannerly, impolite, rude. (See "nomannussubble").

A GULLAH GLOSSARY

ONNUH—(n. and v.) honor, honors, honored, honoring.

ONNUHRUBBLE—honorable.

ONRABBLE—unravel, unravels, unraveled, unraveling; untangle.

ONREASUNNUBBLE—unreasonable.

ONSAA'T'N—uncertain.

ONSATTIFY—unsatisfied, unsatisfying.

ONTEL—until.

ONTIE—untie, unties, untied, untying.

'OOD—wood, woods.

'OOMAN—woman, woman's; women, women's. "'Ooman iz uh
sometime t'ing"—Woman is a fickle, uncertain
creature, sometimes one thing, sometimes another.

OONUH—ye, sometimes you. (See "wunnuh," etc.).

OSHTUH—oyster, oysters.

OSHTUH RAKE—long-handled rake or tongs for gathering
oysters.

OUGHTUH—ought, ought to, ought to be; as: "Man oughtuh
t'engkful"—man ought to be thankful.

OUT
OUT'N
}—to go out, put out, extinguish; as: "Uh out de fiah"
—I put out the fire. "Uh out'n'um"—I put it out.

OUT'UH—out of, out.

OX—oxen.

OXIDIZE—to turn into an ox.

OXIN—ox.

P

PAA'D'N—(n. and v.) pardon, pardons, pardoned, pardoning.

PAA'DNUH—partner, partners.

PAA'KUH—Parker—a low-country family name.

PAA'LUH—parlor, parlors.

PAA'SIMONY—parsimony, also avarice or rapacity.

PAA's'N—parson, parsons.

PAAT'—path, paths.

PAA'T—(n. and v.) part, parts, parted, parting.

PAA'TY—party.

PALABUHRIN'—palavering—soft talk of a philanderer with
the gentler sex.

THE BLACK BORDER

PAPUH—(n. and v.) paper, papers, papered, papering; also a
written instrument, a note or letter.

PARRYSAWL—parasol, parasols.

PASHUN
PASHUNT } —patience; patient, forbearing.

PASSOBUH—Passover.

PASS'UM—pass, passes, passed, passing him, her, it, them.

PASTUH—pastor, pastors; pasture, pastures.

PATTY-AUGUH
PETTY-AUGUH } —piragua, pirogue.

PAWPUS—porpoise, porpoises.

'PAWTUN'
'PORTUN' } —important.

'PAWTUNCE
'PORTUNCE } —importance.

PEACEUBBLE—peaceable, peaceful.

PEAWINE—peavine, peavines.

PENITENSHUS—penitentiary.

'PEN'PUN—depend, depends, depended, depending upon.

PERUSE—to saunter, walk in a leisurely manner, as: "Da' gal
him bin peruse 'long de road en' 'e nebbuh study
'bout nutt'n';" also investigate, examine, consider.

PESSLE—pestle, pestles; a double-headed wooden implement
for beating rice.

PHOSKIT
PHUSKIT } —phosphate, commercial fertilizer; also "de
Phoskit," the phosphate mines.

PIGGIN—a small cedar pail in universal use among Negroes
of the coast.

PINCH'UM—pinch, pinches, pinched, pinching him, her, it,
them; sometimes gripping, as of pain.

'PIN—spin, spins, spun, spinning.

PINDUH—pindar, peanut, peanuts. (See "grunnot").

PINELAN'—pineland, pinelands.

'PINION—opinion, opinions.

P'INT—(n. and v.) point, points, pointed, pointing; direct,
etc.

'P'INT—appoint, appoints, appointed, appointing.

318

A GULLAH GLOSSARY

'P'INTMENT—appointment, appointments.

'PISKUBBLE—Episcopal, Episcopalian.

'PISTLE—Epistle, Epistles (Bible).

PITCHUH—pitcher, pitchers.

PIT—put, puts, put, putting.

PIT'UM—put him, her, it, them.

PIZEN—poison, poisons, poisoned, poisoning.

PIZEN-OAK—poison-oak, or poison ivy.

'PLASH—(n. and v.) splash; to splash, splashes, splashed, splashing.

PLAT-EYE—a ghostly apparition, common to the Georgetown section of the coast.

PLAY 'POSSUM—to make believe, to fool, deceive.

PLEASE KIN—please can—a redundancy; as: "please kin gimme"—please give me.

PLEDJUH—pleasure, pleasures.

PLEDJUHR'UM—please, give pleasure to him, her, it, them.

Po'—poor, also thin, lean, low in flesh.

Po'BUCKRUH—a poor white man, the poor whites.

Po'BUCKRUH-NIGGUH—a Negro who had formerly belonged to the poorer whites, or those not of the "quality."

Po'CH—porch, porches.

POLITICKSUS
POLITICUSS } —political. (See "cawpsus politicksus").

POLLYDO'—Polydore—a favorite man's name among the Negroes; used also for Apollos.

Po'LY—poorly, describing health.

PON PON— the lower Edisto and the region south of the A. C. L. Ry., opposite Jacksonboro.

POOTY
PUTTY } —pretty.

Po'R—pour, pours, poured, pouring.

Po'R'UM—pour, pours, poured, pouring it, that.

Pos'—(n. and v.) post, posts, posted, posting.

POSITUBBLE—positive, positively.

POSSIMMUN—persimmon, persimmons; the tree and fruit.

Po'TRIAL—Port Royal.

PRAISE-MEETIN'—prayer-meeting.

319

Pray—(n. and v.) prayer, prayers; prays, prayed, praying.

'Pread—spread, spreads, spreading.

Preechuh—preacher, preachers; minister, ministers.

Preechuh on de sukkus—the circuit or traveling preacher.

Premussiz—premises.

Presinck—precinct.

Pres'n'ly—presently.

Prezzydent—president.

Priblidge—(n. and v.) privilege, privileges, privileged.

Primus ward—ward primary.

Prizzunt—present, presents, presented, presenting.

Prizzunt aa'm—present arms.

Projic'—to "monkey with," to hazard.

Prommus—(n. and v.) promise, promises, promised, promising.

Proobe—prove, proves, proved, proving.

Proputty—property, wealth.

'Publikin—Republican.

Puhceed
Pusceed } —proceed, proceeds, proceeded, proceeding.

Puhhaps—perhaps.

P'uhjec'—project, projected, as; "W'en da' 'ooman bex, him p'uh'jec' him mout' at me"—When that woman was angry she stuck out her mouth at me.

Puhjuh—perjure, perjures, perjured, perjuring.

Puhliclituh—solicitor, solicitors; the dreaded prosecuting attorney of the Criminal Court, held in awe by all low-country Negroes.

Puhlite—polite, politely. Also a popular Negro name, as "Mingo Puhlite."

Puhshay—Porcher—name of a low-country family.

Puhtek—protect, protects, protected, protecting.

Puhtekshun—protection.

Puhtettuh—potato, potatoes—usually sweet. (See "tettuh").

Puhtickluh—particular, particularly.

Puhwide—provide, provides, provided, providing.

A GULLAH GLOSSARY

PUHWID'N—providing, also provided.

PUHWIDUH—provider, providers.

PUHWISHUN—provision, provisions; ration, rations.

PUHWOKE—provoke, provokes, provoked, provoking.

PUHWOKIN'—provoking.

PUHZAC'LY—exactly, precisely.

PUHZISHUN—position, positions.

PULBLIC—public, the public.

PULL WOOL—to pull the kinky forelock in salutation to "de Buckruh."

PUNKIN—pumpkin, pumpkins.

PUNKIN-SKIN—pumpkin colored or mulatto Negro.

PUNNOUNCE—pronounce, pronounces, pronounced, pronouncing.

'PUNTOP
'PUNTAP   —upon, on, on top of.
'PANTAP

'PUNTOP'UH—upon top of, on top of, at.

PUPPUS—purpose, on purpose.

PUSS'N
PUSSON   —person, persons.
PUSSUN

PUSS'NULLY
PUSSONULLY   —personally.
PUSSUNULLY

PYAZZUH—piazza, piazzas; porch, porches; veranda.

PYO'—pure, also fully, absolutely; as: "de pyo' nutt'n'!" absolutely nothing.

Q

'QUAINTUN'—acquainted, acquainted with.

'QUAINTUNCE—acquaintance, acquaintances. (See "acquaintun'").

QUARRIL
QUAWL   —quarrel, quarrels.

QUARRILMENT
QUAWLMENT   —quarrel, quarrels, quarreled, quarreling.

321

THE BLACK BORDER

QUAWT—quart, quarts.

QUAWT'LY—quarterly.

QUAWTUH—(n. and v.) quarter, quarters, quartered, quartering.

'QUEEZE—squeeze, squeezes, squeezed. squeezing.

QUESCHUN ⎤
SQUESCHUN ⎦—(n. and v.) question, questions, questioned, questioning. Rarely used, "quizzit" taking its place.

QUILE—(n. and v.) coil, coils, coiled, coiling.

'QUIRE—require, requires, required, requiring.

'QUIRE—inquire, inquires, inquired, inquiring.

QUIZZIT—(quiz) ask, asks, asked, asking; to question, questions, questioned, questioning. (See "squizzit," a rarely used variant).

R

RABBISH—ravish, ravishes, ravished, ravishing.

RAB'N—raven, ravens; vulture, vultures; buzzard, buzzards.

RAB'NEL—Ravenel, Ravenels—a family name, also a station on Atlantic Coast Line Railway.

RACKTIFY—to break, breaks, broke, broken, breaking. Confuse in mind: "Da' buggy racktify"—that buggy is dilapidated. "Da' 'ooman racktify een 'e min'"—that woman's mind is distracted.

RAIN—(n. and v.) rain, rains, rained, raining.

RALE—real, very, truly.

RAMIFY—to act like a ram.

RANGE—range, ranges, ranged, ranging.

'RANGUHTANG—Orang-Utan, Orang-Utans.

RAPPIT—rapid, rapidly.

RASHI'N—(n. and v.) ration, rations, rationed, rationing.

RAYRE—rear, rears, reared, rearing.

'READY—already.

REBEL TIME—rebel times—the freedmen's offensive characterization of the period before freedom when their former masters controlled the government of their own states.

REB'REN'—reverend—used also as a noun, as "de reb'ren'."

RECISHUN—decision, decisions.

A GULLAH GLOSSARY

REDDUH—rather. (See "rudduh").
REFEN'—defend, defends, defended, defending. (See " 'fen' ").
REINGE—reins.
REMONIA—pneumonia.
RENITE—unite, unites, united, uniting.
RENOINT—anoint, anoints, anointed, anointing. (See " 'n'int").
RENOINTED—anointed.
REPEAH—appear, appears, appeared, appearing.
REPLOY—(rare) reply, replies, replied, replying.
REPOSE—oppose, opposes, opposed, opposing.
RESPLAIN—explain, explains, explained, explaining; elucidate, etc.
RETCH—reach, reaches, reached, reaching.
'RIAH—Maria.
RIBBUH—river, rivers.
RICEBU'D—ricebird, ricebirds.
RIDICK'LUS—ridiculous, also outrageous, scandalous. (Often so used by illiterate whites).
ROAS'—roast, roasts, roasted, roasting.
ROCK—rock, rocks, rocked, rocking. Also for phosphate rock. (See "de Rock").
ROKKOON—raccoon, raccoons.
ROLL—roll, rolls, rolled, rolling.
ROOS'—(n. and v.) roost, roosts, roosted, roosting.
ROOSTUH—rooster, roosters.
ROZZUM—(n. and v.) rosin, rosins, rosined, rosining.
RUBBIDGE—rubbish.
RUCKUHNIZE—recognize, recognizes, recognized, recognizing.
RUDDUH—rather. (See "redduh").
RUDDUH—rudder, rudders.
RUMPLETAIL—(rumpless) a tailless fowl.
RUN—run, runs, ran, running.
RUPPEZUNT—represent, represents, represented, representing.

S

SAA'B—serve, serves, served, serving.
SAA'BINT—(also "saa'bunt") servant, servants.
SAA'BINT DAY—servants' day—perhaps originally a corruption of Sabbath day.

SAA'BIS—(also sarbis) service, services, use.

SAA'CH—search, searches, searched, searching; also examine, examined, etc.

SAA'F'—soft.

SAA'F'LY—softly.

SAA'PINT
SAA'PUNT } —serpent (Biblical).

SAA'T'N
SUTT'N } —certain.

SABANNUH
SAWANNUH } —Savannah; savanna, savannas.

SABBIDGE—savage, savages.

SABE—save, saves, saved, saving.

SABEYUH—the Savior.

SA'LEENUH—St. Helena Island, on the South Carolina coast.

SAME LUKKUH—(also sukkuh) same like, like, resembling.

SAN'—sand.

SAT'D'Y
SATTYDAY } —Saturday.

SATTIFACKSHUN—satisfaction.

SATTIFY—satisfy, satisfies, satisfied, satisfying.

SAWLKETCHUH—Salkehatchie—upper reaches of the Combahee above the A. C. L. Ry.

SAWT—(n. and v.) sort, sorts, sorted, sorting.

SAWTUH—sort of—after a fashion.

SAY—say, says, said, saying.

SCA'CE
SCA'CEFUL } —scarce.

SCA'CELY—scarcely, hardly. (See "kacely").

SCATTUH—scatter, scatters, scattered, scattering.

SCHEMY—scheming, tricky.

SCOLE—scold, scolds, scolded, scolding.

SCRIPTUH—Scripture—the Bible.

'SCUSE—(noun) excuse, excuses.

'SCUSIN'—excusing, except.

'SCUSSHUN—excursion, excursions.

'SCUZE—(verb) excuse, excuses, excused, excusing.

A GULLAH GLOSSARY

SEAZ'NIN'—seasoning.

SEB'N—seven.

SEB'NPUNCE—seven pence. (See "fo'punce").

SEB'NTEEN—seventeen.

SEB'NTY—seventy.

SECKRITERRY—secretary, secretaries.

SECTEMBUH—September.

SECUN'—second.

SEDATE—sedately, quietly, in a leisurely manner: "De mule walk so sedate uh couldn' plow fas'."

SEDDOWN—sit or set down, sits or sets down, sat or set down, sitting or setting down.

SEE—see, sees, saw, seen, seeing.

SEEGYAA'—cigar, cigars.

SEEM—seem, seems, seemed, seeming.

'SELF—himself, herself, itself, themselves; as: "Him maussuh 'self haffuh wu'k"—his master himself has to work.

SELFISH—selfish—glum, dour.

SENCE—since.

SEN'UM—send, sends, sent, sending him, her, it, them.

SESSO—say so, says so, said so, saying so. (See "susso").

SET—sit, sits, sat, sitting. (See "seddown").

SETTLE'—settled, as: "settle' 'ooman," a settled woman, a Negro woman of a certain age, not a flapper.

SETT'N'—sitting.

SETT'N'UP—sitting up—a Negro wake; a small religious meeting.

SEZZEE—says he, said he.

SEZZI—says I, said I.

SHAA'K—shark, sharks.

SHAA'P—sharp.

SHAA'P'N—sharpen, sharpens, sharpened, sharpening.

SHABE—shave, shaves, shaved, shaving.

SHADDUH—(n. and v.) shadow, shadows, shadowed, shadowing.

SHAME—(n. and v.) shame, shames, shamed, shaming; ashamed.

SHAWT—short—"shawt-pashunt," short patience or irritable, irritability.

SHAYRE—share, shares, shared, sharing.

SHAYRE'UM—share, shares, shared, sharing him, her, it, them. Also for shear, shears, sheared, shearing him, her, it, them.

SHEEPBUHR—sheepburr, sheepburrs.

SHE'OWN—her own.

SHEPU'D—shepherd, shepherds.

SHE-SHE TALK—woman's talk, gabble.

SHET—shut, shuts, shut, shutting.

SHIMMY—chemise, chemises.

SHISH—such.

SHISHUH—such a.

SHO'—sure, surely.

SHOE—(n. and v.) shoe, shoes, shod, shoeing.

SHOESH—shoes.

SHO'LY—surely.

SHOOT'UM—shoot, shoots, shot, shooting him, her, it, them.

SHOULDUH—shoulder, shoulders, shouldered, shouldering.

SHOULD'UH—should have.

SHOUT—(n. and v.) shout, shouts; shout, shouts, shouted, shouting; frenzied outcries of a religious devotee. A plantation dancing festival, frequently accompanied by beating sticks on the floor.

SHOW—show, shows, showed, showing.

SHOW'UM—show, shows, showed, showing him, her, it, them.

SHROUD—shroud, shrouds; also surplice, surplices, as: "De 'Piskubble preechuh pit on 'e shroud."

SHUB—shove, shoves, shoved, shoving.

SHUH—pshaw!

SHUM—see, sees, saw, seeing him, her, it, them.

SHU'T—shirt, shirts.

SIDE'UH—on the side of, alongside.

SILBUH—silver—"silbuhfish," silver fish.

SILBY—Silvia.

SILUNT—silent, silence, as "silunt een co't!"—silence in court!

SILUS—Silas.

SISTUH—(formal) sister, sisters.

SKAY'D—scared.

SKAYRE—scare, scares, scared, scaring.

SKAY-TO-DE'T'—scare or scared to death.

SKOLLUP—escallop, escallops, escalloped, escalloping.

A GULLAH GLOSSARY

Sku't—skirt, skirts.

Slabe—slave, slaves.

Slabery—slavery.

Slabery time—slavery times—before freedom.

Slam—a synonym for "spang," expressing distance, all the way.

Slann' Ilun'—Slann's Island, a tract lying along the North Edisto inlet and Toogoodoo creek.

Sleebe—sleeve, sleeves.

'Sleep—asleep; sleep, sleeps, slept, sleeping.

Slip'ry—slippery.

Smaa't—smart.

'Smattuh—what is the matter?

Snawt—snort, snorts, snorted, snorting.

Snow're—snore, snores, snored, snoring.

Soad—sword, swords.

Sobuh—sober.

Sobuhr'um—sober, sobers, sobered, sobering him, her, them.

Sodjuh—(n. and v.) soldier, soldiers; soldiering, etc. To loaf on the job.

Sof'—soft.

Somebody—somebody's, some one, some one's.

Somebody'own—somebody's own.

Sonnylaw—son-in-law, sons-in-law.

Soon-man—a smart, alert, wide-awake man.

Sooply—supple.

Spaa'k—spark, sparks.

Spang—all the way, expressive of distance.

Sparruh—sparrow, sparrows.

Sparruh-grass—asparagus.

Sparruhhawk—sparrow-hawk or hawks.

'Spec'—expect, expects, expected, expecting; suspect, suspects, suspected, suspecting.

Specie'—species.

Specify—from specify, but greatly extended to include almost all meanings of "specifications"—proving inadequate, not coming up to expectations, etc. (See Introduction to this Glossary).

Speckly—speckled.

Spen'—spend, spends, spent, spending.

THE BLACK BORDER

SPERRITUAL—spiritual, spirituals, the Negro religious songs.
'SPERIUNCE—experience, experiences, experienced, experiencing.
SPESHLY—specially, especially.
SPIDUH—spider, spiders; also a cooking utensil in universal use among the Coast Negroes.
SPILE—spoil, spoils, spoiled, spoiling.
'SPISHUN—suspicion, suspicions.
'SPISHUS—suspicious, suspiciously.
'SPIZE—despise, despises, despised, despising.
'SPLAIN—explain, explains, explained, explaining.
SPLOTCH—blot, blots; stain, stains.
'SPON'—respond, responds, responded, responding.
'SPONSUBBLE—responsible, also used emphatically or specifically; as: "Tell'um 'sponsubble fuh do da' t'ing."
'SPOSE—expose, exposes, exposed, exposing.
S'POSE—suppose, supposes, supposed, supposing.
SPO'T—sport, sports; also sporting man.
SPO'TIN'
SPOT'N' } —(n. and v.) sport, sports, sported, sporting.
SPO'TY—sporty.
S'PREME—(n.) supreme—only in "s'preme co't."
SPUHR—(n. and v.) spur, spurs, spurred, spurring.
'SPUTE—(n. and v.) dispute, disputes, disputed, disputing; contest with.
'SPUTE'N—disputing.
SQUAYRE—(also squay) square—also a parallelogram in a ricefield divided from other squares by irrigation ditches.
SQUESCHUN—question—sometimes used for the more common "quizzit," which see. (Also see "queschun").
SQUIZZIT—a rarely used variant of "quizzit," which see.
STAA'CH—(n. and v.) starch, starches, starched, starching.
STAAR—star, stars.
STAA'T—start, starts, started, starting.
STAA'T NAKID—stark naked.
'STABLISH—establish, establishes, established, establishing.
STAN'—stand, stands, stood, standing; look, looks, looked, looking.

328

A GULLAH GLOSSARY

STAN'—a stand, stands; deer stands, etc.

STAN'LUKKUH—stand, stands, stood, standing like; to look like, etc.

STAN'SUKKUH—stand same like unto, same meaning as "stan'-lukkuh."

'STEAD'UH—(also 'stidduh) instead of.

STEAL—steal, steals, stole, stealing.

STO'—store, stores; shop, shops.

'STONISH—astonish, astonishes, astonished, astonishing.

'STRACTID—protracted, as a " 'stractid meet'n'," a protracted meeting.

STRAIGHT'N FUH—make for, made for, making for; run quickly or swiftly.

STRANCE—trance, trances.

STREE—three; as in "seb'nty-stree." Rarely used. (See "t'ree").

STRENGK—strength.

STRETCH-OUT—stretch out—extend. (See " 'tretch-out").

STRIKE—strike, strikes, struck, striking. (See " 'trike").

'STROY'D—destroy, destroys, destroyed, destroying.

'STRUCKSHUN—destruction.

'STRUCKSHUN—construction.

'STRUCKSHUN STRAIN—construction train.

STRUCTID—struck, striking.

STUBB'N—(also stubbunt) stubborn.

STUDY—think, plan, ponder.

STUHR—stir, stirs, stirred, stirring.

STUHSTIFFIKIT—certificate.

STYLISH—stylish, meaning also appropriate, dignified, suitable, as: "uh stylish grabe," being a grave ornately decorated with broken china or glass.

'SUADE—persuade, persuades, persuaded, persuading.

SUCK—suck, sucks, sucked, sucking.

SUCK-AIG—suck-egg—as: "uh suck-aig dog."

SUCK ME TEET'—and "suck 'e teet' "—a contemptuous gesture, frequently indulged in by the fair sex.

SUDD'NT—sudden, suddenly.

SUFFUHRATE—separate, separates, separated, separating; also divorce, divorcing, etc.

SUH—sir.

Suh—that, say. (See "susso" and "sesso").

Suhciety—society, societies.

Sukkle—(n. and v.) circle, circles, circled, circling.

Sukkuh—(a contraction of "same lukkuh" used by rapid speakers) same, same like, resembling.

Sukkuhr'um—same like, or like him, her, it, them.

Sukkus—circus, circuses.

Sukkus—circuit, circuits.

Sukkus-preechuh—circuit preacher.

Summuch—so much, so many.

Summuh
Summuhtime ⎰—summer, summers, summer-time.

Sump'n'—something.

Sump'n'nurruh—something or other.

Sundown—sunset.

Sunhigh—late morning, about the middle of the forenoon.

Sunhot—sunshine, heat of sun.

Sun-lean—period of the day when the sun begins to decline, and its declining: "sun-lean fuh down."

Sun'up—sunrise.

Supploy—supply, supplies, supplied, supplying.

Suppuh—supper.

Supshun—substance, sustenance, strength of food, as of a juicy roast: "Da' meat hab supshun een'um"—that meat has much nourishment.

Susso
Suh-so ⎰—say so, says so, said so, saying so. (See "sesso").

Sutt'n—certain, certainly.

Sutt'nly—certainly.

Swalluh—(n. and v.) swallow, swallows, swallowed, swallowing.

Swalluhr'um—swallow, swallows, swallowed, swallowing him, her, it, them.

Swawm—(n. and v.) swarm, swarms, swarmed, swarming.

Sway'
Swayre ⎰—swear, swears, swore, swearing.

Swaytogawd—swear to God.

Sweeth'aa't—sweetheart, sweethearts.

A GULLAH GLOSSARY

SWEETMOUT'—sweetmouth—blarney, flattery.

SWEETMOUT' TALK—soft talk of a philanderer with the gentler sex.

SWELL—swell, swells, swelled, swelling; swollen.

SWELL-UP—swelled, swollen up, puffed up with anger, importance or authority.

SWEET'N—sweeten, sweetens, sweetened, sweetening.

SWEET'NIN'—"sweetening."

SWIF'—swift, fast.

SWIMP—shrimp, shrimps.

SWINGE—singe, singes, singed, singeing.

SWINK—shrink, shrinks, shrunk, shrinking.

SWONGUH—"swank," swagger, swaggering, boastful.

T

TAAR—(n. and v.) tar, tars, tarred, tarring.

'TACK—(n. and v.) attack, attacks, attacked, attacking.

'TACKTID—attacked. (See "attacktid").

TACKLE—(n. and v.) tackle, tackles, tackled, tackling; arraign, hold accountable.

'TAGUHNIZE—antagonize, antagonizes, antagonized, antagonizing; arraign, arraigned, etc.

'TAIL—(n. and v.) entail, entails, entailed, entailing.

'TAKE—(n. and v.) stake, stakes, staked, staking.

TALK'UM—talk, talks, talked, talking; talking it, speak out, etc.

TALLUH—tallow.

TALLYGRAF—(n. and v.) telegraph, telegraphs, telegraphed, telegraphing; telegram, telegrams.

'TAN'—stand, stands, stood, standing.

'TAN'UP—stand, stands, stood, standing up.

'TARRYGATE—interrogate, interrogates, interrogated, interrogating; question, questioned, etc.

TARRYPIN—terrapin, terrapins.

TARRIFY—terrify, terrifies, terrified, terrifying.

TARRUH—t'other, the other. (See "torruh," "todduh").

TAS'—task—a measure of distance as well as of area: 105 feet or 105 feet square. A "tas'," or one-fourth of an acre, being the daily task during slavery on a sea-island cotton plantation, in "listing," "hauling," or hoeing sea-island cotton, a task being frequently completed before noon, when the slave was free for the rest of the day. Used as meaning distance of a shot; as: "My gun kin shoot two tas' "—My gun can kill at 210 feet (70 yards).

TAS'E—taste, tastes, tasted, tasting.

TAS'E 'E MOUT'—put a taste in his, her or their mouth or mouths; meaning something appetizing to eat.

T'AW'T—(n. and v.) thought, thoughts. (See also "t'ink").

'TAY—stay, stays, stayed, staying.

TAYRE—tear, tears, tore, tearing.

TAYRE'UM—tear, tears, tore, tearing him, her, it, them.

TEDAY—today.

TEET'—tooth, teeth.

TEET'ACHE—toothache.

TEK—take, takes, took, taken, taking.

TEK'CARE—take-care—as: "Tek'care bettuh mo'nuh baig paa'd'n"—Take care is better more than beg pardon; meaning an ounce of prevention is worth a pound of cure.

TEK'ESELF—take, takes, took, taking himself, herself, itself, themselves.

TEK ME FOOT EEN ME HAN'—"tek him foot een 'e han' "—Took my foot in my hand, took his or her foot or their feet in his, her, or their hand or hands—meaning hastened, hurried, speeded up.

TEK'UM—take, took, taken him, it, them; as, "tek'um en' t'engky."

TEK'WAY—take, takes, took, taking away.

TEK WID'UM—taken with, pleased with him, her, it, them.

'TELL—till, until.

TELL'UM—tell, tells, telling, told him, her, it, them. "Tell'um huddy fuh me"—tell him howdy for me.

'TEN'—attend, attends, attended, attending; intend, intends, etc.

A GULLAH GLOSSARY

TENDUH—tender.

T'ENGKFUL—thankful.

T'ENGK'GAWD—thank God!—thank, thanks, thanked, thanking God.

T'ENGKY—thanks, thank you.

TENIGHT—tonight.

'TENSHUN—attention.

'TENSHUN—intention; as: "Uh 'tenshun fuh go"—it is my intention to go.

'TEP—(n. and v.) step, steps, stepped, stepping.

TETCH—(n. and v.) touch, touches, touched, touching. Also a remnant, as: "T'engk Gawd, 'e lef' uh leetle tetch een de bottle."

TETCH'UM—touch, touches, touched, touching him, her, it, them.

'TETTUH—potato, potatoes—usually sweet. (See "puhtettuh").

T'ICK—thick.

'TICK—(n. and v.) stick, sticks, stuck, sticking.

T'ICKIT—thicket, thickets.

'TICKLUH—(n. and v.) particular, particulars. (See "puhtickluh").

T'ICKNESS—thickness, thicknesses.

'TICKY—sticky.

T'IEF—(n. and v.) thief, thieves; steal, steals, stole, stolen, stealing. "T'ief iz bad, but t'ief en' ketch iz de debble"—It is bad to steal, but to steal and be caught is worse.

T'IEFIN'—thieving.

TIE'UM—tie, ties, tied, tying him, her, it, them.

TIE UP 'E MOUT'—tie, ties, tied, tying up his, her, or their mouth or mouths; meaning held his, her, or their speech.

TILLIN'ASS'—Tillinghast—a low-country family name.

T'ING—thing, things.

'TING—sting, stings, stung, stinging.

T'INK—think, thinks, thought, thinking.

T'IRTEEN—thirteen.

T'IRTY—thirty.

T'ISTLE—thistle, thistles.

TITTIE
TITTUH } —sister, sisters (informal).

TOAD—a young female dog (old English).

TOAD-FROG—toad, toads.

TODDUH
TUDDUH } —the other, t'other, the others. (See "tarruh," and "torruh").

TOL'—rare, for told. (See "tell'um").

TONGUE
TOUNG } —tongue, tongues.

TOOGOODOO—a short tidal creek or river in former Colleton, now Charleston, County.

'TOOP—stoop, stoops, stooped, stooping.

TOOT'—tooth, teeth.

'TOP—stop, stops, stopped, stopping.

TOP—(n. and v.) top, tops; top, tops, topped, topping.

'TOPPUH—on, on top of.

TORRUH—(also tarruh and todduh) t'other; the other, the others; as: "Dem todduh one"—those other ones.

'T'ORUHTY—authority.

TOTE—"tote"—carry, carries, carried, carrying.

T'OUS'N
T'OUZ'N } —thousand.

TOWN—Charleston, "the City." (See "Chaa'stun").

TRABBLE—travel, travels, traveled, traveling.

'TRAIGHT—straight.

'TRAIGHT'N—straighten, straightens, straightened, straightening. " 'Traight'n fuh"—straighten for, to hurry or extend oneself for a certain point.

'TRANGLE—strangle, strangles, strangled, strangling.

T'RASH—thrash, thrashes, thrashed, thrashing; thresh, threshed, etc.

T'RASHUH—thrasher, thrashers; thresher, threshers.

TREDJUH—treasure, treasures.

TREDJURUH—treasurer, treasurers.

TREE—(v.) tree, trees, treed, treeing.

T'REE—rarely "stree"—three.

T'REE-TIME—three times.

'TRETCH—stretch, stretches, stretched, stretching.

A GULLAH GLOSSARY

'Tretch-out—stretch out. (See "stretch-out").

Trigguh— trigger, triggers.

'Trike—strike, strikes, struck, striking.

Trimble—tremble, trembles, trembled, trembling.

'Tring—string, strings, strung, stringing; " 'tringbean"—string or snap-beans.

T'roat—throat, throats.

T'row—throw, throws, threw, thrown, throwing.

T'rowbone—throw "bones" (dice) play craps.

T'row'd—threw, thrown.

T'row'way
T'ruh'way }—throw, throws, threw, throwing, thrown away.

T'ru—through.

Trubble—(n. and v.) trouble, troubles, troubled, troubling.

Trus'—(n. and v.) trust, trusts, trusted, trusting.

Trus'-me-Gawd—a narrow dugout canoe, so cranky that one who ventures forth upon the waters must have faith in God to bring him through.

Trute—truth.

Trute-mout'—truth-mouth—one who will not lie.

Trybunul—tribunal, tribunals.

Tuckrey—turkey, turkeys.

Tuh—to.

Tuhbackuh—tobacco.

Tuh dat—to that—as: " 'E chupid tuh dat"—he is stupid to that extent; he is that stupid. "Ef him maussuh lub'um tuh dat"—if his master loves him so greatly.

Tuhgedduh—together.

Tuhreckly—directly.

Tuhr'um—to him, her, it, them.

Tuk—took. (See "tek").

Tummuch—too much, intensely, ardently, fervently.

'Tump—(n. and v.) stump, stumps; stump, stumps, stumped, stumping.

'Tump—stub, stubs, stubbed, stubbing.

'Tumpsuckuh—stump-sucker, a crib-sucking horse or mule.

Tu'n—(n. and v.) turn, turns, turned, turning.

T'unduh—(n. and v.) thunder, thunders, thundered, thundering.

T'UNDUHSNAKE—thundersnake, thundersnakes.

TU'NFLOUR—turned flour, scalded corn meal, mush or por-
ridge; same as Italian polenta.

TU'NUP—turnip, turnips.

TU'N UP—turn, turns, turned, turning up.

TUP'MTIME ⎫
TUP'NTINE ⎬ —turpentine.

T'URSD'Y—Thursday.

TWELB'—twelve.

TWIS'—(n. and v.) twist, twists, twisted, twisting.

TWIS'-MOUT'—twist mouth—twist-mouthed.

TWIS'UP—twist or twisted up.

TWO CHUESDAY, TWO T'URSDAY, etc.—the second Tuesday or
the second Thursday in the month.

TWO PLACE—second place, in the second place. NOTE: Other
numbers used similarly.

TWO TIME—two times, twice.

TWO-T'REE—two or three.

U

UB—of. (See "uh").

UBTAIN—obtain, obtains, obtained, obtaining.

UB UH—of a—"Uh debble ub uh mule"—a devil of a mule.

UH—I; a, an. Also of. (See "ub").

UHHEAD—ahead.

UHHEAD'UH—ahead of.

UHLLY ⎫
YUHLLY ⎬ —early.

UM—him, her, it, them.

UP TUH DE NOTCH—up to the notch—to the Queen's taste,
perfect.

US—we, our.

USE—use, uses, used, using; also for game or cattle fre-
quenting certain feeding grounds. (See "nyuse").

USE'N ⎫
UZE'N ⎬ —used to be, in the habit of.

USE-TUH—used to, accustomed to.

A GULLAH GLOSSARY

W

WAAGIN—wagon, wagons.

WAA'MENT—"varmint, varmints," destructive animals or birds.

WADMUHLAW—Wadmalaw—an island of the Carolina coast.

WAH—war.

WAIS'—waist, waists.

WANJUE-RANGE—sometimes "Banjue-Range"—Vendue Range,
the old Charleston slave market.

WANTUH—want to, wants to, wanted to, wanting to.

WARRUH
WADDUH } —what, what is that.

W'ARY—weary.

WAS'E—waste, wastes, wasted, wasting.

WASH-UP
WUSH-UP } —worship (religious).

WATUHMILYUN—watermelon, watermelons.

WAWM—(n. and v.) warm, warms, warmed, warming.

WAWN—(n. and v.) warn, warns, warned, warning.

WAWSS'—wasp, wasps.

WAWSS'NES'—wasp's nest.

WE—our, us.

W'EAT—wheat.

W'EAT-FLOUR—flour, wheat-flour.

WEDDUH—weather, weather; to rain or storm, in such phrases
as: " 'E gwine tuh wedduh"—it is going to or looks
like rain or storm.

WEDD'N'—wedding, weddings.

WEEKY-DAY—a week day.

W'EEL—(n. and v.) wheel, wheels, wheeled, wheeling.

W'EELBARRUH—wheelbarrow, wheelbarrows.

WEGITUBBLE—vegetable, vegetables.

WEH—where.

WEHR'AS—whereas.

WEHREBBUH—wherever.

W'ENEBBUH—whenever.

W'ENSD'Y—Wednesday.

WE'OWN—our own, ours.

WERRY—very. (See "berry").

THE BLACK BORDER

WE'SELF—ourselves.

WESKIT—waistcoat, waistcoats.

WESTIBLUE—vestibuled—the fast "limited" or tourist train.

WHOEBBUH—whoever.

WICTORIA—Victoria—also victorious.

'WICE—(also "exwice") advice, advices.

W'ICH
W'ICH'N } —which.

W'ICH EN' W'Y—which and why—as: "W'ich en' w'y talk"—contradictory talk.

WICKITY
WICKIT } —wicked, wickedness.

WID—with.

WIDDUH—widow, widows.

WIDT'—width, widths.

W'ILE—while, awhile.

WIL'CAT—wild cat, the bay-lynx of the Southern swamps.

WILLUH—willow, willows.

WIN'—(n. and v.) wind, winds; wind, winded.

WIN'—(n and v.) wind, winds, wound, winded, winding.

WINDUH—window, windows.

WINE—vine.

WINEGUH—vinegar.

WINNUH—winnow, winnows, winnowed, winnowing.

WINNUHHOUSE—winnowhouse, winnowhouses, where in the old days rice was winnowed.

WINTUHTIME—winter, in the winter season.

'WISE—(also "exwise") advise, advises, advised, advising,

WISH DE TIME UH DAY—"pass de time uh day"—a salutation, greeting.

WISIT—(n. and v.) visit, visits, visited, visiting.

W'ISKEY—whiskey; formerly used, now an obsolete vocable among the Gullah.

WITCH—witch, witches.

'WITCH—bewitch, bewitches, bewitched, bewitching.

W'ITE—white.

WOICE—voice, voices.

WOODPECKUH—woodpecker, woodpeckers.

WOODPECKUH LAA'K—woodpecker lark—the flicker.

WROP—wrap, wraps, wrapped, wrapping.

A GULLAH GLOSSARY

WU'D—word, words.

WUDDUH DA'—what is that.

WUFFUH—what for, why.

WUH—what, that.

WUHEBBUH—whatever.

WU'K—(n. and v.) work, works, worked, working.

WU'LL'—world, worlds.

WUNDUH—(n. and v.) wonder, wonders, wondered, wondering.

WUNT—won't, will not.

WURRUM—worm, worms.

WUS'DEN'EBBUH—worse than ever.

WUSS ⎫
WUS' ⎬—worse, worst.

WUSSUH—worse.

WUT'—worth, is worth, was worth, etc. "Ent wut'"—a dis-
    paraging characterization.

WUZ—was.

W'YMEKSO—what makes it so, why.

Y

YAA'D—yard, yards.

YAA'N—yarn, yarns.

YAAS—yes.

YAAS'SUH—yes-sir.

YALLUH—yellow.

YALLUHHAMMUH—yellowhammer—the   flicker   or   golden-
    winged woodpecker.

YALLUH YAM—yellow yam—a variety of sweet potato.

YANDUH—yonder.

YEAH—ear, ears (corn or other grain); also year, years.

YEARIN'—hearing.

YEDDY ⎫
YERRY ⎬—hear, hears, heard, hearing.

YEDDY'UM—hear, hears, heard, or hearing him, her, it, them.

YELLIN'—yearling, yearlings.

YENT—(ent) ain't, is not, are not; so pronounced when pre-
    ceded by a soft vowel sound.

YE'T ⎫
YU'T ⎬—earth. (See "eart'").

THE BLACK BORDER

Yeye—eye, eyes; so pronounced when preceded by a soft vowel sound. " 'E yeye red"—his or her eyes are bloodshot with anger.

Yez—ear, ears (human or animal).

Yistiddy—yesterday.

Yiz—is; so pronounced when preceded by a soft vowel sound.

Yo'
You } —your, yours.

You'own—your own, yours.

Yowe—ewe. ("Yowe" is in use in Early English).

Yuh—here.

Yuh him—here he, she, it is, or they are.

Z

'Zackly—exactly. (See "puhzackly").

'Zammin'—examine, examines, examined, examining; question, questioned, etc.

'Zyd'n'—presiding; as: " 'Zyd'n' elduh"—presiding elder.

THE TAR BABY STORY
AS TOLD BY COL. C. C. JONES AND
JOEL CHANDLER HARRIS

BUH WOLF, BUH RABBIT, AND DE TAR BABY

Buh Wolf and Buh Rabbit, dem bin lib nabur. De dry
drout come. Ebry ting stew up. Water scace. Buh Wolf dig
one spring fuh him fuh git water. Buh Rabbit, him too lazy
an too scheemy fuh wuk fuh isself. Eh pen pon lib off
tarruh people. Ebry day, wen Buh Wolf yent duh watch
um, eh slip to Buh Wolf spring, an eh full him calabash long
water an cah um to eh house fuh cook long and fuh drink.
Buh Wolf see Buh Rabbit track, but eh couldnt ketch um
duh tief de water.

One day eh meet Buh Rabbit in de big road, an eh ax um
how eh make out fur water. Buh Rabbit say him no casion
fuh hunt water: him lib off de jew on de grass. Buh Wolf
quire: "Enty you blan tek water outer me spring?" Buh Rabbit say: "Me yent." Buh Wolf say: "You yis, enty me see
you track?" Buh Rabbit mek answer: "Yent me gone to
you spring. Must be some edder rabbit. Me nebber bin nigh
you spring. Me dunno way you spring day." Buh Wolf no
question um no mo: but eh know say eh bin Buh Rabbit fuh
true, an eh fix plan fuh ketch um.

De same ebenin eh mek Tar Baby, an eh gone an set um
right in de middle er de trail wuh lead to de spring, and
dist in front er de spring.

Soon a mornin Buh Rabbit rise an tun in fuh cook eh bittle.
Eh pot biggin fuh bun. Buh Rabbit say: "Hey! me pot duh
bun. Lemme slip to Buh Wolf spring an git some water fuh
cool um." So eh tek eh calabash an hop off fuh de spring.
Wen eh ketch de spring, eh see de Tar Baby duh tan dist
een front er de spring. Eh stonish. Eh stop. Eh come close.
Eh look at um. Eh wait fur um fuh mobe. De Tar Baby
yent notice um. Eh yent wink eh yeye. Eh yent say nuttne.
Eh yent mobe. Buh Rabbit, him say: "Hey titter, enty you
guine tan one side an lemme git some water?" De Tar Baby
no answer. Den Buh Rabbit say: "Leely Gal, mobe, me tell
you, so me kin dip some water outer de spring long me cala-

bash." De Tar Baby wunt mobe. Buh Rabbit say: "Enty you
know me pot duh bun? Enty you know me hurry? Enty you
yeddy me tell you fuh mobe? You see dis han? Ef you dont
go long and lemme git some water, me guine slap you ober."
De Tar Baby stan day. Buh Rabbit haul off an slap um side
de head. Eh han fastne. Buh Rabbit try fuh pull eh hand
back, en eh say: "Wuh you hole me han fuh? Lemme go.
Ef you dont loose me, me guine box de life outer you wid
dis tarruh han." De Tar Baby yent crack eh teet. Buh Rabbit
hit um, bim, wid eh tarruh han. Dat han fastne too same
luk tudder. Buh Rabbit say: "Wuh you up teh? Tun me
loose. Ef you dont leggo me right off, me guine knee you."
De Tar Baby hole um fas. Buh Rabbit skade an bex too. Eh
faid Buh Wolf come ketch um. Wen eh fine eh cant loosne
eh han, eh kick de Tar Baby wid eh knee. Eh knee fastne.
Yuh de big trouble now. Buh Rabbit skade den wus den
nebber. Eh try fuh skade de Tar Baby. Eh say: "Leely
Gal, you better mine who you duh fool long. Me tell you,
fuh de las time, tun me loose. Ef you dont loosne me han
an me knee right off, me guine bus you wide open wid dis
head." De Tar Baby hole um fas. Eh yent say one wud.
Den Buh Rabbit but de Tar Baby een eh face. Eh head fastne
same fashion luk eh han an eh knee. Yuh de ting now. Po
Buh Rabbit done fuh. Eh fastne all side. Eh cant pull loose.
Eh gib up. Eh bague. Eh cry. Eh holler. Buh Wolf yeddy
um. Eh run day. Eh hail Buh Rabbit: "Hey Budder; wuh de
trouble? Enty you tell me you no blan wisit me spring fuh
git water? Who calabash dis? Wuh you duh do yuh any-
how?" Buh Rabbit so condemn eh yent hab one wud fuh
talk. Buh Wolf, him say: "Nummine, I done ketch you dis
day. I guine lick you now." Buh Rabbit bague. Eh bague.
Eh prommus nebber fuh trouble Buh Wolf spring no mo.
Buh Wolf laugh at um. Den eh tek an loose Buh Rabbit from
de Tar Baby, an eh tie um teh one spakleberry bush, an eh
git switch an eh lick um tel eh tired. All de time Buh Rabbit
bin a bague an a holler. Buh Wolf yent duh listne ter um, but
eh keep on duh pit de lick ter um. At las Buh Rabbit tell
Buh Wolf: "Dont lick me no mo. Kill me one time. Mek
fire an bun me up. Knock me brains out gin de tree." Buh

THE TAR BABY STORY

Wolf mek answer: "Ef I bun you up, ef I knock you brains out, you guine dead too quick. Me guine trow you in de brier patch, so de brier kin scratch you life out." Buh Rabbit say: "Do Buh Wolf, bun me: broke me neck, but dont trow me in de brier patch. Lemme dead one time. Dont tarrify me no mo." Buh Wolf yent bin know wuh Buh Rabbit up teh. Eh tink eh bin guine tare Buh Rabbit hide off. So, wuh eh do? Eh loose Buh Rabbit from de spakleberry bush, an eh tek um by de hine leg, an eh swing um roun, an eh trow um way in de tick brier patch fuh tare eh hide an cratch eh yeye out. De minnit Buh Rabbit drap in de brier patch, eh cock up eh tail, eh jump, an holler back to Buh Wolf: "Good bye, Budder! Dis de place me mammy fotch me up,— dis de place me mammy fotch me up." An eh gone befo Buh Wolf kin ketch um. Buh Rabbit too scheemy.

THE WONDERFUL TAR-BABY STORY

HARRIS'S VERSION

"Didn't the fox *never* catch the rabbit, Uncle Remus?" asked the little boy the next evening.

"He come mighty nigh it, honey, sho's you born—Brer Fox did. One day atter Brer Rabbit fool 'im wid dat calamus root, Brer Fox went ter wuk en got 'im some tar, en mix it wid some turkentime, en fix up a contrapshun wat he call a Tar-Baby, en he tuck dish yer Tar-Baby en he sot 'er in de big road, en den he lay off in de bushes for to see wat de news wuz gwineter be. En he didn't hatter wait long, nudder, kaze bimeby here come Brer Rabbit pacin' down de road—lippity-clippity, clippity-lippity—dez ez sassy ez a Jay-bird. Brer Fox he lay low. Brer Rabbit come prancin' 'long twel he spy de Tar-Baby, en den he fotch up on his behime legs like he wuz 'stonished. De Tar-Baby, she sot dar, she did, en Brer Fox, he lay low.

"'Mawnin'!' sez Brer Rabbit, sezee—'nice wedder dis mawnin',' sezee.

"Tar-Baby ain't sayin' nothin', en Brer Fox, he lay low.

"'How duz yo' sym'tums seem ter segashuate?' sez Brer Rabbit, sezee.

"Brer Fox, he wink his eye slow, en lay low, en de Tar-Baby she ain't sayin' nothin'.

"'How you come on, den? Is you deaf?' sez Brer Rabbit, sezee. 'Kaze if you is, I kin holler louder,' sezee.

"Tar-Baby stay still, en Brer Fox he lay low.

"'Youer stuck up, dat's w'at you is,' says Brer Rabbit, sezee, 'en I'm gwineter kyore you, dat's w'at I'm a gwineter do,' sezee.

"Brer Fox, he sorter chuckle in his stummuck, he did, but Tar-Baby ain't sayin' nothin'.

"'I'm gwineter larn you howter talk ter 'spectubble fokes ef hit's de las' ack,' sez Brer Rabbit, sezee. 'Ef you don't take off dat hat en tell me howdy, I'm gwineter bus' you wide open,' sezee.

"Tar-Baby stay still, en Brer Fox he lay low.

THE TAR BABY STORY

"Brer Rabbit keep on axin' 'im, en de Tar-Baby, she keep on sayin' nothin', twel present'y Brer Rabbit draw back wid his fis', he did, en blip he tuck 'er side er de head. Right dar's whar he broke his merlasses jug. His fis' stuck, en he can't pull loose. De tar hilt 'im. But Tar-Baby, she stay still, en Brer Fox, he lay low.

" 'Ef you don't lemme loose, I'll knock you agin,' Brer Rabbit, sezee, en wid dat he fotch 'er a wipe wid de udder han', en dat stuck. Tar-Baby, she ain't sayin' nothin', en Brer Fox, he lay low.

" 'Tu'n me loose, fo' I kick de natal stuffin' outen you,' sez Brer Rabbit, sezee, but de Tar-Baby, she ain't sayin' nothin.' She des hilt on, en den Brer Rabbit lose de use er his feet in de same way. Brer Fox, he lay low. Den Brer Rabbit squall out dat ef de Tar-Baby don't tu'n 'im loose he butt 'er cranksided. En den he butted, en his head got stuck. Den Brer Fox, he sa'ntered fort', lookin' des ez innercent ez one er yo' mamy's mockin'-birds.

" 'Howdy, Brer Rabbit,' sez Brer Fox, sezee. 'You look sorter stuck up dis mawnin',' sezee, en den he rolled on de groun', en laughed en laughed twel he couldn't laugh no mo'. 'I speck you'll take dinner wid me dis time, Brer Rabbit. I done laid in some calamus root, en I ain't gwineter take no skuse,' sez Brer Fox, sezee."

Here Uncle Remus paused, and drew a two-pound yam out of the ashes.

"Did the fox eat the rabbit"? asked the little boy to whom the story had been told.

"W'en Brer Fox fine Brer Rabbit mixt up wid de Tar-Baby, he feel mighty good, en he roll on de groun' en laff. Bimeby he up'n say, sezee:

" 'Well, I speck I got you dis time, Brer Rabbit,' sezee; 'maybe I ain't, but I speck I is. You been runnin' roun' here sassin' atter me a mighty long time, but I speck you done come ter de een' er de row. You bin cuttin' up yo' capers en bouncin' roun' in dis neighberhood ontwel you come ter b'leeve yo'se'f de boss er de whole gang. En den youer allers some'rs whar you got no bizness,' sez Brer Fox, sezee. 'Who ax you fer ter come en strike up a 'quaintance wid dish yer Tar-

Baby? En who stuck you up dar whar you iz? Nobody in de roun worril. You des tuck en jam yo'se'f on dat Tar-Baby widout waitin' fer enny invite,' sez Brer Fox, sezee, 'en dar you is, en dar you'll stay twel I fixes up a bresh-pile and fires her up, kaze I'm gwineter bobbycue you dis day, sho,' sez Brer Fox, sezee.

"Den Brer Rabbit talk mighty 'umble.

" 'I don't keer w'at you do wid me, Brer Fox,' sezee, 'so you don't fling me in dat brier-patch. Roas' me, Brer Fox,' sezee. 'but don't fling me in dat brier-patch,' sezee.

" 'Hit's so much trouble fer ter kindle a fier,' sez Brer Fox, sezee, 'dat I speck I'll hatter hang you,' sezee.

" 'Hang me des ez high as you please, Brer Fox,' sez Brer Rabbit, sezee, 'but do fer de Lord's sake don't fling me in dat brier-patch,' sezee.

" 'I ain't got no string,' sez Brer Fox, sezee, 'en now I speck I'll hatter drown you,' sezee.

" 'Drown me des ez deep ez you please, Brer Fox,' sez Brer Rabbit, sezee, 'but do don't fling me in dat brier-patch,' sezee.

" 'Dey ain't no water nigh,' sez Brer Fox, sezee, 'en now I speck I'll hatter skin you,' sezee.

" 'Skin me, Brer Fox,' sez Brer Rabbit, sezee, 'snatch out my eyeballs, t'ar out my years by de roots, en cut off my legs,' sezee, 'but do please, Brer Fox, don't fling me in dat brier-patch,' sezee.

"Co'se Brer Fox wanter hurt Brer Rabbit bad ez he kin, so he cotch 'im by de behime legs en slung 'im right in de middle er de brier-patch. Dar wuz a considerbul flutter whar Brer Rabbit struck de bushes, en Brer Fox sorter hang 'roun' fer ter see w'at wus gwineter happen. Bimeby he hear somebody call 'im, en way up de hill he see Brer Rabbit settin' cross-legged on a chinkapin log koamin' de pitch outer his har wid a chip. Den Brer Fox know dat he bin swop off mighty bad. Brer Rabbit wuz bleedzed fer ter fling back some er his sass, en he holler out:

" 'Bred en bawn in a brier-patch, Brer Fox—bred en bawn in a brier-patch!' en wid dat he skip out des ez lively ez a cricket in de embers."

Printed in the United States
1111100001B/276